Gracie Harris
Is Under
Construction

# Gracie Harris Is Under Construction

A NOVEL

## Kate Hash

DUTTON

**DUTTON**

An imprint of Penguin Random House LLC
1745 Broadway, New York, NY 10019
penguinrandomhouse.com

Copyright © 2025 by Kathryn Hash

Penguin Random House values and supports copyright. Copyright fuels creativity, encourages diverse voices, promotes free speech, and creates a vibrant culture. Thank you for buying an authorized edition of this book and for complying with copyright laws by not reproducing, scanning, or distributing any part of it in any form without permission. You are supporting writers and allowing Penguin Random House to continue to publish books for every reader. Please note that no part of this book may be used or reproduced in any manner for the purpose of training artificial intelligence technologies or systems.

DUTTON and the D colophon are registered trademarks
of Penguin Random House LLC.

Interior art by swarnstudio / Shutterstock

BOOK DESIGN BY ASHLEY TUCKER

LIBRARY OF CONGRESS CATALOGING-IN-PUBLICATION DATA
has been applied for.

ISBN 9798217045457 (paperback)
ISBN 9798217045464 (ebook)

Printed in the United States of America
1st Printing

The authorized representative in the EU for product safety and compliance is Penguin Random House Ireland, Morrison Chambers, 32 Nassau Street, Dublin D02 YH68, Ireland, https://eu-contact.penguin.ie.

For Rob

# CHAPTER 1

I NEVER INTENDED TO BECOME THE QUEEN OF GRIEF.

In fact, until a minute ago, when Maisy Miller referred to me as such, it never dawned on me that I could be the queen of anything. Yes, women sometimes stop me on the street and call me an inspiration. They usually ask if we can be friends, tell me they follow me on social media, or say that they have read *everything* I've ever written. And, yes, sometimes they cry as they spill their own sad stories. But I'm not anyone's guru or spiritual guide, and I'm sure as hell not anyone's queen.

Now, however, is not the time to work through my ongoing identity crisis—not with Maisy Miller, *the* biggest name in daytime television, and her studio audience staring at me. Maisy's perfectly curled, long red hair and deep-green eyes are captivating as she waits for me to speak, but I need to stay focused.

"I love that people relate to my writing so much," I say, grabbing a little tighter onto the edge of the velvet armchair onstage, "but I hope they also see in my words that I'm still trying to figure out how to navigate life after loss just like they are. I'm no different."

The audience lets out a collective murmur of appreciation. Maisy purses her lips, nods, and gives that rehearsed look of understanding that her on-screen personality has mastered.

"That's the humble Gracie Harris your readers have come to love over the last year," she says, reaching across the table between us and placing her perfectly manicured hand on mine. "A year ago, you wrote an essay that went absolutely viral. I'm wondering if you might tell us a bit about the night you wrote it and what you were feeling."

On the night of Ben's memorial service, I was unbearably lonely. The kids were finally asleep, and the house was quiet. I had spent the day receiving more affection than I could possibly absorb. A few times, as someone new leaned in for a hug, I thought I heard Ben's ghost laughing from the front pew, watching me embrace the hundreds of people who had shown up to support me and remember him.

There had been awkward huggers, sincere huggers, people who held on for far too long, and those blessed few who provided the momentary relief of a graceful side hug. It was obvious who, like Ben, thrived on physical touch. Everyone assumed I did, too, or that I would appreciate some extra love that day. My true and old friends knew to grab my hand for a quick squeeze or to put a gentle palm on my back.

The essay that changed my life took shape that night through eyes too tired to cry and a mind too overstimulated to think twice about the words that filled the screen. It took me just forty-five minutes to write the one thousand words that would change everything.

When I woke up the next day, the laptop was by my side. I

popped it open and read the essay once. Then twice. Everything I felt in the aftermath of Ben's death and the overwhelm of the days that followed was captured in those words. Without a second thought, I pulled up the submission form for Modern Love.

This is a story I've told a million times to friends but never in public. I'm grateful for all of the prep work that my publicist, Lucia, and I did to prepare for this moment because, of course, I still don't feel brave enough to share all this with the world. It's still too raw, even a year later. I need to separate my public persona from my private one to get through the days, let alone the rest of the segment. Instead of the whole truth, I give Maisy and the audience an abbreviated story full of platitudes before succinctly wrapping things up.

"I copied and pasted my essay into that form and hit Submit," I say with a nervous smile. "And then everything changed."

Again, the audience takes a big joint sigh, and for a moment my anxiety drifts a bit from the surface. Writing essays for people from afar has an air of anonymity, even after all this time. Talking to this live audience is an entirely different thing—but I can do this.

"Gracie, I love the way you talk so openly about grief and loss. Your willingness to share your journey has inspired and comforted so many people. One thing I've never heard you share is the story of the day you lost your husband. Would you be willing to open up to us about this?"

We knew this line of questioning was inevitable. I take a deep breath to maintain my composure and will my brain to remember the answer Lucia and I practiced over the phone just last night.

"Up until the moment it became the worst day of my life, it had been a completely normal day," I tell her, staring into her eyes, fighting every instinct to run right off this stage. "I took the kids to school, went to work, had lunch with a friend, and then went out to a business dinner. The most normal day, albeit a little busier than usual.

"That's the thing about losses like mine," I say, before turning to the audience and gesturing toward them, "and like so many of those that y'all have faced. Sometimes we get to plan for a loss or at least a long goodbye, but sometimes they are sudden—so painfully sudden—that it feels like from that moment on there is only the before and the after. That day felt like the end of one life and not just Ben's. I've had to completely reimagine what my life was supposed to look like. I'm honestly still working through that, as my readers are well aware."

Maisy smiles and puts her hand to her heart as the audience claps in approval. I've given them an answer without giving them anything of value. Not a single material detail about Ben's death. As rehearsed, as practiced.

"You and Ben have two children, is that right?" Maisy asks.

"That's right—I have a son and a daughter," I answer nervously. We kindly requested that my kids be kept off the discussion list, but an acknowledged request isn't the same as a promise.

That's when Maisy unleashes. Her questions come fast and hard. *What are you doing to support them? What have you gotten wrong along the way?*

I stammer through the answers as best as I can, but quickly my right leg starts to vibrate. At first, it's a manageable rattle, but soon it transforms into the telltale rapid shake. I discreetly spread out my long dress, hoping to hide the tic that has plagued me for months.

It also quickly becomes the least of my worries because Maisy doesn't relent. *Are the kids in therapy? Are* you *in therapy? What's been the hardest thing for them about losing their dad? What are your greatest fears about raising them without Ben?*

Maisy's questions about the kids strip away my ability to perform a safe version of grief. She has adeptly wrested control from my carefully prepared hands. And once she has it, I lose myself completely.

The edges of my vision begin to blur as I talk about my kids' mental health. *Breathe*, I think. *You have to breathe*. I struggle to fill my lungs as I talk about holiday concerts and family dinners always being one person short. Before I can answer the last question, however, I feel the room start to spin and voices drift away.

"Maisy," I say in a low, desperate voice. "I need a minute."

Over the last year, grief has taught me that it's rarely the obvious things that send you over the edge. It's not the anniversaries or the birthdays or even the missed soccer games. Today, on this stage, it's divulging how the single empty chair at the dining table breaks my heart in two every night. Sharing this delicate detail with a room of strangers was all it took to send my stress, nerves, and sadness over the edge.

The other truth about grief—deep, visceral, unrelenting grief—is that it puts observers into their own state of shock. Maisy is staring at me with a lethal cocktail of horror, pity, and fascination.

I put my head in my hands, close my eyes, and simply try to breathe. *In through the nose, out through the mouth*. Maisy tries to speak and I put my hand up and gently shake my head. Minutes feel like an eternity. Quiet whispers passed between audience members become white noise.

Finally, I sit up and open my eyes. I've regained my composure, but if the goal was to keep my dignity, I'm fairly certain that's off the table. Nobody stops a Maisy interview with the cameras rolling.

"I'm sorry. I'm not used to *talking* about these things," I say, rubbing my clammy palms into one another. "Maybe that's why I'm a writer."

A soft, nervous laughter travels around the studio. Maisy squints, recognizing she's only got one question left to ask. The audience might turn on her if she attempts to go for round two. I also sense a hint of disappointment that I didn't actually keel over, although this is still certain to be *a thing* when the episode airs.

"Do you ever regret going down this path . . . sharing so much with the world?" she asks.

"*Regret* is a strong word, but I do sometimes wonder if I've taken on more than I can handle," I say. "I guess only time will tell."

"Well, we wish you the best of luck," she says, before turning to look directly into the camera. "Don't forget—in addition to reading Gracie's essays twice a month, you can now preorder her memoir!"

I force a smile, just in time for Maisy to turn to me one last time and add with a smirk, "Maybe this will make the book?"

I quickly remove my mic and rush backstage to safety.

---

"THAT WAS A complete disaster," I say to Jenny once the door to the greenroom closes behind me. The wide eyes of every production assistant that I passed on the thirty-second walk between the stage and my best friend's arms told me all I need to know. Total. Disaster.

"You stayed strong," Jenny whispers in my ear. "Even when it looked like things were going bad, you stayed tough."

I don't feel strong. In fact, I feel quite literally on the verge of collapse. The weight of my head on her shoulder makes that clear. Why did I agree to fly to Nashville on short notice? And why did I assume Maisy would be nice to me? I should've known better.

Jenny guides me to the leather armchairs a few feet away, loudly dragging one to fully face the other. My hands instinctively find hers as we both sit, our foreheads pressed to one another.

"What happened out there, Gracie? It was going so great—really, it was—and then suddenly . . . it wasn't."

"Everyone just assumed I'd be a natural at this part. I'm good with words on paper, not this," I say angrily, not answering her question. Instead, I pose one of my own. "Why couldn't she just stick to the script?"

"Those were very personal questions—borderline inappropriate, to be sure—but I've never, ever seen that happen to you in the thirty years we've known each other. *What happened?*"

Her emphasis on those last couple of words lets me know she is not going to let this go. Jenny's concern is clear from the wobble of her voice and the way her hand is now softly stroking my arm.

"Anxiety attack? Pure panic? Good old-fashioned exhaustion?" I answer, trying to be funny but failing to conjure any humor. It all comes out flat. "Or maybe it's just that I'm a mess and trying so damn hard to pretend that I'm not."

"I need you to be very honest with me," Jenny begins, tilting her head to make eye contact with me. "Has this happened before? Is this something we need to worry about?"

This isn't the first time I've had an unexpected meltdown—just the first time so many other people have witnessed it. Usually, I can muster the strength to wait until I'm home, or in my office, or safely tucked in a bathroom stall. Not today. Maisy is probably proud of herself for cracking me in such a public way.

Still . . . almost blacking out? This part *is* new.

"No, it's not normal," I finally tell her. "Usually, the worst of it is whatever the stress tic of the month is, which goes on for an hour or two, and then I move on. This was not normal. Not at all."

The air between us sits still for a moment. We've supported one another through the best and worst life has to offer. She stood beside me when I said "I do" to Ben and again, nearly twenty years later, in that same church to mourn him. The ways that she has met me in the dark corners of life over the last year feel as impossible as they do miraculous.

"We need to revisit last night's conversation," she says, breaking the silence. I feel her hand squeeze mine tighter than ever. "You need to go."

"Can we please not do this now?"

"We absolutely are going to do this now—this is exactly the right time. You almost blacked out on television. This is not you, Gracie. Something needs to change, and there is an easy option staring you right in the face."

"You really think a change of scenery is the answer? You think it's that simple?" I ask. "What if I get there and it's all the same problems just mixed with a bunch of new ones? That doesn't seem like an Easy Button. It seems like a recipe for more disaster."

"When will you ever have this chance again? A break from work. Kids safe. Long hours to write and figure yourself the hell out?"

"And I can't do that at home?"

"No, I don't think you can. What you've been doing hasn't

worked—it's time to try something new. Your body and mind are begging you for a change."

---

A FEW SHORT hours later, Jenny and I are giving each other one last hug before we go our separate ways at the airport.

"Thanks again for flying down here on such short notice," I tell her as we pull away. "I needed you—even more than I thought I would."

She grabs my hand before I can turn to go. She's got her serious eyes on.

"Gracie, the last few months have been particularly rough," she says. "I've been in complete and total amazement watching you this last year, but I have a request. You know that thing that they're about to say to us on the plane about putting our own oxygen masks on first?"

"Jenny," I interrupt, my patience with the world worn thin. "You know I had to get masks on the kids first. You know that."

"I do, sweetie," she reassures me, "but I'm not sure that you ever put your own mask on at all. Like, ever. Today was proof. I think it's time to focus on you. Go to Canopy."

She pulls me in for one last, big hug and I whisper that I will take her advice under close consideration.

"Next time I see you, you're going to be gigantic," I add playfully, touching her belly and trying to end this quick, complex visit on a tender note. "Be sure to tell this peanut how much I love her every single night, okay?"

"Will do," she says. "Last piece of advice: in the coming days try to think about the first ten minutes of that interview, not the last five. When it was good, it was really good. I'm proud of you. You should be proud of yourself—I know Ben definitely is."

Ninety minutes later, I'm on my flight back home. Back to my kids, my real life, the last month of school, and another summer without Ben. It's been just over a year since we lost him, but last summer it was all so fresh, passing by in a haze of grief so thick that sometimes it felt hard to breathe. Last year there was bereavement leave, frozen dinners made by sweet ladies from church, and a fledgling writing gig that I was convinced would disappear as quickly as it had arrived. The meals and official mourning period ended, but the writing thing stuck around.

When I quickly grab a magazine from my bag to read, out slides a laminated commemorative essay that was given to audience members today. It's an extra signed copy that Maisy gave me to remember the appearance—as if I could ever forget what happened.

I study the photo at the top. It's a casual shot of Ben and me on one of those magical nights out with friends when everyone was able to line up babysitters and no one needed to cancel due to last-minute work obligations. It's the last real photo I have of us, and if I knew how widely the essay would end up being shared, I probably would've chosen something less meaningful.

I'm perched on a tall bar stool staring up at him with a big smile while he stares down at me with a playful grin. A finger is snuck between buttons on his shirt and I'm pulling him in close. His arm is tucked behind my back, a hand resting on my hip. My long, dark-brown hair looks shiny and full of body. A good hair day, for sure. There's a visible twinkle in my eyes.

Ben is in desperate need of a haircut in this photo, but his wavy brown hair makes him look younger, despite the flecks of gray that were on a slow, steady march from temples to crown. I swear I can see his freckles, even though the lighting in the restaurant is terrible and our friend took the picture from a few feet away.

I like to look at this photo whenever our last hours together come to mind. I like remembering him like this: full of life and happiness and with so much to live for. He'll be stuck at this age forever, whereas I've already celebrated a birthday without him. What I wouldn't give to look—no, to feel—as happy as I do in this photo.

My eyes drift to the essay itself. *The* essay. I haven't actually read it since the morning I sent it to *The New York Times* for consideration. The morning that set this new life into motion. I take a deep breath and begin.

> Some people are born huggers. I am not one of them.
>
> One of my earliest memories is being told by my parents, aunts, and sundry extended family about what a good baby I had been. I slept, I ate, I smiled, I did my duty as a human with very little fuss. A dream, they would say.
>
> As I grew older and my introversion fully blossomed, I became convinced that my infant self quickly assessed the situation and decided that being wholly agreeable would mean less physical touch from those around me. A quiet baby is left alone on the blanket. A non-fussy baby doesn't get rocked for an hour before bed. No hugging required.
>
> In my life, there have been few people I've hugged without reservation. I require a connection so deep that it's almost an impossible standard to reach. My children. My favorite

aunt, Sandy. Friends who have appeared in my life at the perfect moments as if sent by a higher power, like my best friend, Jenny. Most of all, my husband, Ben.

Ben and I met in college and were immediately inseparable. The first time he suggested we spend the night together (as in sleep over—the deed had long since been done), I was confused. Two people, all night, in a twin bed? I didn't understand the physics.

But I loved him from the moment he sat down next to me in our Introduction to Anthropology class, and this felt like a test. Not a test he was giving me (that wasn't Ben's style), but one I was giving myself. Was I capable of this level of intimacy? Of being wrapped up and consumed into someone else's space and embrace—literally and figuratively feeling the weight of their affection?

Yes, it turns out. With Ben, it was possible.

I promised myself the summer before my freshman year that, no, I absolutely would not go to college, fall in love, and spend four years tied to another person. I was annoyed to meet Ben three weeks into the semester but too stubborn to give him away. One thing I've always had a talent for is recognizing a good thing when it's right in front of me.

I realized that all of the things that scared me—marriage, kids, big commitments—were not scary at all with someone next to me whom I trusted without reservation. I felt instantly known and understood by him. He respected and was, perhaps, even a bit charmed by my love of physical boundaries.

In today's cultural lingo, it would be easy to devolve this to love languages. His, touch. Mine, not touching me on purpose. As most couples do, we learned how to meet in the middle. Our hugs became a secret language. Every marriage has its own dictionary, and ours was the physical attention we each needed or didn't need in a given moment.

I knew when he had a tough day at work and needed me to crawl silently into his lap on the sofa and wrap my arms around his neck. He knew when to hug me from behind and bury his face in my hair after a particularly stressful visit from family. He never got it wrong, not once. He read my cues, and I read his. Ben's love of affection softened me in ways that mattered, in ways that made me a loving, affectionate mother from day one. A better daughter. A better friend.

I thought of Ben and our secret language whenever I met a new set of sad, teary eyes at his memorial service.

*He was too young. I'm sorry this was so sudden. He loved you and the kids so much. I can't believe this has happened to you two. You were perfect together.*

Inevitably, each person would bring me in for a hug. Each time, I had to remind myself that the hug wasn't for me. It was for them. It was for Ben. The guy who would've lined up and gladly taken a hug from each of these mourners and remember some minute detail about their life and tell them, genuinely, that he was happy to see them despite the circumstances.

Ben and I shared a dark sense of humor, and when we were feeling particularly stressed out, we would play a game called "The Reasons You Can't Die." We would call out clever things whenever they came to mind, like him admitting the kids would never see a summer camp enrollment or doctor's appointment without me. I would follow up by conceding that I would need to learn to pump gas again and how to operate the breaker box. Remembering birthdays without his prompt reminders would be impossible.

One night a year or so ago, we were lying in bed, exhausted, and playing the game after finally getting the kids to bed. After Ben added a few hilarious new items to the list, I looked at him earnestly and said, "You can't die, because I will turn to stone." He pulled me in close and we fell asleep tight together, like we were in his old twin bed.

The well-intentioned hugs at his memorial service only reminded me of what I'd lost. I could feel my heart and soul calcifying in real time, just like I had predicted.

Of course, the truth is, I would gladly become a hugger. A giggler. A walking human-interest repository, if it meant that I got just one more hug from Ben. To feel known and understood simply by the way he held me. I know the hug he would give me right now to make it all feel better, and yet I can't have it. I will never have it again.

I would do anything to look over at this empty space in my bed and see his blue eyes, convincing me with his wry smile that, yes, two people can inhabit this small space if we hold tight.

You'll love it, he would say, just like he did when I was eighteen. And I would.

# CHAPTER 2

"YESTERDAY AT LUNCH, GEMMA SAID THE ONLY REASON you're famous is because Dad died," Ava blurts out while we work together through the morning routine. We both pause and stare at one another, our matching hazel eyes locked. "And that you're probably glad it happened."

"Wow, sixth-grade girls are harsh," I respond while pulling my hair into a low ponytail. "I can't imagine thinking something so terrible and then having the gumption to say it out loud."

I know, of course, that twelve-year-old Gemma did not form this thought on her own. It smells of an adult opinion spilled in earshot of an impressionable kid. At least now I know what her mom thinks of me. If I weren't so physically and emotionally exhausted, I'd probably be angry. It never occurred to me that a daytime TV appearance would impact Ava's life. It's been two weeks since my Maisy interview aired, and parents are still stopping me at school to talk about it.

I glance at my sweet girl, the child who made me a mom, as she twirls her own dark-brown hair around her finger. She's ruminating on what Gemma had said, clearly. She was probably up late thinking about it. We can look each other in the eyes now, thanks to her last growth spurt and the height she inherited from Ben. In a few years she'll tower over me.

"Number one, I'm not famous. Writers don't get famous-famous, but I'm flattered Gemma thinks I am. Number two, let's be clear. I already have fifteen thousand presales of my book, which will likely make us very rich by this time next year," I say, raising my eyebrows playfully to impress her. "I would give it all up to have your dad back for a day. An hour, even! That's what I would actually be glad about."

I responsibly channel my now-simmering rage by being honest about bringing back Ben while also *slightly* inflating my presale numbers, so Ava will repeat them, and Gemma's mom will feel like garbage.

Ava hates when I opine or try to give advice (ironic, given that's all strangers want me to do), but I can't hold back.

"A real friend would never say that to you. Tons of inappropriate thoughts and ideas fly around your brain as a preteen, but part of life is learning when to keep your mouth closed and just"—I take a breath—"say nothing."

I look intensely at Ava, my spitting image with Ben's personality infused into every fiber of her being. I wonder what it must be like to have the worst thing happen to you so young: losing the person who understood you the best. Some people probably ask the same thing about me.

She smiles. "I know what you're going to say next: bottle this feeling up and remember how your heart and body feel. Make sure to avoid making someone else ever feel this way." She laughs because she's right, and her impression of me is uncanny. "It's not that serious, Mom."

Her tone is unconvincing. Gemma is popular and it's obvious Ava is wounded. I don't ask, but I assume other kids were around to hear it, too. Ava, like Ben before her, is a feeler. Comments like these go in one ear and out the other for me—which has proven useful in my new, unexpected life as a writer and semipublic figure. For people like Ava, those comments stick around.

"Maybe it's not a big deal," I say. "But your dad and I also believed that someone's true nature is shown in the small things. The day-to-day acts of friendship and life matter. You know this. And that statement"—I'm dramatically waving my hands at this point—"is not the work of a good nature. That is all."

I make a mental note to tell my therapist about this conversation and silently thank God we are in the last week of school before the summer break. This year has been too hard. For me, for the kids. So many firsts without Ben—birthdays, holidays, school events, trips.

What I really want to do right now is give Ava a few ideas of things she can say if the conversation reemerges today at school.

*Well, Gemma, your mom isn't going to get famous if she keeps losing PTA elections.*

*Your dad seems very interested in my mom's fame every time he sees her.*

*Don't be such an asshole, Gemma.*

I file these away as things to say to make Ava laugh later, if needed, because I know that my beautiful, loving, smart, and empathetic daughter would never say something quite so mean-spirited. She isn't me, after all.

Lost in my thoughts, I realize it's 7:25. We needed to be out the door three minutes ago.

"Benji, it's time!" I call to get my son's attention from the living room. He is a seventy-year-old man trapped in a fourth-grader's body. He was up, dressed, lunch packed, and breakfast made before Ava or I rolled out of bed. He is quiet, resourceful, and slightly obsessive. He's the inverse of Ava—looks like Ben, but every personality quality and quirk has come from me. I used to get up early, too.

---

ON THE WAY home from car pool, I make a stop at Pageturner, my favorite bookstore-meets–coffee shop in town. The college students cleared out when the semester ended a few weeks ago, and Franklin Street is blissfully quiet. I snag a parking spot right in front. *That's a lucky way to start the day*, I think.

A sign with beautiful script writing greets me at the entrance. *Books: your reward for having an attention span.* I'm a sucker for clever signs anywhere, and Pageturner is very good at them.

Coffee in hand, perched by the front window, I finally let myself take in that this is a big day. June 3. It's the first official day of my sabbatical from work. For the last year, I have somehow pushed through a full-time job, an unexpectedly popular biweekly column for *The New York Times*, drafting my memoir, and—oh yeah—somehow kept my and the kids' lives on track despite losing the person we loved most in the world.

I wasn't sure Carol, my real-life boss, would even agree to let me take a three-month sabbatical after my month of bereavement leave a year ago. I'm the lead marketing manager for a state tourism magazine, and the staff is small. Every person matters. Marketing doesn't fully capture what my three-person team does—we also run social media, email promotion, and special events. All on a shoestring budget and lots of desk lunches.

Carol is nothing if not a consummate saleswoman, and having a fame-adjacent writer on staff (but, ironically, not writing for the magazine) became something she could brag about. Also, she definitely wants a reason to nepo her freshly graduated niece onto the staff as a paid intern. Win-win.

What Carol doesn't know but probably intuits is that today starts my trial run to see if I can just be a writer. I think she's onto me, though, because yesterday she offered to pay me freelance for an essay about my "summer vacation in the great state of NC," as she called it. When she said the word "vacation," my leg twitch briefly acted up.

I can see the headline of my article now. "Lonely in the Mountains of NC: The Top Ten Hikes for Depressed Widows." Maybe I can include some tips for finding bears and offering yourself as a sacrifice.

Most people take a sabbatical to get away from work, but it feels like I'm diving headfirst into more work than I've ever had before—including the final push to get my memoir out the door for editing. Nothing about writing tens of thousands of words for my unfinished memoir sounds like a vacation. But if the full manuscript draft is not done by mid-August, we will not hit our aggressive printing deadlines, and if that happens, a late-spring release for next year is out of the question.

I'm deep in thought when a short, middle-aged woman quietly approaches me.

"I'm sorry, I don't mean to bother you, but are you Gracie Harris, the writer?"

I nod and smile, aware that this conversation is about to be equal parts endearing and overwhelming. This isn't my first rodeo.

"I just wanted to come say hi. My name is Dee. I live in town, and I kept hoping I'd run into you one day. I follow you on social media and I just love your writing. It got me through a really dark time when my brother died last year a few months after your husband. It's been so hard, but you've helped so much."

I relay my usual sentiments—that I'm humbled to be a part of her journey, that hopefully she's realized how strong she is, and that grief really is a son of a bitch. Everyone always laughs at that last part.

A year ago, I would have never believed you if you told me that I would be comfortable (and even welcoming) with strangers approaching me in coffee shops and grocery stores and doctors' offices. Because of the first essay, people usually don't try to hug me, but I often initiate or at least shake their hands after a little conversation.

For the first few months after the regular column started, I was able to remain completely anonymous—just a random sad widow with a byline that showed up in the Thursday Styles section of *The New York Times* twice a month. Sometime around Thanksgiving, things shifted in a big way. All it took was a few more essays going viral and the subsequent social media followers hopping on board for things to change. My feed was full of pictures of me, Ben, and the kids. For a decade, my Instagram was just me sharing silly and sweet family photos with a hundred people, but once readers started to follow me, a shift occurred. They could put real faces to the sad story. I don't post the kids anymore to help with their privacy, and I've hidden the old family posts, but my face is now easy to find.

Here in town, people sometimes look at me in public with that strange side-eye that says, *I think I know you, but I don't know how*, and they plaster on a friendly smile, wave, and walk away. Most people who do approach me are like Dee, and over time, I've come to appreciate them. On a few occasions when I've felt particularly tender, I've invited the person to join me for coffee and to talk a bit more about what we're both going through. The weird thing about grief is that it's often easier to open up to strangers. Grief is reflected back and forth, but it's not personal. They don't know Ben, and I don't know their loved one. It's the grief alone that binds us.

When Dee politely excuses herself after a minute, I snap myself back into reality and remember that today is also a big day because there is something else I need to do. I can no longer put off the task that's been at the top of my list for a month: call James.

James is my real estate agent. Well, not my agent here at home, but the one Ben and I used to buy our vacation house in Canopy, a cozy mountain town four hours west. The place where *we* were supposed to spend our summers while the kids attended sleepaway camp. The place where *we* would celebrate Thanksgiving and maybe even Christmas some years. Where our future grandkids would come to spend weeks with *us*. It's not that anymore.

It's just a stupid house with a million problems that I need help with.

Rather than call James, though, I open my laptop and email him instead. Chicken.

Hi James,

Thanks again for keeping an eye on things over the past year. I've decided to keep the house, at least for this summer. I need time to figure out what to do in the long-term.

As you know, the house is what can be generously described as a hot mess, and I would rather spontaneously combust than attempt a single DIY project. It's livable, but barely. I've got a list of things I want done, but of course, I have no connections. Do you have any GC recommendations? People you trust? You know, just someone who can do electrical, plumbing, drywall, and literally every type of general repair.

Gracie
P.S. At least it has Wi-Fi!

# CHAPTER 3

CANOPY IS A CLASSIC MOUNTAIN RETREAT THAT SWELLS every summer with visitors and families dropping their kids off at sleepaway camps. The locals blend with seasonal visitors and backpackers alike, creating an atmosphere that's vibrant, jovial, and intensely charming. It instantly feels like home.

That's how Ben and I discovered Canopy several years ago—dropping Ava off at her first one-week introductory camp session after she finished first grade. I was a camp kid, but Ben was not, and he was too nervous to leave the area, so we booked a house a few blocks from downtown. By the third day, we had both fallen in love and decided that we would buy a house for the family there as soon as we could afford it. It took some time, but we made that dream a reality.

We saw the house on Wilson Street for the first time on a rainy February afternoon last year. It was the first of three houses we toured with James that day and the one that turned into the obvious choice.

Ben wanted a house close to downtown. He wanted to be able

to walk a few blocks and grab coffee, lunch, or a new book. Ever the social butterfly, he felt it was crucial to have easy access to other living, breathing people he could strike up conversations with. I was much more interested in the idea of multiple acres of privacy a little farther away from town. Something that would offer complete quiet and relaxation in the mountain air—something different from what we already had at home.

Like so much else in our married life, the house on Wilson was full of willing compromise. Ben wanted to go for a modern, new home on a lot nearby (that they had torn down a perfectly adorable ranch house to build). I wanted the secluded old farmhouse with tons of character five miles east.

Wilson Street was the best of both worlds. A gorgeous Craftsman built in the 1930s that miraculously had only had three owners in all that time. Ben got his location; I got my character.

Cedar shingles covered the top story of the house, offset by freshly painted white brick on the first floor. A porch swing hung off to the side of a gracious, sturdy concrete porch. I sat on the swing, closed my eyes, and smelled the rain in the air. Heaven. The crisp, clean exterior tricked us into thinking the inside would be similarly polished. Not so.

When we walked through the front door, I was caught between two simultaneous and contradictory thoughts: this house has been so loved; this house is so gross.

A ratty green carpet greeted us in an empty living room. The sun and time had faded the parts of the carpet not covered by furniture, leaving the impression of a ready-made floor plan. I remember thinking the layout made a lot of sense for the space as I stared at where the sofa should have been. There were holes in the wall where paintings and photos had once hung, a cable sticking out over the fireplace where a TV had blared the weather report each morning.

Everything in the home was so worn, but you could feel *life* in it.

As I peered around the corner into the dining room, James told us he had spent some time here as a kid. His childhood best friend's aunt lived in the house for forty years and would invite them over after school. "She would feed us and then insist we go into the backyard and leave her alone while she read a book."

I stared at a long, dark wooden buffet in the dining room. It was the sole piece of furniture and, as such, conspicuous. James caught me staring.

"Bess, my friend's aunt, gave all her furniture away to family and friends before she moved into her new facility—except for this. She insisted that it stay. Her uncle and cousins had lived in the house before and they inherited the buffet from the original owner. It's the one thing that's stayed put."

While Ben inspected the obvious water damage and tested whether the windows would open and close properly, I ran my hand along the buffet. It was mostly smooth, broken only by the occasional water ring in the wood. That piece of furniture had witnessed so many moments in the room. I felt happiness there.

In the moment, I was pulled back to a decade prior when we were looking for a house in Chapel Hill. It was a few years after the Great Recession and there was an overwhelming amount of housing stock to consider. We toured house after house, and I developed a belief that you could quickly assess a home's energy after a few minutes in the space. We walked into one old house close to downtown, and Ben's eyes immediately bugged out.

"This house has bad energy," I said dramatically as my own eyes widened. "I do not think we should spend time here." A Google search later in the day told us that some grisly things had occurred there in the 1980s. From that moment on, Ben trusted me when I gave my energy assessment.

That's why I caught him looking at me as I meandered into the only first-floor bedroom, a smile on my face. "Good energy" is all I said. I felt it from the moment I walked through the door. He did, too, although he would never admit to feeling energy. Somehow, Mr. Feelings drew the line at vibes.

A door frame in this room had been used to track the heights of some number of children. The most recent one I could find was dated summer '98. I saw "James '95" and wondered if it was possible that we were walking through the house with a once-boy who measured himself against this wall.

"Bess—what was she like?" I called to the other room.

James appeared. "The best. She never had kids but loved kids. I was lucky to be one of the many she gave her attention to. As a parent now, I realize how good she was at knowing when friends in her life were overwhelmed and needed to offload their children. She was everyone's aunt."

He spoke about her in the past tense in a way that told me she wasn't still here but that she wasn't really gone, either. James had spent the last ten minutes walking around the house, caught in his own memories, and suddenly remembered why we were there.

"If it makes you feel better, I can tell you that under every nasty carpet is hardwood floor, even upstairs. And the foundation is solid."

Ben and I wandered for another half hour, finally meeting in the upstairs hallway.

"I love so much about this house, but there's a lot of work to do," I said, twirling my hair, a habit that Ava and I share when we are deep in thought. "The price is amazing, but I'm not sure we can take on these repairs."

"I can do it," Ben responded without a moment of hesitation, catching my eye and seeing a dubious expression cross my face. "Well, I can figure out most of it and we can pay someone to do the rest. Plus, the kitchen renovation is fairly recent, and that would be the hardest thing to do on our own."

Ben didn't know how to do anything the house needed, but he had a famous ability among our friends to learn new skills from watching a single YouTube tutorial. So, though he'd never so much as repainted a bedroom, I had no reason to doubt he could pull this renovation off.

One thing that Ben and I had in common was that *no one* would describe us as impetuous, especially with big decisions. We agonized over when to have kids, when he should go back to get his MBA, and when to buy our first home. But this felt right. It felt happy. And safe. Like it belonged to us.

"Mr. Harris, I think we should buy the house."

"Mrs. Harris, I think we should, too."

---

I REMEMBER FORTY-FIVE days later. After we closed on the house, Ben's parents came to stay with the kids for a long weekend so that we could drive to Canopy and do lots of planning. We measured every inch and discussed options and projects until we couldn't keep them straight anymore. Ben made six trips to the hardware store on Main Street to get tools he didn't really need but thought were essential to have in the house.

Our first night there, a Friday, was spent on an inflatable mattress in the living room. We were due to pick up some basic furniture the next day, but for that one night, it was like being twentysomething again in one of our first apartments in Chicago. His long legs dangled off the end while I curled up tightly against him. We laughed all night, trying to lie perfectly still, but inevitably one of us would readjust and displace the other.

By the time we left on Sunday after breakfast at our new favorite spot, we had cataloged every repair needed, categorized them based on difficulty, and prioritized the list. We had a plan, a checklist. We would work remotely from Canopy all summer while the kids were at camp. Ben would spend every free minute repairing the house, and I would spend my time slowly decorating it. Making it ours. It might take a summer or two (or three), but that was fine. We had time.

The drive back home was perfect. We took the scenic route and kept the windows down until we hit the interstate. When we could hear each other again, we talked about everything we had done and built together. We had our vacation house in the mountains—a place to spend summers and make memories. Everything was so right.

Except, it wasn't, really. Ten days after we got home, Ben was dead.

# CHAPTER 4

MY PHONE BUZZES, AND WHEN I SEE HIS NAME, I SMILE. Obviously, James has decided to respond to my email with a phone call because that's what small-town people do.

I texted him a few weeks after Ben died. We—us and the kids—were supposed to be back in Canopy to do more planning and tackle some easy projects as a family. James was insisting on taking us out to lunch in celebration of the new house. I don't know why, but it was one of the most challenging texts I had to send during the whole initial ordeal. A call was out of the question; I learned quickly that I would fall apart during those conversations.

Ben and James had hit it off during our home search. It started six months before we found the Craftsman, during a frustrating lull in the market. They would talk about college basketball and hiking while I walked the houses, hoping to manifest the magic feeling that we had found *the one*.

James was devastated by the news. Like many of our friends and coworkers, he saw himself in Ben—in his forties, young kids, successful career. All gone. Poof. He and Ben got on so well. I also suspected that James felt the loss of a future fishing buddy and missed a potential friend that he never really got to know. James proceeded to check in on me at least once a month via text, usually wrapped in a compliment about my most recent essay. The thing about good, nice people is that they can be painfully sincere. More than once, his messages and commentary on my writing made me cry. Okay, sob.

I remember one text a few months into this internet-famous-because-my-husband-died-and-now-I-write-about-it roller coaster: Good news: I have everyone in Canopy hooked on your writing and they can't wait to meet you. Bad news: everyone in Canopy is a fan and can't wait to meet you. Something about that message captured the essence of my existence at the time.

I slide my finger across the phone and take the call.

"Hey, James."

"Gracie Harris, it is so nice to hear your voice!" He's speaking in a raised voice because at least two of his young kids are loudly running around in the background. "It's been too long, but I feel like we've seen each other because Kendell saw your segment on *The Maisy Show* and recorded it for me."

Kendell is his equally sincere and wonderful wife. She sent a stunning floral arrangement after I shared the news with James. *Deepest sympathies from Kendell, James, and frankly, everyone in your new home away from home*, the card read. I have Kendells in my life, and I know it pained her that they missed the memorial service for someone they didn't really know but would've loved if given the chance.

"Please tell me that you were too busy to watch it," I say, feeling my ego take a hit before the conversation even gets started.

"You were great," he said. "Maisy asked you way too many personal questions and you handled them with grace."

"I appreciate that you're skipping right past the part where I blacked out in front of a studio audience," I respond, laughing—mostly at myself.

"Sure, it got a little rocky, but you kept going," he says in a stern but still caring voice. "Which is certainly more than I would've been able to do in your shoes. You were brave—don't let anyone tell you different."

After the episode aired, people in my real life and online had lots of opinions about the interview. Some felt Maisy was too tough, or I was too sensitive, that I should never have been let on in the first place, or that the show should've cut the part that showed me crashing out. It seemed that everyone could find someone to share a stance with them. The truth is that I mostly felt numb. Empty. Embarrassed. And far from brave.

"I appreciate that, James," I tell him. "I assume you're calling to do more than just say unreasonably kind things to me?"

"Indeed. I've got good news—a solution to your problem." There is a quick pause as if James is psyching himself up. "My brother."

"Your brother?" My tone is curious and cautious.

"Yup. He has all the skills you need and more. He can jump right into any work you have."

This seems too easy. I expected the search for a contractor to take some time and to be told everyone was backed up for months. Supply chains! Demand! Labor shortage! James just happens to have a brother available to help? My stranger-danger flags are being hoisted up the flagpole.

"Is he a recently released convict or something? How does he have time to do this?"

James laughs in the way that only a brother can when they've heard a solid burn at a sibling's expense. One of his boys stops to ask, "What's so funny, Daddy?" but James shoos him away.

"Actually, he's a GC and has not broken any major laws since reaching adulthood. He runs a very successful building company and spent the last five years working nonstop. Like, literally no breaks—builders like him have been in high demand. We all basically did an intervention and forced him to take a break for the entire summer so he doesn't drop dead."

You don't realize how often a turn of phrase like that is used until you experience the literal version of it. Nobody can say those words around me without instantly feeling like garbage (despite the fact it doesn't bother me, because people like Ben do indeed drop dead), so James quickly adds, "You know, he needs to get some hobbies, take it easy."

I throw him a lifeline. "How's that going for him?"

"He's bored out of his mind, Gracie. Wakes up at the crack of dawn, goes on long runs, and then is twiddling his fingers by nine a.m. I'm afraid if we don't find something for him soon that takes just a little of his time, he will sneak back to work. I've never wished a video game addiction on anyone before, but he could use it. The man needs a break. His pace was not sustainable."

"Do you remember the inside of this house? It doesn't sound like much of a break to me."

"Gracie, he was working seventy-hour weeks for years. Running from site to site, meeting to meeting, issue to issue. A few hours a day at your place, working at a reasonable pace, *is a break*. Trust me—plus, the type of work your house needs is the problem-solving stuff that Josh loves."

So, the brother has a name. Josh.

A real-life GC has landed in my lap. The house could actually be nice by the end of the summer. If I decide to keep it, I'll have a beautiful home to enjoy and share with friends. If, more likely, I decide to sell it, I might actually be able to make a significant profit, thanks to the repairs.

I let the silence go on too long, and James seems to sense I'm not entirely sold on the deal.

"How about this? I'll have Josh do the most obvious thing that I'm sure is at the top of your list: the green carpet in the living room. We know there are wood floors under there. He'll tear up the carpet and refinish the floors on the first level. They'll be done by the time you get here next week. He'll just charge for materials. If you like the work, I'll bring him by, and you can discuss the rest of your list."

Before the end of summer, I need to write thirty thousand words of my memoir, crank out essays for one of the biggest newspapers in the country, and do about a hundred interviews that I've put off to help grow my personal brand, develop my author persona, and hopefully build my confidence back up. The house, as it stands today, is the least creatively motivating space I can imagine doing this work in.

Like many writers, my approach is to brainstorm, procrastinate, and write feverishly at the last possible second. I know at least twenty thousand words will be written in the last few weeks (although I will *think* a lot about writing beforehand). By that point, the space will be exactly what I need.

This brother—Josh—will be in my space a lot. What if he's not sincere, kind, and self-aware like his brother? Worst of all, what if he's really good at home repairs but a complete dick? Is home resale more important than a peaceful work environment?

I think momentarily about asking for more details about Josh, but I decide it won't change my mind. I really do care about the resale value.

"Okay, James. I'm sold. I really hope he's not a weirdo."

# CHAPTER 5

MY LITERARY AGENT GIVES ME EXACTLY THREE DAYS TO enjoy my sabbatical before insisting on flying down to Chapel Hill from New York to discuss my book and summer plans. She arrives in time for lunch on my final day of freedom before the school year ends. Felicity is nothing if not determined to keep me on schedule.

When the book offers came flying in after my viral Modern Love essay, I naively assumed that I would get to dictate the direction of the book. The initial pitch was a memoir composed of essays (different from my regular column, but still essays), which the publisher rejected outright. Essays are a comfort zone for me, if that's not obvious.

"They want you, but not *that* book," I remember Felicity telling me, emphasizing that we would find the right formula for everyone.

Eventually, we landed on a traditional-style memoir, but one that would be focused on a single year of my life: the one I'm living right now. The goal is for me to write in as close to real time as possible, mirroring the raw and unsteady tone of my essays. The end product, hopefully, will tell the honest story of the first year or so of grief. Someone at the publisher said, "Think Joan Didion for millennials," and I just about had my own heart attack from the anxiety of living up to that.

I'm twirling the straw around in my sweet tea when I see Felicity bound into this Mediterranean café—pushing through the double doors with flair instead of just calmly opening one. Here's what you need to know: Felicity Hines is a classic New York creature. That is, at least what we non–New Yorkers perceive they all look like. If I were to write a novel set in New York City, Felicity would be my protagonist. She's tall, slim, always dressed in black, and her perpetually tan skin is glistening like she just left her facialist. Her hair is pulled tightly into a low bun.

This woman just got off an airplane! When I get off a plane—even after a quick flight—my skin is dried up like a roasted almond. She looks perfectly dewy and fully rested, despite the fact she was probably up around 5 a.m. to get to the airport in time for her flight.

I wave her over and stand to greet her with a big hug. I like Felicity—she's honest, funny, and knows her stuff. I can't think of a better person to have in my corner, even if she is sometimes the messenger of bad tidings between the publisher and me.

"It's so wonderful to see you in real life," she says. "Video chat doesn't do you justice, my love."

"Likewise. I'm glad you were able to get down here on such short notice," I respond as we take our seats on the bistro-style chairs.

"Anything for my current favorite writer," she says with a devious smile. "Plus, I'm going to visit my old stomping grounds down the street in Durham."

Felicity did undergrad at Duke but left for New York the week after graduation and never looked back. And yet even people who aren't particularly nostalgic find it fun to return to the places that made them into adults. If you close your eyes in the quad, you can almost feel young again. What I would give to be eighteen again with Ben.

"Let's order," I say firmly. "And then we can get down to business and talk about the book. I assume you're here for a reason."

She nods. It's a Greek salad for me and falafel for her. She wastes no time jumping into book talk.

"Okay, let's start with the stats. Where are you?" she asks.

The answer to this question is not Chapel Hill. It's not North Carolina. It's not even a state of persistent stress and delusion. She means how many words have I written—this is the currency we deal in.

"Fifty thousand words done," I answer, pretending to be proud despite the fact that when combined, those words as a whole are a disjointed mess.

"Phenomenal," she replies, borderline giddy. "Most of my authors are not as on the ball as you are, Gracie. I'm basically begging for words. Do you still feel good about the mid-August deadline for the first draft?"

I nod but add, "I'm not sure what condition the overall narrative arc will be in. You and Jeannie will really need to help me work through this. I know the timeline is tight."

Jeannie is my editor. She has helped birth five bestselling memoirs in as many years and has a sixth sense for what works and what doesn't. She's the one who killed my book-of-essays idea. I still remember what she said: "We can't be so obvious and predictable." She's a tough but fair editor and the type of person I claimed I needed to get me through my debut book. I don't need her to hold my hand; that's what Felicity is for.

"Have you thought any more about her prologue idea?" Felicity asks, avoiding both eye contact and any emotion in her voice as she reaches for a piece of freshly baked focaccia from the basket between us.

Jeannie is *convinced* that my prologue needs to be an emotional kick in the balls: a no-holds-barred description of Ben's death.

"I know why she wants it and what it adds," I say, looking directly at Felicity so that she knows I'm serious. "I won't pretend that I don't, but I haven't been able to bring myself to write it just yet."

That's a lie. I've just lied to her face.

I've written Jeannie's prologue concept three times and deleted it *completely* three times. I can't be certain, but judging by word counts before I hit the Delete key, it was nearly the exact same each time. Each detail. Each memory. Seared into my brain. But as long as I keep deleting it, I keep protecting myself.

The biggest concern the publisher has about my manuscript is that it will be too close to the content of the *New York Times* essays. I've never written about Ben's death, so using that for a prologue seems like a truly fresh idea. Bonus stress: after an underwhelming essay a few weeks ago, my editor at the paper has now voiced concerns that I'm leaving the good stuff for the book.

And today, a few days before I need to throw two camp trunks and tons of luggage into the back of my SUV and get myself and the kids to Canopy, I'm sitting here trying to convince Felicity that I've got the memoir fully handled (I don't) and that I will be emotionally strong enough to write about the worst day of my life (I won't be).

"To be clear, though, you do agree that it's a strong and captivating way to start the book, right?" she asks with the tone of a rhetorical question. "There's a reason Maisy tried to get you to share the story. It's the type of emotional pull that will make someone buy the book if they pick it up in a store and read the first few pages. That matters, Gracie, because memoirs are a tough sell even with an online following like yours."

*My following.* Felicity is referring to the nearly five hundred thousand people and counting who now follow me on Instagram. Every time an essay goes viral or I do a notable media appearance, my follower count grows by a few thousand more. Organic new followers trigger algorithmic magic that can, over the span of a few days, turn five thousand people who found me from my latest column into triple that number. One of the only good things to come out of the recent appearance on *The Maisy Show* was the nearly fifty thousand new followers in just a few days.

My followers are mostly women, almost exclusively between the ages of thirty and fifty years old, and people with expendable income to do fun things—like buy books. It's impossible to truly quantify, but Jeannie believes that nearly all of my presales can be attributed to my social media following. When it comes to the book and prospective sales, my followers matter. A lot. But hopefully, they won't be the only people who buy the book.

"I trust the experts," I say. "I will write the version that Jeannie wants to see, but don't be surprised if I deliver the manuscript with an alternate beginning in there as well."

"Fair enough," Felicity responds, although it's obvious she also thinks the death scene will be money in the bank for all of us. It just doesn't feel right.

"Are you going to ask me about the interview?" I jump in, knowing she won't want to be the one to bring it up.

"Honestly? I'm not sure there is anything I could say that you haven't probably already heard," she states matter-of-factly. "You must be sick of conversations where people tell you it wasn't that bad—and you don't believe them, obviously."

"You've only known me for a year and yet you know me so well."

"Maisy has always been one to go off script just a bit," she reminds me. "There is a lot of pressure on her to figure out how to grow her audience. I'm not surprised they booked you—your readers are exactly the people they want. She certainly got their attention."

"She sure did," I respond, before adding, "You'll be happy to know that, at my request, Lucia has lined up lots of small-time interviews for the summer. I need to work my way up to another big appearance like that. *The Maisy Show* was *a lot* for me. I want to be fully ready for the big time by next spring when the book comes out, and I need to get better at speaking off the cuff."

"I will say this," Felicity begins. "If there is one thing you know how to do, it's capture the internet's attention for a day. There are worse ways to sell books."

"For my sake, let's hope I don't discover what any of those are."

We both let out a laugh. If it had been *really* bad, Felicity would be honest with me. The fact that she's being so casual about it makes me think that perhaps it really was just *normal* bad.

With business out of the way, Felicity smiles and adeptly changes the subject to our favorite thing to commiserate about: our dating lives. She prods me for details on my latest blind date with the brother of a friend. It's funny how everyone you know suddenly has single brothers and cousins the second you're back on the market with the low standards of a woman on the ultimate emotional rebound. Also, everyone is trying to help me "get back out there." Felicity is single after her divorce a few years back, and for every hilarious story I have, she always has a way to one-up me. Dating in New York sounds incredibly entertaining and absolutely dreadful. I imagine she thinks the same thing about dating in the limited pool of a college town.

Dating is particularly hard for me because all of my friends are married and can't relate to the modern dating scene. To be fair, until my first date late last year, I didn't understand the current condition of the dating scene *at all*. When my friends go right to deep questions after first dates, I recall every time that I did the same to them over the years. Karma will always get you. Conversations with Felicity are a breath of fresh air. I get to be lighthearted and unserious—she never asks me if I've met the future Mr. Gracie Harris. She's the one who I can truly dish with. She reminds me a lot of Jenny before she met her husband.

Through giggles, we inappropriately and loudly discuss our body-hair preferences in men. I'm shocked to discover she likes the high-maintenance men who wax or shave their chests. Give me all natural, I respond, with a cackle that makes us both laugh so hard the old ladies sitting nearby shush us. Out comes my phone so I can show her a photo of Ben at the beach a few years ago. Some people share baby photos. I brag about how cute my dead husband was.

"Gracie, I get it," she says with a knowing smile, before adding, "He really was a good-looking guy."

After an hour and a half, Felicity pays the bill, and we share a big hug before she heads to meet a friend in Durham and I return to the house.

"You've got this," she says to me, sensing my general anxiety. "And I don't just mean the book, Gracie. I mean *all* of this. I was going to try to convince you to get away for a bit, but it sounds like your friends already took care of that. It's the right choice, and I think it's going to blow your mind how good it feels. Write a ton in the mountains, but girl, try to get some fresh air, too."

"I'll do my best, as always," I respond with a smile. Fresh air sounds good right about now.

---

TODAY'S THEME OF consulting with experts continues with my 3 p.m. therapy appointment. It's my final to-do before heading out to get the kids from the last day of their after-school program.

Prior to Ben's death, I had never seen a therapist or psychologist (confession: I didn't know the difference), but it became clear to me very quickly that I needed an impartial third party in my life if I was going to get through this.

Everyone told me that I should see a local therapist. They wanted someone whose cushy armchair I could curl up in and share my innermost thoughts, but I hated the idea of dropping into the hippie grocery co-op down the road for an orange or some fancy cheese and running into the person I'd previously confessed deep secrets to. This project—me—requires distance.

A friend of a friend who I followed on social media lost her husband a few years before Ben died. She talked a lot about how important her therapist was to her "healing journey." As much as the phrase made me want to gag, I still reached out for the recommendation.

I liked Dr. Lisa from the moment we met via little rectangular boxes on our laptop screens. I liked the safety and distance that virtual therapy offered. Me, in the comfort of my own home. Her, in her cozy home office somewhere in the Pacific Northwest. Portland, maybe? She told me once, but now I forget, and it feels rude to ask again.

In our first session, she told me to call her Lisa. I confessed that I liked formality in these situations to keep the lines from getting blurry. We landed on Dr. Lisa, which makes me feel like I'm visiting my kids' pediatrician, but it helps me with boundaries.

With fifteen minutes left in that first session late last summer, she'd asked me something that I hadn't expected.

"Have you had your great unravel yet?" she inquired.

"My what?" was my question as answer.

"A lot of times—most times, actually—after a sudden loss like this, someone experiences what I've learned to call the great unravel. It's that moment when everything hits you at once. Different types of people have it at different times. It's a mind- and body-altering experience, insomuch as you aren't in control of anything," she explained.

"Well, I mean, I've cried a lot," I said, "including many nights curled in a ball, sobbing myself to sleep. Is that what you're talking about?"

"That's normal behavior, given what's happened," she started. "But no, that's not what unraveling feels like. It's been my professional experience that we don't really start 'moving on'—although to be clear, that's a loaded phrase—until this happens."

"Maybe I'll be the exception to the rule," I respond.

"Everyone says that," she told me. "You are doing a wonderful job working through your feelings, Gracie, but you also have a lot of commitments that compromise the potential of your emotional processing power. I believe we will come to a point where you experience this unraveling, and when it happens, I'll be here for you."

I remember being annoyed at her insisting I was hurtling toward an inevitable breakdown, but I've made it a practice to believe experts when they tell me things. So, I filed that into the back of my mind and kept moving. Nearly a year later with Dr. Lisa and no unraveling yet. Just my janky eye twitches, leg shakes, and near blackouts on television.

During our regular weekly appointments, I still talk about my grief a lot but have also graduated to generalized griping about work, writing, family, dating fails, and this emerging internet fame of mine. We'd been on a lighthearted streak for a few months, but for the last six weeks, my appointments have all been double sessions. First came the anniversary of Ben's death, then the Maisy interview (in real life), followed by my friends practically staging an intervention to convince me to get out of town, and finally—the icing on the cake—the airing of the Maisy interview. It's been a lot to unpack. I almost took this one back down to an hour, but as the session creeps into the second hour, I'm glad for the extra time with Dr. Lisa.

"How are you feeling about the impending move to Canopy for the summer?" she asks, adding, "I know it's something we've talked about a lot, but it's only a few days away now. Still feeling that it's the right decision?"

"I am. Once my friends helped me see the light, it's been clear that it's the right choice—I'm genuinely excited now," I respond without hesitation. "I desperately need a place that allows me to be a little more anonymous. I know that some people might recognize me, but it will be rare. I need to be someplace where my grief isn't right there on the surface for the taking. I feel like everyone here knows my business."

In Chapel Hill, everywhere I go people ask me how I feel, putting a hand to their heart when they ask with such predictability it's comical. Most people—me included, before Ben died—have no idea how to be around someone who is deeply sad, so they perform a version of grief support that feels safe.

I sense a friendly reminder coming from Dr. Lisa, so I preempt her commentary.

"I'm very aware that this is about more than just 'hiding' my grief. If I make a few friends or even friendly acquaintances while I'm there, it will be nice to have people who get to know Gracie the person, not Gracie the sad widow," I say.

"That's the right attitude," Dr. Lisa says. "You are an incredible woman, Gracie, and this is a beautiful opportunity to meet new people and be your own person for the first time in a long while."

Dr. Lisa comes back to this a lot. Ben and I got married young and, as is prone to happen, grew up together in a way that we became "Ben and Gracie." Not Ben, not Gracie, but an inextricably linked duo. Finding my own way has been hard, mostly because I desperately don't want to say goodbye to the Gracie that Ben knew and loved.

"You texted me that your agent was making a last-minute trip to see you. How did that go?" she asks, changing the topic.

"Pretty good," I respond. "Felicity is wonderful. She's my age, she understands me, she builds up my confidence every time I see her, and we have so much in common, but . . ."

"But . . ." Dr. Lisa adds for dramatic effect. I love when she does this. It's a gift of more time for me to find and rehearse the right words in my head before I speak.

"She brought up my editor's prologue idea again," I say in a despondent voice. "I get it, I really do, but it feels so gross to share such a private moment. If my kids were older and I could get their permission as informed adults or even teenagers, maybe I would, but there is a reason I've never written an essay about it."

I say this a lot—this line about wanting to protect my kids' privacy. Yet every time I hear my voice say it out loud, something feels not quite right about it. Don't get me wrong—I'm being honest, but I can't help but feel like there is something else going on, too. Every time, though, I tuck that concern neatly back where it came from and direct my energy to the nearest distraction.

"I understand that," she says. "Even if you don't publish it, there could be value in being brave and writing what you remember. Memories get fuzzy over time, and as hard as it might be to read, you and your kids might find value in having it documented."

I don't admit to Dr. Lisa my little secret of having already written the death scene three times—omniscient-narrator style, of course, because I wasn't there for most of it. I know she's right, but I'm just not ready to hit Save on that story yet.

"I feel afraid," I say, utilizing a straightforward feeling statement like she has coached me to do. "People love to play the Grief Olympics with me. Just last week a woman came up and started telling me how helpful my writing was to her 'much more tragic than mine' situation. There is a subset of people that use loss and grief like they're a competitive sport—if they do that *after* reading about Ben's death, I won't be able to control myself."

"Grief Olympics," Dr. Lisa repeats. "That's a clever way to frame what you've just described. I see it a lot in my line of work, as I'm sure you can imagine."

Before that moment, it never occurred to me to give that experience a name, but Grief Olympics is pretty good. Immediately I start turning questions over in my head: What leads people to minimize others' grief? Why do some believe we've codified a hierarchy of grief—kids, partners, siblings, parents, friends, pets . . . in that order? Why is it only human loss we factor into the Grief Olympics? What sort of coping mechanism is this?

I'm smiling by the time Dr. Lisa and I say our goodbyes a minute later. This is how every one of my essays—particularly the popular ones—starts out. All it takes is a simple line of questioning with myself, usually mulling over a phrase or experience in my mind until it forms into the crux of an argument or a point awaiting a counterpoint. This concept of Grief Olympics has the legs to be both good *and* viral. I start jotting down notes in preparation for later tonight, when I'll sit down to type out a draft of my next essay once the kids are asleep.

---

MY FAVORITE ESSAYS and book chapters that I've written fall into two distinct categories: they either flow hot and heavy like an erupting creative volcano *or* require the patience and extraction techniques of an archaeological dig. Some stories come easy, but others want you to work for every single word that hits the page. Both are rewarding.

"Can We Stop Competing in the Grief Olympics?" falls into the category of fast-moving lava. An eighteen-hundred-word draft is done and dusted in a little over an hour. My own editing takes just another hour on top of that.

As usual, I spend the most time agonizing over my targeted pull quotes. If my career in marketing taught me anything, it's the importance of a killer hook. Plus, sometimes consumers need to be guided to the best choice for sharing. I try to put one or two obvious "quotable" lines in every essay. These are the quotes that my social media intern (yes, I have one of those) will drop into graphics and share across social platforms.

These are the lines I *expect* people will latch onto the most. Pull quotes are what help essays go viral, which means more readers, which brings more social followers, which results in more book presales. The marketer in me knows that pull quotes are the kindling that lights the Web-traffic and book-sale fire. They matter. Today's pull quote has my classic marriage of contemplative and humorous tones.

> *Grief isn't a competition. If it were, it would look something like a bunch of us trying to win the heptathlon without ever training. We lack the skills for every piece of the competition and only manage to get to the finish line by observing and learning from the ways we all crash and burn. That's no competition I want to be part of.*

I text Danny, my beloved editor at *The New York Times*. New essay incoming. I think this is a good one . . . I hope you enjoy it.

With a few steps still remaining in my complex nighttime skin-care routine, I hear my phone buzz from the bedside table.

This is a classic Gracie essay. Thank you. Edited version in your inbox by tomorrow evening.

# CHAPTER 6

A FEW DAYS LATER, TRADITION DICTATES THAT THE KIDS and I pile into Ava's room to kick off their sibling sleepover. This started Ava's first year of camp, when then five-year-old Benji was distraught over the thought of her leaving for so long. That first year of camp was only a week long, but in his sweet little mind it must have felt like forever. A few years later, neither of them got a good night's sleep because Benji was so excited for *his* first camp experience that our usually quiet kid couldn't keep his mouth shut. I remember Ben and I leaving the room around 10 p.m. in a fit of giggles while Ava playfully pleaded with Benji to *please stop talking*. Last summer? They didn't go to camp and we missed more than just this tradition. It felt like we were missing the world.

For an hour, I lie on the floor talking with them about their hopes for camp while they drift off to sleep. I doze off for a few minutes but then wake up and walk quietly to my room for one more good night of sleep in a familiar place before I spend the summer getting to know a new one all alone. There is a strange sense of nostalgia for this home I haven't left yet. Ben is everywhere here—not just in the photos on the wall, but in every decor choice (he loved buying ridiculous carved-wood animals everywhere we went) and furniture arrangement. We built this house together. It feels inconceivable to say goodbye to it, even for just one summer.

A predictable but still miserable wave of sadness hits me as I lie down in the bed, fully clothed, to wonder if this life I'm living will ever get a little easier. Unfortunately, easy is not on the agenda tonight.

---

THE FETAL POSITION gets a bad rap. Too many people view it as emblematic of a complete collapse. The reality is more nuanced.

For me, it's the ultimate act of self-preservation that acknowledges all shades of the devastation color wheel while simultaneously easing my body out from the stresses of the world. The curved spine, the tucked head. It's a brilliant act of release against the rigidity of the worst seasons of life.

One side of my body gets warm against the crisp linen duvet while the other feels the fresh breeze from the fan above. I am stifled and free all at once. It's the best position for that sticky mix of exhaustion, overwhelm, and loneliness that I feel this evening.

Of course, the fetal position is how Ava finds me an hour after I leave her room.

"I couldn't stay asleep—I'm too excited to leave tomorrow," she says, cracking the door slightly to witness tonight's mental malaise. She raises her eyebrows when she sees me. "Is everything okay?"

I've mostly hidden my worst moments of grief from the kids,

but it's a delicate balance. I want them to know it's healthy, normal, and admirable to experience grief. If you tuck away grief too much, it makes it harder to deal with when it jumps out at you when you least expect it. Being open and honest about our grief is something that we've handled pretty well as a downsized family of three.

Tonight's situation is an entirely different beast. It's a full-body-and-mind grief-induced exhaustion that borders on paralysis. Despite my best efforts, a few times over the last year Ava has found me in a variation of this scene: curled up in my trusty fetal position, fully clothed, lying on the unmade bed, trying to muster the will to get up, do the nightly skin-care routine, and crawl back into bed with a whisper of hope that tomorrow will be better.

Early on it was fairly common for me to be fetal and sobbing. Lately, however, I can't seem to cry. Maybe it's the sensory overload of my life or maybe I've just cried so much since Ben died that there are no tears left in my body. Tonight, I'm mostly numb.

"Have you sent a note to the group chat?" Ava asks, crawling into the bed to face me, tucking a lock of hair gently behind my ear.

"Do I look that pathetic?" I ask back.

"You look like you need Aunt Jenny," Ava says, examining me with the curious and judgmental eyes that only preteens can fully master. "Maybe even Keke."

I smile through the stress. The group text has ten amazing women from all stages of my life. The local girls are the ones who jump in when I need a night out or a meal delivered. Friends who live states away are often the ones who take long or late-night phone calls. Different time zones are an unexpected gift after years of bemoaning long-distance friendship.

Jenny is my oldest and closest friend. I've known her since we were ten years old in Charlotte. Although she's not my actual sister, she's Ava's godmother and practically family. Keke is a clinical professor of psychology. The fact that these are the two people Ava thinks I need tonight—well, it suggests things look even worse than they feel.

More times than I care to admit over the last year I've sent a note to the group text akin to a bat signal. I need to talk. Today was the worst. I can't believe I have to live without Ben forever. If I have to decide what to make for dinner one more night, I'm going to lose it. Will I ever have free time again? To be fair, those last two sentiments were shared in the pre-widow days, too.

Every time, without fail, a video chat request comes through from one or more of the girls within minutes. Some of my friends are more lighthearted, like Jenny, and others are more serious, like Keke. The universe always seems to find exactly the right friend for me to talk to in the moment.

"Where's your phone?" Ava asks.

I gesture to the nightstand, and she rolls over to Ben's side of the bed to grab it.

"Is there anything in particular I should say?"

"It's everything and nothing," I quickly answer. "That's probably enough."

Ava taps away, kindly places the phone next to me, and kisses my forehead. She mumbles something about not staying up too late on the phone and quietly walks back to her room. I glance down at the text thread and see Mom is freaking out about the summer. Someone please call her, she looks pathetic. Love you all. She read me like a book. The message is lighthearted enough, however, for me to know that she's not *too* worried.

While I'm reading Ava's message, Jenny responds with a heart and quick On it note. This will keep the other girls from stressing out and save their Friday night from becoming a widow-filled bummer. I know my friends don't really feel that way, but I do.

A few minutes later, a FaceTime comes in from my dearest, most trusted friend. Before I can say a word, she jumps in.

"Did you put that oxygen mask on?" she asks, skipping the normal pleasantries and asking a question she already knows the answer to. "Tell me everything."

"It is *everything*, Jenny," I begin. "I'm already missing the kids for the summer, I'm sad to leave this bed and the imaginary Ben smells, I'm weirded out by the new routine I need to manage and nervous about spending months in that crappy house."

"It's a lot to handle, and it's completely understandable," she responds. "From your text the other day, I assumed that the house was getting fixed up?"

"It is," I answer, "assuming James's brother actually knows what he's doing, but I'm losing my mind about everything. I'm really scared about the book not living up to expectations. I don't want to disappoint everyone. I want to honor Ben's memory."

She's uncharacteristically quiet for a split second, and it's clear I've given her a useful nugget to work with.

"Listen, Gracie, I'm not going to pretend that the book and the column aren't a big damn deal, because it still blows my mind what my best friend has achieved," she says in her no-nonsense voice so that I know she's serious. "But I've also never been more sure of or more confident in someone's ability to get a job done. You've totally got this. Ben would be so proud—of the column, of the book, of everything you managed to make happen this last year."

"A year ago, when I agreed to all of this, I thought it would make me feel closer to him, you know?" I share. "I thought that writing about Ben all of the time would be this invisible tether to keep him right here where he belongs. It's all just so much more complicated than that."

"I get that; I do," she says. "Don't get mad at me for asking, but are you getting out enough? You know that I would never tell you that you need to 'move on,' but sometimes an escape is a good thing."

"Both my and Ben's parents watched the kids a bunch last month," I answer. "I went on three dates and two girls' nights out. Getting out is not my problem."

"Three dates?" she responds in a curious voice, jumping on the one non-bummer detail that I've offered her. "Any potential?"

"All very nice. Two doctors and a lawyer. Nothing special."

"Anyone special . . . enough?" she asks with a giggle, clearly trying to lighten the mood and genuinely wondering if I slept with any of them. Jenny found her husband in her late thirties, so she spent most of her adult life dating. As such, she has a very different view of casual hookups than I do. She's always telling me not to take things so seriously. I try to embrace that, I really do, but it's not easy.

"I'm not sure my intimacy-starved need for attention makes someone truly special, but you could say they were enough of something."

"I'll take that as a humble yes that you got lucky," she says with a subtle smile. "I'll also say this to my humble friend: you are smart and funny, curious, and immensely talented. I know dating is hard and feels meaningless right now, but you are a catch and there is someone else out there for you. I know it."

"I just keep hoping Ben will walk back through the door and tell me there's been a big mistake or he just wanted the life insurance money," I say wistfully. "I wouldn't even be mad."

"Gracie, that breaks my heart. I wish that were possible, but you know it's not," she says, injecting that jolt of reality I know is right but that makes my chest ache. "Have you talked to your therapist about this?"

"She could drop all her other clients and I'm pretty sure I could keep her in business," I answer. "I'm embarrassed how much I still need you all—you, the girls, Dr. Lisa—to keep me from sinking," I say.

"Sweetie, when's the last time you cried?" she asks me with genuine concern, acknowledging the dry eyes staring back at her. This seems more like a Keke question, and it makes me wonder what conversations they've had without me.

"Three months ago," I respond.

"What about Chicago?" she inquires with an incredulous tone that isn't judging but is genuinely curious.

Ben and I kept saying for years that we needed to take the kids to the city where we met. Chicago held so many wonderful memories for us. But as happens with life, things got busy. Holidays were usually spent with family, spring break meant trips to warm locations, and we never got around to Chicago as a family of four.

So a month and a half ago, the kids and I spent the one-year anniversary of Ben's death in the city where we'd met two decades ago. The place that started it all. I needed to be away from the endlessly well-meaning friends, family, neighbors, and strangers who would certainly check in. I needed the phone on silent and just to be with my earthside reminders of the man I loved. Still love.

I booked three plane tickets on a whim a week before the anniversary and texted everyone our plans. I asked for privacy on the day. I know you'll be thinking of us, I told them.

We stayed in a fancy hotel downtown, visited museums, and ate endless amounts of food. On the day of his death, we took a cab to campus. Benji still talks about the cab ride being his favorite part of the trip. He loved watching the city pass by through the windows of the car.

I walked the kids into the building where we met, pointing to the long-since-replaced row of lecture-hall seating where Ben first introduced himself to me. We ate a deep-dish for dinner at a mediocre place near campus that we used to go to when we were broke.

As we sat in that sticky pizzeria booth, I told them about the young, perpetually irresponsible version of their dad. The guy with the wavy, usually crazy hair and freckles who would stay out all night with friends and somehow manage to make it to an 8 a.m. class. The comically unprepared frat boy who attempted to run a half-marathon without any training on a dare and cramped up afterward so bad he could barely walk for a week. They howled with laughter at the story of the time he went to an evening class dressed as a hot dog so he could go to a Halloween party immediately after.

Benji and Ava heard about the crappy town house that we rented the year after my graduation. I told them how it had kitchen cabinets too high for me to reach anything useful and how Ben, with his six-foot-two frame, would come up behind me and say,

"Whatcha need, beautiful?" and then kiss me before going back to whatever conversation or work he'd been in the middle of. I told them how Ben made life easy. He made loving him so easy. Missing him is the hard part.

"No, not even in Chicago," I tell Jenny. "The kids were so happy to be in this place they'd heard so much about. More than that, though, Jenny, anniversaries are the easy part in some ways. It's the small moments like tonight when I feel like my heart might explode."

Jenny takes a deep breath. She and I have always been good at silence. Sometimes, during our otherwise wild college years when we were a thousand miles apart, we would sit on our respective dorm phones and just hang out in silence while we did our homework, occasionally offering a "Hey, you still there?" to ask each other for synonyms or biology terms or simple commiseration. Silence is the deep intimacy of friendship.

"Do you want me to plan a visit to Canopy?" she asks with a hint of genuine worry in her eyes. "I think it's going to be a relief for you to be in a new place, but I will get something on the calendar if you need me."

"No," I quickly answer. "Absolutely not."

Jenny lives with her husband in Michigan now. She spent weeks away from him last summer when they were newlyweds to help take care of me and now she's five months pregnant. Thinking back, I realize her visit to Nashville for the *Maisy* interview is probably more than I should have asked of her.

"I'll be fine," I say with increased firmness. "I will be a boring hamster on a wheel writing nonstop, living in a construction zone, and taking breaks only to heap handfuls of candy into my mouth for sustenance. My agent, Felicity, will probably pop down at some point, and I promised Dr. Lisa that I'd *try* to make new friends."

"Gracie, I love you, but you can get really antisocial without a bona fide extrovert like me or Ben around," she says with a smile. "Promise me you *will try* to meet new people and carve out something fresh for yourself? Maybe even go on a date?"

"I'll do my best," I answer. "Thanks for this, Jenny."

"Not sure I did anything special, but tell Ava that I solved everything, okay?" she jokes.

"You can do no wrong in that girl's eyes, but yes, I will. Good night, love," I say, hitting the little red button before willing myself out of bed and into my pajamas.

---

OUR HOUSE SITTER, Casey, and her boyfriend come by early in the morning to help me get all of the heavy camp trunks and luggage into the car for the drive. It's not a pretty job, but it fits. One more thing I definitely could not have done on my own.

We also do a lap around the house so that I can give Casey final instructions to make sure things don't burn down this summer. I remind her of the cleaning and landscaping schedules and also give her the phone number for the former.

"I'd prefer that you not have any raging parties, but if the house gets disheveled for any reason, just call them and they'll take care of it," I tell her. "They auto-debit my credit card, and I likely won't even notice."

Casey is the most responsible teenager on the block, so I'm not too worried, but sometimes it helps to let people know you won't disown them if they make a mistake and proactively give a solid solution to potential problems.

"Don't worry, Mrs. Harris," she says. "I'll take good care of it, and remember that my parents are right across the street. I'm sure they're watching us on their front door camera right now."

The kids walk past us with their survival supplies—tablets, snacks, travel bingo boards—for the four-hour drive. I hand over the keys and do one last look inside the house before joining Ava and Benji in the SUV, which has not an inch of free room to spare. They roll down the windows and wave. Casey is their favorite babysitter.

"Good luck this summer, Mrs. Harris," she yells from the front step as we pull out of the driveway and start our journey.

## CHAPTER 7

THE DRIVE INTO CANOPY IS AS BEAUTIFUL AS I REMEMBER, and I'm instantly thankful we decided to make the trip during the morning. The last little bit of the drive is a gorgeous country highway full of rolling hills and mountain views. It all feels like a ceremonial changing of the guard. I instantly feel lighter and less stressed. The mountains have always had this effect on me, but I realize that I haven't spent enough time with them as an adult.

"Benji, Ava, we're almost there," I yell to the back seat. Like magic, they put down their devices and seem to notice the beauty outside the windows for the first time. This will be Ava's fifth year coming to Transylvania County for camp, but for Benji it's just the third. They would each have an additional year under their belt if I hadn't kept them home last summer. It felt too soon for us after Ben's death to be away from one another.

They both still get transfixed by the mountains and beautiful scenery that we pass and take turns pointing out horse farms tucked into the valleys. When we pass a road marker indicating downtown Canopy is only three miles away, I flip into parent mode.

"Now, remember what we talked about," I say, starting a classic mom talk. "The house is a mess, and the guy who sold it to us and the guy who's going to fix it will both be there when we arrive. Please be polite and try to imagine what it could look like once the repairs are done."

We pass the small women's college and the performing arts center on the outskirts of town. We turn off the two-lane highway onto Main Street and Canopy's small town "skyline" emerges. My heart swells as we pass my and Ben's short-lived favorites: the lunch spot; The Drip, a fantastic coffee shop; an amazing little bookstore. It's all so quaint and perfect but without any pretense or pretending. Canopy is just itself. The streets are bustling with guests and residents having lunch.

I steer the car down Wilson Street and pull into the rough concrete driveway, listening to pebbles bounce around under my SUV. Two trucks are already here, which I assume belong to the Anderson brothers. One is a perfectly clean and polished navy blue that you might expect from a real estate agent who needs to make a good impression. The other is a decidedly more worn-in, slightly muddy white work truck with a few dents that are noticeable as I get closer. Maybe I'll end up being wrong, but I'd make a hundred-dollar bet right now that I'm right on which vehicle belongs to which person.

I take a deep breath. Home sweet home—for the summer, at least.

Before I can even turn off the car, the kids are jumping out and James is emerging from the house. If it were anyone else, it would be strange to see someone walking out of *your* house to greet you, but James makes it feel normal.

"Oh my goodness, this must be Benji and Ava," he says. "I've heard so much about you both."

They both seem to have registered my mom talk from a few

minutes ago because they politely say hi before running into the house to look around. It's hard to believe, but neither of them has been here before. They've only seen the house in photos. As I climb out of the driver's seat and greet James with a hug, I hear shrieks of delight and curiosity from inside.

"I think they saw your new floors," he says with a smile. "Welcome home!"

I dive into questions about Kendell and his kids as we walk toward the door, but I lose all sense of propriety when I see what the kids were raving about. The floors are glistening as far as my eyes can see. The oak has been sanded, varnished, and sealed to perfection.

"How is this the same house? The floors make it look almost like new," I say dramatically, turning to stare at James, before noticing another person off to the side of the living room. We lock eyes and share a moment of *something*. This must be Josh.

"Gracie, this is my brother, Josh," James replies, seeming not to notice any special moment. "And he's the one responsible for making these floors look amazing."

"You're hired," I say, smiling, trying to forget the moment we just had or at least that I just felt. "It's nice to meet you."

As he walks closer to us, I take a guess that he and James must be just like my kids. Each child so closely physically mirrors one parent that you have to really stare to find the similarities between the siblings themselves.

Both brothers have subtle freckles, easy smiles, and similar mannerisms, but that's where the obvious commonalities end. While both are in shape, it's in different ways. James is shorter but clearly actually works out. Josh is taller by a handful of inches and has a slimmer frame—he's toned but in the way someone gets only through the work they do. James has light-brown hair to Josh's dark, almost reddish hair. The big difference is their eyes—James's blue eyes to Josh's brown ones.

James is dressed for an afternoon of showing houses in a polo and neat khakis, but Josh is wearing worn jeans, work boots, and a T-shirt that looks like he took it out of the package this morning. I imagine it was older brother James who told him to look presentable.

Josh holds out his hand to shake mine. "I've heard a lot about you, Gracie Harris," he says bashfully. "And I'm happy you like the floor so much."

Before I can respond, James cuts in. "I wanted to be here when you arrived, Gracie, to make this introduction, but I need to run off and show two different sets of clients some houses. I assume the two of you can take it from here?"

We both nod.

"Don't let this quiet guy fool you," James says as he's leaving. "Once he gets to know you, he won't shut up. Prepare to lock yourself in that writing room to hide from the endless banter."

Josh playfully punches him in the arm as he passes by. James is out of the house in a flash, but not before promising he'll see me around town and insisting that Kendell wants to have me over for dinner. Josh breaks the silence that follows once the door closes.

"Two really cute kids introduced themselves to me a few minutes ago, but I haven't heard a peep since. Anything to be worried about?" he asks. I suspect James's kids have given him cause to stress during uncle babysitting nights over the years. The thought makes me smile.

"Nothing to worry about," I respond. "They go to camp tomorrow, where they will be internet-free for eight weeks. I guarantee they are huddled in a corner somewhere funneling the last bits of blue light into their brains."

"Gotcha," Josh says with a natural smile, those dark-brown eyes staring intently at me. "So, where should we start?"

"Right here," I say without a hint of sarcasm, and start pointing out the things I remember from my and Ben's planning trip. Josh has his cell phone out, dutifully taking notes in a bulleted list of to-dos. Felicity, my agent, once said the sluttiest thing a man could do was take notes on things that she liked so that he could remember them in the future. One guy even wrote down her preferred take-out meals from favorite spots. She never told me why that relationship ended.

As I stand here beside an attractive man who is about to make my house look amazing, watching him take notes on everything I say ... it's *something*, for sure. Then I remember I'm paying him to be here, and some of the magic wears off.

We walk through slowly—because in this house, there is something broken in every single room ... basically every corner of every room—and I point to things and give them a quick and very official ranking of "That grosses me out," "Please make this better," and "I literally can't even." You know, to help him prioritize the work.

When we venture upstairs, I slip on a loose board and Josh braces me with his hand on my back. He pauses to add it to the list. I pause to make a mental note to tell Felicity that chivalry and list making at the same time hits a certain kind of way.

We find the kids in the room that will become Ava's, sitting on opposite ends of a small single-sized bed. James generously brought it over a few months ago when his oldest daughter grew out of it.

It's the only piece of furniture in the room so far. A few newer items are due to be delivered next week.

"Just like I said, rotting their brains before nature heals them this summer," I say, looking at Josh, who smiles back.

In Ava's room we talk about the closet. Wallpaper needs to be removed, walls sanded, new shelving put in. Ava pipes up to share some feedback without breaking her eye contact with the tablet. Through it all, Josh types dutifully into his Notes app.

Benji pauses for a few minutes to watch us find more things to repair in the room. Then he interrupts with a classic ten-year-old-boy question.

"How old are you?" he asks Josh.

"I'm thirty-seven, little man. Why do you ask?" Josh responds, comically furrowing his brow with suspicion.

"That's pretty close to my mom, but you look a lot younger," Benji says, making me feel about a thousand years old. I put my hand on my hip in mock anger.

"Do you have kids?" I ask, turning to Josh even though I assume the answer is no. Josh has too much of a cool-uncle vibe. He lacks the worry lines and early gray hair that come from parenthood.

"No, I don't," he responds with a chuckle.

"There's your answer, Benji. The man hasn't been aged by children who chronically get lost in crowds or go off the high dive at the pool or get sent to the principal's office over arguments about *Star Wars*," I respond with a heightened sense of dramatics. I want Josh to know I'm not being serious.

We leave the kids, but not before I warn them while cackling in an evil voice that their remaining screen time is slowly melting away.

They groan in sync as we walk out of the room. We spend another twenty minutes in the other two bedrooms and one bathroom upstairs. The last room we hit isn't technically a bedroom, since it has no closet.

"I plan to make this my writing room," I say. "It doesn't need much besides the basic cosmetic improvements, but I haven't really made any plans for it yet. This old desk is just a placeholder until I find the right thing."

Josh peeks around the corner into the tiny room. Aside from the save on the stairs, this is the closest we've been to one another. I decide that it's good to get this out of the way. He's going to be here all summer. I need to get used to him in my space and close by. I can't let my imagined tension be a third wheel for the next few months.

We convene in the spacious upstairs hallway, and I announce that it's time for us to discuss everyone's favorite topic: money.

"James indicated you wanted to do a set weekly fee," I say matter-of-factly. "What should it be?"

"I don't know—a few hundred bucks," he suggests nonchalantly.

"What?" I ask, incredulous. "Be truthful—what's the catch?"

That big, easy smile crosses his face. It's just like the one his brother has.

"Gracie, I know James told you about my actual situation. This is a way for me to pass time without going crazy. So, two hundred and fifty dollars a week?"

"Absolutely not. The lowest I will go is five hundred dollars, and I need you to know I will feel bad about that paltry amount every single day."

"That seems high for a guy just trying to kill time."

"Josh, you realize I've googled your work, right? You are, like, a construction and remodeling genius. I don't deserve your talents for five hundred dollars a week."

This causes him to blush and push his hands into his pockets.

"Well, five hundred dollars it is because I won't charge more than that."

Deal, we agree, shaking hands for effect. Then I remember the list in my purse. I reach in and hand it to him.

"I almost forgot. This is a list my late husband and I worked on a year ago right after we bought the house. Most likely we didn't miss anything today, but it's probably good to have it just in case.

He unfolds the notebook paper, and I watch those dark-brown eyes travel up and down as he skims the list.

"Did you write this?" he asks with an interested look on his face.

"No," I answer bluntly in a tone that says this thread of conversation is *done*. Ben wrote it, but I don't tell him that. He probably assumes it's my dead husband's handwriting.

---

NOW THAT WE'VE established the ground rules for how this will work, I decide to give him a bit more information about my life and the slightly frantic version of me he should expect to see. It feels important to stress that the person he's about to spend the summer with is an amped-up, anxiety-ridden version of my usual self, just so he knows I'm not always like this.

"The other thing is that with me being here alone, without my kids, trying to pound out tons of writing, all the days are the same to me," I explain. "So, you should feel comfortable working on the days that are best for you . . . weekday, weekend . . . no difference.

Just promise not to judge me for the amount of food I'll be ordering in or that I might not change my clothes for days in a row. I'll be very focused on my work this summer."

"Got it and I promise," he responds. "Anything else I should know?"

I think for a minute and realize, yes—there's a bit more. "A few times a week at noon I'll need quiet for around an hour. I need to do some press interviews as a way to promote my column and a little bit of the book, too. I've given my publicist the noon hour as the one time frame she's allowed to use because I'm not usually in my creative flow around lunch."

Josh stares at me like he's trying to connect a few new puzzle pieces that have just appeared on a table. "James told me you're a writer, but interviews and a publicist? Am I just standing here ignorant to the fact that a famous person is in front of me?"

"It depends on how you define *famous*," I say with a broad but slightly embarrassed smile on my face. "*Internet famous* is probably the accurate term, but I hate it. There is an argument to be made that I'm *actually* famous for a segment of the thirty-five-to-fifty-year-old female population that is chronically online."

"That is oddly specific, but I also get it, which is slightly terrifying," he responds with a quick laugh. "Can I ask what sort of interviews you do?"

I take a few minutes to explain that I will be subjected to every type of interview possible to help build my confidence back up for the eventual wider onslaught that will be the book tour next spring. Podcasts, women's magazines, regional newspapers, public radio—if they are willing to talk to me, I will do it. I'm promoting the column but also practicing so I'm in good shape for the major leagues next year. Gracie Harris, the brand, reporting for duty.

"It's all part of the plan to 'build buzz' until—if I manage to hit my writing deadlines—the book comes out next spring. I've mostly avoided doing interviews until now, so this is a new layer to the work and definitely not my favorite part," I add. I leave out how I've got a seven-layer dip's worth of anxiety about opening up to journalists and "content creators" over the next few months. This is the Gracie Recovery Tour after my visit to Maisy last month. If I'm going to fail, I need to fail small, learn from it, and recover quick. I cannot be in this condition next spring.

"Cool. No problem on the interviews," he says, and then pauses. "The walls in this house are solid, but I'm still gonna be pretty noisy with some of the work. I don't want to get a fame-adjacent writer out of her creative flow. Should we have a bat signal or something you can throw up if I'm annoying the hell out of you?"

If I didn't know any better, I'd say he was now obviously flirting with me. Remembering terms that I just used, like *creative flow*, and being concerned about my writing process? I make a note that this behavior is also very attractive to me. I recover quickly and play it cool.

"No need to worry," I explain. "I grew up in a busy house and I'm a mom to two kids. I can block out any and all noise, but I appreciate you asking."

He starts digging around in his back pocket and pulls out the little gold key to the front door. Just as he's about to hand it over, I wave him off.

"It'll be convenient for you to have that. If I'm working from The Drip, you'll be able to come right in and I'll see your truck in the driveway when I get back, so I won't have to worry when the door is unlocked."

He slips it back into his pocket and a look crosses his face that I can't quite put my finger on. I suspect it has something to do with me expressing stranger-danger concerns to his brother a week ago (which James surely told him about) and now hearing me tell him less than two hours after we've met that he can keep a key to my house.

"Most days I'll get here around nine if that's okay with you," he says.

"Totally fine. I'm an early riser. The kids used to wake us up so early when they were young, and my body never really adjusted back," I respond. "Honestly, I'll be up and around by seven most days. Don't be shy."

"Got it," he says as we walk toward the door.

We exchange the typical pleasantries that new acquaintances share when saying a first goodbye. I stand in the doorway just long enough to do a stiff, unnatural wave when he turns to get into his truck. Then I close the door and snap back into mom life.

"Benji, Ava," I call up the stairs. "Time to go explore town for a bit and grab an early dinner before camp tomorrow!"

In the five minutes it takes to wrap up their tablet games, I fire off a note to the group text. They were all convinced James was setting me up to be the subject of a true-crime podcast with some story about an imaginary brother.

> Good news—the contractor is REAL and is going to work out. Definitely not a serial killer. With all due respect to James, he is not the cuter brother. Lots of work from the coffee shop for me! NO DISTRACTIONS. Finished memoir, here I come!

# CHAPTER 8

I KNEW THIS MORNING WOULD BE HARD, BUT FOR SOME reason I foolishly thought that the excitement of spending the summer writing and just having *me time* would make it all a little easier to bear. How wrong of me.

Instead, it's 5:30 a.m., and I've woken up with tears already rolling down my face just thinking about leaving the kids in a few hours. My subconscious got so sad that it made me cry *while I slept*. On the upside, at least my tear ducts are fully functional again. I can feel the stress building in my body, too, because the leg twitch that's been bothering me since the *Maisy Show* appearance is on the brink of reemerging.

The scared mom in me wants to run into their rooms and yell, *Camp is canceled!* but I know they need this summer just as much as I need mine. They missed camp last year because of Ben; they can't miss it this year because of me.

A few weeks ago, Ava came into my room after lights out and asked if she could talk. As any parent of a twelve-year-old can tell you, the conversations that follow "Can we talk about something?"

vary wildly from hilarious to heartfelt to horrifying. Crushes, broken hearts, girl drama, grief, test jitters, SEX. I didn't know where this one was going to land.

"The first thing I want to say," she started, "is that I really love and miss Dad. So much."

I told her, of course, that we all do.

"The thing is, I'm tired of being the sad girl that everyone pities because her dad died," she said bluntly. I could tell that she'd been working herself up to the conversation for some time. One thing she and I have in common is our need to rehearse conversations in our head before we have them out loud.

"Camp is my first opportunity to just be me again," she added. "I don't want the sad faces and people checking on me constantly. I want to be able to talk about stupid, fun stuff with my friends. I want people to be able to complain about their parents without suddenly looking at me and feeling bad because I don't have half of mine anymore."

"I get that," I assured her. "Trust me—I understand more than most."

She sat straight up and gave me her serious face. "What I would like you to do is call the camp and ask them not to bring it up. And definitely not to pull me into the nurse's hut for an 'emotional check-in' every few days. Ask them to just let me be *normal*."

Her entire life, I had thought of Ava as Ben's mini, but here she was admitting to the same internal dialogue that I'd been having for months. The Maisy interview may have tipped the scales, but *this* is the thing that kept me from selling the house, kept this wild plan on track to go on sabbatical and to live in Canopy for the entire summer. The ability to be *free*. To be me. To not be the woman with the dead husband's ashes on her bookshelf. To go into a damn grocery store and not run into someone who says, "Oh, sweetie, how are you doing ... *really?*"

I looked forward to the anonymity that Canopy would give me. Sure, I expect to run into readers and others who know about my situation, but it's fundamentally different.

The first time I went on a short work trip to Charlotte four months after Ben died, I sat at the hotel bar to have a drink after a busy day of meetings. I made small talk with a sweet old couple sitting on the stools nearby. We covered the normal topics: what we were doing in town, where our favorite dinner spots were, and what future travel plans we had. Then the question that always comes along eventually with sweet old couples on a trip together: "What about you, Gracie—are you married?"

I took a breath and answered, "No. I'm a widow."

The wife said, "Oh, what a shame. You're so young, though; I'm sure you'll find love again." And then, the next thought came out: "Gracie, you seem like a woman who would know about the new exhibit at the Mint Museum. Am I right about that?"

They didn't pry, which I appreciated, but what also struck me was how dispassionate the response had been ... in a *good way*. There was no emotion tied to it, unlike every single person I ran into in Chapel Hill. Being loved and appreciated in my adopted hometown is great, but it can also be stifling. At that moment, with the Fahertys from Richmond, Virginia, I felt free to be me for the first time since Ben died.

So, as I lie here in bed waiting for the kids to wake up screaming with excitement about the next eight weeks at summer camp, I remember those two conversations: the one with the Fahertys in Charlotte and with Ava at home in my room. This summer in Canopy is a gift, and as long as I can get through this morning drop-off, I will be able to bask in the glory of just being me for the next few months.

---

TWO HOURS LATER, the kids and I are standing behind the SUV doing a final review of all their camp luggage—trunks, duffels, pillows, portable fans, and creature comforts to last the summer—which is all staged on the driveway. I let them both get their trunks out of the car yesterday. Casey, her boyfriend, and I had struggled to get them in in the first place, and now I'm wondering how on earth I'll manage this on my own.

About the moment I consider knocking on the door of the neighbor whom I haven't yet met for help, Josh pulls up in his truck.

"Need help?" he asks after seeing our predicament.

"Yes, please," I reply in a grateful tone. "It's always easy to get these trunks out but much harder to get them in."

I bend down to grab one side of the first trunk, but Josh waves me off. In one swift motion, he grabs both sides of the camp trunk and hoists it into the SUV. He repeats it again for Ava's purple case.

"Dude, you're strong," Benji says, impressed by the quick work.

"I work on construction sites some days. I lift a lot of crazy stuff that I probably shouldn't. These are easy," Josh responds.

We do one last verbal inventory of what's crammed into my

SUV and the kids are finally satisfied that we haven't missed anything. Josh is hanging close by, ready to help if we need something.

"All right, guys, I think we're ready!" I say with forced excitement.

"Take care of my mom," Benji says to Josh in a serious tone after we close the liftgate. He's pointing at him and raising his eyebrows. This is Benji's no-nonsense expression.

I throw a glance at Ava to commiserate at the latest ridiculous thing to come out of Benji's mouth, but now she's looking at Josh and adding care instructions.

"She works too hard. If she looks stressed, ask her if she's had enough to eat."

"You two make me sound helpless. I'll be fine, and Josh is not here to take care of me. He's here to make our house look spectacular."

Josh fist-bumps Benji and says to both kids, "Don't worry—message received."

I mouth *sorry* to Josh, but he just smiles as he walks toward the house. The kids are overflowing with adrenaline for camp, and before I'm even fully in the driver's seat, Benji pulls himself halfway out of his already-rolled-down window to yell goodbye to Josh.

"He's really nice," Benji begins. "I'm glad you'll have a nice person around all summer to hang out with. It's important to have friends around."

"I didn't see a wedding ring on this hand," Ava chimes in.

"Ava!"

"It's just an observation, Mom. Don't freak out."

"I appreciate y'all worrying about me, but my job this summer is to finish my book. My job is definitely *not* to make friends or worry about the marital status of the people I meet."

"Don't be so strict with yourself, Mom. Please have some fun. If your letters to camp are all emo, I'll make up an excuse to leave early," Ava says. "And maybe go on a few dates this summer. There's a whole new batch of people here!"

One of my biggest concerns after Ben died was parentifying my children. I've spent the last year hyperfocused on their health and wellness. Home-cooked meals despite the fact that I hate to cook, showing up to sporting events, helping with homework. I made sure all of those parent jobs were fulfilled by me, and I didn't ask them to grow up too fast. Benji has always been a little adult, but I didn't want him to go overboard. Driving in the car now, I'm wondering if I still somehow failed at this.

"We just love you and want you to be happy," Benji says tenderly. Both kids get a little soft in the last hours and minutes before camp starts.

We stop for donuts on the way, and after thirty minutes, we arrive at Camp Canopy Valley. A mile-long gravel driveway leads up to acres of open space, a lake, cabins, and lots of activity huts. This is kid heaven.

Within thirty seconds of pulling into our parking spot, a SWAT team of teenage and twentysomething camp counselors rushes to the car. Benji jumps out and heads to the back to play foreman, instructing the counselors which trunks and bags go up the hill to the boys' side of camp and which go down the hill to the girls' part.

First, we walk up to Benji's home for the summer—his cabin is already full of loud boys unpacking their clothes and towels in a very disorderly fashion. Ava and I help Benji make his bed with his favorite superhero sheets and get him settled in. A few minutes later, he's shooing us out. I sneak in for a few last big hugs and kisses before leaving to take Ava to her cabin.

"By next year he'll probably be too old for his superhero sheets," I say wistfully as we walk back down the hill.

"Probably, but it'll just be some silly cartoon or anime theme after that. It'll still be cute," she says back, trying to make me feel better.

Ava's cabin is noticeably calmer and less messy than Benji's. That is, of course, the difference between twelve-year-old girls and ten-year-old boys. I help her make her bed on the top bunk and get her toiletries organized. A friend she's spent three summers with shows up, and they fall into a quick hug and then sit on the bottom bunk to start catching up. After a few minutes, I tell Ava I should probably go. She excuses herself and says she'll walk me back to the car. She's never done this in all of her years of camp.

"Write to me at least twice a week," she instructs. "If you fall in love with Josh or some other guy, I expect a separate letter, please."

The kids have asked about my dating life a lot lately. Dr. Lisa and I agree the reason is twofold. First, they genuinely want me to be happy and in love again. They are old enough to understand the ways that relationships can enrich your life. I'm certain Ben's absence has made them realize this in a sad way. The second reason they care so much is that all they've known is a traditional family structure. At the end of the day, they want someone to play the father figure. This thought breaks my heart.

I give Ava the biggest hug and tell her I love her about twenty times. Then she turns around and walks back to her cabin and her summer of freedom. I reluctantly climb into the car, feeling like I've lived a hundred years this morning.

---

"NO INTERVIEWS TODAY," I tell Josh when I arrive back at the house so he knows that he's free to make as much noise as he needs. "It's my last day of relaxation before I dive into the work, so I'm going to sit on the creaky, old porch swing and finish this book that's been on my nightstand for over a month."

He tilts his head and raises his eyebrows at the book I've just held up. "You're reading a book *that* thick while also writing a book? Very brave," he playfully observes.

"I'm writing a memoir, and ironically, it's not been my favorite genre of book to read over the years," I explain. "So I've spent the last nine months reading memoirs to get a better sense of how I want to structure my book and learn what sorts of techniques I do and don't want to use."

"What sort of techniques?" he asks. I can tell the question is genuine and he's interested in my process. James did tell me that Josh is a process guy.

"Well, for example, this book isn't told in chronological order. It skips around and there are *a lot* of flashbacks," I say. "The writing in this book is superb, but as a reader, I struggle with this narrative structure. My memoir is shaping up to be more linear."

I take a moment to decide if I want to add on the next thought and just go for it. "This book is also written at about a thirtieth-grade level. It's very literary and beautiful, but it's not something everyone will pick up and enjoy. It's definitely not a book you buy at the airport. Most people don't like needing to look up new words every few pages."

"So, will your book be more accessible?" he asks.

"It will," I answer, deciding that I like that word: accessible. "My column in *The New York Times* is written so that as many people as possible can relate to it, and I think that's part of what's made my work so popular and occasionally viral. Why mess with a good thing?"

He nods. "Well, then, with all that in mind, I think I'll stop on the window casings for now and switch to the cabinet repair above the refrigerator. That's going to be loud as hell and not easy, so good to take care of it today when you don't have work stuff," he says. "But if you hear me cursing from the comfort of your swing, don't worry."

I wish him luck and grab a fluffy sofa pillow off the only piece of furniture currently in the living room to make the swing a bit more comfortable. I lie down, place the pillow behind my head, and hang my legs over the opposite armrest. I open to page 363 and promptly fall asleep.

When I'm startled awake what feels like a minute later, it's because Josh is trying to quietly sneak out of the house. He sees me open my eyes and wince in pain from being in one position for too long. What time is it? I'm not *that* old.

"Sorry," he says with a tense smile. "I was trying really hard not to wake you."

I look at my watch. Holy shit—it's been two hours. If he's been doing loud construction inside, I somehow slept through it. I close the book that has been spread across my chest without progress.

"Please tell me you were silently working in there," I say, embarrassed.

"Do you want me to tell the truth?"

"I guess I didn't realize how tired I was. The last few weeks have been relentless."

"The good news is that the cabinet is fixed and securely attached to the wall. It was never installed properly in the first place. You don't have to live in fear of it crashing down anymore."

"Thank you. Thanks for everything you're doing here this summer. I still feel so terrible about how little I'm paying you."

"Remember—it's helpful to me, too. I'll be back tomorrow morning for a full day of work."

I sit on the porch swing and watch him drive away. Then I grab the pillow and book to go inside, read a few more paragraphs, and fall asleep once again.

# CHAPTER 9

I LEAVE A SMALL NOTE TAPED TO THE FRONT DOOR WHEN I leave the house bright and early at 8 a.m. so that Josh will know to let himself in. *Working from The Drip this morning. Back at noon for an interview.*

Chapel Hill is a small town, according to most people in my life (who nearly all live in big cities), but at home I would never broadcast "Hey, my house is empty—come on in!" like I feel comfortable doing here in Canopy. Josh seemed sensitive to invading my space and hesitant to keep the key, so this feels like a small token of welcome that I can leave. The guy is repairing my run-down house, after all.

Initially, I wanted a place farther removed from downtown, but today I'm appreciative that we landed a few blocks from every creature comfort that I need: restaurants, bookstore, gift shops, and, my favorite, an utterly charming coffee shop.

The Drip is a converted single-family home on Main Street, and it's only a three-minute walk from the house. The front is a glass-enclosed porch that I assume at one point must've been open. The dark steel frame of the sunroom contrasts against the light-gray paint that covers the rest of the brick house. To the left, a large gravel patio is filled with tables and chairs of all sizes. A few early risers have already set up shop with their laptops and books by the time I arrive. It's a perfect morning to work outside, with a slight chill still hanging in the air before the day heats up. My mind, however, wanders in the fresh air, so it's best if I stay indoors to kick off my summer of writing.

I open the door and walk inside. It's just as I remember it from over a year ago when I was last here with Ben. The café has a purposefully mismatched decor style that looks like a loving grandma made every single piece. Local art and photography cover the walls. Places like these feel comfortable to me. The wood floor creaks ever so slightly as I advance toward the register. It's so cozy and welcoming in here—perfect for my writing process. This will be my second home for the summer. Thirty thousand more words, here we come.

A friendly face greets me at the counter and says, "Welcome in. What can we make for you this morning?"

"An iced Americano with a splash of almond milk, please." This is my go-to drink. I imagine that by the end of next week I'll be regular here enough that they'll start making it when I walk through the door. That's what I'm hoping for, at least.

I spot a small table in the corner of the shop, walk over, and plug in my laptop, even though it's fully charged. A minute later, the barista kindly walks over my drink instead of calling my name and leaving it on the counter. There is a quiet, unfussy hospitality here that makes me feel welcome and comfortable. I smile, say thank you, and open the laptop, ready to get to work.

My editor, Jeannie, is giving me wiggle room with the period that the book will cover. The "first year" of widowhood memoir approach is less of a strict timeline and more of a rough guide. Whatever it takes for the story to come to a natural conclusion of some sort. When I got invited to *The Maisy Show* I imagined it would be the perfect, triumphant end to the tale of my first year without Ben. Things obviously didn't end up that way. I'd like to at least *try* to end the book on a neutral or positive note, so a bit of summer just might creep in. The ultimate goal is to construct a cohesive narrative that flows and brings together strong themes around grief, motherhood, and midlife reinvention. Lofty stuff.

That goal line still feels pretty far down the field. I'm supposed to deliver somewhere in the neighborhood of eighty thousand words, and I've got fifty thousand "done," but right now nothing feels complete. The chapters aren't connected, and there's no narrative arc quite yet.

Part of what has made my essays in *The New York Times* so popular is that my writing is raw, real, and unsettled. Every essay is about grief, and while there are sometimes neat resolutions or clear advice, for the most part it's me saying, *I experienced this new, unexpected aspect of sadness and loss! Let me tell you all about it!* None of my published essays are retrospective. Everything is written for the here and now. It's what my readers love.

Writing for the memoir is a bit different. There is something entirely unique, but similarly special, that happens with my prose if I wait a few weeks to reflect. I'm able to see events and emotions in my life just a little more clearly and gain a perspective that my essays don't have—and one that's important for the tone of the memoir *and* to set it apart from the column.

For most of the year that approach worked for making progress on the book—wait a few weeks, then write about it—but the fact is that I'm nearly two *months* behind at the moment. I didn't plan for this to happen. I've blamed sports banquets, real-life work deadlines, and the end of the school year. The truth is a little more nuanced. The last thing I wrote about was a date gone terribly wrong in early April, and ever since I haven't felt the urge to reopen the manuscript. Until now. I scroll through the document and relive the experience that halted my progress.

It was a first date at one of my favorite restaurants, a cute Thai place a few blocks from the heart of downtown. Most of my dates come courtesy of colleagues, friends, or even friends of friends. The thought of installing an app makes me want to hurl, so it's all word-of-mouth setups or meet-cutes in bookstores for me. The meet-cute thing hasn't happened yet, to be clear, but I'm holding out hope.

A colleague connected me with her cousin, and I was happily impressed when a handsome, recently divorced doctor sat down across the table. He had just relocated for work a few months prior and hadn't grown up in Chapel Hill or even North Carolina, so there wasn't the typical small talk to make and no seven degrees of do you know so-and-so. Instead, we talked about our work, our lives, our kids. It was perfectly lovely. And then.

Right about the time the server came by to grab our plates after the main course, a woman who looked to be in her sixties strolled up to the table. Her body posture and confidence made me think that my date must have known her, so I smiled. But she just stood there, staring directly at me without breaking eye contact.

"You should be ashamed of yourself" was the first thing out of her mouth. I was shocked.

"I'm sorry—do I know you?" I stammered out. "What is this even about?"

Her tone had caught the attention of people at the nearby tables, and I saw our waitress staring at me from a nearby station with a *WTF is going on?* look. I sure didn't know.

"I've been a regular reader since the beginning, and I just want to say how disappointed I am in you. I didn't expect to see you out here being a floozy with some random man so soon after your husband died," she said, gesturing toward the cute doctor.

I just stared. Then glared. Then raged. But I could not find the words to meet the moment. My date across the table looked completely horrified.

My first thought was to tell this woman, *Actually, this is probably my tenth date since Ben died, and by the way, it's all been traumatizing, and even so, I've occasionally managed grief sex rather than anything even remotely resembling real connection.*

Thankfully, I had the sense to realize that putting my business out like that in public was probably not the best path forward. This was two months after a dating-related essay that ruffled a few feathers and made me realize some things really should be left private. But all I could do was sit there in silence.

"Ma'am, I'm going to need you to leave us alone," the cute doctor said, swooping in to rescue everyone involved and those simply stuck witnessing the moment. "You are being incredibly rude."

"Well, she's being a whore," the terrible woman responded, shocked that she'd been confronted and clearly expecting me to apologize for *something*. That's the weird thing about even lightweight fame—people think they know you, that they have a right to you. It's screwed up, actually.

She was escorted out of the restaurant by the manager as her clearly embarrassed husband gathered up their things and tried to pay the bill. Their server said something to the tune of *I would rather die than take your money*.

"That . . . was not normal," the cute doctor said, trying to rescue what until then had been a perfect first date, knowing, of course, that no good relationship—even a casual one—could ever grow from such a sour start, even if we had nothing to do with it.

That's the thing about normalcy, though—it can all be swept away in an instant. Trust me, I'm an expert.

Life was just starting to feel manageable when that happened and it made me question, well, everything that I was doing and how public I had made my life. Just like I ended up doing a month later onstage with Maisy, I hit a roadblock and completely shut down. So, I tapped a mental pause button and stopped writing the memoir because, of course, it was obviously about so much more than just that one date. Dr. Lisa is the only one who knows about this. I conveniently left my little writing hiatus out of my recent lunch conversation with Felicity.

Also, I know myself. Eventually, I always sort things out, and a lot has changed since I last stared at the blinking cursor on this document. This is my first real day back writing this memoir. I simply refuse to wallow. Today has the potential to set the tone for all of the writing I need to get done this summer. It is critical to plow forward and get going again. So, I make the decision to cheat and skip right past the anniversary of Ben's death and the bombed interview and head to my sweet spot—a two-week retrospective. I'll deal with the heavy stuff later.

When I was an English major in college, a creative-writing professor told us that the best skill we could master as creators (he was ahead of his time—the concept of being a "creator" didn't exist in the early 2000s like we know it now) was the ability to sit down and produce *something*. You're an artist? Be able to sit down and paint. Photographer? Find a photo to take. Writer? Create an essay, poem, or short story on demand.

This professor was clear that most of what we created would be throwaway, but you never knew when inspiration would strike or how a bunch of mediocre creations could be pulled together into something more cohesive and shiny. I've spent the last two decades being a marketer and not a writer, but his advice has served me well in my career. Today doesn't need to be perfect and it doesn't even need to end up in the finished book . . . it simply needs to say something, anything. Words on the page. Ideally, heading in the direction of progress.

I close my eyes and think about the ways that most of the month of May was oddly comforting. There was a long list of to-dos that I was able to prioritize and accomplish—shopping lists for camp, final parent-teacher conferences, spirit weeks, and, after I decided to spend the summer in Canopy, ordering furniture online for the house here. Retail therapy always helps. I was able to casually slide into a version of life that almost felt normal.

The return to normal, I think. That's worth writing about.

As I write, I'm aware of people coming and going from The Drip. The little bell on the door rings out every few minutes. Friends and neighbors greet one another and start up conversations. The young barista behind the counter who brought me my drink welcomes more than a few people by their first names. The quiet hum of the place turns into the background white noise that I need to get the closest I've been to a flow state with this memoir in a long time.

I spend the next few hours massaging a chapter about the beauty of mundanity. When you've had a year like mine, boring is a gift. Predictability feels like a warm hug. The everyday tasks that usually drive parents to insanity at the end of the school year? A welcome distraction. Returning to routine is essential—at least for me—to finding anything resembling equilibrium. It's also what excites me so much about my summer here in Canopy. I get to dive into the deep end of a routine. Yes, it's a new routine in new surroundings, but there is comfort in it.

It's not my best writing, but even in the moment I know that this will be an important transition chapter that leads to the final portion of the book. The prose can be polished later. Morning number one has been perfectly adequate.

## CHAPTER 10

I ARRIVE BACK AT THE HOUSE WITH JUST A FEW MINUTES TO spare before my interview. Today I'm chatting with a freelancer for a content factory focused on women's lifestyle topics. Like I said, we're using these early interviews to build my confidence back up. No glamour here.

Josh emerges from a back room wiping his hands on a towel, but some of the putty is clearly not budging.

"I got that big ugly dent on the wall patched in the guest room. Depending on how fast it dries, I may be able to prime it before I leave today."

I thank him, remembering where the dent came from. Ben and I found a gorgeous four-poster bed at an antique mall one town over on our planning trip. We managed to get it into the truck bed and home without losing any pieces. Getting it into the house and room was another matter. The door frames are skinnier in older homes, and I have the upper-body strength of a fifth-grader. We bumped into the walls, and I had to pause every two feet to stop laughing or I was definitely going to pee my pants. The headboard was the final piece, but my tired hands lost their grip, and it flew into the wall. Ben stared at me with fake annoyance. Then he took out the project list and a pencil from his back pocket and added *Fix dent in guest room wall.*

Josh interrupts my daydream. "I brought lunch today. Is it cool if I eat at the dining table while you do your interview? I'll put earbuds in and a podcast on so you don't think I'm eavesdropping."

He's worried about my privacy, but I'm more worried about embarrassing myself in front of this mostly stranger, so I tell him that would be great.

I pull myself onto a stool at the kitchen island and open my laptop for the second time today. With three minutes left before noon, I google the writer's name and skim the headlines from her recent stories. Mostly fluff, I confirm. Instantly, I relax, and the tension melts a bit from my neck and shoulders. My calendar notification pops up with a virtual meeting link. I throw in my own earbuds and click on it.

We exchange the usual pleasantries before Maya jumps right into her questions—and immediately I realize this is going to be a nightmare. The questions are all over the place. Did she even go to journalism school? Stupid content farms—all quantity and zero quality.

*My kids are my top priority, and their mental well-being is something I prioritize even over my own. I know the whole "put on your oxygen mask before others'" advice that people give, but they're my focus.*

*Blush and mascara . . . Oh, favorites? I grew up on drugstore brands, so CoverGirl mostly.*

*I haven't watched a lot of Netflix over the last year—most nights I use to write. Writing is sacred to me and really important to my healing. I'm sure it's similar for you.*

*Sky blue? I guess that's a paint color I use a lot.*

*I'm not sure I'm the best person to give dating advice, but I guess my top recommendation would be to be willing to go outside your comfort zone. Be willing to not have a type, or don't be so attached to a type if you have one.*

*A cute spot called Regina's Café.*

*Wow, um, well, my mortality is mostly tied to my kids' well-being, to be honest. Confronting my own mortality means the potential that I leave them alone, and I just can't let that be an option right now.*

Interview one is utter fucking chaos. Very auspicious.

---

I SPREAD MY arms out clear across the kitchen island and put my forehead on the counter with just enough force to make a noise. A long, frustrated grunt-moan sound emerges from my chest. I won't deny it—this is dramatic. Without looking up, I can tell my theatrics have stirred Josh's curiosity. It's confirmed a second later.

"Everything okay over there?" he calls from the dining room on the other side of the wall with a hint of sarcasm in his voice.

"Why am I so bad at this?" I say to nobody in particular, not really answering his question.

"You're bad at interviews? I thought you were this fancy writer from the big city," he says with a mock twang as he walks into the room, trying to pull me from my brief fit of despair. Which, of course, makes me realize I'll be spending every day this summer with one of those people who tries to make everyone smile and laugh when things go a little sideways. This is clearly not a man who wallows.

How do I explain this to him? *Well, person I just met two days ago, I've spent pretty much the entire last year avoiding doing interviews as a form of self-preservation to ensure that I wouldn't lose my shit talking to a random journalist about my life, my struggles, and what an absolute mess things have been.* I respond in a way that captures the spirit of honesty.

"I put off doing any sort of press for the better part of a year so that I could focus on my writing, my job, and my kids. Then I had a very tough public interview about a month ago, so I made a deal with my publicist that I would start doing press this summer to build my confidence and get better at thinking on my feet. I need more column readers so I'll get more followers so I'll sell more books," I release at the speed of sound. "I'm going to dread every one of these. My confidence is a wreck."

He stares and squints his eyes like he's studying me to decide the right next thing to say. Like he's deciding between a joke or something endearing. He opts for the latter and starts nodding his head like he's figured out the final clue on a crossword.

"Gracie, I'm a person who likes to get to the root of a problem. Not to use a lame building analogy, but it works here—I can't really make a house look nice until I fix all of the stuff underneath. The water stain will always reemerge if you don't identify where the leak is coming from. So, what is it about interviews that you hate so much? You won't be able to make it better—or at least make it *sound* better—until you know that."

He's still staring at me, and I'm laser focused back on him. He genuinely wants to talk about this. Two days ago, I was stuck comparing him to James, so this is the first time I've let myself observe what he truly looks like. His short, thick brown hair looks a little crazy, which I assume is from wearing the alarmingly beat-up baseball hat that he's holding in his left hand. There's a tiny piece of putty stuck to his right temple. He's got one of those permanently furrowed brows that comes from always being deep in thought, and his smile is both gracious and charming. He's got the tiniest gap between his two front teeth, which gives him an instantly unique face. I consider how unpolished he looks and yet how relaxed his demeanor is. This is a guy totally comfortable in his skin.

When it comes to his offer of assistance, the rational part of my brain is telling me to say, *Don't worry about it*, but the Jenny-on-the-shoulder side of things is reminding me that I need to ask for help more often. People want to be helpful. I take a deep breath and opt for the spirit of honesty again. Not the whole truth, but enough of it.

"The answer is twofold. First, I'm terrible at small talk."

"Should've grown up in a small town," he says before I can finish the thought. "We're great at it."

"And second," I continue, undeterred, "interviews are absolutely wild. The questions are everywhere. Some journalists do it to throw you off your game, and others are just naturally all over the place."

"How so?" he asks as he slides onto the kitchen stool beside me.

"The interviewer just now asked me my favorite place to get coffee in Chapel Hill in one breath, and then her follow-up was 'How has Ben's death caused you to confront your own mortality?'"

Josh lets out a bolt of laughter. It's one of those loud, honest laughs that naturally gregarious people have. The type of laugh that belongs to someone who isn't afraid to be the center of attention. He apologizes for laughing.

"If this were happening to anyone else, I would have about ten jokes right now," I say so that he won't feel bad. "What article is she even writing with that collection of information?"

It's a strange feeling to be in such an honest, intimate conversation with someone I just met. At home, I'm so focused on making sure everyone knows that I'm definitely okay. This business of blurting out my misery to someone besides Jenny or Dr. Lisa isn't my style.

"Well, I can't really help with the crazy stuff the journalists ask you," he says bluntly. "But I do have an idea to help with the rest of it."

I sit up straight and correct the depressed slouch I've held since the interview wrapped. My home-improvement contractor has a solution to my existential crisis? A solution to the creativity-sucking nonsense that these interviews are shaping up to be three times a week for the foreseeable future? I turn my head to the side, indicating that I'm waiting without saying it out loud. A hint of a smile emerges from the corner of his mouth.

"Number one, every day, you need to get out and make small talk with someone in town. Coffee shop, lunch place, post office," he instructs. "In fact, tomorrow I need you to go set up an account at the hardware store for project supplies. While you're there, try to get to know Br— Nope, not gonna tell you his name. The guy behind the counter. Same thing at The Drip."

"Small-talk practice," I say. "That's your advice?"

"Absolutely. You'll be a pro before you know it," he responds, then pauses. "You might get a reputation for being friendly, but that's a problem you can worry about down the road."

He laughs again, clearly proud of the joke he just made. I let a smile creep across my face and realize that small-talk practice is probably a good idea. It'll help me get better about thinking on my feet. "Okay, done," I respond.

"Second thing," he starts but hesitates, like he's really trying to decide if this is going to be a good idea. He raises his arms to run his hands through his hair before putting his hat back on, and I notice a tattoo peeking out from the bottom of his T-shirt sleeve. "I don't mind learning things about people, and I've been known to be awkward at times. So, I can help with interview practice during lunch hours when you don't have time booked with the professionals. Off the clock."

It's a sweet gesture, and he's probably on to something with the concept of interview practice. I make a mental note to ask my publicist, Lucia, for a media trainer to help take the edge off my obviously terrible interview etiquette and sound bites. Practice won't make me perfect, but it will make me acceptably mediocre at this part of the job.

When I don't respond right away, Josh takes matters into his own hands.

"Anyway, let's take your mind off the train-wreck interview. What's your favorite cocktail and why?" he asks innocently.

I cradle my chin with my hand and put my elbow on the counter, mocking a good "thinker" face, even though this is the easiest question I can be asked. Before Ben died, there was no happy-hour invitation that I would turn down. It's one of the few guaranteed social events that I will attend.

"A freshly made margarita. It's heavenly on a hot day and never gives me a hangover."

Without missing a beat, he follows up with, "Have you ever considered that you'll never find love again after the sudden death of your husband?"

My eyes go wide, and my mouth opens. You see it happen in movies—someone's jaw drops—but there are so few moments in real life that shock us this way. This is one of those times.

"Well played," I say in a tone that makes no mistake that I'm legitimately impressed.

"Would you like to reconsider my offer?" he responds with a smug *I told you so* grin on his face.

"Interview hour starts tomorrow at noon," I state without hesitation. "Don't be late."

He smiles big, puts his earbuds in, and walks back to the guest room to tackle the next repair.

# CHAPTER 11

I'M A WOMAN WHO HAS ALWAYS LOVED A GOOD HOME-work assignment, so it's no surprise that I'm at The Drip right at 8 a.m. to start my morning of small-talk practice. I've decided to begin here, write for a bit, and then move on to the hardware store on the way home.

"Good morning. It's nice to see you again," the petite blonde behind the counter says. "What can we make for you?"

"Iced Americano, splash of almond milk," I say.

"Are you new to town or just passing through?" she asks, beating me to the punch.

This is a trick question for me at the moment, and I think of clever ways to explain the circumstances that have brought me here, but that is not small talk. Josh would probably say I'm overthinking it. Keep it simple.

"New to town for the summer," I say. "I own a home on Wilson Street, and I'm spending the summer here while my kids are at camp. My name is Gracie."

I hold out my hand to make the introduction formal, and a look of recognition comes over the barista's face.

"Oh, you're Gracie Harris!" she exclaims. "Josh is a friend of mine, and he mentioned that he was working at your place. I'm Sunny—I own The Drip."

"You own this slice of heaven?" I respond, mirroring her excitement. "I hope you're ready to see me here almost every day this summer. Something about the vibe in here just works for me."

This makes Sunny glow with pride. She then shares something that I don't expect.

"I'm really glad Josh has someone new to keep him company—I hope that's not weird to say. It's just that he's had a rough few years, and a new face is sometimes helpful," she says, while making my coffee.

*Don't I know it*, I respond in my head at first but then decide to share it out loud. Open and honest, just as Dr. Lisa would like it.

As Sunny works, I slide down to the pick-up area. A moment later when she hands me my coffee, she adds, "I'm only here a few days a week, but if you ever need a break from writing, just pop over to the counter. I can give you all of the good Canopy gossip and gush about how much I love your work. A little while back, Kendell—James's wife—convinced our book club to read a handful of your essays instead of one of our normal selections. I've been hooked ever since. I can't believe I didn't recognize you at first!"

"I haven't met Kendell yet," I say with a smile, "but I'm fairly convinced she's my unofficial hype woman."

I walk over to the same table as yesterday and it dawns on me that Sunny's name is literally perfect for her. She brightened my day and gave me the slightest bit of confidence that, yes, I am capable of the small talk needed to survive my interviews and maybe even enjoy Canopy this summer.

I set my phone alarm for two hours, open my laptop, and get to work.

---

IN THE BLINK of an eye, the two hours are up. I'm in a groove, so I hit Snooze on the alarm a few times. Slowly but surely, I *will* catch this memoir up to the present day. I just need to take it word by word, page by page. In a few weeks, maybe a little longer, I'll officially be living in real time with my writing. That also means I'll need to find and fix all the gaps and, even more intimidating, figure out how to end the book. All problems for future Gracie to worry about.

I repack all of my stuff and walk the dirty glass to the bar, thanking Sunny and telling her I look forward to seeing her again soon.

It takes just a few minutes and one corner to get to the hardware store. From what I can tell, the store doesn't have a real name. There's just a big sign outside that reads HARDWARE. Speaking as the least handy person on the planet, I appreciate the simplicity.

The bell rings as I open the door, announcing my arrival. Looking around, it appears that I'm the only customer in the space, when a man with a kind face and workman's apron walks up to greet me.

"Mornin'. Welcome in," he says. "What can I help you find?"

"You," I respond, then instantly realize it is a slightly strange thing to say, so I try to fix it with a smile.

Hardware Man gives me a funny look and holds up his hand so

that I can see his ring finger. This makes me giggle. I like him instantly.

"My name is Gracie," I say with a huge grin on my face. "My contractor, Josh, has sent me in to set up an account so that he can come in here and shop to his heart's content like some kind of kept man."

Now it's Hardware Man's turn to chuckle. His head tilts back as he laughs and says something quietly about Josh having his hands full this summer.

"Josh certainly can be high-maintenance, but I think you'll be able to handle him," he says. "Let's get this sorted out. Follow me. I'm Brian, by the way."

We weave our way through the tight aisles of the store. What it lacks in size it makes up for in perfect curation. There might not be a hundred of everything like in a big-box store, but the variety is astonishing. Someone like Josh—or Ben, for that matter—could get lost in a place like this, thinking up tons of projects to do just for fun. It's obvious now why Ben bought all those tools. He couldn't help himself once he stepped into this man's paradise of plywood and power drills.

While Brian and I pass my credit card back and forth and I fill out forms, he asks me lots of little questions about how I found myself here in Canopy for the summer.

I stick to the short version of my very complicated story, and he listens intently. Bought a house, husband died, became a writer, got internet famous, needed to escape to the aforementioned house but realized it was a mess, used limited connections to find resources, and ended up here in this very hardware store to tell the tale.

"Gracie, I bet you're a good writer. I'm going to have to google you. You sure can tell a story," Brian says sweetly, before adding, "I'm really glad someone like you got that house. The last owner was loved by many of us, and it's good to see it in the hands of someone determined to restore it to its proper glory and not turn it into a short-term rental. We hate those."

"That means a lot to me, Brian," I respond, purposefully saying his name back so it will embed itself in my brain and I won't forget. "My late husband and I spent a lot of time looking with James for the right place, and the Craftsman was perfect for us. Well, now just me and the kids, of course, but still perfect."

"Life sure can be unpredictable," he says in a soulful way that conveys there is no need for me to respond.

He's about to wrap up when I decide small-talk practice should really end with me asking Brian a perfectly simple question.

"What's your favorite thing about Canopy, Brian? If I told you I was leaving tomorrow and had just one day to do something or eat something while I was here, what would it be?"

He doesn't even stop to think, just dives right into an answer after glancing at his watch.

"When you leave the shop, turn right instead of going left back to your house. Walk to Lenny's Diner on Main Street and order the BLT. The ripest, thickest tomatoes and homemade garlic mayo. It's pure heaven. Nothing makes it feel like summer quite like a Lenny's BLT."

As if on cue, my stomach growls and I tell Brian that my best friend's mom used to make BLTs for us as kids, so this will be a hard barrier to clear, but challenge accepted nonetheless. He walks me to the door and just as I'm about to leave, he says, "Josh loves those BLTs. Why don't you grab one for him?"

IT'S 12:45 BY the time I walk back through the front door. Josh is at the sink, rinsing out a paintbrush for what must be the fifth time in the short period he's been at the house. Apparently, my approach of just buying new brushes isn't the only option. Ben used to tease me relentlessly about this.

"I have good news to share," I say triumphantly. "Not only did I write a full chapter this morning, but I kicked some small-talk ass."

I walk to the kitchen island and put down the Lenny's take-out bag, which catches Josh's attention, and I watch his eyes dart between jealousy and hopefulness thinking about the contents of the bag. I would've been home sooner, but Lenny and I spent a half hour talking about our college basketball fandoms. We talked for so long that he had the kitchen remake the sandwiches so they would be fresh.

"You've been quite the social butterfly," he says in a knowing tone. "Brian, Sunny, and Lenny all texted me to say what a nice woman I'm working for this summer."

"I am a benevolent and kind employer, Josh," I say in the most faux charming voice possible as I reach into the bag and pull out two huge BLT sandwiches. "One for me and one for you. The giant fries are to share."

A look that can only be described as pure childlike joy crosses his face.

"Occasional deliveries of my favorite food in the entire universe definitely make up for the terrible working conditions," he says playfully.

I toss a fry at him, and he ducks with alarming reflexes, but it still hits him in the shoulder.

"Just so you know," he adds, picking the weaponized fry off the counter and eating it, "there is absolutely no way to eat this sandwich gracefully. Just embrace the mess."

"I was about to grab a fork and knife," I say.

He shakes his head in mock disgust and tells me in no uncertain terms that this behavior simply won't be tolerated. Before I dig in, I grab my instant camera from my bag on the other stool. I carry it everywhere with me, despite the fact that it's bright pink with stickers all over it, courtesy of the kids.

"Listen, I think the BLT is a thing of beauty, but are you really taking a photo of it?" he asks with a puzzled look on his face.

"Ava and I started this tradition her first summer at camp, and now I do it for both kids," I explain, lowering the camera to the sandwich's level so each layer will be clearly visible. "Any time I write them a letter, I take a photo that captures exactly what I was doing at that moment. Ava said it kept her connected to us without making her homesick."

"Well, now I feel bad for teasing you, because that's about the sweetest thing I've ever heard," he says.

"This one is for Benji," I say, gently fanning the developing photo. "He is a sandwich connoisseur. I'd put a hundred dollars on the table that his letter back insists we go to Lenny's the same day they get out of camp. I'll write him a quick note when we're done."

The last thing I do before I take a bite is grab my little notebook, flip to a page in the middle, and make a quick mark under Benji's name.

"They are siblings," I say with a sigh. "They are definitely comparing the number of letters that I send them."

"You are a very smart mom," he says as he realizes what the tally marks are for. "So, what did you learn about the art of small talk today?"

"There is an alarming tendency deep inside of me to overcomplicate every conversation—to try to explain everything or find the right words. Today, I tried to take your advice and keep it light. It worked great," I declare.

"Any surprises? Were all the conversations the same?" he asks.

"No, they weren't the same. Sunny and I had a short, friendly conversation, but I imagine we'll chat a million times over the summer. She and I will get to know one another bit by bit. Brian asked me lots of questions, and I let him guide the conversation. Lenny and I were just all over the place, which was fun but also chaotic. I just kind of went with the flow."

"Are you usually a go-with-the-flow sort of person?" he asks, the side of his mouth going up in a knowing grin.

I pretend to launch another fry in his direction. Of course I'm not a go-with-the-flow sort of person.

"I'm trying out some new things this summer," I respond.

Josh might be the fastest eater I've ever seen, because he's done with his entire sandwich before I'm even halfway through mine.

"We shouldn't lose track of our other goal for the summer: interview practice," he says while walking his container to the trash. "Finish up your sandwich because it's time to get down to business. Should I ask a question?"

"Let's do it," I respond confidently.

"I tried to think of questions that you might actually get asked. First up, what's the hardest thing about writing a memoir?" he inquires while keeping those brown eyes on mine.

The fact that he's put thought into these questions makes me feel unexpectedly warm in my chest. The tender kindness of it catches me off guard.

"Without a doubt the hardest thing so far has been including stories that I would prefer to keep private," I respond, "but knowing that those stories enrich the bigger narrative and will ultimately make the book better."

"Any examples?" he follows up.

Deep breath. The obvious story is the one from April where the horrible woman ruined a perfectly good first date. I stare at Josh. He stares at me, and I sigh deeply. He starts to indicate that I don't need to share, but I put my hand up to interrupt him. "You're doing me a favor," I tell him. "I have three interviews in the coming weeks with journalists that are particularly interested in my process. This question is bound to come up eventually."

So I dive into the story. Because it's Josh and we've got this great mix of a new friendship and no baggage, I go into detail in a way that I certainly won't with journalists and, honestly, even some of my friends at home. My friends are always quick to worry intensely about everything. So I leave no sordid detail untold. As the story progresses, I see Josh switch into a defensive posture; his shoulders tighten, and he sits up bolt straight. As someone who carries tension in my neck, it's like I can see stress travel up his body just from hearing the story. He tries to keep a poker face, but it's morphing just like his body language.

When I finish the story, he quietly tells me he's sorry that happened and that part of my job means sharing it with the world.

"Maybe you don't have to share that?" he asks. His body loosens slightly, but it's just obvious he's had a physical reaction to my experience.

"It's an important piece of my lived experience from the first year after Ben died. And the truth is, I was starting to get cold feet about being away from Chapel Hill all summer before that happened. Between that date and a particularly bad interview situation, I knew that I really needed to get away for a bit," I add quietly.

We exist in silence for a minute while I gather my own empty container and take it to the bin under the sink. Josh breaks the quiet.

"Okay, one more question before I get back to work. I've decided just now that every interview session should end with a fun question so that we don't have to be so serious. What is your least favorite movie of all time?"

"So easy. This terribly long movie with Russell Crowe where he's on a ship for, like, three hours and the dialogue goes on forever and your brain wants to explode from boredom."

Once again, those brown eyes home in on me like laser beams.

"For real? That is easily one of my top three favorite movies of all time," he says, hand to his heart like I've just broken it.

Then he immediately bursts out laughing and tells the truth. "James made me watch that movie, like, ten years ago, and yes, my brain almost exploded. I'm pretty sure I disassociated for the last hour. That's a solid terrible-movie choice."

We have a moment of shared giggles over our dislike of the same film, and then he thanks me for lunch before disappearing upstairs to work on the next project. With the sounds of his hammering in the background, I flip open my laptop to do some furniture shopping online and realize this has been one of the best mornings of my post-Ben life—filled with small talk and new friends. Who am I?

# CHAPTER 12

THERE'S NO DENYING IT: I'M SLOWLY LEARNING TO LIKE the interview process. The days I get to chat with Josh are, by far, my favorite days, and thanks to our practice sessions, I'm even learning to like the real interviews just a little bit. It's been a solid week of our new repertoire, and it's adding a bit of fun and unexpected joy to my day-to-day routine. The first few days he was tentative, asking just two or three questions. Now we spend the entire lunch hour together.

"Josh, you'll never guess," I say, barging into Benji's room, where he's working after my lunchtime interview with a journalist for a women's magazine. "She asked me the same question you asked a few days ago. The one about 'What's one thing you wish you said but never did?' In your exact words. You should write fluff articles for a living!"

Josh smiles and gives me what I now know is his trademark *I told you so* look. Initially, I refused to answer the question when he asked it. My argument was, and continues to be, that people just love to ask me these revisionist history–type questions. If you could change one thing. If you could do one thing differently. If you could go back in time and say something different. People *love* hypotheticals based on time-traveling powers.

He pushed the issue, so I answered with the most honest thing that came to mind: "Ben, I'm not sleeping with you until you go to the doctor."

"Really, that's the one thing you'd go back in time and tell your husband?" he asked, incredulous.

"Yes, one threat of withholding sex and he would've been at the doctor's office like this," I said, snapping my fingers. "Men are not as complicated as you guys like to think you are."

Now he's asking me, "What was her response?"

"Very similar to yours. She laughed, but then I explained *why* I would go back and say that. So many women and wives are tired of being the nags in their families and work lives. It's like we're the human reminder list for everything and everyone. I had countless days where I felt like I only nagged—my kids, my colleagues, my husband. Sometimes we just give up. I honestly just wish I forced the issue with the doctor's visit. I torture myself wondering if maybe he would still be here if I had. It led to a great conversation about the expectations of women in modern relationships."

"Well, I'm glad that my practice interviews are useful," he says with a sad smile, given what I just shared.

"Ugh, they are annoyingly helpful. Even when it's not like today and the exact same question, I still find myself using a lot of the same 'sound bites' or whatever you want to call them. Thank you."

"Get ready, Gracie—I've got some doozies forming in my big ol' brain for tomorrow," he says, packing up his things and calling it an early day.

At the same time, my phone vibrates, and when I glance down, the summer camp caller ID stares back at me. Instant panic. I swipe the screen and answer in a flash.

"Hello?"

"Is this Gracie Harris?" the voice on the other end of the line asks me.

"Yes. Is everything all right?" I respond, my voice rising and full of concern. I've never once gotten a call from them during a summer camp session.

Things get quiet, and Josh freezes in place and keeps a sharp eye on me. I can see a hint of worry and concern crossing his face.

"Things are fine—don't worry," the voice assures me. "This is Sheila, the camp director."

"Right, right—sorry, Sheila. I didn't recognize your voice," I respond, my heart still pounding. I'm a mom, and unexpected calls from the person currently responsible for my kids' safety immediately sends my worry gear into overdrive.

"I'm calling because Benji took a tumble while riding one of those longboards down the big hill," she calmly tells me. "He had on a helmet and some pads, but it was a big spill."

"Does he need to see a doctor or get stitches or anything?" I ask, now in full panic mode.

"He's fine; nothing is broken," she tells me slowly and with a hint of annoyance. "No need for stitches, but he's got a lot of small cuts and bruises. I didn't want you to be surprised next time you check the camp photo feed and see him looking like he lost a fight."

She laughs at her joke, trying to take the pressure off. Josh can only hear my side of the conversation, and he's listening intently.

I'm focused on the phone, but I see the stress in his face loosen a bit as the tone in my voice changes.

"That's good to hear," I say, trying to slow my heart rate. "Does he need me? Should I talk to him?"

"No, no," she says abruptly. "You know we prefer campers not to chat with parents if at all possible. It just makes them homesick. Normally the nurse would have called you, but I'm just holding up my end of the bargain to keep you personally informed, given the, uh, situation."

*Situation.* An interesting word choice. A situation is time limited; whatever this is that the kids and I are in feels very permanent.

"I appreciate that, and I promise not to freak out when I see a photo," I say, trying to simultaneously sound normal and calm myself down. "He's doing well, though, on the whole?"

"He is. Ava came and hung out with him while we bandaged him up. His counselors are keeping a close eye on him, as promised, and he's having a good time," she tells me, not giving in too much to my overbearing questions. She probably regrets agreeing to call me personally.

"Sheila, thank you for calling me—I appreciate it," I tell her.

"Happy to do it, Gracie. I hope you're having a good summer so far," she says, before adding, "Have a good rest of your day and try not to worry."

"I'll do my best. You have a good day, too."

I put the phone down and take a deep breath. I'm not sure I've taken in air since that call started. When I look up, Josh is slowly approaching. He's clearly trying to discern what sort of friendship intimacy we have and how to handle the moment.

"You okay?" he asks, pointing to my leg.

My stupid leg. I don't even remember sitting on the edge of the bed, but clearly at some point I did. If I had been in my right mind, I would've moved out of sight or at least stayed standing. The shake is always less obvious when I'm upright. But instead, I'm sitting on the edge of this unmade bed with my stupid right leg shaking relentlessly.

"Yeah, totally fine," I respond, only hoping that I'm hiding the lie. "This just happens when I get nervous, and that call from camp caught me off guard. I just worry about the kids a lot."

Josh stares at me for a moment too long, catches himself, and begins to turn away.

"Maybe I could get you a glass of water or something," he says, not really asking. "Or make you a margarita?"

I'm mildly distracted and charmed upon hearing he remembered my drink order. I tell him water is fine and attempt to focus on my breathing. I will myself to remember the calming exercises that Dr. Lisa and I have practiced time and again. When he comes back into the room and hands me the water, I plaster on a fake smile that convinces neither of us that things are okay.

"I live in a constant state of worry," I tell him as he sits down beside me. "Losing Ben so suddenly put me perpetually on edge. I'm still learning to ease back into some normal state of existence and retraining myself not to expect that every phone call bears tidings of catastrophe."

"I can't even begin to imagine what that's like," he tells me, keeping eye contact and doing his best not to look concerned. I know this look, though, because I've gotten it from friends many times over the last year. He's worried. Genuinely worried. As Jenny has reminded me repeatedly over the last year, part of the reason I try to avoid emotions is because I wear them like a clown suit—impossible to miss, impossible to hide. I have no emotional camouflage.

"The only time I feel truly calm is when I'm writing," I share. "It's like I can disappear into my mind and nothing else matters. I need to figure out how to harness that power into my day-to-day life, that's for sure."

"Is there anything I can do to help?" he says.

"A distraction or conversation usually works," I say. The only hope of stopping this stupid leg shake is if we convince my brain to focus on something else. "Maybe an early preview of your interview questions for tomorrow?"

"Let's try something else. Tell me about Benji," he says. "What's he like when he's not causing the camp to call and stress you out?"

I smile and launch into a long-winded response, telling Josh that Benji sometimes feels like two different kids. He's incredibly responsible and a good listener. He's always the first one up and you usually don't have to ask him more than once to do something, unlike Ava, who needs constant reminders. He's also a ten-year-old boy, so when he goes outside or gets around friends, he is adventurous and open to anything. If you dare him to do something, he'll shrug his shoulders like it's no big deal and give it a try. He's as happy to fish quietly in a lake off the side of a boat as he is to longboard down a big hill and crash and burn. Perfectly adaptable to the conditions in which he finds himself. As I talk, Josh interjects to ask questions or make jokes, and before I know it, fifteen minutes have passed of him just listening to me babble on about Benji.

"Maybe all little boys are the same on some level, but he sounds a lot like me as a kid," he says. "I drove my parents nutty."

He glances down at my leg and smiles. "Hey, look," he says, pointing. "No more shake."

That was fast. Usually, it takes an hour for things to really calm down, but sitting here talking about Benji did the trick.

"See? I told you it would help," I say confidently, even though I didn't think it would actually work so quickly. How about that?

I've likely made Josh late for whatever lunch meeting he was trying to get to, but he doesn't rush to leave. I thank him again and walk across the hall to the writing room to collect my thoughts.

Josh is the first person to successfully talk me through a stress tic. Jenny, my mom, Dr. Lisa—they're all almost always focused on trying to get to the root of the problem or downplay my mental spiral that they don't take time to just talk me through it. Frankly, I didn't know a calming conversation was an option. Josh was surprisingly adept at de-escalating the situation and acting like it wasn't a big deal.

I sit down at the desk and think about an essay from five months ago. Over wine and a late-night phone call, Jenny and I basically cowrote the equally loved and maligned essay called "Rules for Dating a Despondent Widow." It was a mostly tongue-in-cheek look at what it means to date someone who is both very sad and very new to the realities of dating in the modern era. It included tips like *Don't mention anything to make them cry* (spoiler alert: you won't know what those things are until they start crying). It was all based on real experiences of mine in the first month I got back into dating. It was a sensation. People shared it with comments like "Also goes for divorcées" and "Literally peed my pants reading this."

Some readers without a sense of humor declared that I was a terrible person and mom for attempting to date within the first year after Ben's death. I have no doubt that the horrible woman at the restaurant was one of them. Meanwhile, Ava read it and laughed so hard she snorted. "Wow, Mom—I didn't know you could be so funny," she said with so much preteen honesty that I didn't know whether to be offended or honored.

That piece is on my mind because now I'm thinking of new rules—rules for distracting a despondent friend. I reach for a pen and notebook and jot down three things that Josh did really well.

Rule #1: Don't make it about you.
Rule #2: Engage them on a topic that always brings them joy.
Rule #3: Let them decide when they feel better.

I like where this is going. I reach across the desk for my laptop and open a fresh document. I type for long enough that I see the mailman drive up one side of Wilson Street and come back down two hours later to my driveway. That means he's done most of downtown; I'm at the end of the central route. A true creative flow. The pull quote for this one is easy:

*Perhaps the most important rule of all is this: don't try to solve the problem. The problem is a bigger and more tangled mess than you can imagine. Be there, be present, be aware. That's what we need when we're down.*

Aside from Ben and the kids, the only other people who have inspired essays for me are Dr. Lisa and Jenny. I take this as a sign that this is a genuine friendship blooming. Something about this summer in Canopy really, truly matters. I won't tell Josh, though; it might go to his head. I also conveniently leave mention of my leg shake out of the essay. That isn't something I'm ready to share with the world just yet.

---

I EXPECTED THAT yesterday's minor freak-out on my part might've scared Josh away for a day, but we're back to the normal routine like nothing out of the ordinary happened at all.

"What's your biggest fear?" he asks me over today's kitchen-island lunch. I'm nibbling on toast with almond butter (which Josh claims isn't even a real meal) and he's got a turkey sandwich.

"Do you mean like a very in-the-moment fear that camp calls me about another injury, or, like, I'm afraid of heights?"

"Probably aiming for something in between those two," he begins. "But glad to know I shouldn't take you on any hikes with tall peaks."

"Definitely not," I say playfully before turning serious. "Honestly, Josh, my biggest fear right now is dying—and not in the sense that I'm afraid of death *for me* or have issues with mortality. I'm desperately afraid of leaving my kids orphaned. There were many days, weeks probably, after Ben died when I stayed up at night just panicked at the thought. Suddenly it's just you standing between some semblance of happiness and total childhood devastation."

"How do you work through that?"

"You know me well enough now. There's a practical answer and a more philosophical one. Practically speaking, I got my will rewritten within the first month of Ben's death. I talked to designated caretakers instead of just writing it down and assuming it would never matter. I made sure beneficiaries were listed on literally every insurance policy and retirement account. Just tons of stuff like that, so at least if it happened, they would be taken care of in the legal and financial sense."

"What about the nonpractical stuff?"

"I try to decrease risk as much as possible in my life. I used to love traveling around not just the state, but the country, for work. Now I try not to be far from them. The few trips I've done to New York City for book stuff, I'm there and back in thirty-six hours or less. I turned down an amazing writing residency in Italy this summer in part because my kids didn't want me so far away."

"Wait. First of all, that's still a practical answer. Second, are you telling me that you could be in Italy right this second?"

"Tuscany, to be exact. Probably getting served a drink by some handsome Italian man asking me if there is anything else he can do to help me finish my book," I say, giggling and raising my eyebrows in a very unsexy attempt to convey romance.

"I would argue that getting your house remodeled is way more valuable than whatever *that situation* would've been, even if it means you have to watch me sloppily eat sandwiches a few times a week," he replies, seeming almost disappointed on my behalf that I'm not in Italy.

"Canopy isn't a consolation prize," I firmly tell him. "My mom and best friend, Jenny, both thought I was insane to turn down the residency, but the truth is that I knew after the first few days here that I made the right decision. This all feels meant to be. I feel strongly that Ben would want me here finishing the book, even if I do have to watch tomato juice drip down your chin with alarming regularity."

The other truth is that I can't imagine a better summer than the one I'm having. I feel lighter, happier, and more productive than I have in years—not just the last year.

"Canopy is happy you're here," he says, before adding, "I'm happy you're here, too. You should know that. This whole situation we've got going on has been good for me, too."

This makes me smile. Big. It's hard for me to keep my classic Gracie poker face with Josh. We speak so openly and honestly to one another that playing it cool has become nearly impossible.

"You can't distract me with that smile, Gracie," he says, looking maybe just a little off his game. "Next question: Did people say or do anything after Ben died that annoyed you?"

"You mean aside from the standard 'He's in a better place' or 'The universe has a plan for us all' sort of crap?"

"I hate when people do that."

"It's the worst, but over time I came to realize that most people just have no idea what to say in grief-filled circumstances. Americans are terrible at grief. We let ourselves go to a funeral or memorial and then fold the grief up in our pocket and try to never take it back out again. I'm the worst offender."

"Is that what made you start writing?"

"I have no idea what possessed me to write the first essay. Honestly, it was like an out-of-body experience. But it was like floodgates opening. I suddenly had so much to say. I think it's the reason I agreed to start writing the biweekly column. I wanted to make a space to talk about grief and to share what it's like to live and exist in the thick of it, especially when there are no easy answers."

"Was there anything people said or did that genuinely surprised you?"

"I mean, I guess I was surprised by how many people wanted to give me advice for 'moving on' or 'getting back out there' who had never themselves experienced anything like this. You learn a lot about people watching them try to help and console you. Even my closest friends missed the mark on this one."

"What made you decide to write a memoir? Writing a book looks like a lot of work."

"So much work. Honestly?"

"Honest answers only."

"The book advance. I got a huge—well, huge to me—advance. It doesn't come all in one check. It's broken out into four payments. I saw the advance offer and the consistent income for a few years and decided that I had to do it. Again, practical."

"So damn practical. You didn't have even a moment of wanting to be a published writer?"

"I did think it would be pretty great to hold a book in my hands with my name on the cover. I do get more excited about that as time goes by. That, and leaving my kids with something tangible and important that tells this story of me and Ben."

"Last one for today before I get back to work. What's the single most important thing you want to get out of your time in Canopy this summer?"

"I really do want to finish the book here. It feels important but also right. I can't explain it. I want to leave here knowing myself just a little bit better, too, because I am still figuring out who I am without Ben."

"I can't speak to who you were before," Josh says, piercing me with those eyes. "But I like the person I'm getting to know. I think all of your new friends here would agree."

I smile and look down, bashful and feeling my cheeks getting red. I've always been this way with compliments. Flushed cheeks and a nervous smile. He jumps in for one final question.

"Actually, one more," he begins, rescuing me from my embarrassed flush. "I'm curious about something after the call from the summer camp yesterday. Do interviewers ever ask you about your kids? It dawned on me that I don't hear them come up during your interviews."

"No, not usually," I respond, grateful for the serious line of questioning to help tackle my rosy cheeks. "Mostly because Lucia, my publicist, sets ground rules with journalists."

"Rules?" he asks, tilting his head. "You can do that?"

"It's pretty common to put expectations on the table ahead of an interview—things I'm willing and not willing to talk about," I explain. "Of course, there's no guarantee that people will follow rules, but for the most part, journalists do."

"Can I ask why not speaking about your kids is one of the ground rules?"

"I want to protect their privacy and their mental health," I tell him. "And I never want to tell their stories for them. They lost their dad and it's been really, really hard on them. They don't owe anything to anyone. I accidentally made my life available for consumption, but not theirs. I don't even post photos of them on social media anymore."

"You said 'not usually' a minute ago," he follows up. "So, someone broke those rules? What does angry Gracie look like when someone breaks the rules?"

I think back to the spring and the appearance on *The Maisy Show*. She sideswiped me with those questions about the kids and suddenly that cozy velvet chair felt like a prison. I stuttered, struggled through my answers, and made a fool of myself. If this conversation with Josh happened first, I might have been ready. Although, who is ever really ready to share the worst parts of their life on national television?

"Well," I say, taking a deep breath. "You know Maisy Miller?"

"I'm a culturally plugged-in man, Gracie," he says with a laugh and slightly offended look. "With a mom who watches a lot of daytime television."

"I'm just checking," I respond, smiling. "A little over a month ago, I was on her show—another writer had to cancel, so they dropped me right in their spot. My publicist had only floated my name to their booker, like, two weeks before, so this was a big deal. We didn't have a lot of time to prepare, and I had to jump on a flight to Nashville with very little notice."

"Number one, I'm impressed. My mom would be beyond starstruck. You are indeed a fancy, famous writer," he says. "What happened?"

"I was so nervous," I begin. "And I got on that stage and the first few questions were easy enough, but then she asked about the day Ben died. I don't really share that. It feels too intimate, too private. But Lucia and I had practiced how to artfully dodge that, so I was feeling confident. I didn't expect the next line of questioning. She asked if my kids were in therapy, what I've gotten wrong about guiding them through this loss, and what the hardest part is for them—when we all miss Ben the most."

Josh takes a long, deep inhale as I continue.

"I'm more than willing to talk about motherhood, challenges from my perspective, and things I'm doing, but not about my kids' feelings and experiences. Some people can't see the difference, but as a mom, it's an obvious line in the sand."

"How did it go?"

"Not good. An absolute train wreck, if we're being completely honest," I tell him. "That leg shake you asked about? Stress tics have been an ongoing issue since Ben died, and they've presented in different ways. That shake started earlier this year and for the six weeks prior to the Maisy interview, I had a long stretch of no issues. Those six weeks were a big achievement for me—and my therapist."

We both let nervous smiles escape. I'm always finding ways to make light of the serious stuff. I think Josh appreciates it. At the very least, he gives me space to make light of these moments when I choose to.

"But it kept getting worse. I had trouble catching my breath, and my vision got blurry—I had to ask her to stop the interview so I could get control of myself again," I share, feeling my mind and body reliving that day. "So in summary, 'angry Gracie' is a big wimp with a stress tic. That's why I'm doing all of these interviews. I need to figure myself out. Hopefully, I'll be ready by next spring, and if not, the internet can just have its way with me."

"Writing a book, doing these interviews, renovating a house," he begins, looking me square in the eyes. "That's stressful stuff, Gracie. I think you should go easy on yourself."

"To be fair, you're the one renovating the house," I say, pointing at him.

"True," he laughs. "But you're still living in the chaos of it all."

We both take quiet sips of our drinks, feeling the natural end to today's conversation. It's never awkward with Josh. One of us inevitably excuses ourselves to take care of a real task, and we pick up where we left off the next day, or the day after that. It's the easiest friendship I've had in a long time. Maybe I need more straight male friends.

"Thanks," I tell him.

"For what?"

"For being the one person in my life who hasn't seen that interview and can let me tell the story completely from my point of view. Please never watch it."

"You're welcome, and I won't," he says. Then he pauses, clearly weighing whether or not to continue. "Gracie, are there any ground rules *we* should have? For my 'interview' questions, I mean." He adds air quotes to *interview*, which elicits a smile.

I'm surprised by how quick my response comes, and how true it feels.

"A couple of weeks ago, I didn't know you, and now you're the one person I can just be completely honest with. I like that I don't have to think before I speak with you. Probably not the best for you, but it's good for me. No rules."

"The gloves are off," he says, pivoting us back to our usual lighthearted banter. "Now I'm off to do more work. Thanks for indulging my questions, as usual."

# CHAPTER 13

JOSH IS OUT OF TOWN VISITING HIS PARENTS FOR THREE days, so I spend three mornings in a row at The Drip, writing and talking with whichever barista is feeling chatty.

Sunny is here today, but instead of standing behind the counter as usual, she's perched on a high-back chair at the bar, looking out the window with a grumpy expression on her face. After I grab my coffee, I walk over to say hello.

"Gracie!" she shouts. "Rescue me from the monthly accounting reconciliation."

"I really have to write today," I tell her, instantly registering the disappointment in her face before adding, "but I can make five minutes for the woman who keeps me caffeinated."

Sunny is one of those free spirits who is magically both a good listener and someone who can talk forever. No topic is off-limits for her because she can introduce any subject in a smooth, honest fashion that never feels forced.

"As you know, I'm a big fan and I've read most of your essays," she begins, "but I'm anti–social media, so I can't look you up on

Instagram. Do you have any photos of you and Ben? Now that I know you, I'd love to know what he really looked like."

*Looked like.* The past tense is accurate but always so hard to hear. I do love sharing anything and everything about him when given the chance, however, so I grab my phone and open up an album of about fifty of my favorite photos of the two of us.

Sunny scrolls through a few photos, staring intently, before putting the phone down and looking me in the eyes.

"He was superhot," she says with a straight face before we both erupt in giggles. She picks the phone back up. "Seriously, why do men look so good with salt-and-pepper hair? You look like two very down-to-earth movie stars together."

She turns the phone around to show me a photo of us dressed up for a black-tie holiday party his company hosted a few years ago. The photo is framed on the mantel in our living room at home because it is objectively the best photo we took in our last few years together. We do look good.

"For the longest time, Ben was a tall, lanky guy," I tell her. "In his late thirties, he put on some weight due to normal life stuff. He was sensitive about it, but obnoxiously, he somehow looked even better with extra pounds on his frame. He could be weird about the gray hair, too, but same thing—it just made him hotter."

"Men are infuriating like that, aren't they?" she says, before asking, "How did the two of you meet?"

"In college," I begin. "I was in my very first semester taking an Intro to Anthropology class. He was a junior trying for the second time to pass the class after failing as a freshman while pledging a fraternity."

She smiles and asks who made the first move.

"Ben, for sure. I'm way too shy," I tell her. "I learned over time that he had slowly been moving down row by row in those first few weeks to get closer after he spotted me on day one. I clocked his accent to North Carolina right away, and I think we were both goners after that. Chicago felt like a long way from home, for both of us."

A bit of sadness creeps into my voice. That happens a lot when thinking about Ben and remembering those carefree early days, months, and years. Sunny quickly pivots to keep things light and fun.

"Your hair was so short!" she says, turning the phone around again so we can admire a photo of Ben and me out with friends nearly a decade ago. "The bob is cute, but I like this longer flowy style you have now. No surprise, me being a hippie and all."

"It's grown extra long over the last year out of pure neglect," I tell her. "But I kind of love it. I had to keep it short while Benji was young because he constantly pulled on it."

"Is it possible you got younger over the last few years?" she asks.

"Bougie facials and Botox," I respond. "They go a long way."

I can tell the instant she reaches the one photo that she's already seen before. It's the one at the bar—me looking at Ben, him looking at me.

"I remember this from the first essay," she says with a sweet but sad smile.

Lastly, she taps on a photo of us and the kids at a beachside restaurant. Ava and Benji look so little, even though the photo was only taken three years ago. We forgot the sunblock that day, so we'd all flown past sun-kissed and were turning slightly red. It's a perfect family photo and one I look at a lot. We're full of joy and completely in the moment.

"Josh told me your kids are adorable," she relays. "You and Ben gave them good genes."

She hands the phone back and turns to look at her screen. It seems we both have deadlines to work against.

"Thanks for sharing," she says. "And if you're looking for another tall and dashing leading man, there happens to be one working in your house every day."

"I appreciate the sentiment," I tell her with a big smile, "but we're just friends. Plus, I need to write, not date."

---

I'M NOT ASHAMED to admit that today marks my third lunch in a row at Lenny's. I enjoy the food and equally enjoy chatting with him and the staff about everything and nothing. Today I've heard the updates about the new merchant moving into the empty storefront next door (a pottery shop), rumors of a torrid (but hilarious) affair in a nearby fifty-five-plus community, and the plans for the peach festival at the end of the summer. Lenny is not a fan of this year's tagline: "Peach for the Stars."

A buzz rattles against the bar and I look down at my phone. It's another text from Josh. He keeps asking me questions about Ava's room. He got three-quarters of the way through a project before he left town, and it's clearly driving him crazy that it's unfinished. I text back Stop staring at your phone and hang out with your parents and shake my head.

"Lenny, you've known Josh all of his life. Is he always this obsessive about his work?"

"My dear, you do realize the entire reason that guy is even available to renovate your house is because he burnt himself out at his regular job, right? He's a workaholic through and through," Lenny confesses.

"We haven't spent a ton of time together, but it's crazy to me because he's so laid-back in conversation any time he's not working."

"So, y'all spending some time together outside of work, are you?" Lenny says with a playful look in his eye. Most of the last hour was spent with me listening to Lenny share the latest Canopy gossip, and this is the last thing I need in the rumor mill. Men like Lenny always make the best worst gossips. Yes, that's a thing.

"Nice try, Lenny," I say, dramatically rolling my eyes for full effect. "We often eat lunch together and chat, but then he disappears to different rooms to work his magic. I just don't get to see the intensity for myself very much."

"You need to spend a lot of time with someone to get the full picture of who they are. Except for me," he jokes. "You could have lunch here every day for years and I'd still have my secrets."

"Dang," I say in response. "I bet you have really good secrets."

"Speaking of Josh, I heard some particularly good intel about your handyman and his ex," Lenny says, looking at me with a knowing glance.

Except, I don't have a clue what this could be about. An ex? Gossip? Josh, thus far, has struck me as the least controversial person on the planet. He's basically the man version of strawberry ice cream—not too plain but nothing over-the-top.

"Not sure I follow, Lenny, and I think that maybe *you* think I can read between the lines," I say. "Josh doesn't really tell me much about himself."

I say it out loud and realize it's a bit of a silent confession. So far this summer, Josh has shown nothing but interest in me and my story. Yet I really know so little about him. That's something I should fix—if only so I can better navigate the gossip mill.

Lenny nods and stares. He's obviously doing the mental math on whether he should share. In the end, as always, his need to talk wins out.

"A few old-timers were in yesterday, including her parents," he begins, still not giving the ex a name or any description. I'm not being let into the full story—that much is clear. "Now, it's not my business, but it sounds like she's coming back to town after some big life changes or something. If she's not here now, she will be sometime this summer."

"That doesn't seem like a big deal," I reply a little too quickly. "I mean, maybe she's just coming to see her parents?"

"Not getting worried, are you, Gracie?" he asks, trying to pivot the conversation.

"We've been over this," I say. "Just friends."

It takes just a little extra effort on my part to say the word "friends" in a convincing tone. Why does it feel weird to hear about his ex? Josh is a grown man with a whole life. I've known him for only a couple of weeks.

"Well, if you do learn anything, be sure to let me know," he says. "Not having the full picture drives me crazy!"

He gives me a big hug (and I'm surprisingly okay with it) before I leave and tell him to enjoy his Sunday off tomorrow. On the short walk home, I pop into the hardware store to say hi to Brian and pick up a few things that Josh has asked him to set aside for his next project.

"How many times do you think he'll be in when he gets back?" Brian asks me with a smirk on his face. "It was four times in three days this past week."

"I think he just likes hanging out with you, Brian, because there really is no other logical excuse for it," I say back. I've officially moved into the friend zone with Lenny and Brian when it comes to their teasing about Josh.

"You're probably right. Josh and I go way back. He was two years behind me in school. He's a good friend. He helped me get the finances straight here when my dad retired about five years ago. Good Lord, it was a mess in here," Brian tells me.

I'm probably right that Josh enjoys taking breaks and coming to the hardware store to talk to Brian. It's a three-minute walk, and he's an old friend. It also dawns on me that Josh likes supporting the business and will do everything possible not to go to a big home-improvement store if he can give the money to Brian instead. Josh does seem to love his people.

After I pay, I lift a Lenny's take-out bag onto the counter. I know from previous visits and chats with Josh that Brian skips lunch most days to help keep staffing costs down. Brian's eyes get big and excited just like Josh's did the first time I brought a BLT home for lunch.

"Gracie, you did not," he says in a surprised voice.

"Just a treat from your new favorite customer," I say with a smile, walking to the door before he can try to give me something for free as a thank-you.

I GET BACK to the house and have five minutes to relax before my midafternoon session with Dr. Lisa. I've been in Canopy for two weeks and am fully immersed in my new routine. This is the first time I'm able to get a session with Dr. Lisa. She made a special exception for me to meet on a Saturday.

"Gracie, it's lovely to see you. I've been looking forward to our time together and hearing all about your first couple of weeks in Canopy at the new house. How has the adjustment been?"

"It's gone surprisingly well. Everything about life is easy and comfortable here. I've fallen into a wonderful routine, and I have a great person helping around the house."

"You look wonderful. I can tell you're getting better sleep. You were carrying a lot of stress about the house in the lead-up to summer. What has changed?"

It's not like Dr. Lisa to make comments on my physical appearance, so I know the difference must be dramatic. The depression and exhaustion that followed Ben's death were not how I expected to reclaim the bone structure of my twenties. But good rest and the bits of sunshine from my walks into town seem to have made a difference.

"The truth is that I expected the broken house to be a buzzkill. Not to be obnoxiously poetic, but I thought it would be a painful reminder of the work-in-progress sign I have hanging around my own neck. Instead, I feel possibilities. Potential. I haven't really felt those two things since Ben died."

"I was very hopeful this would happen. A change of scenery is often the best medicine in a situation like yours. Now, you mentioned someone helping you around the house. Tell me about them."

"His name is Josh, and he's the brother of my real estate agent here."

I dive into the story of why Josh is available, making a joke that he could likely benefit from his own therapist who helps him set boundaries. I tell her about my meltdown with the first interview and his offer to help. I share bits and pieces of the conversations that he and I have had and how much I like them.

"It's nice to get to know someone brand-new, from scratch," I tell her. "Maybe it's more accurate to say that I like someone else getting to know me in that way. He knows my story, of course, but it doesn't feel like baggage."

"After a traumatic event, it's important to have all different types of friendships. Your old friends are critical to your healing, but new friends are key to helping you grow as well. Aside from Josh, have you gotten to know anyone else?"

"Yes, but I'll be honest that it's only because Josh pushed me to do it. He told me I needed to work on my small talk, so now I have new friends at a few different spots in town that I visit often."

Dr. Lisa is usually good at keeping a straight face, but the small-talk comment brings a genuine smile to her face. She knows I'm an overthinker and that my small-talk skills are, let's just say, an identified area for development. We talk for a good while about my new daily routine and how I'm building space for rest and meditation. With five minutes left in our abbreviated session, she poses one last, seemingly innocent question.

"Gracie, is there anything else you would like to share?"

"Yes," I say, but with hesitation and a frustrated sigh. "I hate to admit this because it's the least independent-woman thing I could ever say, but I like having a man around the house again. I like having someone to casually talk to, to fix things, to make me laugh when I need it. The energy in my life feels balanced out."

"You spent half your life in a relationship with Ben. I'm not surprised you feel comfort in having a situation that allows you to get some companionship back, even on this smaller level."

Then Dr. Lisa nods quietly for a moment before continuing with a zinger of a follow-up. "Is it having *a* man or *this* man around that feels good?"

I am genuinely caught off guard by the question. So much for curveball prep.

I remember back to earlier in the year when my dad came to stay with us for a week. There were tasks around the house that needed to be taken care of—gutters, old light fixtures, bathroom grout—and he offered to hang out and tend to the household chores. Despite the fact that I had spent eighteen years of my life sharing a house with him, I was annoyed and ready for my own space by the end of his visit.

It isn't just that on my mind, though. I think back to the many men I'd been out on dates with and the few I even brought back home for a night. It never crossed my mind to invite them around again—there was no appeal to having them in my space. Still, I can't decide the right answer to her question, because I'm not sure.

"Maybe a bit of both," I start, tipping my chin up slightly and genuinely thinking through how I feel about this line of questioning. "I guess if you made me pick one, though, I would say this *type* of man." It didn't strike me as a big deal as I was saying it, but as soon as I finish, it certainly feels like a confession.

"Interesting," she replies. Dr. Lisa's favorite word and her kind way of drawing out more explanation from you. I don't bite, so she continues. "Gracie, I want you to explore this. Pay attention to how you feel when he's around. I don't mean surface-level stuff—like, *Oh, this is nice to not eat lunch alone today.* No, I want you focused on the emotions down a layer or two. Why does it feel nice? What about Josh makes you feel this way? What empty cup has this filled? Don't overthink it, but I know that's easier said than done."

Dr. Lisa has just insinuated that I might be into a guy like Josh . . . romantically. I'm already into the way he does home repairs. She's dropped a bomb into my psyche and has the audacity to follow up with *Don't overthink it*? I will think of nothing else until we talk again in a few weeks.

# CHAPTER 14

EVEN THOUGH HE'S BACK IN TOWN, I ASSUMED THAT JOSH would take Sunday off before coming back for a week of work on Monday. Instead, he texts me first thing in the morning and asks if it's okay if he comes over.

He pulls into the driveway right at nine. I unlock the door and open it for him.

"You really are a workaholic; I'm glad they did that intervention," I say when he walks through the door.

Josh shakes his head and rolls his eyes. "James is so dramatic," he starts. "The truth is that I *hate* when things are unfinished. Once I get a picture in my mind of how to solve a problem, it's really hard for me to walk away until it's finished. That's how I'm feeling about Ava's room. I know you have big plans for decorating it."

"Here I was thinking that you just missed my charming personality," I respond with a smile.

"Obviously that, too," he starts. "Mostly, Lenny told me to come back before he started telling you his secrets. Three days in a row, huh?"

*That's interesting,* I think, *because Lenny was definitely fighting the urge to share* your *secrets while you were gone.* I don't say that out loud, though, because the quality of the information is dubious at best and lacks any detail worth sharing.

"Lenny belongs on the big screen," I say to keep the conversation in a safe place. "So much personality and so fun to be around. I wrote some heavy stuff while you were away, and my time with him was like a breath of fresh air."

With that, he starts gathering tools from the various spots he stashes them on the first floor. I remember one important thing I need his help with today.

"Josh, it's actually a good thing that you showed up today," I say. "Remember the writing desk I told you about last week? The guy is going to deliver it sometime before noon. I am a strong, independent, and capable woman, but I have abysmal upper-body strength. Can you help him get it upstairs?"

"I'm here to serve," he says, mimicking the tipping of a cap. I playfully punch him in the arm as he walks by. It's nice to touch him, I think, before instantly making myself forget it.

Two hours later, while I simultaneously tend to business correspondence and watch mindless videos on my phone, the guy from the vintage shop in Asheville texts me that he's a few minutes away. I run up to grab Josh, who is sanding the final patch job on the bedroom walls.

"We will *finally* be ready to paint these next week," he says, before adding, "And by *we*, I clearly mean me."

We sit outside on the front porch swing to wait for Aaron, the furniture guy, and it squeaks as we slowly rock together.

"I'd add this to the list if it weren't already on there," he says with a laugh. "There is always something to fix at this house."

Aaron pulls into the driveway in a large pickup truck. I expected a proper delivery truck and it dawns on me that Aaron is likely making a special exception for delivery today. The desk is protected by a thick fabric wrap and cinched down in the truck bed. Josh and I rise from the swing to greet him. Well, I'm there to greet him and Josh is there to do the actual labor.

"Nice to see you again," he says to me before turning to Josh. "Nice to meet you. Are you Gracie's, uh, husband?"

Josh doesn't miss a beat. "She wishes," he says, laughing. "No, man, I'm just here to help."

Something like a look of relief crosses Aaron's face. He's almost as tall as Josh, with sandy-blond hair and a slight hipster vibe. He's a little young—probably late twenties—but he's definitely cute. Josh's eyes narrow ever so slightly, and it dawns on me that his energy has shifted into protective mode. Interesting.

They both instinctively reach for the closest end of the desk, which is the toughest job given the need to support the weight as it's slowly pulled from the truck bed. Aaron gets there first and makes a point to tell Josh he should take his time to make sure he's got a good grip. Josh lets out a huff and I stifle my laughter at the apparent impromptu strength competition I'm now witnessing. As we proceed up the front stairs and into the house, I give the dueling men quiet instructions and warn them whenever a step or slight change of direction needs to occur. They easily maneuver the desk up the stairs and around the corner to the writing room. Right in front of the window, I instruct, and then it's there.

"I'm gonna get back to work," Josh says before stepping out and heading back to Ava's room.

Aaron stands in the room with me to admire how amazing the desk looks in the space. The windows are perfectly centered over the dark, turned-wood furniture. Despite being vintage, the desk has a modern flair to it. It could not be more perfect.

"This desk belongs here," Aaron says. "I'm glad you scooped it up before someone else did."

"Me, too," I say with a big grin. "This desk might be the exact place where I finish my debut book."

Spontaneously referring to it as my debut makes me happy, because it silently telegraphs that I expect there to be another. I make a mental note to do that more often.

Aaron rocks back on his heels and then turns to me and says, "Sorry if this is weird or inappropriate, but would you ever want to grab coffee or a drink sometime? I'm down in Canopy and nearby towns a few times a week. My treat, of course."

This makes me blush. I hate to admit it, but a much younger guy hitting on a woman my age is a certain sort of compliment. The furniture shop belongs to Aaron's family, and while they mostly sell vintage pieces, he does design and build some newer ones. When I was in the store a week ago, we had a great conversation about our respective creative processes. He was a bit of a flirt, but I thought he was just trying to sell the desk.

When I started dating again and friends would ask for my parameters, I decided not to worry about age at all. I only go out with people once and lack the emotional fortitude to get serious with anyone, so why stress about something as basic as age? I've been out with a twenty-seven-year-old and a fifty-five-year-old and plenty of ages in between. Men are men.

"I'd like that, but I'm keeping a pretty tight schedule this summer to write. Why don't you text me next time you're in the neighborhood and we can see if it works out?"

"Sounds like a plan," he says as we start walking back toward the stairs. "I'd really like to see you again."

He delivers the second part just as we pass by Ava's room, and it feels surprisingly like a shot fired at Josh.

AN HOUR LATER, Josh and I are at the kitchen island ready for the next set of questions. I'm a little surprised by the first thing that comes out of his mouth.

"Do you always have teenagers in skinny jeans hitting on you?" he asks without a hint of sarcasm.

"Josh, I detect some judgment in that question."

"Not at all—I'm just curious."

"I will answer this way: ever since I stopped regularly wearing my wedding ring—which I still get emotional about, just so you know—I get hit on by men of all ages, and I can't quite figure out why. My guess is that Aaron is in his late twenties, which is flattering, but dudes firmly in the AARP age bracket ask me out, too. I never thought of myself as having an approachable aura. My resting bitch face is real, but it's not the deterrent I thought it'd be."

Josh gives a half-hearted laugh and smile. He looks at me briefly in a way that unsettles me a bit.

"You don't have a resting bitch face. More like a persistently contemplative face. There's a big difference. Will you really go out with him if he texts?"

"Maybe. Hard to say. He seems nice enough, but I'm really trying to stay focused on the book."

Something about that seems to lift Josh's spirits a little bit, and now I'm trying to decipher what is really happening at this moment. Is there a chance Josh likes me? He would've asked me out already. Is this a protective-big-brother sort of situation? Dr. Lisa has put too many thoughts in my head. Josh clears his throat.

"Hey, you asked me to come up with some personal-life questions for you in preparation for stuff you have coming this week, and I thought of a few," Josh says before getting a nod from me that conveys I'm ready to go. "What's it been like being a single parent?"

"Different than you might expect. On one hand, not as hard as I thought, but that's only because I've got family around. My support system is industrial strength. My parents bought a small condo in Chapel Hill right after we moved back to North Carolina so that they could be in town without being in the way. They hate driving to and from Charlotte, where they still live. Ben's parents are two hours east, so they have a key to the condo now, too, and use it once or twice a month. They all take turns having the kids over for grandparent sleepovers for entire weekends and even some school nights. It's the only reason I ever have time to fully decompress. Never in a million years did I think my kids would still have four grandparents but not their dad."

"That's all fairly practical, so I assume there is another angle to it as well?"

"Yeah, the shitty angle and, basically, exactly what you'd expect. It's a lot of pressure to be two parents at once and try to do everything on my own. Between school events and sports teams and birthday parties, it's just a ton to manage. Not to mention my work and writing schedule. That's before we even get to the emotional side of things—therapy for me, therapy for the kids. I have no idea how single parents do it without such amazing friends and family willing to pitch in."

"I only met them briefly, but your kids seem pretty great."

This makes me blush and fills me with pride. Like a lot of parents, I think my kids are spectacular. What we three have been through in the last year has only deepened our bond.

"They really are fantastic. Ava is like a mini Ben in personality. She's inquisitive, super friendly and social, and loves to try and see new things. Benji, of course, you know a bit about now. He really is a riot, but he's naturally more introspective, like me."

"I always thought it would be fun to have kids," Josh admits, "but life seems to have other plans." He doesn't elaborate, and I don't push him.

He starts to ask questions about my family, my job, and how I see my life in a year or two if the writing path works out for me. It feels good to share a bit of my life story with him and to imagine what might be waiting for me down a future road. All I can really think about, however, is how happy I am to have him back in the house after his few days away.

---

BEFORE HE HEADS out a few hours later, Josh catches me staring at the walls in the dining room.

"What's going on in here?" he asks.

"Just thinking," I reply, rotating my body completely around to consider the space and view from every angle.

"Do you usually brainstorm while staring at empty walls?" he says in a joking but curious tone.

"I'd really like to do a beautiful wallpaper in this room," I tell him. "It feels like a spot in the house to do something fun and different, and I could choose a vintage pattern to fit with the era the house was built in."

"What's your hesitation?" he asks. Last week, I shared with him how it's strange to make so many decisions by myself after two decades of always having Ben around to bounce ideas off of. Now he tries to act as a sounding board every time I have trouble with a new design choice.

"Wallpaper isn't everyone's thing," I explain. "And I don't want to do anything to hurt the resale value."

The vibe in the room palpably shifts when I drop the words *resale value*. Josh takes a quick half step back away from me, and I realize that despite our hours of conversation and the deep secrets I've shared, never once have I mentioned getting rid of the house.

"You'd really sell this place?" Josh asks in a tone that makes his disappointment clear.

"Yes," I say, before instantly adding, "Maybe? I don't know."

"I thought I was fixing this place up for you," he says in a gruff voice, "not for random people that I'll never meet."

So far this summer, there has never been a time when I felt the need to manage Josh or his emotions. He's just not that kind of guy. Right now, though, it feels necessary to keep our friendship on track. The whiplash between the Aaron thing followed by a heartfelt conversation and whatever is happening now is throwing me for a loop. I'm not proud to admit it, but my tactic is to play the dead-husband card.

"Ben and I bought this house and then he died, suddenly," I tell him, or maybe remind him. This isn't a fact that sits top of mind for most people. "That's not me being dramatic, either, Josh. Literally ten days after our only other trip here, he died. For about nine months, texts from James were the only reminders that I actually owned a second house. My brain compartmentalized so many things, and I just couldn't think about it."

"That makes total sense," he allows in a gentler tone. He's been blindsided, though, so feelings are slipping through his usually calm demeanor and mannerisms.

"I guess I didn't realize how attached to the house you are," I say. "My intention wasn't to make you upset or think that I don't love the house. It's really complicated."

"Maybe I'm attached to the thought of you and your kids getting to enjoy it," he says, immediately diverting his eyes from mine. "So many people come and go from Canopy, and I wanted to give you a reason to hang around."

I smile at the sweet sentiment, but he's done making eye contact.

"It's important to me that you know I appreciate everything you've done—that you're doing—for me. Please don't be mad."

"I'm not mad, but I should go," he says.

And just like that, he walks out the door without resolving the first disagreement of our friendship.

# CHAPTER 15

"ANY BIG PLANS TODAY?" JOSH ASKS WHILE DROPPING OFF supplies for tomorrow's next big project. "Any chance you've got a free couple of hours?"

"No interviews and no major writing plans aside from getting letters out to both the kids," I answer. "Why do you ask?"

"It's just that I've not really seen you leave the house, The Drip, or Lenny's since you got here," he says, giving me a smile that tells me he's trying to be nice as he delivers a mildly judgmental take on how I've been spending my time. "As soon as I leave here, I'm going on one of my favorite hikes to a place called Triple Falls. It's a little steep but not technically challenging. The views are great, and I think it would do you good to come with me. Picture it like a two-hour version of *Walden* to reinvigorate your creative process. It would be good for us both."

I think back to something Felicity told me when she came to Chapel Hill earlier this month before I left for Canopy. *Try to get some fresh air.* I've walked downtown more times than I can count, written thousands of words, supervised tons of home repairs, and crossed almost everything off my to-do list. Fresh air? Not so much. Plus, after yesterday, some new scenery might help to get our friendship back on track. I can't even pretend to be offended by his invitation.

"For someone who bought a house in a cute mountain town, I haven't really done much of the mountain thing yet, have I?"

He lets out a laugh and nods his head in quick agreement.

"You promise not to judge me?" I begin. "Because I haven't so much as rolled out the yoga mat since I've been here. Not sure where my cardiovascular health stands at the moment."

"I promise," he says, holding up three fingers to mimic the Scouts' sign. "Your legs will burn, but I did this hike with my seventy-year-old aunt a few months ago, and she's had a hip replacement. You'll be fine."

"Great, no pressure," I joke. "Let me get changed and grab my backpack."

---

AS USUAL, JOSH is right, and I know it the second we step out of his truck in the trailhead parking lot. The sound of the rushing falls greets us in the echoes of the forest. They are out of sight but teasing us with their presence nearby.

"Pretty cool, right?" he asks, noticing me close my eyes for a second to take it all in.

"I love the sound of water," I respond. "Which is ironic, because I'm not big on swimming or boats or most water activities—but the sound of water instantly calms me."

"For me, it's the sound of the leaves rustling in the wind on these mountain trails," he shares, handing me my bag from the back seat.

"First you mention *Walden* and now you opine on rustling leaves?" I offer playfully. "I think you've got a hidden poet somewhere in there."

He smiles and gestures to the path.

"A mile up, a mile back," he says, before adding, "The way back is much easier."

We're quiet for the first few minutes of the hike. I'm easily distracted by a handful of fly fishermen, equally spread out as though they are obeying unwritten rules about space and territory. One guy lets out a yelp of excitement, and I turn to see him dropping a small trout into his net before snapping a quick photo and letting the fish back in the gushing stream.

"Do you fish?" I ask, assuming the answer is yes because there doesn't seem to be an outdoor activity that Josh hasn't tried.

"I do, but not by myself," he answers. "To me, fishing is synonymous with spending time with James, my nephews, my dad, or my uncles. You?"

"I've tried it a few times, but it's never been my thing. Ben liked it a lot and would take Benji out. They rarely caught anything but always managed to have the best time ever."

We round a bend in the trail and are greeted by an impressive incline.

"A little steep, you said?"

"The elevation comes in waves. We'll go slow and talk the entire way. You'll barely notice these little hills. Plus, the first payoff is at the very first landing, so it's instant gratification."

"If I make it there alive!"

Josh playfully rolls his eyes, mimicking one of my classic facial expressions. Before I have time to elbow him, he jumps into conversation.

"What else did Ben like to do?" he asks.

I'm surprised by the question, but just like when Sunny recently asked about Ben, I welcome the opportunity to tell Josh about him.

"For fun? Ben loved sports," I say at a somewhat rapid pace, thanks to my embarrassing shortness of breath. "Basketball at the Y, pickleball with retirees, coaching Ava's soccer team. He always had to be in motion. He kept all of us active."

"I can relate to that," Josh shares. "Although for most of the last few years, it's only been a few hikes here and there . . . and fantasy football. Not sure that counts."

"What is it with grown men and fantasy football?" I ask with a smile. "Ben was obsessed."

"We all think we could run a professional sports team better than the actual professionals, and fantasy exists to humble us," Josh jokes, before pausing to ask, "What did Ben do for a living?"

"He worked for a medical-industry tech company in product development," I answer with a quick, labored breath. "Just a dude with a totally normal corporate gig."

"That's why he liked sports and the outdoors so much," Josh says, as though he's just connected two pieces of a puzzle. "He had to balance out all that time in front of his screen."

He says this with a deadpan look, staring straight into my eyes before breaking into a big laugh.

"I know you're trying to be funny," I say while wiping sweat from the side of my face, "but you're right. Some days it feels like my laptop is my mortal enemy."

"Well, be glad you got out of the house today," he says, grabbing my shoulders and turning me toward a clearing that's just appeared. "Because this is your reward."

The view is spectacular. Triple Falls is a series of three beautiful, cascading waterfalls. Most of the hikes we've done with the kids have been to what I would now consider tiny waterfalls with accessible pools at the bottom for them to splash around in. The vista in front of me is expansive and more rapid and powerful than I expected. I close my eyes to listen and breathe.

"I can see why you like this," I say, opening my eyes. I follow Josh to a rocky alcove seating area behind us. The view of the falls gets obscured by other visitors, but the sound stays.

"A half mile up the trail is an even more intense fall," he says after a minute of rest. "And most people don't bother to venture up once they've seen this, so it's more peaceful. Are you ready?"

I nod and enjoy the next few minutes of relatively flat terrain before we begin another incline. All the while, Josh and I never stop talking. He asks me more about my family, what my book agent is like, and how we found Canopy in the first place. I ask him questions, too. I want to know how he got into building homes, why he doesn't mountain bike anymore, and how he got the five-inch-long scar on his right arm. Turns out, my last two lines of questioning are related.

These conversations flow quick and easy like the water in the streams all around us, and before I know it, we've reached High Falls. Unlike the orderly triple drop we saw below, High Falls is dramatic and harsh but still utterly beautiful.

I slide my backpack off my shoulders for the first time to grab a quick drink of water and my instant camera. I snap two photos and walk over to the rocky seating area nearby. As the photos develop, I pull out two note cards and a pen.

"Do you mind if we sit here for a bit, and I write notes to the kids?" I ask.

"Not at all. This is one of my favorite spots. I fell asleep sitting up here about a month ago. Kind of like you on that front porch swing," he says with a sweet grin before turning his attention back to the falls.

I don't usually snap and send the same photo to the kids, but I know they will each appreciate this in different ways. Benji is my contemplative kid. He feels, he sees, and he imagines things with such depth and complexity that it sometimes feels like he's not on his first visit to the mortal coil. He'll appreciate the poetic nature of the landscape.

*Benji,*
*Hugs to my best guy from High Falls, which is just about twenty minutes from the house. This waterfall looks like something from one of those nature shows that you and Dad love to watch. I'm starting to think he kept us on the beginner trails as a family so you boys wouldn't have to hear us complain on long hikes. This one was tough! There is a covered bridge at the very top that I promise to take you to after camp—it's high, so I'll need to be brave.*

*The water is so powerful that I can barely hear myself think to write this note. I imagine it's similar to living in a cabin with eight other boys.*

*Love, Mom*

Ava will want to know about the people I saw on the trail, if I overheard any funny conversations, and how much she would've hated the hike but loved the view. It will definitely pique her curiosity that I came here with a boy. A boy! Preteens are nothing if not hilarious when it comes to imaginary relationships.

> Ava,
> I decided to consume air from outside of the house today. Amazing, I know. After four thousand words in the last week, I felt like I earned it. The hike to this view kicked my butt, but I didn't complain out loud because I wanted to seem tough in front of Josh and the other hikers. He told me it would be worth it, and I hate to admit it, but he was right. The sound up here drowns out all of my other concerns, so it was worth the sore legs that I will <u>definitely</u> have tomorrow.
> I hope camp is going great. You owe me a letter!
> Love, Mom

"All done," I say, turning toward Josh. "I've learned to keep camp letters short and sweet. They won't read anything much longer than a paragraph anyway. The thing they want most is the 'Love, Mom' at the end."

We sit in peaceful silence for a few minutes, sharing a bag of trail mix and taking deep breaths anytime a slight breeze comes by to cool us off.

"Hey, before we go down, can I ask you a question?" I cautiously inquire.

"You know me—I'm an open book. Mostly."

*Mostly*, I think, remembering the brief conversation with Lenny about an ex. But that's not the direction I take my questioning. There's something else I want to know.

"James introduced you to me as his workaholic younger brother and made jokes about doing an intervention to save you from your job, but I've never heard the real story about the series of events that led you to my doorstep."

Before he can answer, a group of college-aged friends arrive at the landing and gawk over the view. A few are in the middle of complaining that it's too hot today and the hike is too hard. "Stop complaining," another in the group yells while heading over in our direction. She asks me to take a photo. I pop up and, after taking a few regular shots, insist that they strike silly poses while yelling, "Hiking is fun!" This makes the group laugh, and I snap what will definitely be their favorite. They immediately head back down to the relief of the complainers.

When it's just the two of us again, it's obvious that the brief diversion gave Josh time to think about how to respond. He dives in.

"Success is strange—you know that better than anyone, and it's part of the reason why I think we're able to talk and be open like this. We're meeting each other on the same level," he says, looking me in the eyes before he turns back toward the waterfall with a bashful grin.

"When I started my business a decade ago, I dreamt of success like this, especially the money part. At first, I just did small remodels, but within a few years, I had a team and had moved on to high-end ones. Business was solid from the start, but then a friend asked me if I would consider building a house for his family. That changed everything. Their house ended up in some regional home magazines and on websites. Things just took off. I mostly stopped doing real work at that point and focused on running the business."

"You do realize running a business is still real work?" I interrupt to ask him, while leaning over to bump our shoulders in jest.

"You know exactly what I mean," he replies, shaking his head. "No hands-on work anymore, just decisions and paperwork and meetings with clients. That's all important, but it's not what really fulfills me."

"I still don't understand how things got so crazy," I say. "You have a good team, right?"

"There was some stuff in my personal life about five years ago that made work a mostly healthy coping mechanism for a while. It was a distraction. But things kept getting busier and more intense, and I kept going deeper into it. I didn't hire other high-level people to help me out; I just took on more. A year or so ago, it was clear that I couldn't figure out how to slow down. It wasn't just the work, but the pressure. There were so many people counting on me. The company builds fifty custom homes a year; we employ and contract with tons of people. We support local suppliers. Livelihoods depend, in part, on me making the right choices."

When he mentioned his personal life and needing distractions, I sat up a little straighter. That had to be about his ex. I want to know more. The truth is that I want to know every detail, but he shifted to discussing work stress too fast, and there is now no way for me to bring the conversation back. Instead, I open up a bit about my own experience.

"It's *definitely* not to the same scale, but when I hired a social media intern, and my personal publicist, and a part-time virtual assistant all in the span of two months, it literally changed my life," I tell him. "It freed me up to do the pieces of my work that I love the most."

"That's why everything you do looks effortless," he tells me, which brings out a grin that I can't control, because in reality, nothing ever truly *feels* easy. "Because you were smart enough to get help. I mean, maybe it took you a bit, but you did it."

"So, what was the breaking point?" I ask him, sensing that in this moment of vulnerability, he might share the one thing I've been most curious about since we became real friends. Yes, this is even more important to me than details about his ex.

"One day in April, James and I were out on a run together and I had a full-blown panic attack out of nowhere," he says, shaking his head nervously. "We were deep in a trail with no cell service, and it was really scary. James told me later that he thought I was having a heart attack or an undiagnosed asthma attack. He legitimately thought I was going to die out there."

It dawns on me that about the time I was reeling from a particularly chaotic early spring, Josh was in the midst of his own crisis. There is a long pause, as if Josh is trying to decide whether to share something or not. He turns his body fully toward me before continuing.

"I have no doubt your husband was on James's mind, and he was really freaked out," he adds. "A week later, I walked into what I thought was dinner with his family, but the kids were gone and my parents and a few good friends were there instead. It didn't take much convincing for me to agree that I needed a break. Together we came up with a one-month off-ramp plan. My buddy Tommy stepped into the role of director of operations—which, honestly, I should've done for him a long time ago—and he's hiring a few more people to help run things."

"Have you thought about how to get back to work? Is it possible?" I ask.

"Part of the reason James flung me in your direction is because he wanted me to remember what I really love to do," he tells me. "I need to be in the mix, planning things out, and working with my hands. The whole business will always be mine until I decide differently, but I think I may need to let other people handle the back-office stuff while I do a small side business of historical-home restoration. One house at a time, at my pace. That's what I'm leaning toward."

"I like that," I say, because it's true. That work would suit Josh perfectly. "Canopy and the other towns in the county have no shortage of houses for you to choose from, either. You'd be so great at that."

"Thanks," he responds, before adding in a playful dig. "Every time I talk you out of a decision to get rid of a historical feature in your house, I feel closer to my true calling."

We both laugh and take one more sip of our waters. He packs his bag, stands up, and holds out his hand.

"We should head back down."

The walk toward the trailhead is quiet and contemplative compared to the way up. When we get back to the truck, there's a twinge of sadness in my gut that the morning adventure is over.

"Thanks for inviting me here and showing me this beautiful spot," I say, tossing my backpack into the cab. "This is the first time in forever I haven't been obsessed with checking the next thing off my list."

I fight the urge to bring up or apologize for our conversation yesterday afternoon. It feels like our trip out into nature has organically calmed that tension.

"It was fun to have you here," he says, before adding with a wink, "even if you did slow me down a bit."

"You know, Josh," I say, "I told you today wasn't a workday, but we've just spent this entire hike doing interview practice."

"This was getting to know each other, Gracie."

---

THE MORNING SPENT with the waterfalls and trees does wonders for my mind. I didn't intend to write at all today, but I've learned over the last year to let loose when creativity strikes. Something about writing those letters to the kids today brought a memory to the forefront of my mind that had been hastily buried in the aftermath of Ben's death.

I've mostly ceased being surprised or amazed at the way grief impacts my mind and body, but it's overwhelming to think that today's foray into nature has brought this all back to life. I scroll quickly through my manuscript to the very early chapters to insert a new one.

*Letters*, I type as the chapter heading.

A month after Ben's death, I asked his mom, Cecily, to take the kids for a weekend. It felt like if I didn't write down everything that I remembered about Ben and his best advice, it might fly away without the kids ever hearing it. In a perfect world, Ben would've had time to write these letters himself. Now it was up to me.

I wrote the letters by hand so that I would labor over every word, choosing each one with purpose and meaning. I wanted letters that the kids would treasure as they hit different stages of their lives. Words that would mean one thing to a teenager and another to a recent college grad and another to a new parent.

The contents of the letters will always remain private, so after describing them in broad strokes, I share a handful of the playful names I wrote on the outside of each envelope.

*Your dad in college (and other things you should never do).*
*How to fall in love.*
*Our first year as parents.*
*How to stay in love.*
*Dad's tips for being brave*
   *(or how to scream like a girl when killing spiders).*
*How to be a good friend.*

The full list went on and on. In less than forty-eight hours, I wrote twenty letters for the kids. They were ostensibly full of Ben's advice, but looking back now, I realize it was all stuff he and I had talked about together. So, there it was again. *Ben and Gracie. Gracie and Ben.*

As I folded each piece of paper into an envelope and tucked it into a fancy oversize gift box, it felt overwhelmingly like a symbolic first step to wrapping up *us*. All advice from then on would come directly and solely from me.

# CHAPTER 16

A FEW DAYS LATER, I WAKE UP IN A TANGLED MESS OF sweaty sheets. I'm a hot sleeper, so this is not a new sensation, but something isn't right. Thanks to a heat wave, humidity was something out of hell's kitchen overnight, but it should not be so hot in the house. Then it hits me. The weird noise outside last night—it was the stupid AC unit on the side of the house. Crap, the AC is broken. Glancing at the clock, I realize it's also 7:55.

Not a moment later I hear Josh's truck pull into the driveway. Of course this would be the one day he comes a little early. I throw my hair into a quick, messy bun. It had to happen at some point—Josh seeing me looking like a disaster.

I'm jogging down the stairs when he walks through the door. That's when I remember I'm in tiny black cotton shorts and a tank top that doesn't leave much to the imagination. He glances at me quickly and then immediately averts his eyes.

"Sorry, I just woke up," I explain. "And I think something is wrong with the AC. It's miserable in here."

"That AC unit is crazy old, but the good news is that most of the time they can be easily repaired, unlike some of the new ones," he responds, grabbing his cell phone from his back pocket. "My buddy Billy owns an HVAC company. I'll text him to see if he'll be in the area this morning."

He seems happy to have a task to divert his attention. I, on the other hand, realize that the temperature isn't going to get any better here and decide to prioritize time at The Drip this morning. My new writer's desk upstairs will have to wait.

"A quick bite to eat and I'll be out of your hair," I say as I move into the kitchen.

Never one for a big breakfast, I grab an apple out of the bowl on the counter, rinse it, and take a bite. I prop my phone on the counter against the fruit bowl and start reading news, bent over at the waist, happily eating the apple like no one else is in the house and I'm not dressed in a quarter yard of fabric, max.

Out of the corner of my eye, I catch Josh staring out the corner of *his eye*. Or maybe I'm imagining it. Damn Dr. Lisa and her ideas about this maybe being a potential romantic situation. Josh is hot; my butt looks fantastic in these shorts. Those two things can be true without two people being interested in one another. Right?

"What's on the project list for today?" I inquire, attempting to free us from this unexpected eye-catching fiasco.

"Today I'm replacing all of the outlets and switch faceplates on the first floor," he responds, all business. "Thankless, boring work."

"Thank you," I respond with a bit of sass. "So, life here is just boring now."

With that, I grab my partially eaten breakfast and run upstairs for a change into a light, flowy sundress. After that, a quick stop to throw my laptop in my bag and bolt out the front door before Josh and I stumble into another uncomfortable situation.

---

I SPEND THE first thirty minutes at The Drip procrastinating big-time in conversation with Sunny. Always on the lookout for things to tease Josh about, I prod her for stories about him in high school and college. It's all pretty tame except for learning that he and his high school friends dressed up as the Backstreet Boys for Halloween one year. I practically beg her to find the photos, and she promises to try to dig through her old scrapbooks for proof.

We're both firmly on the happy-to-be-distracted-from-work train when I decide to follow up on what I learned from Lenny. The conversation that Josh and I had during our hike earlier this week has only made me more curious, more desperate to find details.

"Can I ask you a random question about Josh?"

"Always," she tells me, a big smile opening on her face. Just like Lenny, she seems to be on the hunt for any opportunity to discuss the emerging friendship between us.

"No surprise, but I spent lunch with Lenny the other day, and he was brimming with this news that Josh's ex is in town or coming to town," I share with her. "He overheard it from a group that came in for lunch. Honestly, I'm not even sure that he has any of the details right, but it seemed like a big deal."

Sunny's face makes a quick and uncharacteristic shift to an expression of concern—and for the first time since we've met, I see her face without a smile or hint of optimism. The last year of writing has sharpened my observation skills, so even after she adjusts to a more neutral expression, I know there is something beneath the surface.

The next skill set I need, however, is a little deeper than simple observation. I need to pry. As much as I share about my own story with the world, digging into other people's lives does not come naturally to me. Thankfully, I've had the opportunity to learn from the best. Nobody in my life can get to the heart of a story quite like Dr. Lisa, so I pivot into therapist mode.

"You seem awfully quiet," I say, letting a silence fill the air, hoping Sunny will feel the pressure to fill it. "Anything you want to share?"

She takes the bait.

"It's complicated," she says, her eyes now darting around The Drip. I assume she's looking for an unexpected chore or task that didn't seem important until just this moment. I remain quiet. After a few seconds that feel like hours, she continues.

"The thing is, Gracie, as much as I love our fun small-town gossip, there are just some things I really don't think are my business to talk about," she tells me. "That was not a good situation."

Sunny has been an open book since the moment we met. I know most of her life story, and she happily answers every little question I ask about people in town. This also makes me realize how little I've really learned about Josh outside of the bits I've known about his very recent life. This town and these people have their own history—and I simply don't have a clear view to it.

"It's not like you to be at a loss for words," I say, trying to keep my best Dr. Lisa poker face but starting to freak out a bit that something is going on here I'm not privy to. I'm still an outsider, after all.

Buying a house here clearly doesn't automatically pull me into the fold.

"Josh really is a good guy," she tells me, taking a deep inhale and clearly teeing up something that might lead me to think otherwise, "but he has a perpetually bad habit with his girlfriends."

Good Lord. Bad habit? What does that even mean? Maybe my convict joke wasn't that far off. I've obviously exhausted my poker face capabilities, and now Sunny can see the worry on *my* face.

"You're getting to know Josh on a real level," she jumps in to say, putting her hand on mine, "without any of the baggage or nonsense. Whatever Katrina's reasons are for being here or reaching out to Josh shouldn't change your view of him."

With that cryptic response, she gets up to go behind the counter and help a customer, having spotted a fair excuse to escape our conversation. The only new piece of information I've learned is her name—Katrina—everything else is just more mystery. When Lenny first told me the news, it didn't have much impact, but every day Josh becomes more important to me. His friendship is maintaining my sanity. I don't want a former flame to swoop in and take this from me. I need him, but it's also clear that the self-proclaimed open book of a man that I share lunch with some days just might have a bad habit or two that I haven't seen quite yet.

As if on cue, a message comes through from him. Not a lost cause, but he needs to pick up a special piece for your AC. He'll be back after lunch and knows to wait for my all clear.

I've only been away from the house for an hour. I'm shocked his friend has been there and diagnosed the problem so quickly. It really is who you know in towns like these. Trust takes time to build. While Sunny and I are friendly, I'm still a newcomer. After a minute, I finally grab my laptop out of the bag, open it, and stare at the screen for another twenty minutes trying to look busy. Mostly, I'm turning over in my mind the conversation that I've just had with her. Why do I care so much? More importantly, why am I letting this impact my writing?

Thankfully, I've got coping mechanisms teed up specifically for times like these. I've learned to give myself prompts. The content can't usually be repurposed, but it makes me feel productive.

Before things got serious, hearing Sunny talk about high school and college Josh made me smile. Isn't it strange how far away younger versions of ourselves can feel? Yes, it was me who did shots off a friend's belly in Barcelona. Yes, it was me who bungee jumped off a bridge. Yes, it was me who once passed a biology exam while still fully drunk from the night before. But really, who was that person? She doesn't feel like me anymore.

I open up my brainstorming notebook and give myself today's prompt: Remember the twenty-year-old version of Gracie. Write about her. This isn't a note full of wild stories; instead, it's about me. The things I liked to do, how I made big decisions, when I knew that Ben was the one for me. It's a sweet, meandering journal entry on a previous version of *me*.

Ava is owed a letter, and this will surely entertain her. I pull out the instant camera to snap a photo, taking an extra moment to get the composition just right. The stylish, moody wallpaper is sure to catch her attention. It seems like every girl her age loves things that are "aesthetic." The Drip definitely has a vibe.

I tear out the pages and reach back into my packed laptop bag to grab a Post-it, envelope, and stamp. On the Post-it note, I scribble

*Had writer's block today, so I wrote this instead. Enjoy.* The camp mailing address is committed to memory.

I might not have added any words to my manuscript, but I have successfully unblocked whatever I was feeling after my conversation with Sunny. Remembering the younger version of myself has also momentarily made me feel light as air.

There's just one problem: I forget to set my alarm.

---

I BURST THROUGH the door and obviously scare Josh when I do so. He pulls his earbuds out of his ears and stares. It takes a second for me to register that he's working without a shirt on. It's hot as Hades in the house, so I can't blame the man, but good Lord.

Unlike when he adeptly averted his eyes this morning, I can't stop staring. He's more fit than he looks with a shirt on, and his subtle six-pack is staring at me. Wisps of dark hair cover his upper chest. Over the past year I've claimed many times that I don't really have a "type" as a newly single person in her forties. But in this moment, I realize if God has created a man who is physically more my type than Josh, I can't imagine it.

"Sorry," we say at the same time, then laugh.

"I forgot to text you that I'd be back to do an interview. The Drip was crowded, and I completely lost track of time," I say, grabbing my wireless headphones from my bag.

"No worries," he says while looking around for what I imagine is his shirt. "This is quiet work—you won't know I'm here."

I open the laptop and my headphones make that sad little

sound to announce that they are out of battery. Shaking my head, I apologize (again) to Josh and tell him to turn the music up or suffer through one of my interviews. "Ten-four," he responds.

I'm already a minute late when I click the Join button on my calendar reminder. Another day, another interview. Today it's Tonya from *Cosmo*. Here we go.

---

"I'M SORRY. YOU write a sex column?"

Can this day get any worse?

"No—I mean yes. It's more of a digital sex-positivity space. I talk to all types of women—actresses, politicians, entrepreneurs, influencers. The goal is to help *Cosmo*'s online readers feel more confident in their sexuality by hearing about experiences from complex, dynamic, and badass women."

*The Cosmo interview will be slightly different from others*, Lucia had written. Why hadn't I done any research? Screw research—why didn't I just google Tonya's name like a normal person? What am I supposed to say?

"Gracie, I can tell that you're freaking out a little bit. Here's the deal: I interviewed Audrey May for my most recent column, which is online now. Audrey freaking May. She's likely going to be an Oscar nominee next year. Let me tell you, that woman spilled *all* the details, and she's getting nothing but love all over social media. You'll be fine," she tells me, before adding in a direct voice, "Sex positivity."

I'm sitting here at the kitchen island, in a fugue state, when I glance up and look across the room.

Josh has braced himself against the wall, trying to stifle his laughter. He looks over at me with a smile on his face that lets me know he is going to enjoy every second of this. I raise my middle finger out of the camera frame, and his subtle smirk becomes a huge, mischievous smile. He tries to compose himself and puts his earbuds back in, but I notice he doesn't restart his music.

I take a deep, audible breath. Tonya from *Cosmo* wants to talk to me about my widow sex life (which she probably expects will be boring) while my half-naked, incredibly attractive handyman works within earshot. I'm sweating, but I don't know if it's the heat, the hot man, or the stress from this interview. Probably all three.

"Here's the deal. If we're going to talk about sex, I'm going to need to make a drink. Can I have a minute?"

---

"TONYA, FOR A sex-positive journalist, I have to say that's a pretty reductive view of the intimacy that a lot of folks experience in marriage," I say accusingly but still using a playful tone.

We're fifteen minutes into the interview. I've told her about my early sex life—admitting that I had sex for the first time at sixteen, which will surely make my parents blow a gasket retroactively—and now we've hit the twenty-years-of-one-penis commentary.

"Gracie, for a lot of women my age—I'm twenty-six, by the way—the thought of being committed to one man and one flavor of sex for the rest of your life feels daunting, to say the least. I'm trying to understand how you survive that."

"First and foremost, *survive* is a really interesting word choice," I start. "I think the problem is that you're afraid of predictability.

You're young and you want things to be new and exciting all the time."

She nods, indicating that I'm on the right track. I keep going.

"But you're missing one key thing: predictability and comfort are not the same as being boring. There is nothing boring about someone knowing exactly what you like and the next thing you need without even asking. There is nothing boring about being able to roll over on a Sunday morning and have a little fun," I say, recognizing that I'm blushing because the stranger on Zoom and the attractive man in my home are both hearing me talk very openly about my marriage and sex life. But I'm on a mission now.

"You're also assuming that sex stays one way for an entire marriage, and maybe it does for some people, but I can only speak about mine. Ben and I went through a lot of phases depending on what life and work and family stuff were like at the time," and now I pause, wondering if I want to say the next thing that's in my mind. "And when Ben died, we were in a particularly experimental stage."

Her eyebrows shoot up and I know her internal monologue is going something like *Yes—finally the juicy stuff.* Josh has been screwing on the same switch plate since this interview started.

"Now, I *won't* go into any more detail about that," I add with a smile. "I'm just trying to say that the key in my marriage was to be open and flexible. Ben and I grew up together in a lot of ways. He was a total dude and I have no doubt he would be thrilled that a national magazine might post an article broadcasting that he was having dirty sex right up until the day he died. Talk about a cool, after-death way to impress your friends."

"That is oddly sweet and romantic," Tonya says, laughing before continuing. "We only have about ten minutes left, so maybe we should pivot to your sex life now as a, um, widow."

The pause before the word *widow* isn't surprising. I've said the word so many times over the last year that it basically has no meaning, but for most people, it represents a worst fear. Even for the commitment-phobic twenty-six-year-olds.

I've grown to like Tonya over the course of this interview, but I'm not going to spill freely without making her work for it a bit. "What would you like to know?" I ask, tossing the ball back into her court.

"Are you dating yet?" she asks.

"I am," I respond. "I went on my first date about six months after Ben died."

"Interesting," she says. I wonder if Dr. Lisa is her therapist, too.

Again, I'm not going to make it easy for her, so I ask, "Interesting how?"

She pauses for a moment. It's an honest pause, like she's trying to figure out how to word a complex thought she's mulling over.

"I guess I just expected that after twenty years together, you'd need more time before getting back out there . . . that it might feel overwhelming or too hard or even wrong."

"It was all of those things," I say, nodding to affirm her theory. "It turns out everyone you know has a single friend they want to set you up with, but I had no illusions that I would find another Ben on a first date. To be honest, there are some days I'm convinced that I won't find that ever again. As a result, dating this time around is casual and low stakes to me. Not easy by any stretch of the imagination, but casual."

"I walk into every first date wondering if this will be the one where the sparks fly," she admits, seeming to surprise even herself.

"I get that. It's not that I don't take things seriously or have a small fleck of hope deep in here," I say, putting my hand to my heart. "Writing about Ben for the last year has made me realize that I'm much more of a romantic than I care to admit. I want to feel those sparks, too."

"I hope this question doesn't come off as insensitive," she begins. "How have men handled the fact that you're both a widow and have two kids?"

"Everyone I've been out with knows my story—there are no dating-app surprises here since I've mostly been set up," I share. "God bless the friends who sent their cousins and brothers on those early dates with me. They were romantic sacrificial lambs. I cried into my salad and dessert courses more than once. So embarrassing."

This makes Tonya giggle lightly. Humility aside, I've mastered the art of making grief funny.

"What about sex?" she asks, bluntly getting back onto the topic of her column.

"I'm getting back into the swing of things," I respond.

She loses the poker face she's maintained since we started talking about sex and a smile crosses her face.

"At first, I took dates too seriously. My best friend convinced me to lighten up and be more open about the possibilities."

"Good for you," she says. "Have you learned anything revelatory from those experiences?"

"Well, I forgot what it's like to discover a person for the first time," I begin. "Everything with Ben was so familiar. We talked earlier about how I slept with two people before him, but that was a long time ago. I was a literal teenager. It's been fun as a grown woman to see how different men approach intimacy, what they think they're good at versus what they are actually good at, and I do like the newness of it, but..." I trail off.

She's looking at me expectantly, and I realize that she's throwing my approach back across the table—no clarifying questions, no filling the silence.

"I haven't done any second dates yet," I say. "That level of intimacy still feels like a hurdle and something to figure out."

"Would you like to get back to that?" she follows up.

"Absolutely," I answer. "I know that I went viral after writing an essay about how I hate physical touch, but the truth is I miss it all. Maybe one day I'll find it again, but getting my hopes up doesn't feel productive."

We chat for a few more minutes about how I create comfortable boundaries and why I'm avoiding dating apps at this stage of life. With a minute left to go we have time for one final deep dive. "Gracie, what about more than the physical stuff? Do you truly want to have another great love story?"

This question gives me pause. Words are swimming in my brain, trying to find a safe (for me) way to explain how I feel. In the end, I'm just honest.

"Love for me is scary. You need to understand: I wake up every day loving someone I will never see again. I will get wrinkles—well, more wrinkles—and my hair will turn gray, and I will grow old, and Ben will always be this forty-two-year-old man who I want so badly to be right next to me but who I move further away from every day. The pain is a reminder of what I had, but it hurts so deeply right now. Tonya, the world doesn't dole out tragedy fairly. Being ready for the real thing means being willing to accept that this could all happen to me again—to love so deeply and then lose it. That's a lot to ask of one heart."

With that, the interview is over. Tonya stops recording and then tells me this has been one of her favorite interviews so far. I smile and tell her it's the same for me, which is the surprising truth of the matter.

We end the call and I wonder how to transition back into reality after pouring my heart out like that. How do I even look at Josh the next time he turns around after everything he's just heard, that I just shared? He's learned a lot about me over these weeks of our interviews, but that? That was something else.

"Wow," I say out loud to put some movement into the air. "That was certainly something different."

Josh turns and smiles at me, but it's a new look I've never seen before—if I didn't know better, I'd call it a longing expression. Just as I'm about to ask him what he thought as the only audience member to that wild ride, the doorbell rings. His buddy quietly opens the door and his footsteps approach the kitchen. When he sees I'm not on the phone and spots Josh, he says loudly, "For Christ's sake, Anderson, put on a damn shirt."

Then he turns toward me, holds out his hand, and says, "You must be Gracie."

Josh takes the opportunity to walk outside and make small talk with Billy, while I throw back the rest of my drink and mentally debrief on what just happened. Was I too open? Am I going to regret telling her all of that? Is she going to pull out one juicy detail that has strangers obsessing over my dating life again? What on earth does Josh think of all of that?

Before I can fall too deep into the spiral, I hear a guttural noise from outside as the AC kicks back on. The register at my feet begins to blow cool air—finally. As the temperature in the house slowly starts to drop, I sneak upstairs to the safety of the writing room and allow Josh to escape before we unwillingly tip over our awkward interaction quota for the day.

# CHAPTER 17

PEOPLE CAN CLAIM THEY AREN'T LAUGHING AT YOU, BUT let's be honest—you always know the truth. At this moment, for example, I know for sure that Sunny and Jenny are both laughing *at* me as they gasp for air through the biggest laughs I've ever heard.

"That did not happen!" Jenny shrieks over the speakerphone. Sunny is convulsing with laughter next to me at our small round bistro table.

We're hiding out in the comically tiny break room at The Drip so that I can tell them both the story in private, at the same time. I cannot imagine telling this tale more than once. Jenny, of course, will convene the members of the group text as they're available over the next few days and tell an increasingly ridiculous version of the story. That is, if it's possible to be more ridiculous than reality.

"Let me get this straight. Josh had no shirt on, you were being asked about sex, everyone was sweating, and then Billy walked in?" Sunny asks, stifling her laughter to get the words out.

"Thankfully, the interview was over by the time repairman Billy showed up, but my goodness, you guys. It was a comedy of errors," I tell them. I'm not laughing, but I will admit that two nights of sleep have allowed me to see *some* humor in it.

"What does he look like without a shirt on?" Jenny asks once the laughter dies down a bit.

"Jenny! I literally employ this guy," I say to her. "Well, I mean, under the table and with no official documentation, but he works *for me!*"

"Gracie, I'm at the point in pregnancy where I can't cut my own toenails—my husband has to do it for me," she says in a playful tone. "I need to hear something sexy, please."

"I would like to state for the record that I'm a happily partnered woman to a lovely man," Sunny cuts in to explain. "But I can tell you, Jenny, that Josh is very good-looking with and without his shirt. Total babe. Gracie has to be able to admit that."

"He's very attractive," I say in a monotone voice to convey that I'm confirming a fact and not rendering an opinion.

"Gracie showed me photos of Ben," Sunny chimes in. "They don't look alike, but she definitely has a thing for tall guys with good smiles. I think this could work."

"And he knows your whole romantic history now, so there are no secrets or surprises," Jenny adds before howling with laughter once again.

"I think this conversation confirms it," I joke. "I need to sell the house earlier than expected and skip town. Cut my losses. Thanks for the pep talk, ladies."

We hang up with Jenny a few minutes later after even more playful teasing, and Sunny walks me back to the front of the café. Every time she looks at me for the rest of the morning, she bursts into a fit of giggles.

JOSH WAS CONVENIENTLY out of town yesterday for a last-minute hiking trip with James, and it turns out that a little time away has removed any lingering discomfort—outwardly, at least—for both of us after the interview. We are adults, after all. Unlike Jenny and Sunny.

He walks in the door, spreads open his arms, and says, "It's still cool in here!"

"Only because I'm here," I say with a wink. "Heads up: today I have an interview at one instead of noon. It's with a woman who writes a popular publishing-industry blog, so I'm hopeful it's all about my writing process and not my dating life this time."

"I'll cross my fingers for you—actually, for us both—and run some errands so that I'm out of your hair," he responds. "For the rest of the morning I'll mostly be upstairs working in the kids' bathroom, so the downstairs is all yours."

It's still borderline unbelievable to me that a man comes to my house every day and just starts tackling all of the to-dos on a list that I made for him. He's managed to repair most of the older, charming aspects of the house and pulled me back from the ledge of making purchasing decisions that are too modern for the space. It's annoying how he's usually right, but the house does look amazing.

"Do you want me to hang those frames at some point today?" he asks, motioning to a handful of framed art prints that arrived yesterday.

"Don't laugh at me, but I just need them to sit there for a little longer so that I can visualize the perfect place for them to go. I don't have the right feeling about it just yet."

"I thought you weren't a feeler, Gracie Harris," he says.

"When it comes to putting holes in these beautiful walls you've patched and painted, I want to make sure we get it right," I say back, refusing to bite on the playful comment.

He gives me a classic Josh grin, grabs his tools, and makes the first of many trips up the stairs to bring his materials to the second bathroom. I give in to my work and don't see him again until a few minutes before one when he waves and says he'll see me in a couple of hours.

---

I'M CONFUSED WHEN Josh returns from his errands and comes through the door with grocery bags.

"I know we established that I've gone through a relatively long phase of not taking care of my own self, so I can recognize it in others. I can't watch you eat another takeout from Lenny's tonight, Gracie. I can't do it," he says. "Plus, I made a promise to your kids the morning they went to camp to feed you if you got stressed out."

Morning and late at night are my most productive times—a brain trained over twelve years of being a mom. Mid to late afternoon has always been a creative wasteland for me. So far this summer, it means that my schedule is to work all morning, do interviews (the fun ones with Josh or the boring real ones with the real journalists) at noon, and then catch up on my reading or trash TV until an early dinner—which Josh usually catches me eating before he leaves around 5:30. The blue-plate special leads into a few more hours of evening work, which is often my most productive time of the day.

I pretend to consider his offer, despite the fact that I haven't had a proper home-cooked meal in weeks and would do anything for it.

"Only if I can interview *you* while you cook," I finally answer.

"Wait—I offer to cook dinner and I have to pay a cost to do so?"

"Absolutely."

---

AT FIVE O'CLOCK on the dot, Josh is in the kitchen getting ready to start the meal. He doesn't strike me as a guy who eats this early, so I have a feeling it's a kind gesture for my benefit.

"What's for dinner?" I ask, adding with a coy smile, "I hope it's something I like."

"Veggie tacos," he responds. "Nothing too fancy, but I took a guess based on your love of margaritas that tacos would be a good choice."

"You chose wisely. I will make us both a drink to go with the meal."

I watch Josh start his work in the kitchen with an unmasked curiosity. He cooks just like he does home repairs. First, all of the tools he needs are put out on the counter. Cutting board, knives, prep bowls. Then he washes all of the veggies. He is careful and methodical—in direct contrast to the way I move around a kitchen like a hurricane.

"Can you talk and cook at the same time?" I ask.

His big laugh answers the question for me, and I waste no time diving right in while he tends to dicing onions and garlic.

"You know a lot about my dating life now, thanks to Tonya at *Cosmo*. So, now it's my turn to pepper you with probing questions about your love life."

"You're serious?"

"One hundred percent. I want this friendship to be built on equitable ground, and it can't operate that way if you know everything about me, but you're still a mystery. First question: Have you ever been married?"

"Yes."

I wait for him to go on, but nothing is forthcoming. "Yes? I only get a yes?"

"Yes, I was married in my early twenties. My high school sweetheart, Tessa, and I managed to stay together during college even though we were a few hours away from one another. We got married a few months after graduation. It took us about six more months to realize we had made a terrible mistake."

He's now slicing a red pepper while he's telling me this, and I wait until he looks up and catches my eye. Only then am I convinced he's being honest. I'm shocked.

"We stayed married for another year so that our families wouldn't totally freak out, but I was indeed married and divorced before my twenty-fifth birthday."

"Does she still live in town?"

"No. She moved away a while ago. She's remarried and has two kids. We see each other every now and again when she comes home to visit her parents. It feels strange to call her my ex-wife because we really were just kids."

"Josh, I'm not sure I'll be able to top this first revelation. My mind is truly blown right now."

He makes a joke about being an actual man of mystery, but all I can think about is how, aside from Ben, he's the most honest and open guy I've ever met. He grabs the last remaining veggie, a sweet potato, and begins chopping it.

"It's probably breaking the rules for me to ask *you* a question, but how old were you when you married Ben?"

"Twenty-three. Just like you."

"That's the universe for you. For every success story there has to be one failure to keep things balanced out."

He scoops up all of the veggies and drops them in a big bowl, tossing in olive oil and a host of spices to season it all. My stomach growls, and I realize that downing a margarita before my meal likely was not the most responsible decision. I've always been a lightweight. The mental lubrication does, however, allow me to keep on my line of questioning.

"You seem like a guy who only answers the question exactly how it's presented to him, so let me follow up with this: Have you ever been married more than once?"

"No, but I was engaged. To someone other than Tessa, I mean."

"I need all the details on this. Please tell me everything while you cook," I beg.

And he does. While the veggies sizzle on the stovetop, he tells me about his former *fiancée*—the now-infamous (at least to me) Katrina. Lenny and Sunny both somehow left the fiancée bit out for reasons I simply do not understand. Josh and Katrina met when she came to town to teach a few classes at Canopy Community College. It was only supposed to be a six-month contract, but she met

Josh and decided to stay. They dated for five years and were engaged for one more before she sat him down on a completely normal January evening and told him she was leaving. The prime dating years of his late twenties and early thirties were gone, and he felt he had nothing to show for it.

"Six months after she left, business really started to boom, and my love life has been mostly awful since then. I love it here, but small-town dating in your midthirties is not for the faint of heart."

"Josh, I don't know how to tell you this, but at thirty-seven, you're not really midthirties anymore. The technical term is *late* thirties."

He tosses a tortilla chip at me and acknowledges he's older than he likes to admit.

"Not all of us can knock it out of the park like you apparently are."

This makes me throw my head back and laugh. Knocking it out of the park? Are you kidding? I've been writing about my dating life for the book and it's the comedic relief I'll be asked about in every interview once it gets published to balance out the serious questions.

"Josh. JOSH. The last time I dated successfully was in the early 2000s. *Friends* was still on the air—we all actually watched television, not our laptops. Ben Affleck and Jennifer Lopez were dating for the first time. I had an iPod with a spinny wheel. That was the last time I was on the dating scene. What do you think it's been like for me?"

"If you're going to try to convince me that men haven't been lining up at your door, I will simply refuse to believe anything you say."

This makes me blush. And a little angry because, yes, I've been out with some eligible men, but it's been nothing serious and I've been a mess through most of it.

"I'm desperately out of practice, and the men are nothing to write home about. My first date talked for thirty minutes straight without asking a single thing about me, and when he finally did, I cried because my answer reminded me of Ben. A few weeks later, I went out with a guy—a whole grown-ass man—who chewed with his mouth open throughout the entire dinner. I literally left the restaurant and cursed Ben for abandoning me to the weirdos."

"Didn't you ever learn that if you don't have something nice to say, you shouldn't say it at all?"

"Ha! Okay. I did realize, however, that dates would make me better at writing."

"How on earth do bad dates help your writing?"

"I like observing people. It's amazing how much most people will tell you over a date. First dates are nothing if not entertaining. I've learned a lot."

"Have you really not been on any second dates?"

"Not one."

As he finishes up plating the food, I set out napkins and silverware on the kitchen island. The dining table is only a room away, but the island is where we've had all of our good conversations, and I don't want to mess up the energy. I make another drink for me; Josh hasn't touched his yet.

He sets the plates down and we both pull ourselves onto a stool. Instinctively, we turn our bodies to face each other.

"When's the last time you were on a date?" I ask, realizing that most outside observers of this scene could be confused into thinking this was one.

"A year ago. And it was a disaster."

I decide not to pry. Josh is funny, smart, handsome, and runs a successful business. He's also very sensitive. If he's had bad luck dating lately, I don't want to make him feel even worse about it. So, I take a bite of food, savor the delicious flavors for a moment, and then decide to switch things up.

"Changing topics. This question starts with a compliment, so don't make me regret it," I say as a warning. "You and James are two of the nicest people on the planet. I have to know—what are your parents like?"

"The literal best. James and I both grew up thinking we hung the moon, thanks to their support."

"I need more than this, Josh. I'm looking for tips on how to raise good people."

"I don't know if I have tips. I can tell you that we grew up knowing that we were loved completely for who we were. My parents got married right out of high school and wanted to start a family but struggled. They gave up after a few years. James was a surprise when my mom was thirty-four. I came along five years later. They were always just so happy to have us around. We never felt like a bother. There was just a lot of love."

"That's amazing. Did they ever get an explanation for the issue?"

"I'm sure my mom told me at some point, but what I do remember is that it wasn't just one of them. They both had medical things that made kids harder to have. My mom is religious, and she just took it as a sign that God knew the right timing."

"Do they still live nearby?"

"Asheville, so only about a half hour away. James and I bought them a little bungalow there a few years ago. It's all one floor and they can walk to tons of stuff. There are good medical facilities nearby. It's a good spot for their retirement. Their social life is way better than mine."

"Present company excluded."

"Obviously."

We jabber on for twenty more minutes, talking about our families and friends, taking turns to pause while the other speaks, giving us time to eat, listen, and, in my case, sip my drink. Before I know it, we've both cleared our plates and are happily dunking chips into a bowl of store-bought guacamole. We're both double dipping, so we're officially friends. With my second margarita almost gone, I'm rounding the corner to tipsy. Time for another tough question after our light-hearted banter.

"You know the worst thing that's happened to me in the last year or so. What about you?"

"My dog died. He was only eight. Cancer."

"You struck me as a dog guy, and I couldn't figure out why there wasn't one always two steps behind you. Lab or golden retriever?"

"Wow, I'm that predictable. Hammy was indeed a black Lab, and he was gorgeous. Hammy is short for Ham Sandwich, by the way. James's oldest daughter Lucy won the naming rights in a game of Uno when she was seven."

"Did you let her win?"

"Absolutely, but I wouldn't have if I knew what the outcome was going to be!"

"Not to add on to the sad dog stories, but our dog died a few months after Ben. He was super old—a pet we got way too early—but was seriously like a child to us. Buddy was, like, ninety in dog years, and the kids became convinced that he held on so long to personally take care of us after Ben died."

"Jesus. How is that the sweetest and most heartbreaking thing I've ever heard?"

"Welcome to my life," I say, raising my glass.

"Be honest with me, Gracie. Was my dinner better than Lenny's takeout?"

"SO MUCH BETTER. If you tell him that, though, I will deny it."

The intensity of my tipsy margarita voice makes Josh laugh. He glances down at his watch and starts to apologize.

"How is it seven already?" he says. "I've stayed too long, and you've had too many margaritas. I hope you didn't plan to write tonight."

"My current plan is to clean up—you are not allowed to—and then read a single page of my book before falling peacefully asleep entirely too early. I need a good night's sleep more than anything right now."

He tries to insist that he stay and help clean, but I tell him he's already done too much. As we walk toward the door, I realize how much I like having him here. How much I don't want him to leave. Is this romantic? Maybe it's loneliness. Maybe it's because he's the first regular companion I've had in over a year. Maybe I've simply had too much tequila.

I'm lost in these thoughts and my senses are dulled just enough from the drinks that I take a second too long to stop when he opens the front door. When he turns and pauses to say goodbye, we are alarmingly close. He puts his arm up on the door frame in an attempt to make things more casual, but it fails. Miserably.

"We're friends now," I say, reaching out my arms while leaning in for a hug in my own attempt to make things more casual. This also fails.

The moment I tuck my arms around him—feel the warmth of his chest, the firmness of his back, and the comfort of the embrace—I know this is a bad idea. I look up at him before pulling the proper distance away and a subtle flutter hits my heart. Knowing that he'll blame the tequila, I linger a second longer than I should—just to remember the quiet magic of being hugged by a man who knows me.

Throughout it all, he keeps an uncharacteristic poker face. I've spent weeks on the receiving end of his animated expressions. I know the way his eyes get sad when I tell him a story about Ben. I know the way his cheeks lift up when I share a funny anecdote. I know the way he scrunches his nose when I'm heading down a bad train of thought in interview practice and need to pivot. But tonight, there is nothing to read. He has somehow stripped away all expression and left me standing here with my arms wrapped around him, secretly hoping for something more.

"Seriously, thanks for dinner," I say, officially stepping back from the embrace. "It's been a long time since someone has done something like that for me."

He takes a deep inhale once we're separated, and it hits me that for however long we were in that hug, I didn't feel him breathe—not once.

"You are very welcome, fancy writer Gracie. I'll be back here bright and early tomorrow."

# CHAPTER 18

"ARE YOU EVER LONELY?" JOSH ASKS, KICKING OFF OUR lunchtime interview session. At the moment, I can't tell if he's asking out of curiosity or true interview prep.

"This is a hard question, but I'm glad you asked it," I say, taking the question at face value. "Because it definitely feels like something a journalist will eventually ask."

I sit quietly for a minute. It's an obvious yes, but there are so many layers to what I want to say that I'm not sure it will make sense. Josh hasn't taken his dark-brown eyes off me, but it doesn't make me uncomfortable. It's not probing; in fact, it's comforting. When Josh talks to me, I know that I have his full attention.

"The short answer is yes, and the long answer is yes," I begin. "I'm lonely in every way a person can be lonely, I think. I'm lonely because I wake up *literally alone* in my bed every morning, and I'm still not used to it. I'm lonely because my kids are at camp and this house is too quiet. I'm lonely because I'm in a new town. I'm physically lonely."

That last one is my futile attempt to convey the lack of sexual intimacy in my life at the moment. Of course, I'm not sharing that directly with Josh, even after the *Cosmo* interview. It's much better to let him deduce the situation on that one.

"I guess I'm also surprised when the loneliness feels the hardest," I say, diving deeper into my thoughts. "There are things I assumed I grew out of—being scared of the dark or a really bad thunderstorm that shakes the house—but it turns out it just wasn't scary with someone else there. Being here alone in this house at night has made me realize some of that. Honestly, the only time I don't feel lonely is when you're here."

That last part I add on a whim. It's a bit embarrassing to admit, but it's the truth. Dr. Lisa and I are working on being more direct with my true feelings. This, of course, is a reaction to losing someone on short notice and not getting the chance to say everything I wish I had.

Josh's reaction to this is a big, genuine smile I've not seen on him yet. The corners of his mouth go up particularly high, and he dips his head ever so slightly like he's a little embarrassed by it and can't quite make eye contact.

"I spent four years on autopilot," he says, raising his head again so our eyes meet. "Working myself to the bone and ignoring most of the other parts of my life. It wasn't until I slowed down over the past few months that I realized how lonely I was. It was a self-made emptiness that I filled up with work as a distraction. I was showing up to social stuff, but I wasn't really present."

The state of us. I could sense his emptiness like I'm sure he sensed my loneliness. Two sad sacks just trying to figure out what a happy, new normal should feel like. This is the first time it's hit me that maybe these interviews are helping him as much as me.

"Okay, vibe shift," I say with a smile, taking over the interview. "What's your favorite city in the world?"

"You're sittin' in it," he responds. "And before you ask, I'm not messing around. This is my favorite place on the planet. You?"

"It changes," I answer honestly.

For years, my favorite place was Barcelona, the city I studied abroad in my junior year. The buzz of activity, the water, the eclectic architecture with a crazy Gaudí building jumping out where you least expect it. The food, the siestas. All heaven.

Then, a decade ago, Ben and I went back for an anniversary trip, and it felt *different*. I realized the idealized city in my mind was tied up with being twenty-one and who I was then, and what made that person happy. The city didn't fit me like it used to. That was a major moment of growth for me because I gave myself permission to change my mind about things, while honoring the role something played in my past.

I explain all of this to Josh and share other places that have fit the favorite bill. Chicago, London, and even Chapel Hill.

"Right at this moment," I say, "Canopy is pretty high up on the list. I've never felt as creatively energized as I have in this last month. It's just working for me here."

"Okay, back to another serious question. What's the hardest thing about writing," he asks, before pausing and adding, "about Ben?"

This question makes me sit back in my seat. Actually, a lot of Josh's serious questions make me feel this way. It's like they are designed to look into my heart—my soul, for that matter—and dig out the truth. In the few weeks we've been playing our interview game, he's helped me workshop questions that I've been asked by the real journalists. He's preparing me to be strong whether he knows it or not.

"People want me to tell them about a martyr—not a man. Frankly, it's mostly my fault because I'm the one who built up the illusion that he never got things wrong. Nobody wants to hear about how he wouldn't go to the doctor, or how after twenty years together, he still put the lids on too tight for me to open, or how he would start a million home-improvement projects and never finish them. They don't want to hear that he could disappear into his work and not hear me tell him something that was really important for the billionth time. He didn't cheat, he didn't do drugs, he had no crazy vices that I know of. It's mostly all petty marriage stuff—the things any married couple can rattle off," I answer at rapid speed. "But they—my editors, readers, friends, family—want this perfect person, and I feel obliged to give them that. Honestly, that's what I wanted to remember for a long time."

Josh listens intently and gives me a knowing look. "I kind of had the opposite happen when Katrina dumped me. Everyone wanted to talk about how terrible she was, how she was going to hell for hurting me. They nitpicked every time she had ever said the wrong thing or rubbed them the wrong way," he starts, taking a few seconds before continuing on. "The problem was that I secretly thought she was brave for calling it the way she did. Don't get me wrong—it was really hard at the time and was the catalyst for me nearly working myself to death, but I mean, her dad freaking loved me. He referred to me as his son-in-law for years. But she did it anyway, and she's happy now, best that I can tell. I loved her so much, and I hated that people wanted me to destroy her. So, I played the mopey emo guy to get out of the trash talk. I said shit like 'I just really don't want to talk about it.' Because I didn't talk about it, others sort of gave up."

*This is a good man*, I think to myself. I wonder if he still thinks about her, hoping like I do that a lost love will magically walk through the door. It's a real possibility for him, unlike for me. Something about the thought of her potentially being back in town to rekindle sparks with him gives me a brief but noticeable ache in my chest.

"I heard you in an interview last week and you said something about how grief tends to bring out the very best or worst in people—and how you felt lucky to be part of the former group," he begins. "When I left the house that day, it was the first time I gave myself credit for showing my good side in all that grief when she left. I'm not even sure I realized it was grief before that moment."

I take a quiet second to reflect. The intensity of today's chat has caught us both off guard. It feels like this conversation wants more from us and is clawing for something that both of us aren't quite ready to give. Josh swirls his drink around and seems on the verge of saying something when I jump in.

"Wow, that got serious. Um, okay—when did you get the most drunk in your life?"

We laugh and share truly ridiculous stories. Me, in the aforementioned favorite city of Barcelona as a twentysomething. Him, in Asheville for his bachelor party at around the same age. A few runner-up stories make the cut before Josh excuses himself to finish work. "You're not paying me to talk," he says with a smile, but he thanks me for the future blackmail fodder.

I grab my laptop and head outside to the squeaky porch swing, teasing out in my mind something that I said a few minutes ago.

*People want me to tell them about a martyr—not a man.* This isn't a totally new topic. In fact, it's something strangers and I have discussed over coffee many times during the past year. How do you celebrate and honor the real person that you lost rather than remembering only their best qualities?

I've already sent an essay for next week's column, but it wasn't my best. This topic feels juicy, honest, and special. People are complicated—even when someone like Mother Teresa dies, there is a tangled legacy to reckon with. Regular people are no different. No one is perfect, but those of us who are left behind often have to grapple with the fact that nobody wants to hear about the imperfect pieces of our loved ones.

Sometimes I just want to tell friends that the refrigerator door hasn't been left open once since Ben died—it really was him all along! It seems too silly and petty, but it's *real life*. I'm not complaining—this is all part of the banter that makes marriage hilarious and infuriating and joyful and honest.

Once the idea has marinated in my mind for a few more minutes, I open the laptop and start typing. I smile as I tap out sentences about all of the mildly infuriating habits Ben had and how annoying it is to realize how much I miss them. I share all the little things I've learned about myself, too, and how I imagine he would've missed these bits of me had the circumstances been flipped. This essay is a love letter to our imperfections.

I'm sending you something new. If you hate it, just use the one you have. If you love it, put the other one in the bank, I text Danny.

I paste in a link to my Google Doc and, as is my habit, type my preferred title into the subject line: I Need to Be Honest About My Dead Husband. Interestingly, the pull quote for the piece is more sentimental than usual, especially given the comical tone of the piece.

> *What version of our loved ones do we remember when they're gone? Do we remember the martyrs or the men? I don't know about you, but for me it's the messy, perfectly imperfect real person who left the fridge door open all the time. I miss that guy.*

I love it, Danny texts twenty minutes later. Makes me miss my mom so much. This is going to hit people right in the feels.

For the second time, a conversation with Josh has inspired a column. The last one was a smashing success, and this one feels just as strong. This thing he and I have? It works.

---

A FEW HOURS later, I'm deep into a late-afternoon session with Dr. Lisa. We spent the first thirty minutes of our hour together talking about the essay I wrote. I was floating on a high at the start of the session. The mix of how much I loved the new essay draft paired with Danny's quick positive feedback after reading it made me feel invincible. Enter Dr. Lisa to quickly burst that bubble.

"Interesting. I can't wait to read the final product," she said, before pausing and adding, "but can we maybe talk for a bit about some other feelings of anger that you might be holding on to since Ben died? Maybe even anger you have toward him?"

She tried this conversation a few months after Ben died, and I absolutely refused to entertain it. I wasn't mad at my dead husband. Ridiculous. She pushed on it, and I *almost* considered finding a new therapist but came to my senses quickly. There is no one else I can imagine having these sorts of conversations with. Now, nearly a year later, I realize that she's got a bit of a point about the whole repressed-anger-toward-the-dead-husband thing.

"You've been waiting for me to be ready to have this conversation, haven't you?" I ask, already knowing the answer. She gives me her classic therapist smile—it's devoid of actual emotion—but she still acknowledges I'm right with a nod of her head.

"I wrote a chapter last week that was really heavy. It's titled 'I'm Mad.' It's an airing of every grievance that I've had over the last year. I'm mad that I'm a single parent. I'm mad that I rarely have time to myself. I'm mad that people want me to get back to normal. I'm mad that they don't want me to live my life. I'm mad that dating sucks so hardcore. I'm mad that everyone feels bad for me. I was three thousand words deep into being mad before I finally typed it: I'm mad at Ben. I'm mad that he didn't do so much as a virtual doctor's appointment when he felt unwell. I'm mad that he pushed himself so much at work. I'm mad that he didn't have beneficiaries listed on his life insurance, which meant me hacking through all kinds of red tape for *months*. I'm mad that he fucking died. I'm mad that my perfect little life got blown up. But I'm also embarrassed. I'm embarrassed that this revelation happened a year late because I wasn't strong enough to deal with it before."

"Gracie, you're allowed to be mad, but you should not feel embarrassed. You're dealing with it *now* precisely because you've been so strong. Your mind and body knew exactly what to compartmentalize to keep you sane."

It's not easy to be mad at someone you can't fight with, who can't present their side of the story, and who isn't there to offer or receive forgiveness. I've often wondered if any of the tics I've had over the last year have been about me trying desperately to hold this anger in. All I know is that every time a tic starts, it feels like the only thing protecting me from the worst truths of my life.

To address my emerging, but definitely-not-handled, recognition of these emotions, we spend time discussing strategies for fully processing the anger. She also acknowledges that writing it out like I did is probably the best first step in healing this particular wound.

We've covered a lot today. I'm absolutely wasted. It's been one of our most intense and productive sessions so far but also really hard. I'm a few seconds from asking her if we can call it quits, when she jumps in to continue on a different line of reflection.

"You are coming into a phase of real emotional bravery, Gracie. This is an important time for you. You may find it easier to open your heart to people and opportunities in your life."

"What does that mean, really?"

"Gracie, you told me once that your son likes superhero comics. So you're probably familiar with the concept of a canon event. It's something that a superhero goes through that defines who they are and are meant to be. When a canon event happens, there is fundamentally no going back to the old life—the superhero has to make the decision to carry on into the new world and to become a new version of themselves."

"Emotional bravery, canon event—it all makes sense, Dr. Lisa. These aren't complicated topics," I tell her, "but I feel like you're dancing around something here, and I want to give you permission to just say it."

"Gracie, your canon event—Ben's death—closed your heart, but

I believe you are entering a period where you might be ready to be emotionally brave in matters of love. In our last session, you told me that you like having Josh around the house and that you enjoy his company. Did you think any more about that?"

I want to lie. I want to tell her that there's no there there. Josh is just a decent guy who hangs around the house and occasionally makes me laugh. The truth is that there is something about Josh and about the way that I feel when he's around. The moment at the door after dinner last night only underscored how I feel about things.

"I have thought about it. A lot, actually," I share. "Just today I told him that I like having him at the house. It definitely seems like something *could* be there, but we've had those intense moments when he could have said something or expressed interest and he didn't. He's making a choice, and that choice is friendship—and I'm okay with that because this friendship is important to me."

"Maybe he's leaving the ball in your court, given a perceived fragility around your situation."

"Maybe he just doesn't see me as a romantic partner."

"That's possible. Perhaps you're afraid of the potential rejection? But really, what's the worst-case scenario?"

"Well, I could ask him out, he could say no, it could get really uncomfortable, and then I spend the rest of the summer hiding in other rooms while he's working in the house."

"Is that really the worst-case scenario?" she asks.

Dr. Lisa is not messing around today. She is calling me on my shit and taking no prisoners. Why do I feel like she really has been waiting a year for me to be ready to play hardball?

"You think there is a scenario worse than rejection?" I answer, throwing the question back into her court.

"I think the worst-case scenario is that you end the summer having potentially let a love story pass you by," she says so directly that it almost knocks me over.

With that, I hear her quiet alarm chime in the background to let us know the session is over and she needs to prepare for the next client.

"You've given me a lot to think about today," I say, ready to be off this call.

"Gracie, I have just one homework request for you: be brave."

# CHAPTER 19

"WHAT'S ON YOUR AGENDA FOR TODAY?" JOSH ASKS A minute after walking through the door and tossing his keys in the basket on the new entryway table. This is his favorite question to ask almost every morning. He acts like it's to plan out his day around my schedule, but I secretly think he just likes hearing what I'm up to.

"Lots. Today's schedule is a little wonky. I'm going to Canopy Books the minute they open to buy books for the shelves you're about to build," I say, raising my eyebrows quickly in excitement but with a hint of evil genius. "This is a once-in-a-lifetime opportunity for me: go into a bookstore, buy a ton of my favorite books, and then get to bring them home. All in the name of homemaking."

"You are, like, really amped up about this. Not sure I've seen someone so happy about shelving before," he teases.

"A house isn't really a home unless it has books inside. This is going to really make the house feel like mine."

He nods his head in acknowledgment. The repartee Josh and I have flits back and forth between funny, serious, sarcastic, and utterly ridiculous. There's a small expression of excitement on his face now, too, as he realizes that today's project is going to bring me so much joy.

"I know you said you're busy today, but later on—at your usual old-lady dinnertime—my friends and I have a standing Friends' Night Out at a bar in town. You should come. You'll meet some new people."

Josh has been on me to be even more social, and to be honest, I haven't hated his little assignments. But today is jam-packed, and I'm not sure another to-do is in the cards for me.

"My schedule is all flipped around today. I've got a virtual working lunch with my publicist, and then I need to try to write in the afternoon. If I hit my writing quota in time, I'll swing by. When do things start?"

"Five thirty. It's super casual, so people come and go as they can. We get together every other Thursday night. I'll text you the location."

---

WHEN I COME back ninety minutes later, the shelves are almost done, and I squeal in delight. The wall was painted a mossy green a few days ago, and now the walnut shelves look spectacular against the new paint color. My expression of pure joy makes Josh smile, which is a change from the look of frustration he had before. The building instructions left a bit to be desired.

"My trunk is full of books just waiting for a new home, Josh," I say, putting down the first box in the living room. I'm about to head back out to grab another, when Josh interrupts.

"Since it sounds like you'll probably be too busy for an interview today, what if I throw some pop-quiz questions at you now? It'll cheer me up from the hellscape that is putting these shelves together."

"Seems fair. What's up first?"

"How would your friends describe you?"

"Loyal, great at giving advice, lover of dirty jokes, spicy-margarita connoisseur. What about you?"

"We're doing two-way interviews now? All right, well, before I let work take over, they would say I am a good listener, occasional life of the party, a logical thinker that you take your problems to," he answers. "Recently... who's Josh?"

We both laugh at his self-deprecating joke, and I head outside for another box of books. When I get back inside, it's another question that indicates he's going to sneak tough ones in on me. I know his style now.

"How would Ben describe you?"

"Also loyal but silly and open-minded, too. Lover of deep conversations. Unexpectedly adventurous."

"It's interesting how our friends and family see different versions of us, isn't it?"

"It's wild. To be honest, one of the hardest things immediately after Ben died was realizing that not only was the person who knew me the best just gone, but in a lot of ways a version of me went with him. No one knew me like he did."

Over the past few weeks, I've learned to map Josh's expressions to his emotions. The slight frown and direct, piercing eye contact I'm getting right now is his way of telegraphing that he quietly acknowledges the depth of my pain and grief.

He doesn't speak these feelings out loud anymore. Early on, he heard me start comforting him after I shared a particularly sad story—"It's not a big deal, don't feel bad"—and it's like he decided that he didn't want to put me in a situation where suddenly I felt the need to provide him solace. He just lets the feelings and emotions float in the air for a bit. I like it. It's new for me, just sitting with my feelings like this. I'm used to tucking them away.

When I come back inside with the next box, he's ready with the next question.

"Do you ever wonder about the version of Gracie that readers concoct in their minds?"

I stare at him. What made him ask this? It's quite literally one of the biggest struggles I've had with my quasi-fame so far and the thing I'm most nervous about going forward.

"All the time and not just a little bit, either. There are some days it consumes me. The public-persona side of this is really hard. A few weeks ago, Felicity, my agent, told me that we were already getting requests for the movie rights to the book. Can you imagine? My life in movie form."

"I can make guesses about why that's tough, but keeping my journalist hat on, what scares you about that?"

"I've so far controlled my story and narrative. The truth is that essays are just a small sliver of me and how I feel. Same goes for social media—it's all carefully curated. The memoir goes much deeper, but it's still me and my perspective on this crazy, mixed-up year I've had. A movie? I wouldn't write the script and, frankly, wouldn't have much involvement in the process at all. That scares me—there would be a version of me out there that is an artistic creation that people might interpret as real. It's a fine line between fact and fiction."

"Follow-up: Who would play your dashing but underpaid handyman in this movie?"

"Sorry to disappoint you, Josh, but the book is likely to end right before we met. You'll have to wait for your moment onscreen."

To be completely honest, I'm not quite sure when the memoir will really "end." I wrote a bit yesterday about arriving in Canopy and how I feel hopeful for the first time in a long while, but I'm not sure it'll make the cut.

I do give Josh's comment a second thought and then raise my hands to mimic a video camera with him in the frame. "But now that I think about it, you would give Harry Connick Jr. a run for his money in *Hope Floats*."

He pauses, looking at me with his head tilted. "Is that a good thing?" he asks. "I've never seen it."

*It's a very good thing*, I think, recalling late-nineties Harry in those denim shirts and cowboy hats as he flitted around town playing Mr. Fix It. Every preteen girl who managed to sneak into the movie theater had a crush on him, including me.

"It is indeed a compliment, Josh," I admit, trying not to picture him in a cowboy hat. "Don't let it go to your head."

He tosses a piece of foam from the furniture packaging at me and rises to lift up the last remaining shelf. I reach down to start grabbing books, and he shakes his head at me, telling me to be patient. The shelves need to get secured to the wall first. I perform a dramatic pout and head out for the last box of books.

"I think my next question might be a big one for you," he says when I'm back through the door with the final box. "How will you organize your books on the shelves?"

"So many options. I've always wanted a book wall organized by color because it looks so pretty, but it doesn't sit well with my inner librarian—you grow up with the Dewey decimal system, and it shapes your entire worldview. I think I'll group them by genre and then be as close to alphabetical as possible."

"My very first crush was on the school librarian." He's blushing big-time as he says this. I'm not surprised, though. Josh is the most process-oriented, methodical guy I've ever met. A librarian is exactly the sort of person I would expect him to be into.

"If I ever need to be evil and distract you, at least I know what costume to wear," I say, trying to make a joke and also to invite some flirtatious banter. He bites his lip and shakes his head but doesn't take the bait. It's like I told Dr. Lisa—he's just not interested in me that way. Or maybe I'm just bad at flirting? All the possibilities are on the table at this point.

The only thing I've succeeded in doing is making things feel weird again, so I decide to remove myself to the writing room upstairs and brainstorm essay ideas for a little bit before my meeting with Lucia.

"Don't rush," I say. "The books can wait until tomorrow."

---

LUCIA AND I have been hard at work for an hour straight. We spent the first half covering early ideas and planning for the book tour next year. Lucia will be my stand-in to work with the publisher on the book tour. I'm thrilled to outsource that job to her. She'll be more direct when it comes to my preferences and the pace that I want to take.

It's important to me to have a variety of engagements on the book tour. I want big bookstores that can hold two hundred people, small independent shops where I can speak to a group of twenty, virtual book readings, and the ability to stop by actual book club meetings where my memoir is the selection of the month. It's going to be a lot of work, but I can already sense it will be worth it.

Even though it feels like a lifetime away, we click between tabs for my kids' school calendar, the family calendar, and the camp calendar for next year. The goal? Find days when the kids are either on break (and can travel with me) or firmly safe somewhere else, like camp, so that I don't need to rely on childcare from others to make it happen.

Lucia is in her late twenties and doesn't have kids. Her reaction to the logistical nightmare that is my solo-parenting life makes me feel incredibly validated.

"Gracie, I literally don't know how you manage to do all of this. And write essays. And write your book. How are you not snorting cocaine at every free moment?" she asks.

"How do you know I'm not?" I respond with a straight face, at least for a few seconds.

We both laugh at this because I am the squarest square that's ever squared. I smoked pot once in college while in Barcelona, got irrationally paranoid, and decided that drugs were definitely not for me. I told her this story over drinks the one time we've met in person, and she couldn't get enough.

The holds we place on my calendar for tour dates only crowd things up more, and I mentally prepare myself for what a wild year it's going to be. I need to appreciate the relative quiet time between delivering the manuscript and the book being launched into the world.

"Before we get into discussing your interview bookings for the coming few weeks, I want to run an idea by you. Have you considered starting a newsletter? In addition to generating buzz for the book, you could charge for subscriptions and potentially have a steady income stream," she says.

"I have considered it," I answer with a deep sigh. "But right now, I can't imagine committing to writing even more content. Maybe I'll feel differently in August when I submit the manuscript."

"It would go a long way to creating an even stronger bond with your readers, your fans," she pushes. "It wouldn't have to be all about grief, either. It could be about parenting, dating, friendship, and just life stuff. I recognize *The New York Times* wouldn't like you double-dipping content, so if you stuck to different topics, it could be a way to cross-promote your essays between the two platforms."

Lucia is sharing these ideas with me because she wants to help build my brand. The bigger my brand, the more the book sells, the more I need a personal publicist. We all make money, and everyone wins.

I like the idea because it would allow me to diversify my income streams. Even with a sizable cushion in the bank thanks to life insurance and my book advance, everything still feels tenuous. The need to churn out content and keep money coming in matters. I have two kids to raise and another eight years minimum with at least one of them in the house.

"I'll strongly consider it," I finally relent. "It's a great idea, and I know that I should do it. I just want it to be for the right reasons. I promise to brainstorm the second the manuscript is submitted."

"Perfect. In the meantime, I'll dig around to see if there are any consultants we could work with to help you put structure around the newsletter concept when you're ready."

I thank her and prepare myself to move on to the list of upcoming interviews. After the *Cosmo* debacle, I insisted that Lucia give me one or two sentences of context into the angle the journalist is likely to take. We go through the list, and everything in the next ten days feels easy and tame.

"One last opportunity, and it's a doozy," Lucia says, grabbing my attention immediately. "There's a reason I saved this for last."

"I'm intrigued," I tell her. "Not sure I've seen this look on your face before."

"It's with Maisy," she blurts out, her eyes wide. "She's launching a podcast and wants you as one of her first guests. It sounds like a cool show, and it's certainly another great opportunity to expand your reach, but..."

There is never anything good or fun or ego building that comes from someone saying "but" like this, drawing out the word as long as possible while they desperately search their brain to find a kind way to say something difficult.

"Just be honest with me," I say, giving her permission to be direct.

"Your last visit with Maisy wasn't great—it wasn't terrible, but it wasn't great. Something about the two of you just doesn't seem to click. As your publicist, I never want to put you in a situation again where you can't be successful, and honestly, I can't decide how I feel about this."

"Does she think I'm a glutton for punishment or something?" I ask.

"Who knows what she thinks. But let's be clear on one thing: Maisy doesn't care if this goes well or badly for you. She wants to repeat the 'magic' of the last interview—a big social media moment that gets the full attention of a particular corner of the internet. That's why she wants you back. If you decide to say yes to this, it needs to be for reasons as superficial as Maisy's: eyeballs, follows, sales. Period. She expects you to do that exact math—frankly, I *need* you to do that math."

"I have done a lot of practice this summer," I muse, uncharacteristically speaking before I think, "and there haven't been any real fumbles."

I pause. There was one *near* fumble late last week that I haven't told Lucia about. A parenting magazine was doing a standard "guiding your kids through grief" interview. This was such a slam-dunk topic that I put my phone on speaker and started styling the kitchen island for fun while I chatted with the journalist. Things were going well. Then in the final minutes, she shifted to a different line of questioning.

*Do you feel guilty for using your loss for financial gain? What do you think your kids will think about the book down the road? Will they get a final say on what makes the book?* Just like my last visit to Maisy, I got flustered. And fast.

Josh came in from the dining room when he heard things start to go sideways. Just as my leg twitch was starting, he held up a hastily written message on the back of an envelope. *You don't have to answer ~~stupid~~ ~~crazy~~ rude questions.* His scribbles across a couple of words made me smile. I took a deep breath and started giving answers completely unrelated to her questions. Eventually, she got annoyed and time ran out. The article posted online yesterday, and it was completely normal. Crisis averted, thanks to Josh's quick thinking.

"Do you think I'm ready for something like this again?" I ask her.

"It's a little soon," she says, acknowledging the truth of things. "But it is a podcast and not TV. That would certainly take some of the pressure off."

"What are the rest of the specifics?" I ask, needing the very precise details.

"One hour, in her Nashville studio. You'd be paired up with someone else, so you wouldn't be completely on your own. No studio audience or anything, but she is streaming the first five episodes live before pivoting to a traditional prerecorded format. You'd be live. No do-overs. No editing out bad moments. Live."

I can't tell if Lucia is trying to sell me on it or against it. She seems genuinely conflicted. The last Maisy interview was tough on so many levels. If I'm honest, getting the nickname "queen of grief" was the most annoying part of the ordeal. Now *everyone* calls me that. Even Felicity and Jeannie have latched onto it.

The appearance on her show also generated an astonishing one hundred thousand visits to my website in the days after it aired. I had fifty thousand more followers on social media and people telling me very directly, "I'm following you because of Maisy!" I know this is the right thing for my brand. Plus, my confidence is bolstered again, thanks to the summer of interview practice with Josh and the professionals.

"There's more, Gracie," Lucia says tentatively, looking directly into her computer camera. "Maisy wants to know that you're willing to, and I quote, 'go deep.' She wants to be able to ask you questions and get answers that you haven't discussed before. I told them we wouldn't say yes unless I could get that commitment from you."

"What's your honest professional advice?"

"If you say yes, it needs to be because the outcome—the exposure—is worth whatever might go down during the interview itself," she says. "That's my advice. If you're willing to 'go deep' and the outcome is worth it to you, do it. If you're not one hundred percent sure, don't do it."

"Wow—this is a lot to consider," I say. "I'll think about it and talk to some trusted friends to get their opinions. How long do I have to decide?"

"Not very. The interview is in four weeks. You need to let me know within two."

With that, Lucia and I say our goodbyes until the next meeting. I'll definitely need an answer about Maisy by then.

---

THE GRIND OF today has been truly relentless. I've now been at the coffee shop for three hours, and as expected, the late afternoon of writing has been a slog. I am not built for creativity at this time of day and probably should've saved my book shopping spree for now, but desperate times and manuscript deadlines call for grit and perseverance.

There may only be five hundred new words in the document, but at least I can admit that they are solid. Now that I'm caught up chronologically, I'm weaving back through every chapter to fill in gaps and add stories that I missed on the first pass. Today, I revisited an important theme: what it means to take care of people in your life and your community. More specifically, it dives into the unexpected ways you can support people. The kindness of strangers and strangers who become friends, like Josh, really matters.

I've added a few additional paragraphs to a chapter that covers the lead-up to the one-year anniversary of Ben's death, when an acquaintance from church reached out to ask me to coffee. Marley is a sweet lady in her seventies who lost her husband of fifty years five years prior.

"Everyone in my life built up the one-year anniversary as this big dramatic day and completely overwhelmed me," she shared with me, sipping her latte. "Everyone who tried to help actually made it all so much worse. I ended up sneaking out of town and taking myself to the beach."

"I'm already getting one or two texts a day from people asking what my plans are to 'honor' and 'celebrate' him," I responded. "It's so much pressure."

"I figured as much. I know we only see each other periodically at church, and generally speaking, it's not my practice to dole out unsolicited advice, but I wanted to give you permission—if you haven't already given it to yourself—to do what *you* need to do on the anniversary. If it's having a normal workday, do it! If it's playing hooky and taking your kids somewhere, do it! If it's sobbing into a carton of ice cream, that's fine, too!"

Marley and I talked about a great many other things that morning, but we never got coffee again. She waves at church, but her effort to take care of me was in that single moment when I really needed it. It made me think about the different ways a village of people can impact your life. She's the reason I bought those plane tickets and took the kids to Chicago. She's the reason we spent the anniversary in the exact right place for us.

Because the truth is, I did need someone to give me permission to do what I wanted to do. My hope for this chapter in the memoir is to help people better understand what it means to love and support people in times of great distress and, most importantly, how to not center yourself in those situations.

I'm deep inside my own mind when a woman in a cute white sundress and big sunglasses walks up to my table.

"I don't mean to interrupt, but are you Gracie?" she asks.

I nod and smile, expecting the usual routine.

"I'm Josh's friend Lara. He texted the group that he finally invited you to join us tonight. I'm a huge fan of yours and I've been trying to get him to invite you for weeks!"

"It's nice to meet you, Lara. I'm flattered by your sweet comments." I also feel a twinge of disappointment realizing that Josh invited me on behalf of a friend.

"I'm heading over there now," she tells me. "I can totally drive you, and I'm certain Josh would bring you home if you want?"

"I have stuff I need to drop at home and wouldn't want to slow you down," I say.

"It's really no problem. Friends' Night Out is super casual. We all just hang outside when the weather is nice and some people swing by for literally five minutes. The effort is what matters."

This day has been exhausting, but strangely, I feel more excited by the idea of standing up, stretching my legs, and hanging out with new people than I do by the thought of going home and lying on the sofa binge-watching trash TV. So unlike me. But I've been sitting all day, aside from the book run this morning, and my entire social circle this summer has been composed of Josh, Lenny, Brian, and Sunny.

"Okay, I'm in," I say. I need a night to let loose. "Do you mind if I change my outfit real fast when we stop at my house?"

"Not at all—well, only if I can come in and see everything that Josh has done to the place," she says with a big smile, waiting patiently while I pack my belongings. I then swing my bag onto my shoulder and we head out of The Drip.

# CHAPTER 20

WE WALK UP THE STAIRS TO THE OUTDOOR PATIO, AND I spot quite a few familiar faces. Sunny is here. Brian from the hardware store. Shae from the wine shop. This is a reminder that most of my small-talk friends have been Josh's friends all along.

I take in the cute string lights, the classic bar music playing over the speakers, and the welcoming atmosphere. It's obvious everyone here is comfortable with one another. While there are a few young backpacker types who seem to be passing through town, it looks to be mostly locals.

Then I look across the patio and spot Josh at a high table drinking a beer and talking animatedly to a friend. Just when I wonder if he'll look over and notice me, he does. Relief, or something like it, crosses his face. I wave and walk over.

"Gracie, this is my friend Tommy," he says, introducing us. "He's the guy running the business for me during my break."

Tommy and I share quick pleasantries before he adeptly excuses himself to catch up with some new arrivals. He subtly winks at Josh before walking away, but I catch it.

"Hi," I say to Josh, now that it's just the two of us. He makes me feel so comfortable and safe. Normally I hate new social situations, but this just feels easy with him here.

"Hi," he responds. "I'm really glad you made it. No surprise that Lara was the one who scooped you up. She adores you."

"She preemptively invited me to a book club meeting for next spring after my memoir comes out," I say with a giggle. "She said it would make her the most popular mom in the PTA."

"That sounds like Lara," Josh says.

"How many people usually come to this thing?"

"It really depends. On a nice fall day, it could be thirty of us. In the heat of summer and depth of winter, it's usually only ten or so. It's never the exact same crowd."

"Did most of y'all meet in high school?"

"Mostly, and we span about six graduation years or so. Some of James's friends come, and most of mine do. It's a good group. I've been so busy that this was really the only way I got to see people for a few years."

Josh looks down at my hands and notices that I don't yet have a drink and offers to go inside and grab one for me. He doesn't even ask what I'd like (he knows) and heads right in. He's not gone for thirty seconds before Tommy is back at the table.

"Hi again," he says. "Try not to get him too comfortable with easy-street living. We need him back at work at some point."

It dawns on me that Tommy may not know Josh's plans yet, so I take a playful tact.

"I'm pretty good at coming up with projects, but even I will run out of ideas sometime soon. He's making quick progress in the house."

"Yeah, I get that impression."

He quickly glances to the side and sees Josh, his back to the door, pushing his way out with a drink in each hand. Tommy excuses himself and walks away again. Strange.

"What did Tommy want?" Josh asks when he's a few feet away.

"He told me to take it easy on you," I lie, because I'm not really sure how helpful the truth would be.

"I hope the rest of your day went well," he says, sliding my drink across the slick table. "Sounded like it was going to be a busy one."

"Thanks," I say, taking a quick sip before adding, "It was incredibly busy, but it was also mostly good, so I can't complain."

"Mostly?"

I take another gulp of my drink and let out a dramatic sigh.

"Lucia told me a few hours ago that Maisy Miller extended an invitation to this new podcast she's launching soon. It sounds interesting, but I'm not so sure that I'm up to the task. Just another one of those weird situations that I now find myself in—knowing something would be very good for me as a brand but maybe not so good for me, the person."

"I think you're ready," he says without a moment of hesitation and with complete confidence.

"Really?"

"Absolutely. You've spent a few solid weeks getting comfortable with interviews, and James assures me that your appearance on *The Maisy Show* really wasn't *that* bad," he responds. "As you requested, I still haven't watched it."

"James is too nice."

He lets out a quick laugh and shakes his head. "You clearly didn't have him as a big brother growing up."

I return his laughter with my own and think of Ava and Benji. At the end of the last soccer season, Ava's coach congratulated me on raising a "natural leader" who "understands instinctively how to motivate others." Benji was within earshot, and as we walked back to the car, he asked in the most sarcastic tone I've *ever* heard from a child, "Can you please explain to me what *motivation* means? Because I am clearly confused." To everyone else she's Ava, but to him she's a bossy big sister with a short fuse and often very little patience for him.

"You really think I could handle an hour in front of a microphone with Maisy?" I ask, wanting a bit more assurance.

"I do, and I speak from experience that we can do hard things," he begins. "Six months after Katrina left, we were both invited to the same wedding—Lara's, actually. I almost skipped it because I was still pretty embarrassed and sad about the whole thing. But I went and ended up having one of the best nights of my life. A lot of my friends struggled with how to support me when it all went down, but that night things just clicked for everyone. The guys decided to turn it into an epic guys' night. The wedding had a middle school dance vibe in the funniest way possible. Some moments were a struggle, but on the whole? A really good time. I learned that sometimes the only way to get past something is to go directly through. Walking in the door was the hardest part. The rest of the night was a breeze compared to that."

"So, the anticipation might be the worst part—is that what you're telling me?"

"Exactly," he responds. "Plus, if James is lying and that first interview really went as poorly as you *felt* like it did, maybe the better question is 'Could it be any worse?' If the answer is no, then I say go for it."

"I think you have more faith in me than perhaps I have in myself," I say with a gentle smile.

"That's what friends are for," he responds, raising his glass.

*That's us*, I think. *Just friends.*

---

AN HOUR LATER, we've been absorbed into a large group conversation, and most of the friends are a few drinks deep when I look around in shock at what I've just heard.

"Wait, wait. Let me get this straight," I say, turning to Josh. "You have *ten* godchildren?"

Everyone is now acknowledging that this sounds a little crazy, but as a group, they try to insist that it happened organically. It started when James and Kendell had their first a few years after they got married and continued straight through to Sunny's daughter, born just two years ago. In between those bookends are eight other kids of friends from high school, college, and extended family. Over and over people have chosen him for this important honor. A petite brunette named Laney jumps in.

"A few years ago, a bunch of us were on a trip to Mexico—Josh was too busy to come. Anyway, we look around after we board and realize that if the plane goes down, Josh is going to be raising seven kids on his own," she says. "Can you imagine the A-frame bursting at the seams with toddlers and teens?"

This makes everyone laugh uproariously, especially me. While this story isn't new to the group, it's clear no one has heard it in a while. There is genuine joy and laugh-induced tears from folks just thinking about Josh trying to raise all of those kids on his own. I grab on to the new fact that I've just learned: the type of house he lives in. I find myself trying to imagine it. I can't believe that we've never talked about it before, given how much we discuss mine.

Josh takes all of the ribbing in stride and says confidently, "For the record, I would've been great at it."

A few new people arrive, and the group naturally separates into smaller conversations. A couple people, including Lara, start to say goodbyes before they leave. She confirms with Josh that he hasn't been drinking much and can take me home. Then she turns to me.

"Thanks for helping to bring our old Josh back," she says, looking at me with a heartfelt, genuine expression. She gives me a hug before I can ask for clarification, then hugs Josh and waves goodbye.

"Old Josh?" I ask once Lara has walked away.

Josh purses his lips and takes the last sip of a beer he's been nursing since I arrived.

"We've talked a bunch about this, Gracie. The last few years put a lot of money in my bank account, but it all made me a pretty shitty friend. I was here a lot, but not *really* here. James is never going to let me forget it was his idea, but this time off has been really good for me. Apparently, he's not the only one who's noticed the change."

"I'm helping you get in touch with your true self is what I'm hearing. Also, you're rich."

"Something like that," he says with a slightly forced grin, locking eyes with me.

Here we are again. *In a moment.* At least I think we are, but neither of us seems bold enough to call it what it is. Or maybe I just have a crush that is making me see things that aren't really there. No one prepared me for what it would feel like to have a crush as a grown woman. Maybe I've just been confused since day one.

Then the music starts.

"Whitney time!" someone shouts.

"What is Whitney time?" I ask.

Before Josh can answer, Sunny sweeps up behind me to provide an explanation. Every Friends' Night at 7:00, the bar plays "I Wanna Dance with Somebody," and the rule is if you are here, you dance. "No exceptions," Sunny admonishes.

"It keeps us humble and happy," Josh adds.

A few others pop in to explain more. This group of friends has danced through divorces and death. Graduations and even incarcerations. Broken hearts and business failures. James is usually the king of the dance floor, but he and Kendell couldn't find a babysitter for tonight, I'm told.

Josh says as he holds out his hand, "Participation is compulsory."

The entire group has moved to the open space on the patio, and I realize, oh my goodness, we are actually doing this. These friends have danced through tears and sadness, and total happiness and bliss. This is what showing up for your people and yourself looks like. Josh whispers in my ear to explain that even during his lowest days, he was out here on the dance floor.

And it turns out, it has made him a good dancer. Luckily, I am, too. Our bodies move confidently yet playfully on the dance floor. During the chorus, he spins me around and then pulls me in tight. In all of our time together, we've never been this close for this long. I remember how hard it was to back away from our hug after only a few seconds the night he made me dinner. Tonight he smells like cedar cologne—or maybe it's his soap or just what a man who works around the house all day smells like. I'm breathing heavily not from exertion but from the intensity of the moment.

His hand is on the small of my back, even though the current movement makes it awkward. It feels like he doesn't want to let go, and I don't want him to. My dress is thin enough that I can feel the heat of his hand. The moment feels just as hot and heavy, and I glance around, expecting everyone to be staring, but they aren't. Everyone is wrapped up in their own fun little moments with each other. This is our moment, just the two of us.

When Josh moves his hand, it's to turn me around for the emotional crescendo of the bridge. Whitney is singing "somebody who," and we are swaying not entirely to the beat, my back to his chest, lost in our own motion. He has kept our arms entangled across my chest. I tip my head back and think I've given it all away—it's a flash of pure excitement on my part. I'm wondering if he's feeling this, too, when he suddenly turns me back around and keeps me just a few inches farther away. The physical intensity is replaced by the fact that we can now see each other and lock eyes. The song ends, and we join the others in laughing and clapping at the group's collective dance moves.

Josh and I stare bashfully at one another in the sudden quiet, slightly embarrassed by the fun we've just had. It's at this moment that I know Dr. Lisa was right with her advice. I have to figure this out. I like him.

"We should probably get you home," he says. "I wouldn't want to be responsible for messing up your routine."

My writing is the last thing on my mind, but I nod in quiet

agreement and begin saying goodbye to those who I've met tonight.

"Fun fact you probably would've learned eventually in an interview," I say to Josh to break the tension as we walk toward his truck. "But that is definitely one of my favorite songs of all time."

"That tracks," he says. "You were surprisingly on beat." He gives me a side smile and points to where his truck is parked among a sea of other large vehicles.

Josh glides past me, unlocks the door, and opens it for me. "Chivalry isn't dead after all," I say as he slowly closes the passenger door and he smiles at me again through the closed window.

As I watch him walk around the front to the driver's side, I decide to do it. Tonight.

# CHAPTER 21

"YOU'RE A REALLY LUCKY GUY, JOSH," I SAY AS WE TURN onto a now-quiet Pisgah Highway on the way back downtown. My arm is hanging out the truck window, feeling the cool night air. "Your friends are amazing."

He smiles and leans his head firmly against the headrest, turning slightly to make eye contact. "From what you've told me over the last few weeks, you have some great people in your life, too."

It's true. During the past year I've seen just how much people love me and want to see me happy again. Friends have let me cry ugly tears with them, and friends have made me laugh in ways I thought I'd never be able to again. Still . . .

"I do, I do. It's just that most of those people have known you your entire life. They all know you on, like, a cellular level. And while I'm sure there are times it's annoying how well they know you, it's really beautiful." I take a moment before continuing because I'm thinking out loud, and it's surprising how much I'm letting my emotions show.

"I have great friends, but because Ben and I moved around a lot until we landed in Chapel Hill, a lot of my friends are, I guess, 'moment in time' friends. My high school friends know me one way, my college friends another, my Chicago friends another, and so on. My best friend, Jenny, is the only person who knows me like they *all* know you. The love y'all have for each other is so real and organic, and it's got me in my feelings a little bit."

Josh laughs softly and I do, too. "Look at you, letting the feelings flow," he teases.

*Maybe I'm changing*, I think but don't say out loud. Maybe Dr. Lisa is on to something. Maybe I *am* like a superhero who has experienced a canon event—something that fundamentally changes you in a way that can't be undone. It's clear in my writing, my interactions with readers, and especially my conversations with Josh that I'm different. Over the last month in Canopy, something has changed. And that change feels lasting and good.

We drive in silence for a few minutes as I turn over in my mind the thought of telling Josh that I have feelings for him. I want to tell him that I feel happier when I'm with him than I have in a long time. That I look forward to him showing up every day. That he has grown to know me in ways that are new and exciting. I want to tell him all of this before anyone or anything can get in the way.

We turn onto Wilson Street, and I look at him. There's an ache to let him know how I feel, but the risk feels so big. He is the reason my writing is flowing and my heart feels so open. I could ruin it all by saying the wrong thing.

He slips into the driveway and puts the truck in park. "You were thinking some deep thoughts over those last few miles," he says.

It's now or never—that much I know. If I let this moment pass, I may not work up the courage again.

"Can I ask you a question?"

"Is this about the fact that I have ten godchildren? It's wild—trust me, I know."

An honest giggle emerges and lightens the pressure a tiny bit. "Actually, no, but let's put a pin in that and come back to it next time you're here."

Deep breath. "This is from left field, but . . ." I pause, trying to work up the courage to continue. He puts his arm over the steering wheel and fully turns toward me. "Is there a reason this—you and me—hasn't turned into something more?"

He looks stunned. Unprepared, even. He runs a hand through his hair and purses his lips. Suddenly he can't look me in the eyes, and I realize what's about to happen. The energy in this truck has shifted.

"Um, I guess I just never really thought about it because I was doing the work at the house and then we became friends and had this vibe that was really easy and cool and you seem to be in a good place with everything and it's like why mess with a good thing that's working for us both?" he rambles, taking no breaths to deliver a healthy portion of word soup.

I think this must be what people mean when they complain about being put in the "friend zone." I silently thank Jesus that I never had to experience this as an emotionally unformed teenager or twentysomething. At least now I have the coping skills to deal with it. You lose your husband, and suddenly all other disappointments feel inconsequential.

I got the answer that I needed without putting my heart too far out on the line. Not exactly the homework that Dr. Lisa assigned but close enough for me. I have been emotionally brave in a completely safe way. Things will be awkward for a few days around the house, but it will all be fine. We survived the great *Cosmo* debacle; we can handle this.

"Yeah, that makes sense. I was just curious," I say as cool as possible, careful not to raise the intonation in my voice at the end and give away that I was definitely more than curious. I open the truck door and hop out. I turn to look at him, thank him for the ride, and close the door.

I'm on the first step to the porch when I hear the truck door open and shut quickly as Josh gets out. I immediately turn and see him walking the path toward me. Just before I can get a word out, he says in a mildly raised and firm voice, "Why did you ask me that?" I guess I won't get away clean, after all.

"Josh, I'm sorry. I made it weird, and I shouldn't have asked that. That drink clearly got to me and—"

He cuts me off, moving a few steps closer. "Gracie, why did you ask me that?"

"Josh, isn't it obvious?" I respond with a calm, forced smile and then turn back toward the house and begin to climb the porch stairs. I can't face him again or my heart will explode. Except, as I take my first step, I hear the gravel crunch on the ground behind me. Before I can turn my head, I feel his hand firmly grab mine. The next thing I know, he's on the first step next to me and, instinctively, we rotate to face one another.

Before my brain is able to fully process what's happening, his lips are pressed to mine. His right hand caresses the side of my face while his left hand slides behind my back to pull me close. This exact scenario has played out in my mind constantly for the last couple of weeks, and now that it's here, I seem to be without the ability to do anything but be fully in the moment.

I press a hand lightly to his chest and hear him take a deep breath as he momentarily stops kissing me. He angles his forehead down to mine and says softly, "I've been thinking about this since the first moment I saw you."

I remember the bright, brief glint in his eyes when we first met the day the kids and I arrived in Canopy. I remember the moment of undeniable tension when I walked in unexpectedly the day the AC was broken. And I remember how he looked when he saw me arrive at the bar tonight. It hasn't all been in my head. His feelings have been here with us all along.

Now I'm the one pulling him to me, with more intensity. Our hands are beginning to wander out here in the glow of the streetlight and in full view of cars driving by. I have never felt anticipation like this before. I whisper a new question—just two words—in the millisecond my mouth is free.

"Come inside?" He nods without hesitation, and when we pull apart to continue up the steps to the front door, we lock eyes. I feel seen and wanted and known.

---

WE ARE BARELY inside the house when Josh presses me up against the wall next to the entrance. His arm reaches across to lock the door, and something about that action—about being safely inside—causes us both to fully give in to our feelings.

It becomes immediately apparent that Josh told the truth about imagining this moment many times over, because every action, every movement, is too perfect to be created on the spot without planning.

When his hand slides under my dress and up my inner thigh, I can't control my breath. I take a deep inhale and open my eyes to find him looking at me.

"Is this real?" he asks in a way that is so achingly tender and honest that my knees buckle ever so slightly.

"Yes," I reply in a soft whisper—to answer the question and as a way to give permission for his hand to continue rising.

I gathered from our interviews that intimacy hasn't been a part of Josh's life for at least a year, but he is definitely not rusty. He explores me while he pushes my head to the side and kisses my neck. I feel an intensity that I've missed and it makes me realize just how badly I want this to happen.

Nothing over the past year has felt like this. Every hard date, every underwhelming and confusing night has led me to this moment right now. No one has truly known me when I invited them to my bed, and I have never let a man know me after. I have spent the year moving between feelings of pain and confusion, heartbreak and longing. In this moment, however, all I can feel is a sense of what is right and real and meant to be.

It doesn't take long for my breath to quicken and moans to escape as a wave rocks my entire body. I say his name quietly into his ear as I come undone. Before I can fully return to my senses, he picks me up, wraps my legs around his back, and walks me down the hallway to the guest room.

Time stops as it hits us both that this is really happening. We take a few moments just to stare, our foreheads pressed together. I move first to pull his shirt over his head. He reaches behind to unzip my sundress and push the straps to the side so it falls to the floor. When I move my hands to his belt and undo his pants, he moans and tells me how badly he wants me. Through every step, our eyes never leave each other. The intensity of the moment makes me dizzy, and yet before I can lose my balance, we are on the bed.

There is too much anticipation—too much hunger—from us both for this to be delicate. My hands press into his back, and I urge him on. Our bodies move in perfect, forceful harmony. He doesn't hold back, and his moment arrives with a deep ferocity.

After a minute, while his breath is still quick and I feel his heartbeat against my chest, I whisper, "Again."

---

IT'S WELL PAST midnight and we are lying in bed, my head buried in his shoulder and a leg draped over his body. We are tangled, tired, messy, and firmly above the clouds.

Josh breaks the sweet silence and turns onto his side to look at me, locking eyes intently. "I want to tell you something," he says. "Three days ago, James and I were at breakfast, and he asked me when I was going to grow a pair and tell you how I feel."

He's trying to kiss me again in the middle of telling this story. I giggle and pull away just a bit so that he'll stay focused.

"I told him that I recently heard you give an interview—the *Cosmo* one—and you said that you weren't sure you were ready to open your heart and what it would mean to dive back in. I decided at that moment that I would rather spend every day just being around you without it being romantic than doing something stupid to ruin it—I almost did the night I made you dinner," he says, before adding, "Of course, James told me I was being a big baby."

"Did he say 'baby'?" I ask playfully.

Josh laughs. "No, he definitely used a different word. And he gave me a speech about how good timing isn't always what we think it is and a bunch of wise-older-brother shit, but he was right. I guess I just want you to know that this wasn't a sudden thing for me."

I have my hand on his chest and can feel his heart beating briskly under his skin. I say nothing, but he continues.

"I'm also really glad you made the first move because I cannot imagine a world where we are not right here, right now," he says. That might be the most romantic thing a man has said to me in a long time.

"Thank my therapist," I finally say quietly but without hesitation or shame. "In typical 'me fashion,' I was trying to hold my feelings close to the vest but obviously didn't do a very good job. In our last session she told me to be brave and just see what happens. She was obviously right."

"I really like who I am when I'm with you, Gracie," he says. "And that's more special to me than you might realize."

I'm struck at the moment by how there are no walls between us. We are not embarrassed to share how we got here. We have learned so much about each other over this past month, and there is still so much to discover.

"I like you a lot, Gracie," he says.

"Same," I reply, kissing him gently before settling deeper into my pillow.

I close my eyes, realizing all at once how happy and peaceful I feel as I drift off to sleep.

"I NEED TO admit something," Josh says, while we hold our mugs of coffee on opposite sides of the kitchen island as I'm having, *by far*, the best morning-after of my new life. "If I don't tell you now, it could be weird later."

"I'm intrigued," I say, because I am definitely curious where this could go. He obviously clocks my concerned expression.

"It's nothing crazy," he says as a big smile stretches across his face. "It's just that I never really listened to music during your interviews. I just had those earbuds in pretending to be distracted. In reality, I was listening to everything you said."

Now I have a beaming smile, but before I can say anything, he continues on. Heart on his sleeve, this one.

"I liked hearing you talk and learning about you like that. I would try to imagine the question that you were asked to give that answer," he says, dropping his head, embarrassed. "I feel like a stalker telling you this."

"Josh, the jig was mostly up by the day the AC broke and you never even tried to pretend that you were listening to music during the *Cosmo* interview," I begin. "And I definitely caught you listening a few other times, too."

"Not as slick as I thought," he says. "But at least I don't need to pretend anymore."

I'm loving how sheepish and sweet he looks sharing all of this, but I've decided not to let him think he's the only one with secrets.

"Full disclosure, since we're sharing somewhat embarrassing things," I say. "I've considered breaking the AC on purpose about five times just to decrease the amount of clothing you wear in my house. I've thought about that day a lot."

He moves around to my side of the island and pulls me in close. This doesn't feel like someone who has experienced my body for the first time. He seems to know everywhere to touch and how to kiss me exactly right. He pulls away slightly.

"Should I read your stuff?" he asks. "I like getting to know you in real life. James sent me the first essay so I'd know a tiny bit about you, but it's taken a lot of self-control not to read everything else."

I consider this question carefully. My writing is deeply personal and lets readers into my heart and mind—but Josh is already there.

"For most people, I would say yes. Reading my essays is key to understanding where I am and what I've lived through," I begin. "But I strangely don't feel that way about you. I feel like you just know me in a different way. You can read them if you want, but the version of me you know is truer than what I share with the world."

"One last question," he says. "Is it weird if I just stay here and start working on things, or should I go home so there is a break or something?"

I like that Josh feels unpracticed in navigating this moment. It makes me feel like maybe he hasn't done it too many times before. Like maybe this is special for us.

"It's fine," I giggle. "Just leave your shirt off."

He scoops me up and wraps my legs around his waist, just like last night. I let out a playful yelp as he walks us back to the guest room.

"I'm going to be a few minutes late for work today," he whispers in my ear.

And just like that, a man comes to my bed for the second time.

# CHAPTER 22

I KEEP WAITING FOR THIS WHOLE ARRANGEMENT BETWEEN Josh and me to go sideways, but it hasn't yet. In fact, in the week since our first kiss on the front porch, things have only gotten better and hotter. Much hotter.

To keep things from getting too intense, Josh goes home every other night to his house. This has the intended effect that we both get alone time and, in my case, the ability to process the significance of what's happening. It also has the effect of making us *really* happy to see each other in the morning.

Whether I wake up with him in bed next to me or not, the last seven days have all gone a bit like this:

Step one: ridiculously good sex in the morning.

Step two: write for three to four hours at The Drip (this must be done out of the house, or we revert right back to step one).

Step three: lunch together at the house and interviews with either Josh or journalists.

Step four: lazy afternoons spent reading while Josh finishes projects.

Step five: dinner, maybe a little TV, and then more sex.

Most of all, this new routine of ours feels so *natural*. Nothing in or about the last year has been easy for me. Everything has been a slog at some point, but not this. Whatever this is with Josh feels familiar and organic. Are we in the honeymoon phase? Absolutely. And I like it.

Somehow, my writing schedule hasn't been disrupted by all of the distractions from Josh—the opposite, actually. My mornings at The Drip have become my most productive hours of writing ever. I'm starting to wonder if my frustrations with intimacy were making it hard for me to think clearly. Because right now, I'm writing at a blistering pace that has me set to finish the first draft in less than ten days. I've begun editing the first fifty pages to perfection to show Felicity.

The nature of Josh's interview questions has changed, too. We mostly spend our interview time together trying to get some of the standard get-to-know-you things taken care of. Josh and I jumped into serious questions early on, so it feels a bit like we're starting all over again. It's all far less one-sided now, too, with me trying to learn more about him.

Yesterday's questions were a particularly fun attempt by us both to figure out each other's weird quirks.

"Finish this sentence," Josh said. "You can't really know someone until..."

"You see them load a dishwasher," I replied without a moment of hesitation.

"Really? That's your answer?"

"It can be a scary look inside someone's brain, Josh. What's your answer?"

"You meet their family."

"If you were invisible for one day, what would you do?" I asked.

"Probably go hang out with a bunch of wild animals up close. You?"

"My answer is in the future: watch people read my book."

"What is your biggest pet peeve?" he asked.

"People who read their phones at the dinner table."

"A hundred percent the same. One of the first things I noticed about you is how you would go for a long period of time without looking at your phone. You also misplace it more than anyone I've ever known."

Car keys. Phone. Credit cards. If it's small enough to fit in my cross-body purse, I will absolutely lose track of it a few times a day. He got me on that one. I decided to be bold with my next question.

"What is one thing you've thought about with us that hasn't happened yet?"

He got off his stool, walked over, and said in the sexiest whisper I have *ever* heard, "Would you like me to tell you or show you?"

I will never look at the living room furniture the same way again.

I also know that this new routine of ours has an expiration date. The last week has somehow felt like forever and no time at all. At some point, the summer will end, and I will go back to work and Chapel Hill, and Josh will return to his company in some capacity.

A few days ago, I thought about spilling the details to my friends via the group text, but they would be blindsided by the development and ask a gazillion well-intentioned questions. Jenny did get a cryptic note telling her to expect more details when I'm ready. No surprise, she responded with an eggplant emoji.

For now, I just let this be my and Josh's thing. For the first time in my life, I'm allowing myself to be in the moment and not worry about what's down the road. Maybe that's why it feels so damn good.

---

WHEN I OPEN the door and see Kendell coming up the sidewalk, I rush to give her a big hug. We've never met before, but I feel like I know her. Multiple people in town have told me they started reading my column because of her.

Her long blond hair is swept into a low ponytail, and her kind eyes only underscore her loud declaration of "I'm so glad to finally meet you in real life!"

James walks up behind her, and it's hard to believe that I haven't seen him since the day I arrived in town. I suspect he had a sense to hang back—to give me time to settle in and to give this whole brother-as-handyman arrangement time to work out as well. Whatever the reason, it was the right call.

"Obviously, Josh decided about twenty minutes ago that he had enough time to install a faucet in the upstairs bathroom before you arrived," I say. "He'll be down in a minute, I'm sure," I say overly loudly so that he can hear us.

When James walks through the door, there is an unexpected exclamation of "Holy shit." Granted we haven't spent a lot of time together, but I've never heard the man curse. He doesn't strike me as someone who has profanity in his vocabulary. It hits me that he hasn't seen the house in five weeks. Come to think of it, I'd probably say the same thing.

"You guys have transformed this place," he says in total astonishment. "I didn't expect this much progress."

Kendell is equally mesmerized, moving swiftly from room to room in disbelief. She runs her hand along the living room shelving that Josh installed. Not only are many of the first-floor repairs complete, but there are now area rugs and furniture and even some frames on the walls. The one hundred books I bought from Canopy Books are neatly placed on the shelves. I stand off to the side of the living room, watching them admire all of this. It really does look like a home. Almost. It won't truly feel like home until my kids are running through the hallways, yelling for snacks, and hanging out on the porch with me.

"I appreciate you giving me some credit, James, but I've had very little to do with this—it's all Josh," I say. "I owe you big-time, on a few levels."

As if on cue, Josh comes down the stairs, and my heart feels a quiet flutter. He gets to Kendell first and gives her a big hug, then follows that up with a bro hug for James. He comes over to me and wraps his hand around my waist.

"I told you that wouldn't take too long," he says with a smile.

Immediately, I can sense that we're being watched. This thing between Josh and me feels normal to us, but I realize that James and Kendell haven't seen us together before. The new inside of the house, me and Josh together—it must feel surreal to them.

"We should eat," I say, and we all move into the dining room. Tonight's meal is a mix of fancy takeout from a French bistro in town with a few homemade appetizers that Josh and I managed to concoct in the kitchen. Our culinary teamwork mostly consisted of Josh doing the labor while I occasionally chopped a vegetable and read out the recipe instructions. I did take the lead on the Caesar salad. My homemade dressing is famous among my friends.

The conversation flows easily as we set the table and grab drinks. As soon as we sit down, it's apparent that Kendell is bursting at the seams.

"I *really* like the two of you together," she says before dipping a piece of toasted baguette into the spinach dip. "James knew what he was doing."

I cock my head to the side and look at James with inquiring eyes. He knew what he was doing?

"I'm sorry, James—did you set us up? Was this a long con all along?" I ask, pointing my salad fork at him accusingly.

"It's not like that," he says as his cheeks turn a shade of pink to indicate it is definitely *like that*. He rushes to fill the space before I can tease him more.

"Listen. You needed help with your house. Josh desperately needed something to do so he wouldn't be tempted back to work. I knew you would get along, and I thought maybe there was a small chance you'd really hit it off."

Kendell is staring at him with the look of a wife who wants to scream *Bullshit!* at her husband but ultimately decides watching him squirm is more fun.

"Are you serious right now?" Josh asks with fake incredulity.

I know Josh well enough at this point to know he is equal parts amused and annoyed. One more thing his big brother got right. As an only child, I can't relate, but I've watched my own kids over the years and learned that your sibling being right about something is one of life's great tragedies.

"You don't get to be mad—even fake mad—at me," James says in a paternal tone. "You might end the summer with lower blood pressure and a girlfriend, thanks to me."

This makes us all chuckle, and when I turn to look at Josh a moment later, I see an expression on his face as he looks at James that makes me feel instantly warm. It's a look of gratitude, and his eyes are almost glassy. Josh was not happy to be forced by James into his summer sabbatical, and yet it's turning into something no one imagined was possible. Well, except maybe James, as it turns out.

"How's your book coming along?" Kendell asks me.

"Really good," I reply with a huge smile of relief. "I only have about a week of writing left, max, and then I'll edit for a little bit before it's turned in to my publisher."

"Her agent is coming for a quick trip soon to read some of it," Josh adds.

"Why is your agent coming all the way to Canopy? Why not just read it virtually?" James chimes in to ask.

"Most agents probably would do just that," I begin, "but Felicity has a different style. She checks in on me, in person, every couple of months. It's a very nontraditional arrangement that I have—a first-time writer with a book deal and big advance before I ever wrote a single word. She's got a bit more hand-holding to do. Plus, it's a chance to escape the city for a bit."

"Are you feeling good about it?" Kendell follows up. James told me a while back via text that she's a fan of my work, so I don't interpret her questions as prying or pushy. Instead, I suspect she's just hopeful I hit my deadlines so that she can read the book.

"I'm actually feeling really good, which is its own brand of scary," I say. "Felicity will read some polished chapters when she gets here, and her reaction will say a lot about the direction of the next few months."

At the mention of postsummer life, James and Kendell jump into a long dialogue about how busy their fall is set to be: five kids spread between three different schools, competitive sports teams, and a big trip over fall break to see Kendell's family in Tennessee.

"Summer is the only time I get to feel even remotely like a real person," she says. "I try to remember that Lucy is already in eleventh grade and I won't have the kids around forever, but it's still really hard. Fall is always mind-numbingly busy."

"Is it strange not having the kids around this summer?" James interjects to ask. "I can't remember the last time we had a completely quiet house. I can't even imagine it."

"It's ... *different* than I expected," I say with a hint of hesitation. "They've been away at camp at the same time twice before, but I wasn't alone, of course."

Flashes of those two summers fly through my brain. I remember the movies, dinners, uninterrupted conversations, and long walks that Ben and I took—desperately trying to catch up on a year's worth of romantic moments while we had the chance. In many ways, it felt like I was getting to know him all over again.

"To be fair, Josh has been here talking your ear off, just like I said he would," James jokes, keeping the conversation upbeat. "So, I'm not sure how alone you've really been."

"Still, though, spending hours at my writing desk or at The Drip or reading in bed in complete silence feels so strange," I begin. "Sometimes I'm exhilarated by it, sometimes I'm really sad, sometimes I'll think of the kids and my heart will ache, sometimes I feel complete relief about getting to shape my own day. And of course, I find a way to feel bad for whatever emotion is making itself known at the time."

"Oh, a classic mom-guilt cocktail," Kendell says, raising her glass. "We should share recipes sometime."

James chimes in. "Last week, Little James said to Kendell, 'Mom, remember when you missed my band concert a few years ago?'"

"No context, no explanation," she adds. "Just the random thought of the one time I've ever missed a performance. And he just went about his day while I cried on the back deck."

Josh sits quietly as we share about the seven kids that belong to three of us at the table. He seems just a bit sad not to be able to jump in with his own parenting war stories. He's the cool uncle. His stories are pure fun—not the jumbled mix of exhaustion, joy, frustration, and pride that the three of us feel.

Instead, after a few more minutes, he jumps in to share my instant photo and letter tradition. It's a hit with Kendell, who insists she's going to steal the idea when Lucy goes to cheer camp the two weeks before school starts.

"In fact, we should take a photo before you two leave," I add proudly. "My kids instructed me to be more social this summer, so they will be happy to see proof of life of new friends."

We spend the next half hour talking in a hundred different directions about the house, our extended families, current events, town gossip, and everything in between. I liked James from the start and always hoped he would become a friend. Hosting him for dinner in the house he found for us—just with a different person by my side than I expected—is the definition of bittersweet.

While the guys clean up, I invite Kendell upstairs to see the changes on the second floor, but mostly to show her my writing room, as I suspect it will feel extra special for her. She gasps when she sees the vintage wood desk, dark-green velvet curtains, and gold-accented desktop accessories.

"This room has such a vibe, Gracie," she says. "It makes me want to sit down and write!"

"You are totally welcome to," I say back, watching her admire the desk.

She turns around with a somewhat serious look on her face.

"While we're up here and have some privacy," she begins, "I just want to say how happy it makes me to see you and Josh together. He's like a little brother to me. I've known him since he was seventeen, and I've never seen him look this way before. He's completely himself with you, and trust me—he's had issues with that in past relationships. It says a lot about how good the two of you are together."

I blush and think again how lucky Josh is to have such wonderful, caring people around him. I also wonder if this is a bit of what Sunny meant weeks ago when she told me about his bad habit. Still, I sense that there is more that Kendell wants to say.

"Gracie, I have read everything you've published over the last year. I admire you and your work so much. I know there will come a time in the next month when y'all will try to figure out if this can last past the summer. Please know that you can do it and that something great like this is worth fighting for."

"We're mostly taking it day by day at this point," I say, because it's true but also because I haven't let myself think too far ahead, just in case disappointment might be on the horizon. "My life is so complicated. Sometimes I struggle when I think about dragging

Josh into my mess, especially the boring mess—school calendars, soccer games, report cards, preteen drama. Can you imagine him signing up for that after all this time on his own?"

She quietly leans on the desk and takes a deep breath. Her eyes turn soft and watery.

"Josh would be great at that mess," she says with a slight wobble in her voice. "He should've been a dad by now. A husband. The parent who sneaks in Kool-Aid for the kids at the end-of-year party instead of the organic juice boxes the room mom put on the sign-up list. The guy who claims he's definitely not volunteering to coach a team but is on the sideline by the first game. The one who takes his kid for ice cream after a rough math test. Gracie, he'd be absolutely perfect for your mess. I think he longs for it."

"I take it he's been a great uncle?" I ask, because right now I can't imagine someone else being a perfect fit who isn't Ben. My mind knows Kendell is telling the truth that Josh would be a natural, but my heart doesn't want to picture it just yet.

"The best," she says. "He and James share the same core goodness and love for family. James has been the best dad—I would've never had five kids if that weren't the case. I'm sure it's not always been easy for Josh to see his brother get this full family life when things didn't work out the same for him, but he's never let it change how he is with us. My kids adore him."

I realize that Kendell is trying to make a strong pitch for Josh—letting me know that this accidental bachelor might just be able to handle stepping into the complicated world of a widowed mom of two. I fight the urge to let out a nervous chuckle, because I'm quite convinced that I'm the one who needs to make the sales pitch, and it won't be easy.

"We should get back down and take that photo," I say, reaching out my hand to Kendell. "Thanks for this."

We walk downstairs and catch the Anderson brothers goofing off in the kitchen as they load the last of the plates into the dishwasher. Together, in this lighthearted moment, their distinct personalities meld into a moment of pure joy. I instinctively see the goodness that Kendell just described radiating from them both.

And in this one moment, I let myself believe that maybe my mess is indeed a perfect fit. But just as quickly as I let the thought in, I then let it fly away—leaving the future as something to worry about on another day.

# CHAPTER 23

I've only let myself shop in Canopy Books one time this summer—to buy the stacks that I needed to populate the bookshelves at the house. Books are both my sanctuary and top procrastination technique. It's a slippery slope. It starts with just one book before I get back into writing, and then the next thing you know, I'm four books deep and haven't opened my laptop in weeks. How do I know this will happen? Because it was the story of my January.

So, I haven't let myself in the bookstore for nondecorative purposes out of sheer principle until now. I'm only a few days of work (and an annoying prologue) from wrapping up the memoir. Today, I'm buying a reward book to entice myself to write faster so that I can finally read prose again that isn't based on my own sad life or that isn't another memoir (also usually sad). I just want to read a low-impact, mostly-wine-club book-club selection.

I wander down the fiction aisles and head for the "beach reads." I feel an immediate release. The bright colors, the punchy titles. This is my home. Ben used to tease me about my book choices, but the truth was he never made it through many of his yawn-inducing seven-hundred-page nonfiction books. In a year, I could read twenty or thirty books while he struggled to finish a few. I haven't read much of my usual fare lately; life has been too heavy to disappear into the romantic dramedies of fictional characters. As I stand here, I hope I can find joy in this all again. There are two books in my hands to choose between. Both promise the sweet nectar of a juicy romance.

Then suddenly, I see her. What. The. Actual. Hell. It's the horrible, nasty woman who ruined my date in Chapel Hill. Why is the world so small? What twisted joke is this? I duck before I can be spotted over the shelf and practically crawl on my hands and knees to the counter at the front of the store.

The woman at the register is someone that I don't recognize, but there isn't time for an introduction. I slink back behind the counter and sit flat against it with my legs crossed. "Please hide me," I whisper to the woman with a tiny smile so she won't be alarmed. A perplexed and mildly amused look crosses her face. "I'll explain in a few minutes," I add, as if that will make me seem any less crazy.

The counter is deep, so I feel confident that the horrible woman won't see me. Not a minute later, she is up at the register to check out.

"Did you find everything you're looking for?"

"I did; thank you for asking."

"Are you staying in town or just passing through?"

Whoever this woman at the register is, I love her. She's asking the right questions to get me the good intel.

"Just passing through. We live in Durham and are coming back from a week in the Smokies. Dollywood and all! Just beautiful."

"That's lovely. Grabbing reading material for the rest of the drive today?"

"You got it. We thought about staying the night, but there doesn't seem to be all that much here to see."

"Your total is $27.65."

Horrible Woman has hit a nerve because the tone of the lady at the register shifts. *Nothing much here to see? Canopy has everything.* I am sure the cashier is thinking the same thing.

In a few more seconds, Horrible Woman is out the door and I'm free to finally stand.

"I'm so embarrassed, but thank you so much. She's a terrible person that I met—no, wrong word: was accosted by—at home a few months ago. I didn't want another scene."

"I'm Marianne, the owner. You must be Gracie, the famous writer I've heard about."

"This is not usually how I meet people, and I'm entirely mortified."

"On the upside for me, I think you owe me the story of your last interaction with her."

I put my books on the counter to start checking out while regaling Marianne with the terrible tale I've now told three times this summer—once in my book, once to Josh, and now to her. Somehow, it never gets easier.

"If she comes in again, I'm going to slap her in your honor."

Marianne and I spend the next thirty minutes talking about our favorite books, what it's like to pitch and write a book, and what I expect the next few months to be like. She's the first person besides Felicity to truly nerd out with me on all things writing and publishing. Marianne confesses that she's tried to write a novel multiple times in her life, but it's never worked out. So she sells books and supports the dreams of others instead. A customer recognizes me and asks for a selfie—it hasn't happened much in Canopy, but it makes sense that it would happen in a bookstore.

"I know it's probably too early to ask, but please know we would love—LOVE—to host a stop on your book tour here at the shop."

"Only if you promise not to tell the story of how we met."

"Deal."

I give her a big hug and head out the door. I need to spend the next few hours taking care of a backlog of business correspondence with Felicity, Lucia, and a host of others. Before I get to work, I text Josh.

> Marianne at Canopy Books is my new BFF. You won't believe how we met . . .

He calls me and I download the crazy story from the shop. We're on a video call, and I see his initial disbelief and then relief that Marianne was there to help the situation. He tells me she's a great person to have in your corner. After twenty minutes, I beg off the phone. I *need* to clear out my inbox before our big plans tonight.

I'm finally going to Josh's house.

# CHAPTER 24

WHEN JOSH'S PLACE EMERGES AFTER A QUARTER MILE of wooded driveway, I'm in awe. His modern A-frame house looks ripped from the pages of *Dwell*. The house has gorgeous wood siding framing huge glass windows. A dark metal roof goes from the peak of the house to the ground. It's more modern than anything else I've seen in Canopy. Josh told me about it, but it was hard to believe such a laid-back guy could have such stylish taste in architecture.

I park my SUV next to his truck and grab my overnight bag from the passenger seat. As I walk toward the front porch, I admire the craftsmanship of the home's exterior. Before opening the door, I turn around. The view is amazing. The entire drive was on a slight elevation but never dramatic enough for me to realize just how far I'd climbed. From his front door, you see only trees and mountains in the distance. In an hour at dusk, the view from inside the house, out those great big windows, will be exquisite.

Following his instructions, I open the door without knocking. The entire first floor looks to be open space, and he's straight ahead in the kitchen. He looks up and immediately walks toward me with that beaming smile of his.

"It smells amazing in here," I say, greeting him with a kiss.

Every time we look at each other after a kiss or make-out session, one or both of us has a look of disbelief on our face. It's silly, but I think we're still in a little shock that this is all really happening. It is strange at any age to have a crush on someone that actually pans out.

"I don't have an extensive repertoire in the kitchen, but the ten or so things I know how to cook I'm really good at," he says. "Tonight, I'm making chicken Parm."

"Hopefully you're okay making the same ten things over and over because I am a terrible cook," I admit, finally breaking away from him so he can keep making dinner.

I've known Josh for six weeks, and this romance has been sizzling for two—and this is the first time I've been to his house. The Craftsman is convenient and easy, so despite my curiosity, this is the first day we've gotten serious about me coming here and spending the night.

"Can I explore?" I ask, wanting to be respectful of his space even though he knows every imperfect corner of mine.

"Of course. There is a guest bedroom hidden behind us. The stairs take you to a loft, and my bedroom is up there behind it. I'll just be here in the kitchen making you a delicious dinner."

I sneak in for another kiss before heading through a short hallway to the guest bedroom. It's surprisingly large, with a queen bed and a big area rug covering the floor. There's a spacious walk-in closet and bathroom in here, too. I suspect this is supposed to be the primary bedroom but that Josh has decided to sleep up in the trees in the loft area. The walls of this room are covered in art prints from different national parks and forests in the western part of the state. I love it.

In short order, I'm climbing the stairs. There's a small leather sofa facing a huge flat-screen TV at the top of the landing—this is a bachelor pad, after all. Down another short hallway is Josh's room. My guess was right; this room is smaller than the one downstairs. It's also cozier, with high-quality linen sheets that look suspiciously like the ones I have on the bed in the Craftsman. The bed itself is a stunning carved wood in a deep-walnut stain. Josh hasn't mentioned building furniture, but it would not surprise me if he made this bed for himself. Over the bed is a beautiful black-and-white photo of a mountain waterfall. I drop my small bag at the foot of the bed and head downstairs.

"Well, what's the verdict?" Josh asks.

"This house is *so you*. It's like I can feel you in every room and hallway—I guess that makes sense because you literally built it exactly how you wanted it, but it's still pretty cool."

"So no scary surprises lurking that make you second-guess this romantic situation?"

"You are not a red-flag sort of guy, Josh. This house, in fact, only makes me like you more because it's the exact sort of tucked-away paradise I initially thought I wanted in Canopy."

"Really?"

"Yeah. I tried to convince Ben that we needed a rural spot. Downtown reminded me too much of home. We even saw a place just down the road from here. The Craftsman was a compromise at the time—much more of a Ben type of location. Now, of course, I can't imagine being anywhere else. It would be lonely for me to be tucked away by myself up here. I like my quiet time, but I'd be a ball of anxiety on a few acres all alone."

"I can't imagine anyone else in the Wilson Street house besides you, so I think the compromise worked out well. He knew what he was doing."

This is one thing I love about Josh. From the beginning—when we were just strangers asking each other questions—he's been comfortable with me talking openly about Ben. There isn't a hint of jealousy or weirdness.

Suddenly, there is a brief knock at the door followed by it rapidly opening. Two seventysomethings burst in while chatting loudly to one another.

"Josh! We were driving home from Clemson and had to make a stop here to use the bathroom. The old prostate isn't what it used to be," says the man, before looking up and realizing that Josh isn't alone.

The expression on Josh's face is mostly amused but also a little embarrassed. His comfort at the unexpected guests makes me quickly realize these are his *parents*.

"Oh my goodness ... the other car in the driveway ... we're intruding!" says his mom, walking up toward us. "We should've called first, but you're usually home alone on weeknights, sweetie."

I have two kids and irritable bowel syndrome, so there is quite literally nothing people can say to me about their bodily functions to gross me out. My instinct is to make his parents feel comfortable in this awkward moment.

"Mom, Dad, this is Gracie," Josh says, recovering quickly. "Gracie, these are my parents, Jim and Suzanne."

"It's nice to meet you both," I say, giving his mother a quick hug since she is nearby. Josh gives his dad a hug and whispers in his ear something about taking care of his business. We're all laughing, even though Suzanne and I don't hear the full extent of things.

"I'm sorry we barged in. We'll be out of your hair in no time," Suzanne says.

By this point, Josh has taken the chicken out of the oven, and there is enough to feed a small army. He told me once that he makes food in bulk, freezes it, and then eats the same meal every night until it runs out. It's how he survived his busy workload over the last few years. I make small talk with Suzanne for a few minutes, asking about their trip and the traffic they hit on the road.

"There's plenty of food," I offer, gesturing toward the baking sheet full of prepared chicken. "You should stay before you get back on the road."

Jim emerges at this point and heartily agrees. "Is it chicken Parm night? That sounds perfect."

Suzanne and Josh are exchanging the *exact* same look with each other, and it takes no effort for me to start matching the personality traits of Josh and James to their parents. I smile and mouth *It's okay* to Josh. He lets out a sigh, shakes his head, and then nods to his mom. She silently goes over to the kitchen cabinets and nimbly grabs out two more plates, napkins, and sets of cutlery from their respective spots and brings them over to the long wood dining table.

---

WE'RE OVER AN hour into dinner and wine, and Josh's parents are telling me lots of stories about him. Josh wants to pretend like he's embarrassed, but I know he's not. His parents are just like he described—so full of obvious and boundless love for him. Nothing is said in a hurtful or sarcastic tone. It's all so joyful.

"Did Josh tell you that he almost didn't go to college?" Jim asks, looking at me.

"We had to insist on it," Suzanne jumps in. "This guy just wanted to ride mountain bikes for the rest of his life. He wanted to start his own company at eighteen!"

"They told me to go to college, major in business, and learn how to actually do things the right way," Josh adds. "So I did, and I worked summers as a bike tour guide. By the time I graduated, I understood the practical and business sides of things."

"And obviously, we were right," Jim says matter-of-factly. "He started his own company, always operated in the black, and then sold it for high five figures before starting the construction company."

His dad is so obviously proud of him, and it makes my heart swell. My parents do the same for me. They used to keep copies of the tourism magazine on their coffee table with my name circled halfway down the masthead. Now they keep laminated copies of my *New York Times* essays out instead. Once the book is released? Their friends are goners.

"They were right," Josh says in mock annoyance. "It turns out learning how to actually run a business in the classroom keeps you from making stupid mistakes in real life."

"That's enough about us and Josh," Suzanne starts. "Kendell got me hooked on your essays last year, and I know you've spent the summer here in Canopy writing. Tell us about your book and how it's coming along."

I've peppered them with questions and talked very little about myself until now. I know that once you get a parent talking about their children, even adult ones, they won't stop. I wanted intel on Josh.

"Well, I'm really close to wrapping up the complete first draft, which is totally surreal," I begin. "Reading the early chapters now is so wild because it feels like a million years ago. My agent arrives in a few days to read through some of the first chapters."

"Are you nervous?" Suzanne asks.

"A little bit, yes. Felicity is fantastic, but the truth is that no one else has read any of the book, so it's overwhelming to think that she's the first of hopefully many people to see the pages."

"How do you promote a book like yours?" Jim asks. Just like Josh, he's interested in the process.

"Talk about it constantly, which is hard for me," I respond with a half smile. "I'll obviously do a book tour when it actually comes out. In the meantime, we're starting to see more interest from the press in writing about me, my column, and the book. Recently, I found out that Maisy Miller wants me to be one of the first guests on a new podcast she's launching. I'm still trying to decide on that one."

"How exciting is that!" Suzanne says, clasping her hands. "Why the hesitation?"

It's easy to forget that Maisy's daytime show makes her especially popular with the senior-citizen age bracket. She is a superstar to them but is trying to attract more of the demographic that follows me.

"Suzanne, would I be correct to assume that you saw my, um, last run-in with Maisy on her show?" I ask in a bashful voice.

"Of course, dear. It's all my friends and I could talk about for days," she says bluntly but not rudely.

"It was a bit of a crash and burn," I delicately remind her, even though it doesn't seem to be necessary. "I'm not convinced that I'm ready for another Maisy-level interview. Or Maisy herself, for that matter."

"It most certainly was not a crash and burn!" she responds emphatically. "Anyone who thinks that has never experienced a big loss. My usual Thursday brunch with friends turned into a sob fest that morning. You don't reach your seventies without going through some serious stuff in life. It was one of the most honest expressions of delayed grief that I've seen in my life—thinking that you're getting better only for the dam to break at the worst possible time. Unfortunately, many of us have been there before."

Where so many people saw weakness, the Anderson family has told me, without reservation, that they saw bravery and honesty. First James, now Suzanne. Always Josh. I feel my throat tighten, but it's not from anxiety or fear—it's from the emotion of witnessing the pure goodness emanating from the people sitting here with me.

"Josh has been helpful getting me back into the swing of things," I say, worried that I might burst into tears if I let the moment linger too long. "If I do say yes, he's the reason why."

This makes everyone at the table smile, and Suzanne reaches out to squeeze Josh's hand.

"I've been watching that show for years," she tells us. "And that was the first time in a long while that someone truly, deeply moved me."

To be honest, while I don't relish the idea of becoming the main character on the internet again, I know that I will end up doing the podcast. Josh thinks I can do it and so does Jenny, who told me that not everyone gets a "mulligan" on something like this. Both of them think people will forget the first interview entirely if this one goes well.

After giving her a tentative yes a few days ago, I'll text Lucia tomorrow with my final, affirmative decision. It does, however, feel nice to pretend for just one more night that I'm considering not going to Maisy's Nashville studio to record the episode. It makes things feel just a bit more in my control.

We all chat for a few more minutes before Jim's eyes get heavy and he almost falls asleep at the table. Suzanne announces that it's time to go, but I shoot Josh a look to telepathically signal to him that his almost-eighty-year-old dad can absolutely not drive home this late in the dark, this tired. Asheville is only thirty minutes away, but that's twenty-nine minutes too far.

"Mom, Dad, you guys need to stay here. No way are you driving tonight," Josh says to immediate protests.

It doesn't take much for them to relent, though. Jim also doesn't keep much hidden, so after about thirty seconds, he's out the door, grabbing their luggage from the car.

Josh and I insist that they go to bed while we clean up, and the two of us make quick work of the dishes, leftovers, and trash. His mom sneaks out for a good-night hug—including one from me—and retires for the night. Josh and I go upstairs.

"Is it weird if I spend the night with them here?" I ask as we enter his room and I grab my pajamas from my bag.

He shakes his head and lets out a chuckle. "I have no doubt that James has told my mom everything about the progression of things this summer. He's got no filter, just like my dad. I don't think you need to worry."

"Can I ask you something?"

"Of course."

"Do you sleep up here so that they have an easy place to crash?"

There's a pause and then a long answer. "I really do like it up here in the loft, but the truth is, yes—that's why I chose this room. My parents are old, but so are my aunts and uncles. I've always assumed at some point somebody would need to come stay with me for a short or long time. My dad's brother recovered here from a hip replacement two years ago because his house was nothing but stairs. I don't want people I love to feel like they are a hassle to me. Learning to love it up here has made that easier."

"That is the sweetest thing I've ever heard. Can you please stop being so perfect?"

We take turns in the bathroom getting ourselves ready to sleep and then climb into his cozy bed. I turn to face him and he pulls me in for a PG make-out session before we quietly embrace. I have a sudden impulse to tell him that I love him and it takes all of my willpower not to do so. I settle for falling asleep with my head tucked on his chest.

# CHAPTER 25

IT'S NOON ON THE DOT WHEN FELICITY EMERGES FROM the arrivals hallway at Asheville Regional Airport. She looks fresh and beautiful, as always, but—no, it's not possible. Is she wearing cargo pants? With a T-shirt? Shoes with laces?

I wave and smile. Once she's within arm's length, we pull each other in for a hug. When we let go, I take a small step back and playfully twirl her around to fully admire how decidedly *not*–New York she looks.

"Don't be dramatic, Gracie," she says, clicking her tongue in mock annoyance. "You forget that I grew up in Vermont. Just because I'm not actively outdoorsy now doesn't mean I don't know how to live the outdoor life. I like to fit in when I go to new places."

"It's just a shock, but of course you make it look cute," I say, admiring how her cropped tee and jewelry make this Canopy-friendly outfit extremely stylish. I take some mental notes.

The airport is small and she's traveling with only a carry-on for her quick overnight trip, so we are back at the car in no time. I explained to her over the phone that she could drive my car while she's in town because I had other reliable transportation. She read between the lines right away and immediately asked me for details about my "love interest." I told her she had to wait until we saw each other in person.

It's no surprise that the second we're buckled in and exit the airport, she's prodding me for the scoop.

"I need to know everything. Don't skip a single detail."

"Let's start with this: his name is Josh. His brother, James, is the real estate agent who sold Ben and me the house. Before summer started, I reached out to James because the house needed a lot of work, and I was hoping he could recommend people to take on certain repairs. Instead, he told me about Josh."

Felicity raises an eyebrow the same way I did the first time I heard about the magical brother available to renovate a house on short notice. I take a few minutes to explain his situation and why he had the free time.

"So to be clear, an attractive, handy, and successful man landed in your lap?"

I want to laugh and tell her that she's the one being dramatic now, but the truth is, that's pretty much what happened.

"It was a little unsettling at first having someone around the house all the time, but by the end of the first week, we were thick as thieves. He overheard a disaster of an interview and offered to help me with interview practice over lunch on the days that I didn't have real ones."

"Wow, that's a top-tier flirtation strategy. Well done, Josh."

"It worked on a lot of levels," I say with a sly smile. "We learned a lot about each other, and obviously, that only increased the attraction, but it also made me better at the interviews."

"When did you finally hook up?"

"A few weeks ago, and I'll have you know that I was the one who took the initiative."

"And since then?"

"It's hot. It's fun. It's cozy. Like, this is what I was secretly waiting for and hoping for on every terrible date."

After we turn off the main highway and onto the country roads that lead to town, she starts asking me the questions that I expected her to lead with—height, muscle tone, penis size. I'm actually impressed by the self-control she's displayed to make it this far into the drive before asking. I overshare, and we giggle uncontrollably in the car.

For the last ten minutes of the drive, I make Felicity catch me up on how her summer is going. Publishing slows down around now and she tells me it feels like she can finally breathe for the first time this year.

When we pull into the driveway, I admire how adorable the house looks. The ferns I hung from the old hooks on the porch roof last week make the exterior look picture perfect. Josh won't be back until the late afternoon, when he's joining Felicity and me for dinner, so we've got the house to ourselves for now.

As we're walking up the front steps, I tell Felicity to pause. I take out my phone and force about twenty "before" photos on her. She gasps in genuine horror at the photo with the green rug and stained walls.

When I open the front door and she glances inside, she lets out a loud squeal. She walks in and puts her hand to her mouth. This makes me burst with pride—first, for myself, for sticking with the house and making it my own; second, for Josh, who is solely responsible for the physical labor required for the transformation.

"Gracie, this is so amazing. I'm so happy for you," she says, spinning around trying to take in everything within her line of sight. "The fact that a hot man did all of this . . . Girl, you are winning at life right now."

I guide Felicity upstairs to the primary bedroom. Ever since Josh and I got together, it's been all about the first-floor guest room for us. I make a point to show her the kids' rooms and the newly renovated hall bath. That's also Josh's handiwork, of course.

"Will I be protected from the sounds of your copious fornication up here?"

"Only time will tell."

While I give her a few minutes to settle in, I walk across the hall to the writing room to grab the first fifty pages that I've printed off for her. Over the past few days, I've proofread and edited these pages to perfection for my first official reader. This is the first substantial read-through Felicity will have of any piece of the book. I have butterflies—I'm nervous, excited, scared. All the feelings.

When I pop my head back in, she's admiring the wallpaper in the closet. It's a cream color with shiny gold flowers. When I saw a single roll on clearance at an interior store nearby, I knew that I had to have it. The print isn't made anymore, so the closet was the only surface I could fully cover.

"It's the one home-improvement project in this entire house that I did for myself," I brag.

"It's so elegant, Gracie. Everything about this house is so *you.*"

Her comment makes me think. Yes, most of the projects Josh has worked on this summer are the ones that Ben and I came up with together. But everything else—the paint choices, the furniture, the fabrics, the wallpaper—is all me. It's the first time I realize just how much this is *my house*. I've not had to compromise or debate on a single thing. I just *chose*. I have conflicting feelings of pride and loss.

We head back downstairs and out the door for the short walk to The Drip. She requires an afternoon cup of coffee to survive, and I think there is no better place for her to dive into the pages. She assured me on the drive to the house that she ate brunch in the airline lounge and isn't hungry for lunch. I suspect she has butterflies, too.

When we arrive at The Drip, I tell her that I've successfully made it to this point in the writing process primarily because of the caffeine provided here.

"You're entering hallowed ground," I joke. We walk to the counter to order and I settle her into one of my favorite spots. While she reads inside, I'm going to head outside to a broad wire lounge chair in the shade. It's too much pressure to be in the shop while she judges my work.

"Here it is," I say, handing over the stack of pages like it's my firstborn. "Remember: no prologue yet. This is the first five chapters."

Felicity nods, grabs her pen, and gets down to business. I walk out the door with an old copy of *Pride and Prejudice* that I grab off the communal bookshelf.

---

NINETY MINUTES GO by without a peep from Felicity. No head popping out the door, no text messages from inside. Total silence.

I do get a text from Josh that he's back at the house earlier than expected. Come by The Drip, I tell him. You can keep me company until Felicity is ready to discuss the first part of my manuscript.

Jane Austen pulls me right back in the second I put my phone down, and when Josh walks up, I don't notice until he's right in front of me. I pop up and immediately wrap my arms around him. His embrace makes me feel instantly safe and happy. There is such a newness to all of this that we still get bashful about hanging on to those hugs for an extra second.

What catches my eye next, however, is that he's wearing a very clean pair of jeans and a light-blue button-up. This is formal attire in Josh Anderson's world, and he looks very good. He shaved this morning, and now the five o'clock shadow is starting to emerge in the way that drives me insane on men. I am not being discreet at all with regard to my admiration of his look.

"I wanted to make a good first impression on your agent," he says. "Plus, I thought it was good for you to know that I own more than one nice outfit."

We sit down and hold hands while he catches me up on his day. I am still amazed that I have someone to hold hands with again.

Felicity emerges from the inside of the shop twenty minutes after Josh arrives. She is carrying her purse and the manuscript, and her eyes are red. I've never seen Felicity look quite this way. She locks eyes with me and walks directly to me, not even pausing to acknowledge Josh.

"Gracie, this is phenomenal and I'm a mess. I honestly just want to beg you for more chapters right now because these ones were simply so moving and beautiful and literary, and I want more."

It takes a moment, but she glances over and notices Josh. A grin emerges and she looks at me and then back at him.

"You must be Josh. I've heard a lot about you. Sorry to meet you in this condition. Blame Gracie."

He stands and reaches out to shake her hand with a warm hello, and I can tell from her expression that I have set her expectations perfectly right. The two of them sit back down, and she immediately returns to praising the book.

"Gracie, be honest with me. Is the rest of the memoir as good as those chapters that I just read?"

"Yes, I think so. To be clear, I proofread and workshopped those fifty pages hard. Everything else is still pretty raw. But I do think that what you've read is indicative of the style and tone of the rest."

"Perfect, just absolutely perfect," she says, getting teary again, before turning to Josh. "Have you read any of this yet?"

He shakes his head. "I've had the privilege of watching her in action all summer. She's a machine, and I don't want to mess her up."

"You keep protecting our girl's creative process," she says directly to Josh with a stern face before turning to me again. "You'll be done soon, and Jeannie is going to be so freaking thrilled with this. People are going to go crazy for this book, Gracie."

Felicity is not one for bullshit, and neither am I. If she says it's good, it means it's *really* good. To be honest, I've felt that way since I wrote the first chapter in my bedroom nearly a year ago. Having a professional like Felicity tell you that the writing is great, however, is on a different level. I'm bursting with happiness and pride when I realize I'm squeezing Josh's hand extra hard and he's holding me just as tightly back.

A FEW HOURS later, we're laughing over dessert and wine at the French-inspired bistro off of Main Street. Felicity is regaling us with her latest dating mishaps.

"Josh, sorry to put you through this conversation, but Gracie and I have a tradition of sharing our ridiculous experiences. It's the only way a gal can survive being single as she enters middle age," Felicity says in a playful tone.

"I thought you said you were twenty-nine," he says, turning to me and making a puzzled face.

Panic crosses Felicity's face before I can elbow Josh in his side.

"He's joking," I exclaim. Felicity lets out a deep, relieved breath and starts to belly laugh.

When the server brings the bill, all three of us reach for it. I bow out quickly and let equally determined Felicity and Josh fight for the honor.

"I appreciate the sentiment, Josh, but Gracie is about to make me and others a lot of money. This is the least that I can do to show my appreciation."

After she pays, she asks if there are any bars that stay open past 7 p.m. that we can get one more drink at before heading home.

"Just a few blocks away," Josh responds. "It's not *that* small of a town."

On the walk over, Felicity tells us how much she likes Canopy. She's amazed by how much I can walk to from the house. "Everything you need is here, Gracie!" she tells me excitedly. Felicity is already three drinks in, so I make a mental note to only let her have one more.

Despite my love of margaritas I'm not a big drinker, so this is the first time I've made it to the bar—High Tide. It's got a strong hipster vibe, with dark wood walls, a mirrored bar shelf, and bartenders in black button-up shirts. No doubt transplants from some bigger city opened this place.

We grab three stools at the bar. Before I pop into mine, I ask Josh to order me a drink and excuse myself to use the restroom.

A few minutes later, I'm tucked around the corner from the bar on the way back when I hear Josh and Felicity midconversation. I can't see them, but their voices rise above the chatter.

"I'm serious. I'm just so happy she found you, Josh. It really feels like this is all meant to be. This is a new version of Gracie for me. You have to remember that I met her at one of the saddest times of her life. She's just so full of joy and so vibrant now—it's so beautiful."

"You're being too nice. I don't think I had all that much to do with it."

"I'm certain that you did."

There's a brief silence before Felicity says something else in a serious but also decidedly alcohol-infused tone. "Josh, I think she really likes you. Like, a lot. I hope you're as serious about her as I *think* you are."

What Josh says back makes me warm and happy and also inexplicably sad somewhere deep inside.

"Felicity, I was a goner from the first moment I saw her. It took a lot of self-control not to tell her I loved her by the second week at the house. I think she's perfect."

"I'm glad to hear that. She's been through a lot, and she deserves that sort of affection. Judging by the way she looks at you, I suspect that love is flowing in both directions."

I pop back around the corner before Felicity can divulge anything deeper than that. Or maybe I'm more nervous about what else Josh might say.

"I was just telling Josh how much I like this new Gracie. In a crazy way, I feel like I'm meeting you for the first time on this trip," she says.

Last week when I video chatted with my closest friend from Chapel Hill, she said almost the exact same thing. *This is like an entirely new Gracie I'm seeing!*

What is going on in my head right now? This summer. Josh. My writing routine. It's all made things better. I'm happier, healthier, and feeling a lightness that hasn't been present in a long time. Why then do I have the twinge of sadness pinching my insides?

---

AFTER I SAY good night to Felicity and make sure her tipsy legs make it safely up the stairs, I flow back through the house, turning off lights and locking the front door.

When I open the guest room door, Josh is pulling his fancy shirt over his head instead of unbuttoning it. He walks over to give me a perfectly delicate kiss and a hug.

"You okay?" he asks while we're still wrapped together. "Something seemed a little off at the bar."

"I think I just got a little overwhelmed all of a sudden," I say, telling the truth before adding a slight lie. "The impact of what Felicity said about the book just hit me."

"Let yourself be overwhelmed but also enjoy it. You should be really proud of yourself. I'm proud of you. I also know it's a lot to take in."

Despite twinges in my belly and how fuzzy my brain feels, I can't help but melt into Josh. My hands run up and down his chest and around to his back. I gently move my nails down his spine, which makes him arch his back and pelvis toward me. His hands move from my lower back to the front of me, cupping my breasts softly. There is a tenderness to us tonight—as if we're both wrestling with so much inside that our bodies need something gentle.

In quick succession, my sundress is unzipped and his pants are off. He lifts me onto the bed and lays me down carefully. I love the feel of his arms as he does this. Tonight there is no foreplay, just our bodies connected and moving in motion.

Do I love this man? Is this real? Am I ready for this? All these thoughts are running through my mind, when suddenly, I can't think at all.

---

"I DIDN'T HEAR any noise last night, so if you did have sex with that very cute boyfriend of yours, I'm happy to report that the sound doesn't travel up the stairs."

Felicity and I are both adjusting our hiking sandals before setting off on a mile-long trail to a waterfall. Her flight leaves this afternoon, and she refuses to depart without spending time in nature.

"Thanks for the confirmation, because there was definitely fornication last night," I say to make her laugh.

She quickly directs our walking chat to questions about me and how I've managed to climb out of the "widow funk," as she's comically branded it.

"You almost sold the house—which, for the record, would've been a complete mistake. But are you surprised how much this town and these people are really working for you?"

A few weeks ago, I might've answered that I was surprised, but I don't think that's really the case. I keep thinking about how Ben told me back in our early twenties that I was a small-town girl at heart. We were living in Boston after moving from Chicago, and neither of us felt like we were truly in the right place.

*You aren't a big-city girl, Gracie,* I remember him telling me. *You are destined for a small town.*

Eventually, he talked me into returning to North Carolina in his pitch for grad school. Within months of landing in our home state, we were lounging in a hammock in the backyard of our rented house at the time and I told him, *You're right. This feels good.*

The wild thing is knowing that Ben was even more right than we realized, because here in Canopy, in a truly small town, I feel relaxed and able to breathe for the first time in a long while. I tell her all of this as we walk, making the trail seem even easier than I expected.

"I like how much people love being here—living here. My parents trained me to think that small towns were places people ended up in by accident or because they had no other options. Chapel Hill obviously helped me figure out that's bullshit, but being here in Canopy, it's just on a whole different level. Everyone is here because they want to be, me included."

"Do you feel more like your old self here—more like the Gracie that existed before Ben died?"

"No," I respond so quickly that it surprises us both. "I feel more like myself than ever before, but I also don't feel the same. Is that weird?"

Felicity is looking intently at me now as we pass a trail marker that indicates we're halfway there. Unlike usual, Felicity doesn't try to jump in and fill the space. She just lets my thoughts wander out loud.

"I guess," I say slowly, careful to choose each word with purpose, "that being in a new place where I make my own decisions and focus on myself has really been transformative for me. I miss my kids so much, but I've also been able to be Gracie the person since I got here. Not just a mom or a wife or a widow, but a full version of myself."

"There's a noticeable shift in you," Felicity says. "I hope you find it empowering to chart this next journey for yourself, hopefully with a man who loves you by your side."

"It's only been six weeks since we met. I'm not sure he loves me."

"Gracie, be for real right now. That man is crazy about you. I think at our age you just realize things sooner when you meet someone special."

A tentative grin crosses my face. I stop walking for a moment, knowing the waterfall is just a few minutes away and wanting—no, needing—to ask her something before we get there.

"Felicity, can I ask you a question? Like, a really big question?"

"Of course," she says.

"Once this book wraps, who am I?" I ask her. "And I don't just mean a few months from now when the manuscript is officially finalized. Who am I next year after the book tour? Who am I when the interviews stop? What purpose do I serve for anyone if I'm not the sad grief lady?"

More than one question. Quite a few, actually. And now I'm tearing up, choking back my emotions as usual. I'm sure the leg will start up any time now. Felicity doesn't know about that yet; it's a few chapters beyond what she read yesterday. I'm still not certain I'll keep that chapter, but it did feel cathartic to write it.

Felicity doesn't step closer, doesn't move in for a hug. Like me, she's not someone who comforts others with her physicality. Instead, she uses her words.

"Gracie, this book is going to be really important to people. It's going to matter, and that alone is a legacy worth being proud of," she tells me. "Don't diminish what you've done with the book—or your column, for that matter—by calling yourself the grief lady. You are so much more than that."

"Thanks," I tell her, catching my breath. I turn to keep walking and she signals for me to stay.

"I would not have taken you on as a client if I thought you only had one book in you," she tells me.

When the whirlwind after the essay was at its wildest, I met with five different potential literary agents. She was the only one who asked me about my long-term interests, things that I might want to write about in the future, and what crazy dreams I had. At that point, it had only been six weeks since Ben died. Felicity was the first person who gave me an opportunity to imagine a new path for myself.

"You have a gift, Gracie," she continues. "You have a voice and a unique point of view that can't be taught. I think that you are going to write a lot of books. We'll sell some, we'll shelve some—and that's perfectly fine. That's how this all works. But I will believe in you every step of the way. This can be your career—your only career. You could write a dating self-help book next, and people would love it. Or fiction. We have the momentum to take the next step that we want to take."

"Thanks for being my biggest fan, Felicity," I tell her. "But maybe I will hold off on giving dating advice until I make sure I've got good material to share."

Once again, I motion to continue down the path and she stops me.

"What else is on your mind?"

"Why do you ask? You seem to be able to read my mind just fine."

"True," she says with a knowing smile.

"A few minutes ago, you said that Josh is crazy about me."

"Yes, obviously," she says with a nervous laugh.

I turn my head and stare off into the maze of trees around us, closing my eyes for a brief moment to listen for the waterfall set to reward us just a bit farther down the path.

"When I was sixteen, we spent the summer in Maine with some family friends," I start. "I fell in love for the first time with this sweet guy, Marshall. Marshall from Maine. It was special in a lot of ways. He was my first and really important to me. At the end of the summer, I went to my cousin, who was home from college, for advice. I asked all the usual stuff—how do we make this work, what's long distance like, is he going to break my heart? She listened to me blather on for about ten minutes—kind of like you right now. And then she looked at me and said, 'Gracie, sometimes you just need to let summer be summer.'"

I see Felicity's usual neutral expression drop ever so slightly, like she's about to be disappointed by what comes next.

"And she was right. Because as hard as it was to get on a plane at sixteen and feel my heart break into a million pieces, I still to this day think of that summer as pure magic. It was the summer I went from girl to woman, and it's cocooned in this safe little box in my mind. If I had tried to make it something more, I'm certain it would feel very different now. We would have tarnished the shine, the magic. Do you understand what I mean?"

"I do and I get that, Gracie," she begins. "But you're not sixteen, and Josh does not look at you like it's just for the summer—and you don't look at him like that, either. There's a naturalness to the way you two interact. It feels rooted, Gracie, not temporary. There's so much potential there."

"I know and I feel that, too, but what if I'm not really the person that this summer has allowed me to be?"

"Can I say something very honest to you as a friend, not your agent?"

I nod, sensing a seriousness that I haven't yet seen in Felicity.

"Don't make summer an excuse. Frankly, don't make excuses at all. I think you feel stuck because you aren't letting yourself move on. And yes, I know that's a bullshit phrase, but you physically bristled when I said 'I like the new Gracie' yesterday—don't think I was too drunk to notice. You have to figure out who you are after this book and after this summer. These two things are related, girl. And no one can tell you who you are meant to be. You've got to figure that part out. It feels like there is still something holding you back."

"It's strange to have time with my own thoughts," I tell her. "It's like I traded worrying about the kids with all this existential dread for myself. I think I prefer being a worried mom all the time."

"Gracie, you had the top one percent shittiest midlife crisis possible," she says, her facial expression soft again and pivoting us to our comfort zone of joking about disaster. "Cut yourself some slack, and let's keep walking."

A few minutes later, we emerge into the clearing with the waterfall. We quickly glance at each other and run around the waterfall and pool with childlike enthusiasm. Nature has washed away whatever seriousness we were carrying down the path a few minutes ago.

"I really needed a break like this," Felicity says sincerely, grabbing my hand. "Thanks for the invite and thank you for writing a bestselling book. I'm so proud. You are going to figure this all out."

---

FELICITY INSISTS THAT I don't need to walk her into the airport, so I throw the blinkers on and illegally park in the lane for a minute so we can say our goodbyes.

"Two things I want to say before I leave you," Felicity says. "First, you still need a prologue. Don't forget that."

I nod and tell her that when I deliver the final manuscript in a few weeks, both my version (which I haven't written) and Jeannie's requested version (which I need to write for the fourth time) will be in the mix.

"Second, you've got this. All of it," she says, reiterating what she told me on our lunch date at the start of the summer.

"The next time I see you, it will be as an author who has formally submitted her very first manuscript," I say to Felicity, making her light up at the thought. We hug across the seats and she jumps out, ready to go back to her normal life while I try to figure out what in the hell is going on in my new one.

# CHAPTER 26

I'VE SNAPPED OUT OF WHATEVER WEIRD EMOTIONAL FUNK I was in, and in no time at all, Josh and I are back at a Friends' Night Out gathering together. We skipped the last one because it was so early in, well, whatever this is that we have, that we weren't quite ready for prime time. So much has happened in the last month, it's hard to believe we're here again—this time as two people who definitely have something going on. Are we officially a couple? Boyfriend and girlfriend? I'm not sure, because we haven't really talked about it. We're just two planners who have decided to throw caution to the wind and spend every free moment together. It's special but undefined for now. We both know there is nobody else in the picture, so why stress?

We say hi to a few people, including a couple that I haven't met yet, before posting up at a high-top table near the edge of the patio. I wave at Kendell when she and James arrive a few minutes later. They are immediately intercepted by different friends for hugs and quick chats. I imagine that those two are the main glue that holds the broad group of friends together.

Josh and I talk about the dwindling number of to-dos left on the project list for the house. Earlier today, I told him how much I can't wait to see my kids' reactions—especially to their rooms—and he got emotional about it. It all just feels so special.

As Kendell and James slowly get closer to us, Josh gives me a quick kiss and runs inside to get drinks for the two of us. The server on the patio is totally overworked and won't make it over to us anytime soon. Not a minute after he goes inside, a new person that I've never seen shows up, and everyone who is with the friends' group is immediately distracted by her. Lara slides over to me quickly and quietly to tell me, "Oh my gosh, that's Katrina."

In all of my excitement and bliss with Josh over the last month, I'd managed to put my half-baked knowledge that his ex could be back in Canopy out of my mind. I compartmentalized to ensure the fear of that potential situation wouldn't ruin what we actually have going on.

Some people have a type. They move from one relationship to the next with slightly different variations of the same personality. Ben's and Josh's personalities aren't *that* different, so I could probably be accused of having a type to some degree. Josh, however, is not one of those people. He's told me enough about his ex-wife, Tessa, for me to know that she and I are very different. And now, with the ex-fiancée standing just across the patio, I realize she is nothing like Tessa *or* me. I truly can't imagine how anyone, maybe even Josh himself, would put into words the type of woman he's looking for. One of those rare "no type" sort of people, I decide.

Her hair is dirty blond and wild. Before even hearing a word from her you can tell that she will not be tamed. A quiet expression of shock ripples down the patio. Everyone is surprised to see her, except for Sunny, who walks over to give her a polite hug. Knowing Sunny, she did some digging after we chatted and found out that Lenny's dubious gossip was actually true. She's the only one prepared to meet the moment.

I think of Josh inside at the bar, completely unaware of what he's about to walk into. I asked about her a few weeks ago and he shrugged. She had long since fallen away as even a distant topic of conversation that you pull out when nothing else much is going on to talk about. Yet here she is.

I have learned a lot about the human condition over the last year. Life, death, and everything in between. But if there is one subject I've learned about more than any other, it's love. At the end of the day, love is the thing that people talk to me about the most. They tell me how much they miss someone they loved. How they found new love. Love, love, love.

All of my accidental research over the last year has made plain what is in front of me when Josh emerges through the doors with a drink in each hand. My eyes dart from him to her, and I can see it in her expression. The longing, the look. She's here for a reason, and that reason is the man I'm falling in love with.

The pessimist in me is prepared to look back at him and realize in an instant that this romantic situation of ours is done. Instead, he raises an eyebrow and casually walks over to hand me my drink.

"That is definitely unexpected," he says to the rest of the table, which now includes James, Kendell, and me. He is, it seems, completely and genuinely unperturbed by her presence. He hands me my drink and pulls me in for a kiss. I look over at James and see a relieved smile on his face.

It only takes a few minutes for Katrina to walk over to our table.

James and Kendell are on the side closest to her, so she offers them hugs, which they politely accept. She says, "Hey, Josh," with a coy smile and then reaches her hand out to me.

"You must be Gracie," she says, as though she's been thoroughly briefed on me and my situation with Josh. Congrats to her, because I don't think Josh or I have been fully briefed.

She starts up small talk with Kendell and James, asking about the kids and expressing disbelief at how old they are now. She peppers James with questions about the local real estate market; her parents are thinking of selling their house. At some point in that discussion, she very obviously pulls her left hand up to her ear to show off an empty ring finger. After not much time, the surface-level conversations are exhausted, and I expect her to kindly excuse herself and go talk to other people. But she stays and turns toward Josh and me.

He wraps his arm tighter around my waist. It dawns on me that I've never had to deal with a situation like this before. Ben and I met when I was eighteen and he was twenty. The only exes we had were high school sweethearts who didn't amount to much. Josh has an actual romantic history as an adult—an ex-wife and a former fiancée. For all I know, there are other important past girlfriends in his life we haven't even talked about. This is new territory for me.

"Josh, I heard a rumor that you were taking a break from work. That can't be true," she says in a sarcastic tone.

"I'm on a short sabbatical," he responds, not inclined to give more detail.

"What's that even mean?" she pushes back.

"It means that I'm taking a few months off to take it easy and try to figure out how to run my company in a way that doesn't kill me," he responds in a tone that telegraphs this is not really her business to ask about.

They share some icy back-and-forth while she digs for details about his company and the house he ended up building for himself.

"He was supposed to build a house for us," she says, turning to me, assuming I'm the only one who doesn't already possess this information. "But typical Josh, he prioritized doing work for everyone else first, and our little patch of land stayed empty. I always thought that was a little selfish."

"So that we're all clear, I sold that land and built somewhere else," he chimes in.

"Let me guess—one of those horrific A-frames you always wanted?" she says snidely.

She keeps trying to throw insults glazed in passive aggression at Josh, hoping he'll bite and make a scene, but he doesn't do it. The directness of their conversation style is a bit much, even for me. She's trying to engage in a playful, but vaguely hostile, dynamic that they clearly used to have but that no longer appears to exist.

"What brings you back to town?" I ask her in a cheery voice, trying to break the frost that has descended. After all, I'm the only one at this table who's not a part of this clearly messy history.

"I'm visiting my parents, trying to convince them to move out to California with me," she starts. "And since I'm here for a few days, I thought, Why not come see some of the old crew for the first time in a few years? I've been married and divorced since I last saw y'all."

"Married? Divorced?" Kendell asks without really asking. Things like this don't typically fly under the radar of the small-town rumor mill.

"Yeah, the guy I, um . . ." she says, clearly trying to decide whether to continue. "Well, it's all water under the bridge now, so I might as well be out with it. The guy I left Josh for—his name is Will, and it was a blast while it lasted, but we divorced a few months ago. I have, however, stayed in love with California, so that's the upside."

I squeeze Josh's hand below the table. It doesn't matter that years have passed or that he's over her. Learning something like this simply sucks on a million levels. Plus, she's just dropped it in front of me, his brother, and his sister-in-law. That doesn't happen by accident.

I realize that I do not like the idea of her and Josh together. I remember the first few months of Ben's time in business school when a classmate invited us on a double date with his wife. Nice people, I'm sure, but they were loud and wild and their couple energy was just like this: frantic. Ben had to make excuses when future invites came. Their whole vibe just didn't work for me. But here it is again, and I'm realizing this is what Josh and she were like together the entire time they were a couple. What on earth was the appeal? This serious and aggressive dialogue does not fit him at all.

Katrina finally excuses herself with an expression of mild disappointment, and I watch as Josh, James, and Kendell raise their eyebrows and share looks that quietly say *WTF?* That's where it ends, though. There are no whispers or further discussions. The table has silently decided not to let what was clearly a fishing expedition for attention yield the intended result.

Instead, everyone is happy to find a new topic. Kendell and James want the inside scoop on my interview tomorrow with Maisy.

"Are you nervous?" Kendell asks, her eyes glowing with excitement.

"Babe, you don't ask someone if they're nervous," James jumps in. "It will only make her feel nervous if she wasn't already." Their spouse banter makes us all laugh. Mostly because he's not entirely wrong.

"I'm embracing my best friend's approach to this: it's a mulligan. A chance to get it right," I tell them. "Don't get me wrong—my stomach is in knots, but I feel so much more prepared this time around."

The truth is I am nervous. I'm also feeling strangely confident about getting on that flight tomorrow and tackling the interview all by myself. Jenny and Josh both offered to come, but this feels like something I need to do on my own. Well, not fully on my own, because Lucia will be there, but close enough.

"I've been hyping her up all week," Josh adds. "What's our motto?"

"It can't be worse than last time," I say with a genuine smile and a big laugh. All of us raise our glasses for a cheers. The entire time Josh doesn't leave my side. He's always there, in the big and small ways.

Then it's Whitney time.

Josh grabs my hand with a smile that looks like it might explode off his face. Last month, we were here, in this exact place, both fighting off feelings for one another. Today, we're here as a couple that has fully given in to them. He pulls me into a tight embrace, and we start to sway.

"Last time we were here I was trying so hard not to have my heart broken," he whispers in my ear. "I thought if I called you my friend enough times that I might start to believe it. This is so much better. I'm just so happy, Gracie."

"All I wanted last time was for you to spin me around and kiss me," I say back. "I wanted you—this—so desperately."

Josh and I do this a lot these days, admitting all of the little moments when we hoped things might evolve into something more and the moments in which we used all of our willpower to hold back. I never expected to be dating again in my forties, and it certainly hasn't been easy, but what I love about Josh is how open he is with me about how he feels now. He doesn't hold back. He just spins me around to the music and then pulls me in for a kiss.

I glance across the bar patio and spot Katrina watching us. Well, watching him, I'm sure. Whatever the real reason was for her coming here tonight, it's clear from the expression on her face that she understands that Josh's heart isn't on the market anymore. It's firmly tied up with mine.

# CHAPTER 27

IT'S A COOL NIGHT, SO WHEN WE GET BACK TO THE HOUSE after our evening out, we decide to sit on the porch swing for a bit. The lightning bugs are floating through the yard and the fresh air feels comfortable in my lungs. Josh and I fall back into an easy conversation about the interview tomorrow with Maisy.

"I wanted to let you play it cool in front of James and Kendell, but tell me the truth—are you nervous?" he asks, grabbing my hand and tangling our fingers together.

"Do I seem nervous?" I ask with a playful grin on my face.

"We've spent a lot of time together this summer, and I feel like I read your emotions pretty well, but I can't *completely* read your mind yet. It's been hard for me to tell."

"Honestly? All week I've been slingshotting between total confidence and tiny flecks of despair," I admit, realizing that in less than twelve hours I'll be on the plane to Nashville. "I've texted with Dr. Lisa a bit, so I know this is a natural way to feel. Jenny has also been giving me lots of straight talk about it. I've definitely needed your relentless positivity in addition to their reality checks, so you've been playing an important role."

I lean in to sweetly nudge his shoulder. His pivot back to early summer-style interview sessions over the last few days has helped so much. I really do feel more prepared than the last time—and it's buoyed my spirit every time he's yelled out "Nailed it!" when I landed on a great answer.

What's also true is that with Maisy, I really don't know what to expect, and I haven't had a free moment to listen to her first two live stream podcast episodes. Going in blind is best, I've decided, since trying to stick to a prepared strategy didn't quite work for me during my previous visit in April.

Last time, I thought that I was fully prepared and knew what to expect . . . and we all know how that ended up. I don't know what I don't know. Predictions are futile. Yes, the stress is beginning to bubble up, but that might be how I feel before anything this big, and I've got to learn to deal with it.

My support system is also ready to jump in because nothing can change the fact that grief is *weird*. Even a perfectly executed "good" interview could crack open my heart in unintended ways. A poorly executed interview could end up being not so bad on the emotional Richter scale.

"Are you sure you don't want me to hop on a plane and come with you?" he asks, completely genuine. This is not something most normal people would offer someone they've only been dating for a month, but even I know that this thing Josh and I have is anything but normal.

"It's tempting, trust me, but Lucia will be there, and it's barely even a full twenty-four hours. You'll hardly notice that I'm gone."

"That, I'm afraid, is entirely untrue," he says, pulling me close for a kiss as a light breeze blows across the porch.

We sit in silence for a few minutes before Josh admits that sitting outside makes him realize all of the outdoor projects that need to be tackled at the house. This man is never *not* wanting to fix something. The way I love wrestling with words and trying to figure out how to convey a complex emotional feeling for my readers—that's Josh with home projects. See a problem, break it into pieces, and solve it.

I like the feeling of being here with him, just quietly existing together. The crickets are chirping, and you can hear the voices drifting softly down from the restaurants on Main Street that are still open. The nights here are so peaceful. Usually.

"Can I be honest with you?" I ask, rising from his chest, where I've had my head resting for the last few minutes, so that I can look him in the eyes.

"Of course."

"I was nervous when Katrina showed up tonight," I say with an embarrassed half smile. "A little while back, Lenny mentioned that she might be back in town, and then Sunny was super cagey when I asked her about it. I should've told you, but there was no way to make it not weird. There's so much history between the two of you, and I didn't want to spoil anything for us. Tonight, everyone seemed on edge having her back, but you were perfectly normal and made me feel entirely safe."

"I'll be honest with you," he says with a laugh. "I have no idea what tonight was all about. It's the first time she's been back in years. I'm sure someone, probably Sunny or James, will give us the gossip in the next few days."

"That stuff she said about you was so harsh. I don't think or believe any of that. I mean, I know you know that. I guess I just wanted to say it out loud."

"Gracie, when you hear people say that you're good for me, they mean it. For years, I had this terrible habit of sort of morphing into the people I dated. It wasn't only Katrina, although it was the worst with her because of how she operates. I've been single on purpose for the last few years to work through it. To figure out who I am when I'm on my own. When I'm with you, I feel completely myself for the first time ever in a relationship," he shares.

*Relationship.* It's the first time either of us have given this thing we have a formal declaration.

"I definitely can't identify anymore with the dynamic she and I had," he continues. "That's the thing about relationships. We're all different people from one to the next. Katrina's idea of who I *am* is stuck at who I *was* nearly five years ago—before I figured my shit out. The last few years changed so much for me. I'm definitely a different guy than the one she knew. I adapted so much of my personality to her. She's got enough personality for ten people."

"I caught on to that. And, still being honest, it's weird for me because I think of you as the guy who fills the room with personality," I say, and I run my fingers up and down his arm. "It's wild to think you were the shrinking violet in the relationship."

"In retrospect, it's obvious to me that she and I had this really unsustainable energy. It comes down to this: you don't know the same Josh that she did," he says, before nonchalantly adding, "Just like I don't know the same Gracie that Ben did."

For reasons I can't explain, that last part sends a sharp pain through my gut. Suddenly, I can't feel the breeze, I can't see the lightning bugs, and time seems to have stopped. My head starts to throb as he continues in the background. I'm having a physical reaction to this conversation, and I don't know why.

"The one piece of your writing that I have read is the first essay. I told you that James sent it to me before we met. I've spent all summer trying to reconcile the person you described in that essay with the person I've gotten to know. You're not this antisocial person who hates physical touch. You are a kind and open person who loves talking to people. You've made friends in every place you've gone this summer in town. I've watched you hug pretty much everyone. You're different now, Gracie. The version of you that exists now is different."

He says all of this to me like I'm supposed to take it as a compliment—like he's figured out some previously hidden Gracie that no one else was smart enough to uncover.

A new version of me? No. I'm me. *The same me.* I'm the same person. I have to be. Because if I'm not the same person that Ben knew, that means a piece of him is gone, too. Ben and Gracie. That's the me that my friends know. My family knows. My kids know. I have to be the old me. People can claim I'm new or different, but that doesn't make it true. My eyes are welling up, and I don't know what to say or do.

"You're wrong," I finally blurt out without really thinking. "I'm not like you."

"What?" he says, completely confused by my change in tone and posture.

"I'm still the same person as before. The same me that Ben knew. Maybe you change all the time, but I'm still me," I say with breath as thick as molasses. Every word is a struggle.

"Gracie, I don't know what I said that made you so upset—"

"You insinuate that somehow I'm this magical new person. Like, if Ben walked up these steps right now, he wouldn't recognize me."

I see a look of recognition come over his face, but all it tells me is that he knows why I'm mad and not that he's in any way sorry for what he said.

"Can we just pretend that the last minute never happened?" he asks. "All I was trying to say is that I really like you and that we're both the best versions of ourselves around one another. I like the Gracie that I've gotten to know and learned to—"

"There is no special version of me, Josh. I'm just me. You could never understand why even the idea of this conversation is hard for me," I interrupt, using a tone that I instantly regret.

"I just told you in, like, five different ways that I like everything about you, and this is your reaction? You think you're the only one who's ever had something shitty happen to them, Gracie?"

"You've never experienced anything like this."

"Gracie, I was practically left at the altar by the woman you met tonight. I'm over it now, but I was a train wreck for *years*. I took all of that anger and frustration out by working to the point that I almost killed myself from exhaustion. Death isn't the only sad thing that happens to people. You know that. There are lots of ways to lose people."

"Yeah, well, death happened to me, and I survived it. But it didn't change me. I'm not some entirely new person now," I say, knowing how petulant and ridiculous I sound, but I'm fully committed to these feelings that are trying to overwhelm me.

"You need to stop pretending, Gracie. You aren't the same person. You're not. Jesus, every time someone sees you on a video call or visits, they freaking tell you that. They straight up tell you that you're different since you've been *here*. Why am I the bad guy?"

"Because you want to believe that *you* changed me, Josh," I say, looking him square in the eyes. "Like, you rescued me or some stupid shit like that."

"That's not what I think," he says in a quiet tone, shaking his head and attempting to somehow right the situation.

"Well, that's what you're acting like," I say, standing up. "I think you should go home."

"Gracie, please let's just go inside and figure this out," he suggests, presenting the option that I know is right and reasonable.

"This isn't real life, Josh," I yell, raising my voice and surprising us both. Despite all of Felicity's guidance and all of the thought that I've put into how to merge myself into something new, I've decided to take the path of least resistance. The easy off-ramp. I'm making summer the excuse.

"Can we please go inside?" he asks again, and I agree because the last thing I want is a reputation as a yeller in a small town.

As soon as the door closes, he hits me with a question.

"What do you mean this isn't real life?" he asks, hurt spread across his face. "This isn't real for you?"

"The things I feel for you are real," I say, rambling. "But this summer isn't real life, because my life doesn't look like this. I don't spend the morning in bed or write for hours in coffee shops or jump around antique stores looking for a perfect new desk. This is all make-believe. My real life is a fucking grind, Josh. This new version of me that you think you know . . . she's a fantasy."

"This isn't my normal life, either, Gracie," he responds, his own voice annoyed and rising. "I don't work twenty hours a week or take lunch breaks or get to build shit anymore. My normal life is a grind, too. Are you suggesting that maybe that's the only reason why this works?"

"It works for the summer, Josh. It works for the couple of months we find ourselves in these exact conditions," I tell him. "Where do we even go from here?"

"We're adults, Gracie," he tells me. "I just assumed we'd figure it out."

Ben and I rarely fought, but when we did, both of us refused to give up or give in. Both stubborn to our core. I realize in this moment that even this new version of me that everyone keeps claiming exists still won't let things go without a fight. I dig in.

"I don't even live here, Josh. I live three hundred miles away," I press on. "What happens the first time we're supposed to see each other for a weekend and my childcare cancels on me? The first time you've got an important event and one of the kids gets sick? When the book tour next spring eats into the few precious weeks of potential 'us time' we have? What happens as our parents get older and need us to be in all of these different places? What happens?"

"I don't know, and maybe it will be hard," he says with a changed, worried expression. "But, Gracie, I'm crazy about you."

"That's the thing, Josh," I say, making eye contact and immediately fighting the urge to fall into him for a hug. "I'm so tired of things being hard. You probably are, too."

"The hardest thing *for me* is that all this happiness that I feel is the result of you losing the love of your life," he says, his voice cracking with those last few words. "And knowing I would give away everything we have if there were a way to let you go back to your old life—to who you were before—if it meant you were happy again."

"That's not how life works," I say, feeling inexplicable ire rising in response to one of the most truly moving things anyone has ever said to me. My instant regret causes my head to throb and my leg to shake.

"I know," he responds. "Which is why I thought you might settle for a chance to be happy with me."

*Settle.* It's a ludicrous thought because every inch of me thinks it's impossible that he would ultimately settle for the emotional dumpster fire that *I am*. It doesn't matter, though, because I'm still in this for the win, not for the reasonable adult conversation.

"Listen, I need to be up at, like, five a.m. for this flight, and I just can't do this tonight," I say back, now unable to look him in the eye.

"Gracie, please. I don't want to leave you angry."

"I just need the night to myself to think about things."

"Things?"

"Us."

"Gracie, please tell me you don't mean that."

"Just give me a day or two, Josh—please."

With that, he does exactly what I've asked and opens the door and walks back down the path to his truck instead of doing what I really want him to do—hug me while I cry. But I do—cry. For the next hour, I'm inconsolable, and I don't know who the tears are for: Ben, Josh, or me. Maybe all of us? My leg is shaking, but so is the rest of my body.

In the span of a few minutes, I've managed to ruin—or, best-case scenario, taint—the only thing besides my kids that has brought me sustained joy over the last year. This whole time, I was worried about Katrina swooping in to take Josh from me, but she didn't have to take anything. I lost it for myself by not being able to figure out who I am. And what I want. What I need.

"Josh deserves better than me," I say to no one but myself. I put my head on my pillow and somehow fall asleep.

# CHAPTER 28

A FEW DAYS AGO, I CALLED DR. LISA AND ASKED HER TO listen to the live stream of the podcast. If I do end up "going deep" in any unexpected ways, a debrief and maybe even a double session will be required, so why not skip the part where I download what happened? It's better if she just listens to it live and charges me for her time. I look down at my phone as I take my seat and text her a reminder.

> Don't forget. 1 p.m. CST today.

She immediately gives the text a thumbs-up, and I swipe my phone into airplane mode. Maybe it's the stress of the last day or the last year, but I angle my head against the plane window, and the next thing I know, we're landing in Nashville. As if I wasn't disoriented enough, the feeling of having traveled nearly 250 miles without realizing it startles me.

As I reach the arrivals hallway, I see a driver is waiting with my name on a sign. Beside him stands Lucia, my publicist. She got to

Nashville yesterday to meet with another client and insisted on ride-sharing to the airport to greet me. This is only the second time we've met in person, and we greet one another with a great big hug.

Maisy is hosting the podcast sessions from a new small recording studio she had built at her TV show headquarters downtown. I have to give her credit: the concept of the podcast—called *Same Stories*—is actually quite clever. She pairs together two people from different industries, experiences, or walks of life who have experienced a common event or feeling. Unsurprisingly, the theme of today's podcast is grief.

On the forty-five-minute journey to the studio, Lucia briefs me on my interview partner for the day. I've been paired with Darrell Jenkins, a former professional football player in his late twenties who had his career ended earlier last year in the playoffs by a serious spinal injury. One day, he was one of the best running backs of his generation, and the next, he was lucky to be alive. Even luckier to be able to walk. Football, however, is done. Darrell and I both share really shitty canon events for our superhero origin stories, that's for sure. Broken bodies and broken hearts aren't all that different, I know instinctively.

"Is this for real?" I say, staring at the briefing sheet she's just given me when I should be listening to her. The second bulleted item says that we're going to watch alongside Darrell as he views the video of his injury for the first time ever. *Damn*, I think.

"It's going to be intense," Lucia says, basically reading my mind. "That's the type of raw honesty and emotion that Maisy is looking for. If listeners aren't bawling their eyes out by the end of your hour together, we won't consider it a success."

We review the list of potential questions that Maisy's team sent over and go through some preplanned answers, but Lucia is clearly phoning it in. She looks me straight in the eyes and gets serious.

"I mean, it's good we're reviewing this because it may help, but she's going to be on the hunt for 'big feels,' as she calls them. Be prepared for Maisy to go off script from the very beginning."

"I know. Remember—I agreed to this. I've thought about some controversial parenting-through-grief sort of things I can talk about, and I can share some really crazy things people said to me after Ben died," I begin. "Did I ever tell you one of his pickleball buddies offered to 'keep me company'? Ew."

"Major ick," Lucia says, clearly only to humor me. "But I'm not sure Maisy wants ick or funny. She wants emotions, Gracie, so try not to only do your making-grief-funny thing, okay?"

I nod. I feel so fragile after last night with Josh. The fear of today's group therapy session with Darrell and Maisy creeps in. *Breathe*, I tell myself, willing my stress levels to stay down and for my tics and anxiety to keep it cool.

Lucia doesn't miss a beat and continues on with suggestions for how to weave in as many references to the column and memoir as possible. She also recommends how to casually mention that I'm soon launching a newsletter (even though it's not totally official). When all of our business talk is wrapped and with just a few minutes until we arrive at the studio, Lucia asks how the summer is going.

"We don't have enough time left in this car for me to share what this summer has been like—those are definitely big feels for another day," I say with a half-hearted smile. The last twelve hours have made my heart raw, and I'm bone-tired. "The one piece of news I will share is that I will certainly be turning in my finished manuscript by this time next week."

"Well, no matter what else has happened, and I won't pry, just please take a few moments to be proud of yourself for finishing the memoir. I'm proud of you for all you've done and all that is yet to come."

The car pulls into the studio lot, and immediately I get flashbacks of my last trip here a few months ago. I was so nervous and overwhelmed. While I had done a few local-market TV appearances, my time on *The Maisy Show* was my first extended on-camera interview. It was hard talking about Ben with a national audience for the first time. And now, if things don't go well, I certainly can't call Josh for his counsel. Not after yesterday. I'm on my own.

I try to put that all out of my mind as we walk in and are escorted to the same dressing room that I used back in early May. I set my small overnight bag on the floor and use the next half hour to freshen up. Although this is a podcast interview, I try to channel my inner Felicity and make it look like I didn't just get off a plane.

A few minutes before we're due in the studio, Darrell Jenkins pops his head into my room. He's tall, with smooth dark skin and a warm, welcoming smile. He holds out his hand to shake mine.

"Gracie, it's really nice to meet you. I'm Darrell," he says.

"Darrell, it's nice to meet you, too. We get to survive Maisy together today, don't we?" I say back with a tentative smile.

"I hope we do. Did you listen to the one she did with those two activists yesterday? It made me want to crawl into a hole and hide. Or at least cancel for today. We are definitely not getting the touchy-feely daytime host experience."

"Yesterday was a wild day for me, and I did not listen to it," I say, turning to point at Lucia and add, "She's probably glad I missed it; otherwise, I would've probably tried to cancel."

"My advice is that we stay strong and work as a team," he says in a determined tone, "and stop listening to our publicists."

This makes all three of us laugh. Darrell has a good, friendly energy. I'm instantly happy we're in this together. On cue, a production assistant comes to the door and tells us it's time to get things rolling.

"Are you really going to watch the video?" I quietly whisper to him as we walk down the hallway.

"I am. I think it's time, and I needed an excuse to face my fears," he says, taking a long deep breath, before adding with a forced joviality, "Don't get me wrong—I'm freaking out about it, but it's time. What about you? What suffering are they confronting you with today?"

"Don't know yet," I tell him. "I'm sure Maisy will surprise me with something good."

I take my own deep breath, say a quiet prayer, and head to the cozy studio wondering if I will face any fears—and whatever it is that I seem to be running from.

---

THE FIRST FIVE minutes of the podcast go smoothly. Maisy introduces us and throws a few softball questions our way to warm us both up. She calls these her "popcorn questions" because of the quick back-and-forth they allow for. I feel a knot in my stomach when two of the questions are ones that Josh recently asked me. Thanks to him, my answers are there, perfect and ready to go.

The podcast honeymoon, however, ends when Maisy gets to the meat of today's show.

"The theme of today's episode is grief," Maisy begins, signaling that this is the start of the real stuff. "You're both here because of traumatic and catastrophic events you experienced that resulted in significant changes to your life. Darrell, let's start with you. The clip of your injury went viral—watched over seventy-five million times and still climbing—but I read recently that you've never watched it yourself."

"That's true. I just haven't felt ready to do so," he says, nodding his head. "I've been avoiding it for some time. An act of self-preservation, I think."

"Are you up for watching it for the first time with us?" Maisy asks, already knowing the answer.

The clip starts playing on a big screen across from the table we're sitting at. Darrell sits back and takes a deep breath. The clip is difficult to watch, even though I've seen it once before. The hit Darrell takes is the result of a confluence of small decisions and movements that everyone on the field makes. Everyone is trying to win; no one is trying to literally almost kill someone else. The hit is swift and hard. He collapses like a bag of bricks. And then there is nothing. No movement, no thumbs-up. Just Darrell, lying flat, and the players around him manically waving for help.

Darrell is initially sitting with his hands clasped together, but as the clip goes on, he starts to pick at his cuticles and crack his knuckles. A nervous tic of sorts. It's good to know I'm not alone.

Maisy has impeccable timing, so she doesn't let the clip play too long. If memory serves, it will take another minute for the ambulance to get on the field and a handful more to cart him off. The hit itself is the main event, though.

Maisy gracefully presses him with questions about why he waited so long to watch the video and what it means for him to see it now. His family and friends told him about the video and even offered to watch it with him, but he couldn't work up the courage. He could see the trauma on their faces, and that was enough for him. A year later, he was finally strong enough to do it here with us, he explained.

"Sometimes it's easier to do the hard stuff with strangers," he says, echoing what I've learned about grief over the last year. "Of course, with the knowledge that the people who love you are behind the scenes cheering you on."

As Darrell talks, it dawns on me that today's podcast episode isn't just about grief. Turns out it's about the *avoidance* of grief. Maisy's line of questioning with Darrell makes this clear. This is a much more specific niche of the grief world than what I've been peddling.

Darrell has been the focus for a solid fifteen minutes, so I know my time is coming soon. Maisy has allowed me to interject with a few questions of my own for Darrell, giving me time to engage while also having a private conversation with myself about how the hell I'm going to answer questions that she might have. The pivot back to me happens when I'm staring at the studio wall, trying to remember why I agreed to this strange torture.

"Gracie, we're here to talk about grief—you are the queen of grief, after all—but what I find most curious about you and Darrell is how you both avoided engaging with the very moment that changed your life. We've just watched a video of Darrell's injury, but there doesn't seem to be any record or published essay on Ben's death. Perhaps you could talk us through that and the reason for keeping it a secret?"

I start to drop my canned line about privacy, but I can tell she's preparing follow-ups that will render my practiced lines worthless. A quick glance to the control studio, where both of our publicists are posted, delivers a look from Lucia that borders on disappointment. *Go deep*, she mouths.

I can control this, or Maisy can. I can own how this story gets told, or someone else can. Maybe it's the exhaustion, the sadness, or the desperate need for some release, but I have the catalyst I need to do it. I'm going to go deep—so I dive in with reckless abandon.

"Maisy, do you want to know why I don't want to talk about Ben's death? Ben was lively and fun and handsome and so full of life. He had these beautiful blue eyes that could see right into my soul. He was my everything for over twenty years, and then suddenly he was a lifeless body on a hospital bed full of tubes. Gray skin, closed eyes. My Ben was gone. I didn't get to say goodbye to *him*. Not really. I don't want to talk about his death because all it brings to mind is a corpse that can't hug me or love me. That body is the last memory I have in my mind of the man that I loved."

"Gracie, that's so hard," she says with genuine care and emotion in her eyes. "I imagine it takes some serious mental energy to keep something like that inside."

"It has been a struggle. I guess that I don't want anyone—my friends, my readers, and certainly not our kids—to think of Ben in the context of his death. I want everyone to imagine the person that I miss, that I loved, that I sometimes make fun of in my essays for silly little things. It feels so much truer to who he was. To who we were."

"I can imagine that you feel very responsible for his legacy," she says, before leaning forward and pressing again for the answer that I have yet to give. "The secret still seems to be *the how*, Gracie. Would it hurt his legacy for us to know? Is that why you keep it private?"

She thinks *how* he died is the secret.

"What? That's not a secret. He had a heart attack. He had a heart attack at forty-two years old. The secret, Maisy, isn't how Ben died," I say with hot, soft tears now streaming down my face. "The big secret that I've carried for the last year is that I'm relieved that I wasn't there when it happened. I'm glad that he was out drinking with his friend Drew. I'm glad I had a business dinner. Any other night we all would've been at home, as a family. When I try to imagine that happening around the dinner table or while he was kicking the soccer ball with my daughter or reading comics with my son, it's just too much. Our house would've never felt the same again. So, my big secret—the real reason that I don't want to share the particulars—is because the overwhelming sense that I have when I think of it happening the way that it did is *relief*. I've come to terms with the fact that he was always going to die at 7:05 on that Tuesday night. Nothing I could have done would have prevented his death, and I certainly couldn't have saved him. So, the thing I feel is relief that I wasn't there."

There is a long pause in the studio. I look over at Darrell, and he has his right hand covering the lower part of his face. Tears are welling in his eyes. Maisy is looking at me with the same expression that so many people had at the memorial service. It says, without reservation, *I'm so glad this didn't happen to me.*

I've told nobody this. Not my parents or Jenny, Dr. Lisa or Josh. This has been my deepest secret for over a year, and I've just shared it with everyone. This is what I've been running from, avoiding, shielding myself from for over a year. I expect to feel the shake, but it doesn't materialize. Maybe, just maybe, this is what I've been holding in all along. Afraid to blurt this out.

"Part of me thinks it was a strange last gift from Ben to us that it happened the way it did," I add, the one to break the few seconds of silence that felt like eternity. "It seems really selfish to feel this way, but I'm not sure I would've survived being there when it happened, and I think he knew it. I don't think I'm built for that, because I've barely made it through all of this. Every essay you've read, every interview I've given... it's all just been me barely hanging on."

"That's grief, though, isn't it?" Darrell chimes in. "Deciding every day what you have the capacity to handle and what you don't and realizing it's okay—really, truly okay—to put something off for another day if it means getting through this one."

"That's absolutely right," Maisy says. "Four months before you lost Ben, I lost my mom. The way you wrote about your grief allowed me to deal with things in my life. It didn't matter that I didn't know everything you were going through. The things you did share were deeply meaningful to me and to so many others."

Maisy asks a few more questions, giving me time to acclimate to the fact that I've just shared a huge secret. She then adeptly steers the conversation away from the shock and awe of my and Darrell's respective big moments and tenderly walks through the different stages of grief we've experienced.

In the final minutes of the podcast, when it's my turn to share, I embrace the spirit of today and dive right back into the deep end.

"I've been in the denial stage, I think, since day one," I say. "The trouble is that for a long time, I've been focused on one death, one loss, but in reality, what I've actually experienced is something far different. I got married when I was twenty-three. When you get married that young, when you love your partner that deeply, you can't help but envision a world where you're celebrating a sixtieth anniversary surrounded by your kids, grandkids, and a lifetime of friends. Darrell told us earlier that he started playing football when he was seven. Seven! This man built every day of his adolescent and adult life around this game. And the entire time, he had that one goal, that one vision—Super Bowl MVP—driving his life. He was so close."

"Are you saying it's more than just one thing you're grieving?" she asks.

"Yes. Look, I'm grieving Ben. So much," I say, my voice still a little shaky from earlier. "And, yes, Darrell is mourning that one moment and the injury. But you have to understand that it's like the timeline we saw down the road was snipped. Cut off. I will never have a twentieth wedding anniversary with Ben, let alone a sixtieth one. Darrell will never step foot on a field to play again. At least not in uniform. We're grieving the future we were supposed to have. Meant to have. We're grieving the end of one life and trying to figure out how the hell we start a new one. A new one we never expected to have. One we never asked for. And we need a new version of ourselves to do that."

"Where do you go from here? How do you reorient yourself after a loss that sets your life on a different path?" she asks Darrell. He gives a beautiful answer about how he wakes up most days feeling nothing but possibility and how he's not rushing to figure out the next thing. He's also giving himself permission to have bad days, because bad days still do happen. Then Maisy asks me the same question.

"First and foremost, I want grieving people to know it's okay to feel this way," I share. "To feel deeply sad and loudly mad and maybe even a little self-centered. Mourning the end of one life is hard. And it's hard because we don't acknowledge that's what it is—because perhaps the enormity of it would pull us to depths that could be hard to swim out of. In my case, it's an admission that Ben is gone forever and that I will never, ever be the same person again as a result. But I'm not sure it's possible to mourn fully without acknowledging that reality at some point."

"When did you have that aha moment, Gracie?" she asks, staring at me, hopeful for the answer that I know is the honest one.

"Just now."

# CHAPTER 29

Back in the dressing room, I collapse into the lush armchair and curl into a ball. I ask Lucia and the poor production assistant to give me ten minutes alone. I glance at my phone—seventy-five texts and fifteen missed calls. Just as I'm about to toss the phone into my bag, I notice the most recent text message, from Drew. Intrigued, I tap to see the full note.

> Gracie, thank you for sharing that. I've spent the last year feeling sad for Ben that he was stuck with me at the end instead of you. It's been really hard for me to process. Knowing that I relieved you of a burden instead of depriving you of a privilege means more than I can possibly put into words. God, I miss him. He would be so proud of you. Sorry to send such a long message, but I wanted you to know.—Drew

It's heartbreaking to think about the secrets we all keep hidden within ourselves, fearful of the cascade of emotions that they could cause. We end up avoiding the very conversations that could make things better for all of us.

If I had just been honest with myself months ago, I could've avoided this nightmare and kept Drew from constantly reliving his. With this knowledge in my mind, for the second time today, I choose to confront something head on that I've done my best to avoid: the day Ben died.

THE TRUTH IS that Ben was exhausted in the lead-up to our trip to Canopy after we bought the house. The color in his face wasn't quite right, and he complained once (but never again so he wouldn't worry me) that his bike ride one morning had been particularly tough. I wondered if he might have had a bug that gave him weird symptoms—the sorts of things that a fortysomething brushes off because the reality hasn't quite hit yet that you don't have the resiliency or body of a twentysomething. He told me not to worry; work was busy, and he was just tired. I took his word for it.

The other truth is that while Ben was telling me he was fine, fluid was slowly building up around his heart. His bike rides were hard because his heart was slowly drowning.

He was out with Drew when it happened. They were standing at an outdoor beer garden, catching up after a few weeks apart. Talking about college basketball, Drew would later tell me.

"I feel weird," Ben said to no one in particular. And collapsed.

Chapel Hill is a place where at any given moment, you're standing by a number of very smart people. Scholars, lawyers, business leaders, and, yes, as it was that day, a renowned heart surgeon.

I've never actually been on a flight where an attendant came over the intercom and asked, "Are there any doctors on board?" I imagine a doctor in that situation taking a deep breath and thinking, *I just want a break*, as she stands up and says, "I'm a doctor," instead of planning a fast-pass strategy with her eight-year-old on their way to Orlando.

I wonder if that day, the doctor, drinking his beer and trying to catch up with his own friends, thought to himself, *Is this guy really having a coronary on my night off?*

What I do know is that within a few seconds of falling down onto the ground, Ben was surrounded by one heart surgeon, a physician's assistant, and his best friend, a former EMT. If the odds were ever in someone's favor, they were in his right then.

I imagine a world where the odds do go in Ben's direction. The surgeon performs some life-saving techniques right there on the patio of the beer garden. The ambulance whisks him to the hospital just five minutes away, where he is intubated but alive. When I arrive an hour later, it's scary, but I still get good news from the doctor. "He's going to make it," the doctor would say to me. The hero's journey that Ben deserved—nearly losing it all and clawing his way back to the land of the living.

But that's not how things work. That's not the story I get. Not in this life.

Instead, the doctor was yelling at Drew to wake him from the shock that momentarily took over after watching Ben fall. The doctor had seen this too many times before. *Call 911.*

I arrived at the hospital forty minutes later, having raced from the business dinner in Raleigh. The kids were with a babysitter, thank God. Drew heard my voice and ran into the hallway to intercept me.

*He's in there, Gracie, but really, he's gone.* Brain-dead.

My Ben was gone. His body was alive only so I could say my goodbyes. *Should I get the kids? Should I call his parents? What the hell do I do?*

A chair was pulled beside Ben's bed. I sat. I saw tubes and heard beeps. So much was happening. I closed my eyes and leaned down to Ben's ear.

"Why now, Ben? This can't be how our story is supposed to end. This wasn't the plan."

---

IT'S NOT THE story I want to share. It's not the way I want the world to meet Ben in my book. It's not anything that I ever imagined for myself. But nothing good has come of me trying to keep this story—or the way it makes me feel—locked inside of me. On the flight home from Nashville, I will write the prologue for a fourth and final time, and in nine short months, I will share it fully with the world.

A knock on the door makes me raise my head from the back of the chair.

"Come in," I yell.

It's Darrell. "They told me you asked for time alone. I just got done hiding in the bathroom for a bit myself," he says softly.

I stand up to hug him, and then gesture to the two stools by the vanity table. Neither of us quite knows what to say to fill the air. Two hours ago, Darrell was a stranger. Now we've been direct witnesses to big moments in one another's lives.

"I agreed to come on today because I wanted people to know I was better, but also because pro sports are a crapshoot and there are plenty of guys who have had it harder than me. I want those guys to know there can be life after sports. That was really difficult—more so than I thought it would be, if I'm totally honest—but I think in the end we might've helped some people," he says, our glassy eyes locked on each other.

"Me too," I say. "I want to move forward so badly. Not to move on from Ben, but to allow myself to have fullness in my life again. Leaving things behind is painful, though."

"Gracie, it's not fair what's happened to you and me," Darrell says. "But what we had was real and good while it lasted. You're not you without Ben, and I'm not me without football. But maybe we don't leave those experiences and people behind. Maybe we can take it all with us. There's just more for us to discover."

At the end of the show, when Maisy asked where we saw ourselves in a year or two, Darrell answered that he hoped to become a motivational speaker. I know, without question, that he will be fantastic at it.

Me? My answer was that I hoped to still be writing, raising my kids, and maybe, if I was lucky, getting a second chance at love and building a life with someone.

"Can you imagine what it takes to date someone like me?" I asked, laughing, making it almost to the end of the podcast without being self-deprecating, per Lucia's instructions.

"I imagine it takes a strong man," Maisy answered without a hint of humor. "So, can you imagine how wonderful he will end up being when you find him?"

I smiled, thinking, *Yes, in fact—I can imagine that.*

A few minutes after Darrell leaves, there's another knock at the door. Maisy's shiny red locks bounce into the room before the rest of her. She sits on the stool Darrell just left, gently pulling it closer to me without a word. Our proximity feels too intimate. It reminds me of the greenroom with Jenny the last time my life felt on the verge of collapse.

"You're different," she says, looking me square in the eyes. "You're not the same person I interviewed a few months ago."

"No, I'm not," I finally and freely admit when she takes a long pause to study me.

"I never had any doubts that you were a strong woman after all that you'd been through, but there is a fortitude here now . . . a resolve . . . that simply wasn't there before. How'd that happen?"

She could've asked me this while there was a microphone in my face, but she didn't. This is an act of kindness. Now my own curiosity is piqued, and I take time to study *her.* An extended silence grows between us while I look into those green eyes that once scared me. There is a quiet but obvious hunger for information staring back at me.

"Why do you want to know?" I ask bluntly, not fully returning her kindness with my own.

"I really did lose my mom a few months before you lost your husband," she tells me with a slight grimace in response to my brash question. "And the truth is that I can't seem to find my way back to anything close to normal. You seem to have found some measure of equilibrium recently that has completely eluded me. I'm flailing."

Maisy was never trying to be cruel or mean in her questioning. All along she's been trying to find answers. *For herself.* Grief loves to trick us into hiding, give us a false sense of security, and often it makes us wait far too long to ask for help or admit when we feel beyond it completely.

"I stumbled into something very special this summer," I tell her. "Someone, actually. The process of falling in love again has thrown me on and off balance so many times it makes my head spin—and I have struggled."

Here, in this tiny little room, I have just admitted that I love Josh. That I told Maisy before any of my closest friends feels like a joke from the universe—a reminder for me of how quickly we can learn to trust and let go. I continue.

"For the first time since he died, I put myself in Ben's shoes and wondered what *he* would want for me. I had a moment in the studio today when it hit me that Ben wouldn't want me holding on to him so tight that I lose my grasp on everything else that matters. He wouldn't want me losing my balance because of him. I'm sure your mom would want the same for you."

A sweet, sad smile crosses Maisy's face, and she asks if she can tell me about her mom. I nod. At first, she's tentative, and then before either of us knows what's happening, she's overflowing with stories and anecdotes about the most important person in her life.

I've spent all summer talking, telling Josh and anyone who would listen about my life. It's a welcome relief just to fully listen for once. I'm embarrassed I haven't done more of this—simply taking in the stories of those around me. In Maisy's voice, I hear whispers of my own journey. I hear the joy and twinges of sadness that come with remembering someone you love and sharing out loud the stories that capture the beauty of your life together. Thirty minutes pass by quickly, punctuated by tears and laughter from us both.

"Gracie, I need you to know that I never intended for our limited time together in these two interviews to be so full of hurt and trauma," Maisy tells me. "I'd take it all back if I could."

"I wouldn't let you take it back," I assure her, gently resting my hand on her knee. "The last few months of my life have been extraordinary in every wonderful and terrible way possible. No matter what happens, I'm grateful, because without you, I'd still very much be stuck in a really dark place."

"I'm really proud of you. Your personal growth is just brilliant to see," she says, tears still welling in the corners of her eyes. She pulls me in for a generous, honest hug. "It makes me so very hopeful."

"I'm glad to hear it," I say as we break away from our hug. "Because today's interview might be one of the scariest things I've ever done. If it helps just one person—*you*—it was worth it."

"Listen, Gracie," she starts, now holding on to both of my hands. "Next year I'm launching Maisy's Book Club on the show. We're already preselecting, and I really want your memoir to be the selection the month it gets released. I just know it will be perfect for me and my audience."

"I'd be honored," I tell her, taking a deep, relieved breath as I begin to gather my things. "Now, let me go and figure out how to fix some things I've gotten really wrong."

---

LUCIA AND I are sitting at the Starbucks in the public lobby of the north terminal of the airport. Yesterday, after the intensity of the interview, she insisted on buying me a late-afternoon treat and taking me for a manicure, and then she ordered us room service for dinner before I slept for ten hours. This morning, she canceled another engagement to accompany me to the airport. The ultimate act of friendship.

The interview cracked open my spirit in the best way. During dinner, I shared the whole story of my summer in Canopy. It all spilled out, even things I've never admitted to myself before. Now this morning, I'm coming to terms with everything that I said to Josh and all the ways I messed things up two days ago.

"I think I ruined it all. I should've been ready by now, but I wasn't, and I think it's going to make me lose a really wonderful man," I share, holding Lucia's hand, before adding, "Again."

"Gracie, my parents spent seven years in a long-distance relationship before they got married. My mom was in med school and my dad got a job in a different city. I'm the age now that they were in the final years of that arrangement. I couldn't fathom how they made it work, so a little while back I asked my mom what their secret was," she says.

"Something poetic and beautiful, I'm sure," I answer.

"Good people wait and are worth waiting for. He'll be there when you get back. Just be ready to say you're sorry."

With that, she stands to give me a squeeze before I head through security. She reminds me to enjoy submitting my manuscript and the next two "free" weeks. She's cleared the interview calendar.

---

THIRTY MINUTES LATER, and I'm at my gate with just a few minutes to spare before boarding. I sit down and grab my phone to start finally working through my text messages.

"Excuse me, are you Gracie Harris?" the college-age girl across the seating area asks me.

I nod. Two other women nearby—one who looks to be in her

thirties and the other much older—chime in to say, "Oh my goodness, it *is* you!" Before I know what's happening I'm surrounded by a small group of women who have formed a little cocoon around me. Somehow, I'm not overwhelmed with social anxiety.

They take turns telling me how much they loved the interview, even though it must've been hard for me. The college student tells me that the podcast was the first time she ever heard of me—she only started listening to Maisy because she is trying to connect more with her mom, who is a huge Maisy fan. She was googling me in the airport when I showed up.

"I had to look up and down from my phone a few times to convince myself it was you," she tells me. "If you could've seen me yesterday listening to that podcast! Girl, I had mascara running down my face. I think we all did."

When boarding starts, I bring each of them in for a generous hug before we go our separate ways. The interview was hard, but it mattered. It really did. It also might end up being the catalyst for my new life—if I haven't broken it beyond recognition.

# CHAPTER 30

WHEN I TURN THE CORNER ONTO WILSON STREET, I SEE Josh's truck in the driveway. I'm relieved and scared and overwhelmed. As I pull into the driveway, I take a deep breath, steeling myself for the conversation that awaits. I switch off the ignition, leave my bag in the car, and walk up the front path. The stones crunch beneath my shoes.

"I didn't expect you to be here," I say to Josh, barely holding my emotions together.

He rises from the porch swing, not a squeak to be heard. Check.

"I wanted to be here for you when you got back. Please, can we go inside and talk?" he asks, motioning to the door.

I nod and walk toward the door. It's locked. I look at him.

"I didn't want to assume," he says, looking at the ground.

This shatters my heart into a million pieces. I can't believe that I've ruined such a good thing with such a good man—made him doubt that I want him in my home.

Once we're inside, muscle memory guides us to our usual spots at the island. I pull myself onto the stool and turn to look at him. I love him so much it hurts.

"I'm sorry," he says, grabbing my hand. "What I said the other night was insensitive. I thought I was being— No, it doesn't matter what I thought I was doing. I'm sorry that we had that argument and then you had to go and do that interview in Nashville. I feel like the worst person on the planet. All that you've been holding on to is too much for one person."

He's tearing up, and it dawns on me that he's as scared as I am. Scared that the person sitting beside him is going to call it quits. Is going to give up on this good thing. I'm crying now, too. I'm too tired to hold anything back.

"Josh, I just wasn't ready for any of this to happen. You have been the best surprise of my life, but I wasn't prepared for you and what we have between us," I say through sobs. "And the other night I said really terrible things, and I've spent the last two days afraid that I lost you."

He stands up and comes over to me, the realization hitting him that I'm not ready to give up, either. I'm not ending things. He cups my face in his hands and puts his forehead to mine. We stay just like this for a minute. No words.

"I need you. I've never wanted something more than this. It feels like I'm meant to be here, in this house, with you. My own home doesn't feel like it's the right place for me anymore. You are my home, Gracie," he says as we begin to kiss each other delicately through our tears.

"I want this, too," I say, wobbly but standing up so that I can properly embrace him. "It just all feels so unfair to you, Josh. I'm going to be a mess for God knows how long, and we will need to know the answers to some things way too soon. Because I need to have answers for the kids. Or at least some tentative plans."

He looks me deep in the eyes and adds, "Gracie, we can do this. Trust me—I want to know the plans, too. I just want to be the person who gets to check that last to-do on the list."

Check what off which list? He said that like it's supposed to make sense to me, but it doesn't compute. I stare at him with a confused expression, which he registers. He pulls the tattered to-do list out of his back pocket and drops it onto the counter.

"*That* checklist," I say with a deep sigh, conveying that we're now on the same page. "I haven't looked at it *ever*. Ben was in charge of our project-planning list, and ten days later he died. I gave it to you the same way I found it folded in the pocket of his jeans when I cleaned out his closet."

Shock and sadness now cover Josh's face. I've never seen him like this; he's stunned into silence. For months he's had a secret with my dead husband, and I'm about to find out what it is.

"You've really never looked at it?"

"My heart explodes at the most random things, and I knew that if I looked at it, saw his handwriting, and saw all of the things we planned to do to this house, it would break me into a million pieces," I confess. "So, I don't understand what any of this means."

We're both quiet now. After a minute, he clears his throat and breaks the silence.

"Every day, usually multiple times a day, I've unfolded that list and seen the last thing Ben wrote on it," he says in a soft voice, unfolding the piece of paper and placing it on the counter where we both can see it. "It says... *Love Gracie.*"

This breaks whatever bit of self-control I've managed to keep. A flood of sobs escapes me. My hands cover my face, and my knees are so unsteady that I'm seconds from collapse. Instead of falling, I am caught. Josh wraps himself around me.

I am without words. Without the legitimate ability to speak. I feel everything and nothing. I forget where I am, who I'm supposed to be. I'm inside my body and completely separate from it.

I feel myself unspooling, and I know in a deep place that this is the great unravel Dr. Lisa tried to prepare me for. For a minute yesterday, I thought maybe the interview and my great spilling of secrets was the unraveling, but I know better now. It is here and I am gone. It's like all of my grief has been living just below the surface and I've finally given myself permission to let it out. Minutes pass, maybe a lot of minutes, maybe hours. All I can do is fall to pieces.

When the pace of my tears calms slightly, when my body is no longer convulsing, Josh puts his hands on my cheeks again and lifts my head so we can finally see into each other's eyes.

"Truly, all I've ever wanted since the day we met is to be the one who gets to check it off the list," he says, repeating what he's already told me.

I bite my lip and do the ugly-cry thing, gasping for air. Leave it to Ben to leave care instructions for me from the great beyond.

"This is so scary for me," I let out. "It won't be easy. Nothing about this will be easy. It's going to be so, so hard for you. For me. For us."

"I know," he says. "I'm scared, too, but I'm in this. Gracie, all summer I've been fixing up this house, praying that it could be ours together down the road. I cried the night you told me you might sell it, and I hadn't even admitted to myself at that point that I had serious feelings for you. Do you know how crazy that made me feel? I'm so scared that you'll wake up one day and realize you made a terrible mistake."

"That won't happen," I whisper, while staring deeply into his eyes. "I need you."

"I promise that I will work every day to be worthy of a life with you. With your kids," he says, inhaling deeply. "I've never been so sure about anything in my life."

He scoops me up and takes me back to the guest room, which now feels like our bedroom. We taste each other's tears as we fall onto the bed. He runs his strong hands through my hair and down my back, unzipping my dress. I tuck my hands under his shirt and peel it over his head. I have never needed someone more in my life.

There is an otherworldly intensity between us. It is not the forceful intensity of our first night, but a delicate one. I feel not just all of my own emotions, but his, too. Our bodies move together in perfect harmony through deep breaths and moans.

"I love you so much," he says into my ear.

"I love you, too," I say back, staring at him as my world expands and shrinks out of my control.

# CHAPTER 31

OVER THE LAST TWO DAYS, JOSH HAS ONLY LEFT THE house twice—first, to go to his place and grab clothes and toiletries and, second, to grab groceries for us. Otherwise, we've been holed up together in the Craftsman. We talk, make plans, he repairs, I edit my manuscript, and we simply spend time together trying to figure out this new world of ours.

This morning, for the first time ever, I hand him something of mine to read: the prologue for my memoir (Jeannie's version). It was the last thing on the memoir to-do list before jumping into the final pieces of my personal editing process. In the spirit of radical honesty, I don't hold back when I hand the printed pages over to him.

"This is the fourth time I've written these words, and it's been brutal every time," I tell him. "I really don't want it to be how the book starts, but I haven't figured out a better solution yet, and I need to email the manuscript in a few days. Before anyone else reads it, I want you to."

I make myself comfortable on the other side of the sofa while he reads, our legs stretched long and intertwined. He is so engrossed in the pages that he doesn't look up once. I study him in deep appreciation—amazed that this man is mine and that I feel strong enough to share the worst day of my life with him. Yes, everyone will eventually read it, but for a short period of time, the memory—and all of the pain that comes with it—is protected. When he finishes the last page, he takes a deep inhale and looks up at me.

"Gracie, this is devastatingly beautiful," he says, not with sympathy or pity but instead with a mix of compassion and pride. "You are an amazing writer. I can't believe it's taken me so long to experience it for real."

"Thanks. I know it's good, but I can't shake the feeling that it's not right . . . that there is a better way to tell this story."

"Aside from the fact that it shares the worst day of your life—very eloquently, I might add—what is the challenge?" he asks, and I can see the wheels in his brain turning, trying to help me solve this problem.

"Honestly? Exactly what I said on Maisy's podcast. Yes, Ben died, but I hate for it to be the way people are introduced to him. I'm no longer opposed to it being in the book, but it's the wrong first impression. It feels all wrong for who Ben was as a person—a real person—and what he meant to me."

"A lot can happen in a few days, so don't give up hope yet. Is there anyone you can call to try and get inspiration?"

I pause and smile at him. If there is anyone who can help me figure this out, it's her. Plus, she's really owed an update on my summer in Canopy.

"There is actually someone I can call, and I think that's a good idea," I say, crawling over to give him a kiss before I hop off the sofa in search of answers.

---

I PICK UP my cell phone and dial Ben's mom, Cecily. Over the past year, she is the only person who I could truly share my feelings with. My own mom has been wonderful, but Cecily and I both lost a great love of our lives the day Ben died. We usually talk multiple times a week, but the calls have been few and far between this summer. I told her that this would happen with my busy writing schedule. I didn't expect falling in love to be another reason I was so busy.

"Darling, it's so lovely to see you," she exclaims while her image bounces around the screen. I imagine she is attempting to balance her phone against something on her dining table.

"I've missed our conversations so much, Cecily. I'm sorry it's been so long," I say apologetically.

We make small talk for a little while. She shares about the crazy house projects that Ben's dad, Charlie, is attempting to do on his own and how she sneakily calls professionals to swoop in and help. She tells me about my nieces and nephews, including the oldest, who is headed off to college in a month. He's the first kid I've known from birth to college matriculation, and it makes me feel a million years old. I tell her as much.

I share with her all about my conundrum with the prologue, and to my relief, she agrees wholeheartedly with my assessment.

"I truly wish that the first impression your readers have of Ben is one of life and joy," she says, before suggesting a new direction. "Maybe you could tell the story of how you met?"

"That's actually covered in the last chapter of the book, and it works so beautifully in that spot. I don't think I can move it," I say.

"What about the last conversation you had with him?"

"I thought about that," I tell her. "The one that sticks out in my mind is our drive home from Canopy when y'all had the kids for the weekend. I do love the idea of the prologue being a conversation between Ben and me."

"Those are my two suggestions—let life and joy be your guide as you try to figure this out," she adds.

Cecily never lets silence enter a conversation—in person or over the phone. She always has questions or stories. So, when the silence hits after we talk about the prologue, I'm surprised. She stares intently at me, peering over the tops of her cat-eye spectacles.

"What's his name?" she asks, smiling. My shock registers on the video call, and she adds, "Gracie, I always hoped—no, knew—this call would come."

Some people are outgoing and extroverted in a selfish way. They can fill a room but not remember much about the people in it. Cecily is the opposite. She is boisterous and fun but also observant. She always reads your body language and looks you in the eye. Ben got this quality from her and it was something I loved deeply about him. You leave every conversation feeling heard and appreciated. Josh is the same, come to think of it. I shouldn't be surprised that she figured this out.

"His name is Josh," I say with a shaky voice. "And it's all a lot to process."

"Oh, sweetie, start from the beginning. Don't leave out the details," she says with caring eyes and a smile.

For the next thirty minutes, I do exactly that, telling her the story from the very beginning. How Ben and I came to know James, how James introduced me to Josh, the way the summer has unfolded, my creative bursts of genius, the house somehow coming together, the opening of my heart, and my ridiculous attempts to close it right back up again. I paint her a picture of who Josh is so that she can imagine him in her mind's eye.

"He sounds wonderful," she says. "So, what's the real problem here, my girl?"

"It's hard," I explain. I'm crying. "To believe that I am worthy of a second great love. Why me, Cecily? And why so soon after losing Ben? I'm broken and the kids are pretty broken and why is it Josh's job to be here while we fix it all? He deserves something simpler."

I'm a mess again, and I can tell that Cecily is fighting her own emotions. It's also quiet again, making me uncomfortable.

"It's my turn to talk now, sweetheart," she says, breaking the silence and launching into a story that I've never heard before about her first marriage to the father of Ben's oldest brother, Sam. "You've known for a very long time that I was married before Charlie, but the story behind the story isn't one that I've told many people. I met Sam's dad when I was eighteen. I was head over heels in love with that man from the day we met. When he asked me to marry him, I was convinced this was the person I'd be sitting on a porch swing with when I was eighty-five. Of course, it didn't end up that way. I was six months pregnant when he left me for some girl he met on a work trip. I listened to your interview the other day, Gracie—that life you described being snatched away? That was my story, too. Gone in an instant. I had exactly eighteen months of thinking life couldn't get any better.

"Charlie and I had been neighbors since we were little kids. He came home for the holidays that year—his sophomore year at East Carolina—and saw the state of me. Puffy eyes, swollen belly, unceremoniously served divorce papers a few days before Christmas. I thought Charlie was taking pity, judging by the way he stared at me. He had turned into this strikingly handsome guy, and I was a mess.

"It was warm that winter, and I sat out front on my parents' porch swing for a long time, lost in my thoughts. Charlie came over at some point in the midafternoon, and we spent hours talking. It was the happiest I'd been in a long while. His mom gave him a supper warning and we got ready to part ways, but somehow, he worked up the courage to tell me exactly how he felt about me. He'd loved me since we were twelve years old. He had spent most of high school trying to work up the courage to ask me out but could never quite do it. He didn't plan to go to college but went away so he wouldn't have to see me married to someone else. I had been clueless about all of this.

"Then he told me something I didn't think was possible: that he still loved me, deeply, and if I could open my heart to him, he would love me and care for me—and for the baby. I refused to believe it, and that's the whole point of this story, Gracie: I didn't feel worthy of Charlie's love. I didn't feel worthy of God blessing me with another love story—a real love. I didn't feel worthy, period. Charlie had to convince me that I was worthy, and I *still* almost blew it a few times over the years.

"I moved to Greenville to be with Charlie when Sam was only a few months old, and the rest is history, as they say. Forty-seven years and counting. When idiots in town would tell him he was a second choice, he would just brush them off and say, 'Maybe so, but I'm also the final choice.' Charlie has always seen me as worthy of his love.

"Gracie, our Ben was kind and generous and so full of love for you and the kids that sometimes I thought he might burst from it all," Cecily says, tears now rolling down her cheeks. "Our Ben would want nothing more than for you to find love again. Our Ben knows you are worthy of this, Gracie, just like I do and like Charlie knew I was."

*Our Ben.* The first time we visited Ben's parents after getting engaged, Cecily quietly pulled me out onto the patio. She handed me a glass of wine and asked if she could spend a few minutes sharing her philosophy on what makes mother- and daughter-in-law relationships work. By this point, Cecily and I had spent plenty of time together and loved one another. What more could there be to know?

She started off by telling me that she had given this same talk to her three other children by marriage—two other daughters-in-law and one son-in-law. All three of them, like me, adored her.

"The fact of the matter is that *I* have a Ben and *you* have a Ben," she began in a direct tone. "My Ben is the version that a mother sees. My Ben is in my arms as an infant, he's snuggling in the bed as a toddler who is afraid of the dark, he's an outgoing preteen who turns into a sometimes-moody teenager. He's a boisterous young man heading off to college. He is thoughtful but sometimes self-centered. He is caring but sometimes forgetful. He's the baby of the family and all of the things that come with that. He is my Ben. The thing is, Gracie, you have your own version of Ben. I could make guesses as to what that man is like, but it would be clouded by my own judgment. We see our partners in a very different way than their families do—the Ben you've grown with over the last four years isn't the one I know. For the next phase of his life, you will spend more time with him than any other person. We will both watch him grow, hopefully, into a successful professional, a caring husband, and a loving dad. But we will see all of this through our own lenses. Those lenses are different. There is no way around it."

Cecily and Ben shared such a fun-loving, lighthearted approach to life. I remember being caught off guard by how serious the conversation was.

"Gracie, what makes a relationship like ours successful is the ability to see the Venn diagram," she continued. "*My* Ben on one side and *your* Ben on the other. In the middle, the intersection, is *our* Ben. The overlap is where all of the things that we both know and love about Ben exist. It is a shared frame of reference."

Over the years that followed, Cecily and I would share countless conversations about Ben where we would reference *my* and *our*. It was a graceful and ingenious shorthand that allowed us to communicate clearly and without prejudice.

"Our Ben really was incredible, wasn't he?" I say, wiping away tears and glancing at the time. "Gosh, it's four already. Cecily, I don't want to hang up, but there are a few things I need to do to be ready to have the kids back tomorrow."

"Gracie, one more thing before we go," she starts, her voice cracking. "I can't wait to meet him: my future son-in-law."

"Will he get the Venn diagram speech?" I ask through my tears.

"Of course, sweetie, but please don't tell him about it in advance," she says. "Family secret."

---

THE EVENING WITH Josh is beautiful and full of nervousness. We don't know the next time he'll spend the night at the house, the next time we'll fall asleep tangled together or wake up next to each other in bed.

By noon tomorrow, the kids will be home. I will overflow with emotions once again and insist on hugging and snuggling until they beg me to stop. There is so much to show them in the house and so much to hear about their summer that their few, brief letters from camp couldn't possibly explain. I need time with them, and they need time with me. This means, for the first time this summer, that Josh and I will really need to spend time apart.

I kept my promise to Ava. Two weeks ago, I sent her a letter at camp to give her some basic details—so much has happened since then, but somehow everything I told her is thankfully still the truth.

*You were right about Josh*, I wrote, sketching the eye-roll emoji by hand, knowing that she would find it hilarious. I was honest with her that I had big feelings and didn't know exactly where we would go from here. That's all I really could share at that point. I included the photo of us with James and Kendell.

A few days later, I got back a postcard with a sketch on the blank side—a kawaii drawing of a panda with a speech bubble that only said *Squee, I can't wait to hear about it!* with a hundred little hearts.

I know she is happy for me and probably has a million questions—

Benji, too. It's just that I'm certain they will need time just the three of us before they are ready to give their hearts over to someone else. Thanks to an aggressive amount of texting with Jenny over the last few days, I'm letting myself sit in the emotional complexity of the moment without judging myself as a mom or a romantic partner. It will be challenging; it will be okay. This is all possible.

"Please take all the time with the kids that you need," he tells me as we lie in bed, trying desperately to stay awake. "I don't care if you go quiet for weeks and you're back in Chapel Hill before it makes sense to call me. I will be here, and I don't need you to rush."

He is telling me the truth, and I'm letting myself believe that it will be fine because this is what I know for sure: what Josh and I have is real. It is right. And good people wait and are worth waiting for.

# CHAPTER 32

WHEN JOSH'S ALARM GOES OFF AT SEVEN, I PULL HIM IN close and whisper that it can't possibly be morning yet. I think he's still deep asleep, but in a swift motion, he reaches his arm to the side table to silence the beeping and then rolls over on top of me. It all happens so fast that it makes me giggle.

We didn't bother putting on clothes last night, so things are obvious and easy. There is no way to hide intentions in our bed this morning. I put one hand behind his neck and run the other down his chest. The feel of him sends a shiver through my body, and it doesn't take long before we are connected again. I know it won't take much time for either of us to reach our moment, so I desperately try to enjoy every second of this, not knowing when I might be able to feel this way again. He rolls me on top and I rock my hips and kiss his neck. In mere minutes that go by too quickly, we are done.

"What's that smile all about?" he asks me while running his hands through my hair.

"I realized last night that I only know you and Canopy in the summertime. I'm looking forward to seeing you both in all seasons," I say, imagining Josh in a cozy sweater or thermal shirt.

"Fall is my favorite by a mile," he says. "Winter is gray and wet but beautiful. Spring is great except for my allergies."

He kisses my forehead and then we force ourselves out of bed. He grabs his clothes from yesterday off the nearby chair. I let myself admire his body as he dresses. I fell in love with *him* first—his personality, his humor—but I have certainly let myself enjoy all that he has to offer.

"Do you want breakfast before you go?" I ask, knowing that my sparse pantry has very little available. Tomorrow I'll take the kids to the grocery store to stock up on their favorites for our last few weeks in town.

"Gracie, I love that you are trying to find every excuse to keep me here longer, but I should go," he says. "You deserve a few hours to yourself before you get the kids. You'll be happier for it."

I walk him to the door, and we stand at the open threshold for a minute just sweetly kissing before he pulls me in for a final hug. It's the hug you give someone you love at the airport—a little longer and tighter than usual but not too intense, because you know that they'll be back. I watch him drive away and turn around to start my day.

---

DR. LISA IS on the East Coast visiting family, and she's agreed to squeeze me in for an early-morning session at 8. It was a late night for me, and she's still jet-lagged, so we both meet with tired eyes and hands full of freshly brewed coffee.

"Gracie, it's so nice to see you," she says. "I've been looking forward to today's session and more than a little worried about you after listening to the interview."

"I want to talk all about it," I begin, "but before we debrief on the interview with Maisy, I want to tell you what happened the day before and after. I think it matters."

I spend twenty minutes recounting the argument with Josh—how it started, how I knew even in the moment I was being irrational, how scared he seemed by my reactions, and how I sent him home. Every excruciating detail. Dr. Lisa is listening intently, and I see a worried look cross her face. She's learned to like Josh from afar, and I can sense she's worried about where this is headed.

"Believe it or not, although I've only had a few days to digest it, I'm fairly certain the latest Maisy interview might have been the most cathartic experience of my life," I tell her. "I came back with a better understanding of my emotional state."

"I was both proud and concerned, Gracie," she says. "The interview with you and Darrell was incredibly powerful. You both shared some very raw emotions and stories. It was beautiful, but I also know it must have been very upsetting."

"It was," I say, before adding in a half-sarcastic voice, "Maisy was very happy with how our baggage brought social media value."

"Talk to me a bit about what happened when you got home. Judging by your demeanor, I'm assuming that you and Josh reconciled."

"We did," I say, finding myself holding back tears. "We both put all of our feelings on the table. I told him how scared it makes me to be in love again. Neither of us expected this, but I think we're on the road to figuring it out. It's the real deal."

"What concerns or apprehensions do you still have?"

"Not many," I say. "We talked a lot about logistics. We live in different parts of the state, but I'm confident we have a good plan for long distance. I guess that I'm mostly nervous about bringing someone new into the kids' lives. I don't want them to feel like I'm trying to replace Ben."

"What about *you*? What concerns you?"

"I can butter things up in my essays, but it does feel like I'm trying to move on. To move past Ben. Officially. I think that's what I'm still struggling with."

"Interesting," she says. Dr. Lisa's favorite word hangs in the air. I think about what to say next and how I can better explain the complex web of emotions I feel. Love and loss and lots of things in between. She jumps in before I can.

"Gracie, I was on the fence about giving you a very specific homework assignment, but after hearing you describe things this morning, I know for a fact it's the right thing to do," she says.

There's a brief pause and I fill the gap. "You put me on the right track at every point over the last year. Whatever it is, I will do it and trust that you will be right about it."

This makes her laugh—a genuine and appreciative laugh. At this moment, it's clear that no other therapist could do for me what Dr. Lisa has managed to do. She has walked a tightrope, knowing when to push and when to hold back. She has read my cues and engaged in discussions with me that sometimes had no neat answers. Our sessions have resulted in no less than five essays for *The New York Times*. She makes me think. She makes me be honest. She is squarely in my corner.

"Gracie, I would like you to write a letter to Ben," she says, formally assigning today's homework. "Not a farewell letter necessarily, but a collection of your thoughts as you reflect on the last year. Tell him your struggles, your victories, and, most importantly, who you've become while he's been gone. Write it *to him*. Of course, it's for you mostly, but I want you to believe in the spiritual potential of the exercise as you write the letter. Let him listen; let him receive it."

I want to be dismissive of the assignment. I want to make jokes about talking to dead people and writing letters to Santa, but the truth is that something about this exercise feels right. For the last year, I have missed Ben so much. I have missed every silly little conversation that we had, the funny memes he would send me, the dirty jokes he would whisper in my ear, the sticky love notes on mirrors around the house. I have missed his voice, his love—him. I want to talk with him so badly.

"Talk to him, Gracie. It's what you need right now," she whispers. "And then let him go."

We make a date for our next session in a few weeks and then sign off. I have a few hours before I need to leave for camp to get the kids, so I walk upstairs to the writing room and begin my assignment.

I sit down at the desk, take out my phone, and do something that I haven't had the courage to do in months: play Ben's last audio message. His deep, crackly voice escapes through the speaker.

*Hey, babe. The kids are with the sitter and I ordered pizza, so no need to rush home from your meeting. I hope it's going well. I know you told me what it was about, but I forget already. Drew wants to talk about the fantasy football league for next season—already, like an insane person—so I'll be there for a while. If you need me to pick up anything on the way home, just let me know. Okay, well, I think that's it. I love you, obviously. See you tonight. Bye.*

Marriage is funny. You do so many big things together—jobs, relocations, houses, kids—but so much of what makes a happy marriage are the tiny moments. All the interstitial time that ties the threads between minutes, hours, and days. The minutiae of life and marriage can be so heartbreakingly simple and beautiful. And so damned easy to take for granted.

The last sound of Ben's voice that I have is one of those unimportant memos you bounce back and forth. Groceries you need, good-luck wishes for big meetings, reminders about kids' birthday parties, and in the case of the evening Ben died, letting your spouse know that the kids are safe with a sitter and you're about to go have a beer with a friend.

I never got to send a message back. Drew called me in a panic one hour later while I was still at my business dinner, and forty minutes after that, I was holding Ben's limp hand in a hospital bed.

So, I start my letter with the big news, but before I know it, I'm right back into the little things. I tell him Ava is shockingly good at long division, Benji scored his first goal in travel soccer, that I have discovered I actually can keep plants alive, that I was right about the fridge door all along, that I was wrong about who does most of the vacuuming. I tell him about the Canopy house, how right he was about it, and how beautiful it looks now.

I tell him about me—the new version of me. The ways I've changed and grown, and how his death has made me cling to my own strength and faith in ways I never knew were possible. I tell him about therapy and Dr. Lisa, how Jenny has been there for me every step of the way, about Felicity and all the new friends that

I've made, and about the unbelievable reality that is my life of interviews and being fame adjacent. I know that term will crack him up.

I tell him that I spent weeks—months, if I'm honest—being angry and mad and disappointed that life had given me this. But every time I felt ready to give up on the world, I thought of him telling me how beautiful and fair our life had been together. It's no easy feat to meet someone at eighteen and make it work into your forties. We did that. I'm proud of us, I say.

Most of all, I tell him I love him. That he was everything to me while he was here, and he will never, ever leave my heart. We were always meant to be, and maybe this was always meant to be the way our story ended. I hate that for us, but I cannot regret for a second what we had together. I thank him for our beautiful children and for all that we made possible together.

Through tears, I ask him if it's okay for me to move on. Then I hit the backspace key and replace it with *move forward*. Words matter. I don't want to move too far away from him and his love. I don't want to forget it. I want permission that I know he can't really give me to open my heart to someone else. *You need to give yourself permission*, I can hear him saying in my ear.

I tell him that I love him one last time and then stop typing. It is done. I scroll back to the top and read every single word. The letter is hard. It is real. It is us. It is *perfect*.

# CHAPTER 33

I CRY WHEN I SEE BENJI AND AVA WAVING TO ME FROM THE hill where they wait with a hundred other campers to be picked up by their parents. They can't move until it's their turn, so we just wave and smile. Ava mimes to me *Are you crying?* and then jokingly rolls her eyes when I nod yes. Even twenty yards away, her eye-roll skills are unmatched.

When it's finally our turn, they come bursting down the hill and we share a huge, life-giving hug. I then take time to hug them individually and squeeze their little faces. All the while, camp counselors are loading the SUV with trunks and bags and what seems like way more stuff than they arrived with.

"It all fit in on the way here," I yell back. "Just keep shoving it in! We're not going too far."

Camp drop-off is slow and easy, but pickup is a no-nonsense, well-oiled machine. They each get a high five from a counselor, and then we're back in the car for the drive to the house. They roll down the windows and open the sunroof so that they can yell goodbye to their respective sets of friends as we exit on the long gravel driveway.

"I missed you guys so much!" I squeal. "Even though the car literally smells like wet socks already and I will be doing laundry for three days straight."

"Mom, I'm gonna be honest," Benji starts. "Some of my stuff is really funky. I'm sorry."

"Don't worry, buddy," I say. "Tell me everything about camp!"

"Wait, wait, wait," Ava chimes in. "We are dying for some donuts. Can we please stop on the way to the house?"

"Two months without donuts! That should be illegal," Benji chimes in.

We hit the drive-through of a donut chain and get a dozen of the most frosted, sprinkled, and sugared donuts humanly possible. The kids immediately start digging in. Apparently, the cereal at camp did not provide enough sweetness, though I have a hard time believing they've been sugar deprived. They also never stop talking. I missed their quick wit, hilarious observations, and our nonstop conversations.

It's only a thirty-minute drive to the house, but they are both competing for airspace, so I set the timer for ninety seconds, and they alternate back and forth, telling stories. From Ava I hear about rekindled friendships, a two-day camping trip that she was finally old enough to go on, kayaking, and late-night girl-talk sessions. Benji tells me about the wild food combinations he ate in the cafeteria, how he went down the gigantic water slide about a hundred times, zip-lining, and epic games of Frisbee golf.

"Did you guys see each other a lot?" I ask. All summer I've convinced myself that they had each other and wouldn't get too lonely.

"Not really," Ava says nonchalantly. "Maybe once a day or every other day? It was just enough to have a proof of life."

"Ava does have a crush on my counselor, though," Benji blurts out, following it with a comically evil laugh.

"Oh my God, Benji. We've been in the car for, like, five minutes," she says, and I can tell she's blushing without even looking at her. She shrugs in the seat next to me and says, "He had a cute British accent." Lord help me with this one.

As we turn the corner onto Wilson Street, I give them the soft rules for the day. First, don't stress about emptying the car. Yes, it will smell like a locker room for a week as a result, but I just want to spend time with them and not jump into that train wreck. Second, I want to do a grand reveal of the house, so they need to walk through the door with eyes closed and not open them until I say so.

Nothing looks all that different from the outside when we pull up, and they immediately start asking questions.

"Just be patient!" I say as we all jump out of the car and walk up the path to the house.

I unlock the front door and order, "Eyes closed," and slowly guide them inside.

"Okay, open!" I exclaim.

The look on their faces says it all. Benji immediately starts running around the first floor from room to room. Ava is more stuck in space, gawking at everything around her.

"MOM! Is this for real?" she turns and asks me. I nod that it is real, and this is, in fact, our house.

Benji has already run a lap and is headed up the stairs like a hurricane. Ava drops her cool-preteen act and skips upstairs with him. I can hear their squeals of excitement and delight. Benji yells for her to check out his room; she yells back that, no, *he* has

GRACIE HARRIS IS UNDER CONSTRUCTION • 339

to come see her room. I walk up to join them and plop down on Benji's bed.

"What do you think?" I playfully ask, even though I already know the answer.

"I can't believe this is our house," Benji says. "I love this room so much."

"Mom, my room is so cool. Like, can we please just copy and paste it into my room at home?" Ava asks as she walks through the door to Benji's room. She rarely likes to give me such effusive credit, so I know that Josh and I did a good job.

I convince them to come downstairs with me and eat more donuts at the kitchen island. I want more tales of their adventures and friendships from the summer. Just as I take my first bite of a cinnamon-sugar donut, Ava jumps in with an unexpected observation.

"I thought that there would be another car in the driveway when we pulled up," Ava says, staring directly at me.

"Yeah, where's your boyfriend?" Benji asks, catching my expression before adding, "What? Ava told me like an hour after she got your letter."

I try to change the topic, but they won't budge. "You've heard about our summers a little bit; now we want to hear about yours," Ava says. They start grilling me just like Josh and the journalists did all summer.

*Is he funny?* "Yes, he makes me laugh a lot."

*What's his job again?* "He owns a construction company. He mostly builds houses from the ground up."

*Does he have any pets?* "His dog, Hammy, died a little while ago."

*When's his birthday? We should get him a new puppy.* (Not really a question.)

*Where does he live?* "In a very cool house up high on a hill on the outskirts of town."

*Can we go see it?* "Probably eventually."

*Does he fish?* "Yes."

*Does he like kids?* "You won't believe this, but he has ten godchildren! Yes, he likes kids. He can't wait to see the two of you again."

*What's your favorite thing about him?* "We can talk about anything."

*Are there any house projects left that we can help with?* "We'll have to ask Josh."

*Oh yeah, what about your book?* "I'll be done in two days."

Once they get past the surface-level stuff, they fire off a quick succession of deeper questions, some of which I've planned for.

*Will we split time between here and home?* "We won't rush into anything, but the plan is to spend the school year at home, most holidays and summers here."

*Will he live with us?* "Yes, we're going to try that out when we're all ready. He will probably bounce between home and here much more than us for his job. His work will be out here."

*Will you get married?* "It's very possible."

*Do you think you'll have kids together?* "I have no idea."

Then Benji asks a question that I don't expect from my ten-year-old boy: "Do you love him?"

"Yes," I answer without hesitation. "Very much."

"So, I'd like to go back to Benji's original question," Ava says. "Where's your boyfriend?"

"I assumed that you'd want time together with just the three of us, and I wasn't sure what your reactions would be to the news," I say through tears that are now flowing. I'm overwhelmed by their maturity and love for me. "You two are my priority."

"You're our priority," Ava says back with a look of exasperation. "And it's not like we didn't already see him at the start of the summer. I don't want to have to tell all of the camp stories twice."

"Seriously, Mom, this makes us really happy," Benji adds. His face tells me he's not sure why it's such a big deal. "You should invite him over for dinner."

They both hop down from their stools and pull me into an even bigger hug than we had standing in the camp driveway. In addition to becoming a lightweight social butterfly, I'm now also apparently a crier. I can't stop the waterworks.

I walk out to the front porch and grab my phone from my back pocket. I start to text and then realize that I want nothing more than to hear Josh's voice and share how the day has gone down. He picks up on the second ring. He's breathing heavily.

"Hey, I'm out on a run with James. I didn't expect to hear from you today. Is everything okay?" he says. I hear James yell, "Hey, Gracie!" in the background.

"Yeah, it's more than okay. Why don't you call me when you're done?"

"Gracie, you can't tease me like this. What's up?"

I clear my throat, take a deep breath, and try to keep my emotions in check.

"Ava and Benji want to know if you'd like to come over tonight for dinner."

Josh is quiet for a few seconds and then finally chokes out, "Are you serious? Like, tonight?"

"Very serious. In fact, they were disappointed you weren't here when we got home, but to be honest, I think I probably saved you from some serious grilling, and trust me—kid questions are way more unpredictable than journalists'."

"Yes, yes, yes. I will be there."

"The kids only want to order in, so it'll just be pizza or burritos or something, but why don't you come over around five or six?"

"I'll be there. I love you so much."

"I love you, too."

---

I MAKE THE kids shower before Josh comes over. The camp stink is real, but they both look (and smell) mostly presentable when Josh walks in the door at 5:30. He's visibly nervous, which makes me love him even more. I've never seen him quite like this.

Ava and Benji pop up from their game of Uno to reintroduce themselves. They were both hopped up on the pre-camp adrenaline last time they saw him, so neither has a clear picture of him in their mind.

"It's nice to see you guys again," Josh says. "I've been looking forward to it all summer."

"Do you really have ten godchildren?" Benji asks while holding his hand out to shake Josh's.

"It's true," Josh says with a smile.

"Do you know all of their names?" Ava asks.

"I do," he says, before realizing the kids want the full answer. "Lucy, Max, Theo, James Jr., Emma . . . Olivia, Mia . . . Noah, Liam, and Riley."

He has to pause a bit to think on the names in the middle but gets all ten. Benji and Ava are impressed. It's easy to forget the sorts of things that impress kids.

"Mom says that all summer you've been asking her fun questions to get to know her. What's your favorite thing that you've learned?" Ava asks.

Josh's experience as the cool uncle and godfather comes in handy as he considers how to answer this question. He chooses a crowd-pleasing fact.

"Your mom likes to pretend she's all serious," he says, getting down to their level and looking them in the eye. "So, my favorite thing I've learned is probably that your mom loves fart jokes."

This makes them both cackle and say, "So true." Ava claims that twelve-year-old boys don't even find fart jokes as funny as I do.

"Just part of what makes me so special," I say to my adoring fans.

"I was wondering," Benji starts, having held in his curiosity for long enough, "if there are any projects left to do that I could help with. Especially any that I could use some power tools for."

Josh makes a thinking face, and I can tell he's going through his mental to-do list to dig out some mostly kid-safe options.

"Absolutely. I need to put some shelving in your mom's office, so we could use the drill for that. And there are some old boards on the deck out back that we need to cut using a miter saw. I also have a cool paint sprayer we can use on the shed out back," Josh responds.

Benji's eyes light up at the thought of working on projects and using tools. Some parents may worry, but Benji is usually so responsible that I expect him to wear safety goggles, a vest, and gloves without being asked.

"That's the way to Benji's heart," Ava playfully observes. "By the way, I really like my room. Thank you. The whole house is pretty awesome, actually."

"I had a lot of fun fixing things up and spending time with your mom," Josh adds.

"She's the best," Benji says, sidling up to me for a hug.

We spend the next few hours hanging out, eating dinner, and unloading the car. Thankfully, Josh went to camp when he was young, so he's not shocked by any of the clothes, pillows, and blankets that fall out of the SUV trunk. Everything about the evening together feels perfectly normal. Nothing is forced. Sure, there are some clumsy moments for each of us, but that happens in every family.

At 9 p.m., I send the kids upstairs to get ready for bed and spend a few minutes with Josh before he heads out. He gets a fist bump from Benji and waves goodbye to Ava.

Josh and I sit on the front porch swing, and I curl up into him.

"I can't even describe how I feel right now," he says, pulling me in tight and tender. "Tonight was perfect."

"I think maybe in a few days you can spend the night," I say. "Or we could do a camp-out at your house. They would love that."

"There are so many things I want to show them in Canopy. You didn't tell me they were so outdoorsy. Ava will love the scenic outlook on the trail just south of town. And Benji? James and I will take him to the best fishing spot he's ever seen."

I know him. I can see his thoughts moving a mile a minute, formulating fun plans for us. He's got the same childlike excitement he had the first time I brought him a BLT for lunch and this grand adventure of ours began.

"They really like you, Josh. It's so obvious. You have to be able to tell," I say, looking at him in those big brown—and now glassy—eyes.

"I feel like I was meant to be a part of this family. It's going to be the honor of my life if you guys decide to keep me around," he says.

"We're not going to let you go anywhere. Well, tonight we're sending you home, but in the long run, I think you may be stuck with us."

---

I SNEAK DOWNSTAIRS bright and early the next morning before the kids are awake. Nothing feels better for a kid than the first night in a cozy bed after two months in a cabin. My best guess is that I have at least two hours before I hear their little feet tapping down the stairs.

With the coffee brewing nearby, I grab my laptop and set it on the counter. For the second time in two days, I find myself sitting down to write something hard but necessary. My contract with *The New York Times* is up for renewal, and I've decided to call it quits. I spoke with my column editor, Danny, a few days ago to tell him. In the year to come, I need to focus on my family's new life and bringing my baby—my book—into the world. Oh, and the newsletter. I now know that Lucia was right about that. I want to write about lots of things, not just grief.

I would love to do it all, but I can't. I need to focus on a select set of priorities. Ironically, officially quitting my job at the state tourism magazine will be the easy part; the sabbatical helped with that.

Leaving the readers of my *New York Times* column behind is much harder. So, I grab a cup of coffee and settle in to write my last first draft for Danny.

> How do you know when it's time to move on? Maybe not on, but to move forward and to do so with purpose and intent. To move forward with new relationships or jobs. To new adventures or places. How do we close one chapter and give ourselves permission to try something new? I don't have all of the answers, but I've learned a thing or two in the last year.
>
> That's why I know it's time to say goodbye. A part of me wanted to hold on to this column, to keep it as a remnant of a life that I used to live. Over the last few weeks, however, I've discovered there is a real beauty in letting things go free.
>
> Fifteen months ago, I wrote an essay for this newspaper that completely altered the trajectory of my life. It has been an extraordinary privilege to write for you and to share some of our hardest experiences with one another. I'm deeply grateful for each and every one of you who has read, commented on, and shared my essays.
>
> Every other week, you joined me on this miraculous and demanding journey of grief. You met me some weeks when things seemed clear and my advice was firm. You met me other weeks when what I had to offer was hazy at best. Without fail, after every single essay, someone would reach out and say something so magnificently perfect that I knew that whatever it took to write that particular essay had been worth it. You made even the toughest moments worth it.

I'm deeply grateful for the readers who approached me in coffee shops and grocery stores, on planes and in doctors' offices. You would often share your own stories of grief and then apologize for drowning me in your sorrow. But the truth is that your stories did exactly the opposite—they kept me afloat. Because you made me realize that I was never, ever alone.

The essays that you read each week were almost always inspired by conversations with friends and other wonderful people who crossed my path over this last year. So, allow me to express a bit more gratitude.

I'm thankful for television personalities who asked tough questions and the votes of confidence from the pros who prepared me for them. I'm thankful for a small-town community that brought me out of my shell with stories and laughs.

There will certainly never be praise enough for my oldest friends who carried the weight of my loss alongside me and the new friends who gave me a chance to be myself without any baggage at all. My gratitude knows no bounds for the people who told me to dream bigger and those who insisted on loving me even when it was very, very hard.

Yes, I'm even appreciative of those among you who had very unconventional ways of telling me you disagreed with the things that I shared. Looking back, I realize you toughened me up and strengthened my resolve.

When I started writing this column, I naively thought that I'd be the one sharing all the wisdom and helping to expand your horizons around grief, but it turns out it's been *you* all along building *me* back up.

Every time one of you told me that you read my work and valued my words, you helped to construct a new version of me, brick by brick, allowing for a firmer foundation on which I could expand. I now need to focus on spending time with those closest to me to finish out the rest of the work.

For a long time, I tried to hide from the messiness. The hard truths. The things that made me uncomfortable. Of course, avoiding things just because they are hard often makes situations much more difficult. In reality, we don't always get to choose the things that break us down or build us back up again. Often, what's best for us is going down the hardest road. The darkest road. Because on the other side, things seem so much brighter.

I have some plans for this next phase of life, but much of it is still unknown, and that feels unbelievably, surprisingly freeing. And fortunate. What a gift it is to have the opportunity to rebuild myself, to emerge from the depths of sorrow as a new version of who I'm meant to be. Not better, but different. I'm forever altered not just by my loss, but by each of you.

I write to you today as an unfinished Gracie Harris. And you know what? I'm in love with this rough, still-under-construction version of who I am, and I'm not rushing to figure the rest out. It will come with time. I hope that you will continue to find me in new places—not just in bookstores next spring, but on the many different paths that I expect life to take us all down.

As my last act of service to you, let me ask you this: What pieces of *you* need to be reimagined and rebuilt? What's keeping you from fully allowing yourself to grow and change? I challenge you to meet those things head on, let go of anything that's holding you back, and, most importantly, let others help you on your path to get there.

For the last time, I paste in a link to the document, plug in Danny's email address, and fill the subject line with the title: Gracie Harris Is Under Construction.

# CHAPTER 34

LAST NIGHT, AFTER A FAMILY MOVIE AND BEFORE JOSH went back to his place, we told the kids a bit more about how we plan to ease into our new life in the coming months. When we get back home, I'll officially leave my job at the tourism magazine and work as a writer full-time. In addition to writing the newsletter and editing the book, I've started kicking around ideas for a few novels. It's all still in the brainstorming stage, but it's exciting. I've got more than enough savings and anticipated book royalties to give us a few years to see how this new career path goes.

Josh has his own plan, too. After speaking with Tommy and the rest of the company leadership team, he's going to focus on spinning off a new line of business restoring old homes, one at a time. He won't do that alone, either; a few guys are coming over to help out with that. Tommy will run the primary business, and over time, the hope is that Josh will give him part ownership of the company.

The kids are thrilled that I won't need to regularly travel for work anymore. Even those short day or overnight trips in North

Carolina stressed them out. We're all thrilled that I'll have more flexibility in my days and maybe even some actual free time. Josh and I are both excited to own our schedules a bit more, which will make splitting time between Canopy and Chapel Hill a little easier. We all still have lots of questions about how to make this work but are committed to figuring it out as a team.

This morning, Josh and Benji have spent hours outside painting the shed out back while Ava has played video games in her room. Me? I've been editing the final bits of the memoir. There will be many rounds of edits to come once Jeannie gets her hands on it, but at around 11 a.m., I push Print on the last chapter to share with Josh and step away from the desk. There is only so much I can do by myself. It's time to let someone else read it from cover to cover.

I walk outside and call Felicity. We've been through so much together this past year, and she's the first person I want to share the good news with.

"I'm done," I tell her. "The manuscript will be in your inbox by noon."

"Gracie, you can't see me right now, but I'm literally doing a happy dance. My calendar is cleared, and I'm spending the next three days reading your magnificent memoir," she says, before adding, "which I will, of course, be redlining and sending back to you for one round of edits before we send it to Jeannie."

"I would expect nothing less," I tell her. "I truly cannot thank you enough for all that you've done for me over this last year. This book would not be possible without you."

We chat a bit more—including her telling me about her latest date—but then she instructs me to hang up the phone and hit Send on the email right away before she goes crazy.

When I walk back into the house, Josh and Benji are washing their hands in the sink.

"Hey, boys," I say. "How does the shed look?"

"It was a lot of work, but it's done and looks good," Benji says in his sweet voice that somehow has just a trace of a little kid left in it. After Benji runs upstairs, I turn to Josh, and he pulls me in for a generous hug.

"My project is done, too," I say.

"I'm so proud of you," he says, kissing my forehead. "You worked so hard this summer. I can't believe you had time to fall in love with me, too."

"I'm good at multitasking," I say.

"We should do something to celebrate," he says. "What about lunch at Lenny's?"

"Can I read you the last chapter before we go?" I ask, and his eyes immediately light up.

"You sure it's okay for me to hear the end before I read the whole thing?"

"I'm sure."

I've had the last chapter drafted for quite some time. The book doesn't have many flashbacks, but the final chapter tells the story of the day I met Ben. It's one thing that I will fight the publisher to never change—to end on the beautiful story of how my life was set on this devastating and magical course.

I read most of it to Josh and he listens intently, both of us perched on our stools at the kitchen island. When I stop for a few seconds after a paragraph that could easily be the end, he starts to talk, and I interrupt: "Not yet."

For a little while now, I've felt that the ending was missing something. Not closure, per se, but an indication that the new journey I'm on is one worthy of its own story. Maybe it's all of the fiction books that I read, but I've always wanted the story to have a mostly happy ending, even when I wasn't sure it was possible.

"For this last part, I need to put you in position," I say with a sweet but playful grin.

I guide Josh over to a corner of the living room, and then walk over to stand close to the entry. We are positioned exactly where we were the first time we met. An expression of recognition of this fact washes over Josh almost immediately.

"Ready?" I ask.

He nods and I begin.

"I believe in sparks. Sparks of creativity. Sparks of inspiration. Sparks of love. The first time I met Ben, the spark was there. Sometimes our bodies know things before our brains can fully process what's happening. That was how it all started with Ben. I just knew.

"When he died, I prepared myself for the possibility that sparks might never come for me again. *Don't be greedy*, I thought. *You got magic once and it was magnificent.* In the worst of it, I hit a point where I thought all of the new sparks of life might be gone. That maybe I needed to switch my mindset to gratitude for where I've been instead of hopefulness for what might come."

I pause. "But then? Sparks. Lots of them."

I look over at Josh and he's rubbing his chin, smiling big, and quietly walking closer and closer to me. My dashing but underpaid handyman made it into the book, after all.

"The spark of love was subtle this time, as if my body knew that my brain might run away if it sent the message too hard or too quick. It was there on day one, but it whispered to me softly."

I put the printed pages down and let Josh scoop me into a warm embrace. I recite the final few sentences from memory into his ear.

"If you're reading this book and wondering if you'll ever feel sparks again, know that it's possible. Because sparks are flying for me right now, and they are magnificent."

# EPILOGUE

"WE NEED TO LEAVE NOW OR WE'RE GOING TO BE LATE," Benji yells from the front door, ever the responsible grandpa child. He's dressed in his bow tie and fresh khakis so that we know he's taking this *very seriously*.

I jog down the stairs and take a quick look in the mirror by the entry table.

"You look beautiful," Josh says, sweeping up behind me.

"What he said," adds Benji. "Now come on!"

Ava smiles and locks her arm in mine as we walk perfectly synchronized down the front steps. It's a gorgeous spring night with only a slight chill in the air. The sun has almost completely set, and the mountains look magical in the distance. I could not have picked a better evening, a better place, to begin my book tour.

"Are you nervous?" Ava whispers to me while the boys talk fishing behind us.

"A little," I answer. "I'm afraid no one is going to show."

A couple minutes later, that fear is immediately cast away as we turn the corner onto Main Street. We can see a line of people waiting to enter Lenny's.

As we approach, strangers, friends, and everyone in between is excitedly greeting us. Brian from the hardware store gives me a quick hug. Sunny grabs my shoulders and then pulls me in for a tight squeeze. She's simultaneously fighting back tears and smiling bigger than I knew was possible. Everyone tells me how proud they are.

We enter and I see my parents waving from the far side of the room, where most of our close friends have gathered. Josh's and Ben's families are up there, too, chatting away like old friends. Jenny is rocking Baby Coco in her sling as a handful of my girlfriends, including Kendell, coo over her. I also spot Dr. Lisa, who insisted on meeting me in real life and being here for this special night. All of my people, in one place.

The bookstore wasn't quite big enough, and I'm captivated by how much Lenny's has been transformed to host the event. Tables have been removed from the main dining area and folding chairs line every available bit of floor space. Attendees are also seated in the booths that border the diner. Tiny vases with freshly picked flowers have been placed around the room and homemade decorations that the kids snuck out to help with line the walls. *This is perfect.*

Josh and the kids head to their reserved seats, while I chat with Lenny and Marianne to go over the agenda.

"I'll spend five minutes or so introducing you," Marianne says. "Then we'll turn the floor over to you. You can read as much or as little as you'd like, and then we'll pass the mic around for questions."

"This is too much," I respond. "I could not have imagined something more special than this."

"It's nothing at all," Lenny says, shooing me away but visibly emotional. "We're honored."

I walk toward the established front of the room where the acrylic lectern from Canopy Books stands. Set up nearby is a table with stacks of my memoir—*This Wasn't the Plan*—waiting to be signed. A blowup of the cover stands nearby, and a giant starburst sticker at the top proclaims it a Maisy's Book Club selection. At 7 p.m. sharp, Marianne walks to the microphone and gives a tenderhearted introduction to the packed room, describing the first time we met to fits of laughter from the audience, and what the book has meant to her.

Before I know it, I'm up.

"Thank you all for being here today. It's *my* honor to kick off the book tour here in Canopy. I'm eternally grateful to Lenny and Marianne for making this happen.

"I wrote *a lot* of this memoir in town, including about twenty thousand words down the street at The Drip, and even a few at that booth over there—when Lenny wasn't talking my ear off. Some chapters came out neat and without any hassle, but other times I wrote without any idea where it would lead. Finding my voice and finding the story wasn't always easy.

"One thing I struggled with for a long time was how to start this book. A prologue sets the stage for the reader and the journey they are about to take—it was important for me to get it right. Some people had strong opinions. They wanted me to go with shock and awe, and I understand why, but I knew that the true beginning would find me, even if it took a while.

"When I was at a particularly challenging step of this journey, my therapist gave me an assignment. I thought it was silly, but she insisted. My homework? Write a letter to Ben. Tell him about my life and how I've changed. Say the things I need to say—especially the hard stuff, she told me. Then believe that he will receive it.

"One of the most challenging things I've ever done was read that letter back for the first time, but the instant I finished it, I knew my prologue had found me. It's funny sometimes how the beginning of a story doesn't really make sense until we know how it ends—or, in my case, where the new journey begins."

I look out into the crowd and take a deep breath. Sitting in the front row, beaming with pride, are the three loves of my life. Ava, Benji, and Josh. I imagine Ben is here somewhere, too. I felt his energy the second I walked in.

"So, if you'll allow me, I'd like to read the first part of my book—the prologue—before taking your questions."

I sneak a sip of water, clear my throat, and pause for a moment to let all of this love in.

"Dear Ben," I begin. "Big news: I'm a hugger now. I'd like to tell you how I got here."

ACKNOWLEDGMENTS

Thank you to Haley Heidemann, my agent at WME. You responded to a cold query from an unknown, forty-year-old, first-time novelist and completely changed my life. Thanks for believing in me, in this book, and for every editorial comment that enriched the early drafts of the novel. This is the first of many exciting adventures together.

Thank you to Cassidy Sachs, my brilliant editor at Dutton. You are a dream. You simply got this book from day one. Every one of your comments brought the story to new heights. Your feedback made me fall deeper in love with this story and made editing a pure joy. I still pinch myself that I got to bring my debut novel to life with you! Also at Dutton, thank you to John Parsley, Maya Ziv, Stephanie Cooper, Amanda Walker, Jamie Knapp, Caroline Payne, Melissa Solis, Clare Shearer, LeeAnn Pemberton, Gaelyn Galbreath, Ashley Tucker, Christopher Lin, Vikki Chu, and Sarah Oberrender.

Thank you to every assistant behind the scenes at both WME (especially Morgan Montgomery) and Dutton for powering so many of the tasks that help to keep the publishing trains on the rails. I deeply appreciate you.

Sincere gratitude to every teacher and professor who has encouraged my creativity and love of writing over the years. My career has taken me in many directions, but I had the confidence to sit down and write this novel because of the many lessons I learned from you.

To my dear friends who celebrated and toasted my book news at home and abroad. I've been blessed beyond measure to have amazing women by my side through so many seasons of life. To my Italy ladies, in particular—I'm so thankful the universe collected us in Florence at the same time in the early 2010s. My life is better because you're in it.

Thank you to the mountain towns and wonderful residents across western North Carolina that inspired Canopy—especially Brevard, Boone, Cashiers, Hendersonville, and Highlands. In many ways, this novel is a love letter to small towns and the people who make them so special. Western North Carolina has a place in my heart forever.

Just like Gracie says, coffee shops are hallowed ground. Cheers to Cup & Saucer in Brevard, where I wrote the very first brainstorm for this book, and to Lanza's in Carrboro, where I tapped out the finishing touches.

Thanks to my family for being my biggest cheerleaders over the years—especially my mom, who shows up time and again to help make our busy lives feel a little less hectic.

To Livy and Archer for being the best kids ever. I love you both so much and I'm so proud to be your mom.

Last, but certainly not least, to Rob. The only reason I was able to convincingly write two swoon-worthy men for Gracie is because I see you in action every day. You are the bar that my (fictional) leading men must clear.

# ABOUT THE AUTHOR

**Kate Hash** is a debut novelist based in Chapel Hill, North Carolina, who enjoys creating and consuming stories about dynamic women, unexpected relationships, and the complexity that comes with entering midlife. She has lived in Italy, run a business, and even appeared on an episode of *House Hunters International* (one of her favorite "two truths and a lie" facts). During her four years abroad in the early 2010s, Kate operated a popular travel blog and contributed guides to the much-beloved *Design*Sponge*. She's now a homebody who loves spending time with her husband, Rob; two kids, Livia and Archer; and an anxiety-riddled dog, Charlie.